SOULS ALIGNED

NAJEE JAMERSON

ACKNOWLEDGMENT

I'd like to dedicate this book to the woman who stayed up endless nights listening to me rant about writing. Who read and re read Souls Aligned over and over giving me insight to how I can make it better. To my beautiful wife Shay, I love you and thank you for everything you've done. I hope everyone falls in love with Logan and Amaris just like we did. I love you every day of forever.

CONTENTS

CHAPTER

1

"I want you to stay positive, Logan. We've been in this fight for a while now. This is nothing for us. We'll get through this."

Logan smiled as she buttoned her shirt. Her doctor ended their visit with the same line as always. She'd heard the same line for the last two years and she was used to it.

"I know, Doc. I know," she muttered.

"You've made it this far, Logan, don't give up on me now."

"I won't, I promise, Dr. Stein."

Dr. Stein had been Logan's cardiologist for the last few years, and she was a damn good one. If Dr. Stein wasn't available, she wouldn't speak with anyone else; she hated explaining herself.

"Take it easy and tell your mother I said hello."

"I will. Don't work too hard, Doc."

"I'll try not to." After hugging Dr. Stein goodbye, Logan went on her way.

As though her mother had spies who reported Logan's every move to her, her ringtone started to play.

"Hello mom," Logan said, placing the phone to her ear.

"Hi sweetie, how was your appointment?"

"Same ole, same ole. How are you?" Logan's driver opened her door allowing her to slide in her car.

"I'm good. I just had lunch with Daddy. He says hi."

"I will call him later to check on him." Logan looked outside her window as the strip breezed by her; she always loved the architecture of the buildings. Her favorite was City Center—the skyscrapers of buildings could be spotted anywhere. Even though they didn't look like they belonged there, they stood their own ground. The beautiful tall glass buildings fascinated Logan. She loved the fact that she could go to the top of the Eiffel tower without actually going to Paris. She couldn't believe people thought to bring other parts of the world to one place.

"Are you listening, Lo?"

Logan got pulled from her thoughts and she tuned back into her mother's voice. "I'm sorry, what did you say?"

"Don't forget the wedding rehearsal is tomorrow."

"I will be there with bells on, I promise."

Logan's brother was getting married this weekend and everyone was coming out. They were expecting over two hundred people to fill her family estate. It would definitely be the talk of the town.

Xavier, her brother, was a well-known architect among celebrities and his soon to be wife was an interior designer. Together, they opened a very successful business. She was so proud of her brother.

Mrs. Maddox giggled, making Logan smile. She loved to hear her mother's laughter. There was something so soothing about it. "You know, Lo, it's never too late to find someone," she said softly, but sternly. She tried to give Logan the same speech anytime they talked.

Logan listened, but she didn't take it to heart. "Why would I do that mom? You know, with everything."

"So you can have some sense of peace and love."

"How do you know I don't have peace and love? My family's love surrounds me every day. You each call me to check on me. Why do you feel I'm not at peace?"

Mrs. Maddox could hear the irritation in her daughter's voice, so she backed up. "I just want you to be happy. I worry about you."

"I'm fine, I promise." She noticed her car pulling up to her building. "I'm pulling up to the office. I love you mom, I'll call you later."

"Okay sweetie, I love you as well. Don't work too hard."

"I won't." Logan ended the call as her driver pulled into her building.

———— ··●·· ————

"You are gorgeous." Amaris took a shot of the model posing for her. The model was soft and sensual; she allowed her hair to fall over her face as Amaris took another shot. Her beautiful green eyes begged for Amaris to take the picture, but there was also a hint of hurt in them that Amaris caught on film.

"Okay, I got the shot." Amaris smiled as she set her camera down. "You are one beautiful woman, Quelm, you know that?"

Quelm smiled as she wrapped her arm around Amaris' waist, kissing the back of her neck. Then Amaris turned and plugged her camera into her computer to upload the pictures.

"I love when you shoot me. You capture everything." Quelm outlined her body on the computer screen. Amaris watched her outline her own body.

"That's not the reason I took the picture." Amaris started to outline Quelm's face and then her eyes. "This is why I took this picture. Your eyes told a story without trying—those beautiful emerald green eyes I can't get enough of. These are the best pictures," she said, still outlining her eyes.

Quelm tried to hide her smile as she ran her hands through Amaris' thick, curly afro. "Only you can capture what no one else can, Amaris. You have such an eye; it's amazing."

"Thank you, darling." Amaris kissed Quelm gently. "I have to catch a flight out. I have that photo gig in Vegas."

"Vegas! Sounds so fun. Who's getting married?"

"Xavier Maddox and Taylor Kincaid."

"The famous designer!" Quelm said excitedly.

"Yes, her."

"Oh my God, you scored that gig! That's so fucking awesome! That's huge! Why didn't you say anything till now? we could have celebrated." Quelm hugged Amaris tight and kissed her.

"Didn't think it was a big deal."

"That's a huge fucking deal!"

"Thank you. Now you should get going, your husband will be looking for you."

The sadness Amaris saw in Quelm's eyes returned. She was unhappily married to a man she'd been with for ten years. Her excuse was that she was staying for the kids, but Amaris didn't stress it. She wasn't trying to wife Quelm; they had fun and that was it. She was okay with Quelm going home to her family.

"I don't want to go."

"I know you don't, but you have to." Amaris stood Quelm up and helped her to get dressed, while kissing her in different spots and teasing her.

"You're going to make me stay."

"I'll see you next week, lover." Amaris liked their no-strings-attached relationship. She was a free-spirited butterfly and until she found the right person, she liked to keep her options open. Quelm knew she dated other women. Even though she was jealous, Amaris always informed her she had no right to be.

"Have a safe trip." Quelm leaned in and kissed Amaris, allowing their lips to linger.

"I'll text you when I get back in town."

"Okay." Amaris waited by the door, making sure Quelm made it to her car before closing her door.

There she was, alone again with her thoughts. She was nervous about this photo gig. Xavier Maddox had seen a few of her photos in an art gallery and asked for her contact. When she got the call, she couldn't believe he wanted her to photograph his wedding, but the $15,000 he offered her, plus the paid expenses was something she wasn't going to pass up. She'd be a fool to do so.

Amaris headed up to her room to pack and she was happy to get out of LA for a while; LA was so busy for her. From what she was told, she would be staying on the estate in one of the guest houses, which would be really nice. She grabbed her medicine and took a look at it, shaking her head. She hated how dependent she was on it, but she knew that if she left it, she wouldn't be able to function. So, she made sure she slipped it in her suitcase.

"What a life," she whispered to herself.

———— · • ● • · ————

Logan's assistant, Lani, was waiting for her when she hopped out of her car. Logan smiled, buttoning her suit as she headed toward Lani. "Waiting for me now?"

Lani rolled her eyes, but tried to hide her smile. "Your brother is in your office. He's been here for about thirty minutes."

"Did we have a meeting I didn't know about?" Logan asked, heading toward her office.

"No, he just showed up."

She stopped in front of her door and turned toward Lani so abruptly that Lani almost ran into her. "I got it from here. I'll ring you if I need you."

"Okay, Boss."

Logan watched as Lani walked away before she entered her office. Her brother had his back turned away from her as he stared out the window. Logan's office was built to face the mountains; something she made sure her brother knew she wanted before she had him build it.

Logan owned her own publishing company, Maddox Publishing Inc. It was her baby, her pride and joy. Her parents wanted her to go into the real estate family business, but that wasn't where her passion was. She always loved to write from when she was a teenager. Stories would just come to her and she would get lost in them.

Logan received her first book deal at eighteen, but she knew she wanted her own company. So, Maddox Publishing Inc. was created when she was twenty two. She now had twenty authors under her roster; seven of them outside of herself hitting the New York Best Sellers list, which is something she was glad to accomplish.

Logan watched her brother before speaking. Even with his back turned, Xavier Maddox exuded power. He reminded her of her dad so much it was scary. His broad shoulders went up and down as he inhaled and exhaled. He had a fresh cut for his wedding, causing Logan to wonder why he cut his hair so early when he could have had it cut the morning of his wedding. His burgundy suit fit him just right and she wondered who he was trying to impress.

"Brother." She finally broke the silence.

Xavier turned around smiling. "Sup Lo. What took yo ass so long? I've been here, waiting." Xavier made his way over to Logan and pulled her into a big bear hug.

Logan laughed as she tried to escape. "You're going to squeeze the life out of me." Xavier laughed, letting Logan go. "Why didn't you call me? I would have cut my doctor's visit short." she told him.

"You know I wouldn't let you do that." Xavier pulled on Logan's suit, straightening it out.

"I promise you, I need to take some fashion tips from you. Your ass be on one with your suits."

Logan laughed while posing for her brother. She got all her suits tailor-made to fit her. It was very expensive, but she was able to pick the fabric and the way she wanted it to fit her body.

"You know you can never be as fly as me, big bro." she joked.

"Yeah whatever, punk. There's no way my sister should be able to out-dress me."

Logan couldn't help but laugh. Her brother said the same thing to her every time he saw one of her outfits. Logan was a stud and a well-dressed one too. She always made sure her outfits were on point. Even though she usually rocked suits, her comfortable wear was the best.

"Again, step up your game. But what are you doing here? Shouldn't you be planning for the wedding?" Logan walked around her desk and took a seat, not wanting her brother to know that she was exhausted, each step she took, heavier than the last.

"Man, this wedding shit …" Xavier flopped down in the seat as if he was just as tired as Logan. "It's crazy that there's so much to do. So much little shit, man. Taylor is a bridezilla out the ass."

Logan had heard about Taylor's bridezilla ways and had already told Taylor she wanted nothing to do with the wedding. She loved Taylor, but she wasn't going to put up with the bullshit. "Well, it's almost over. It's just two more days."

"I can't wait, man."

"But seriously, what brings you here? You're not one to just show up unless you want something."

"Is that how you view me? " Xavier joked. Logan looked at her brother seriously, but didn't say anything. "I was just coming to check on you."

Logan rolled her eyes. "Did mom send you?"

"No, I sent myself. You're my sister and I love you. When mom told me you had a doctor's appointment today, I came to check on you. So for real, how are you?"

It was as if Xavier was trying to see into her soul, so Logan looked away not able to stand her brother's stare. "I'm good, bro." Logan could see the worry in her brother's eyes and it made her feel bad. "If there was anything for you to be worried about, I would tell you."

"You're up for the wedding?"

"I wouldn't miss this for the world. Are you up for the wedding?" They both laughed. Xavier was such a player before he met Taylor. Usually, it's the guys who sweep women off their feet, but with Xavier and Taylor, it was the other way around. To see their love story unfold was like watching one of those romantic movies. It was a beautiful thing and Logan was so happy for her brother.

"Nigga, you know I am. The bachelor party is going to be something you'll never forget."

"I don't know if I'm going to make it to that one, but I'll be there for the rehearsal dinner."

"Aw come on Sis, you have to come. I got some girls from Palomino and you know how they get down."

Logan smiled because she did know. She'd been to the club a few times with Xavier and his friends and she had to give them props, because the women were really good dancers. "Palomino?"

Xavier shook his head. "Palomino."

"I might have to come out for that."

"You have to." Logan saw how Xavier's playful face became serious and she knew what was coming.

"Anything?" he asked with concern.

He didn't have to say it out right for her to know what he was talking about. "No, nothing yet. But, it's cool. Nothing's going to stop me."

Xavier stood up, walked around the desk, and pulled Logan into his arms. They were best friends—thick as thieves—even though he was older than her. "I love you very much, Sis."

"And I love you. Don't worry, I'll be okay."

• ——— • • ● • • ——— •

Amaris inhaled as she walked out of the airport. She could taste the difference in Vegas air. It tasted and smelled crisper than Los Angeles's smog up air.

It was a nice day in Vegas and Amaris was going to enjoy it. It was neither too hot nor too cold. Thank God they weren't having the wedding in the summer; Amaris didn't know if she would be able to do it. Tonight was the rehearsal dinner and the couple wanted pictures of the rehearsal.

Amaris looked at her watch and realized she had a few hours before the dinner. Then she noticed that the Maddox's family had a car waiting for her once she stepped out.

"Ms. Cole?"

"Yes, that's me."

The driver smiled while extending his hand. "Hello, I'm Charles, one of the Maddox's family drivers. I'm going to drive you to the estate."

"Okay. Nice to meet you, Charles." Amaris shook his hand before he took her bag.

"Did the flight treat you okay?"

"Yes it did, thank you." Xavier had flown her down in first class. Even though the flight wasn't so long, it felt good to be in first class.

"Good. If you're ready, we'll get on the road."

"Yup, I'm ready."

Charles opened the door for her and she slid in. There was chilled champagne waiting for her in the storage compartment. She popped the bottle open and poured herself a glass to calm herself. She had already taken her pill to calm her anxiety prior to her flight, but it wasn't working. Anytime there was something new going on in her life, it sent her anxiety into overdrive. Because this was out of her norm, she needed to get herself in check.

Amaris suffered from severe anxiety and every little thing triggered it. She could go into a full blown anxiety attack for the littlest of things. She hated herself for it; she felt so weak because of it. But she had been living with this since she was ten and her medication helped her function well in her everyday life.

The drive to the Maddox home took about thirty minutes. They were way beyond the strip.

"So, what part of Vegas does the Maddox family live in?" she asked curiously.

"They own land in Seven Hills, a beautiful twenty acre estate they had built." Charles explained.

"Twenty acres." she said, unable to hide her astonishment.

Charles laughed. "Yes, twenty acres. Mr. Maddox built his estate before the area was developed. He has everything he needs on his property. You'll love it."

"Well, I'm here to work, so I don't know what time I'll have to take a look around."

Amaris would have loved to get pictures of Mr. Maddox's property because from the way they did things, she knew it was going to be beautiful.

When she finally saw the property as they entered the massive estate, she couldn't help but let her mouth hang in amazement. There were acres and acres of lush-green, manicured land. She couldn't believe it was actually in Vegas—the desert. She knew Mr. Maddox's water bill had to be some money. Amaris could see the lake in the distance and knew she would get a few good shots with the bride and groom.

As Charles pulled up to the house, Amaris could see the front was lined with exotic cars she figured were Mr. Maddox's; men loved their toys.

"Okay, I'll get your bags out. Mrs. Maddox should be waiting for you in the foyer."

"Okay. Thank you, Charles." Amaris took a deep breath before stepping out of the car. She adjusted her camera strap and pulled it behind her back; she was never without her camera. There was beauty in everything and she loved to capture some of that beauty.

A beautiful older woman was standing in the middle of the room, waiting for Amaris when the doors opened. She assumed it was Mrs. Maddox. Amaris raised her camera and snapped a picture of her. Her chocolate brown skin was flawless; she was the true definition of 'black don't crack'. Her salt and pepper hair fell gracefully around her face. She had beautiful light-brown, almond eyes and full lips that fit perfectly on her.

"Forgive me for just snapping a picture, but you are absolutely gorgeous."

"Flattery will get you everywhere, young lady." Mrs. Maddox gave Amaris a big welcome hug. "Print that picture for me. I'd love to see how it came out."

"Will do, ma'am." The tension in Amaris's body faded a little. Mrs. Maddox's eyes and hug were welcoming, which allowed Amaris to relax. She was so nervous about coming to Vegas to do this job. She knew that sometimes, people with a lot of money were snobs and she didn't know what to expect when it came to the Maddox's. She'd met Taylor and Xavier first, whom she thought were so down to earth, but parents could be a whole different story.

"Please, call me Kayman. I'm glad to have you. I've seen your work. You are quite the photographer. I'll have one of the workers show you to your room. If there's anything you need, please do not hesitate to let someone know."

"I'd love to walk the grounds and get a feel of them, since I'll be taking pictures."

"Of course. I'll have—" the doors suddenly opened, stopping Mrs. Maddox mid-sentence. The smile on Mrs. Maddox's face made Amaris turn around to see what brought her such joy. When her face landed on the woman, she knew why.

"Beautiful ..." she whispered. She was one of the most beautiful women Amaris had laid her eyes on. She had to be the daughter of Mrs. Maddox, because the resemblance was uncanny. Her chocolate skin was smooth and sexy; it looked almost edible.

Amaris imagined shooting her while intimately stripping her naked and pulling her dreads loose to see how long they fell. She'd love to capture the reaction in her beautiful, big brown eyes and would've also loved to see her crack a smile.

Amaris's eyes went to the tie wrapped around her neck; she couldn't lie, she was wearing the hell out of her suit; the material hugged her body as if it didn't want to let her go. The black Louise Vuitton dress shoes that graced her feet had to cost her a fortune, but looking at her, money didn't seem like a problem.

Amaris needed to know who this goddess was and why she was instantly attracted to her. There was a sense of familiarity to the stranger, as if she saw or knew her from somewhere.

"Aw Logan, you made it." Mrs. Maddox's eyes lit up on seeing her daughter.

Logan smiled and kissed her mother's cheek. "Of course I did." Her eyes landed on Amaris for a moment and she felt her heart stop. It was as if something had tugged on her heart, as if her soul had just recognized its other half.

"Are you okay?" Mrs. Maddox said in a panicked voice.

Instead of answering her mother, Logan took Amaris's hand into hers, surprising Amaris. She couldn't explain why, but she needed to have contact with this woman; she needed to feel her skin against hers, which was something new to Logan.

"Do I know you?" she asked with a raised eyebrow.

Amaris felt the energy shift and the butterflies filling her stomach. *Yes, I know you. But from where?* She thought to herself. She knew she'd never laid eyes on Logan or ever had the chance to share each other's presence, but she felt the instant connection.

"I don't know, do you?" she barely whispered. Logan's touch was sending waves of energy through Amaris; it was almost too much to take. Amaris was sensitive to energies; she could share energy with different people. That's why she was always careful with who she surrounded herself with.

Logan was trying to figure out where she'd known Amaris from; maybe it was from a party she couldn't recall. She'd been to so many parties, so it could have been possible, but then again, she knew she would have recognized her. Amaris's beauty was one that couldn't go unnoticed. She had a beautiful, curly afro—Logan could imagine running her hands through as Amaris laid in her arms— and gorgeous, dark-chocolate complexion that Logan wouldn't mind kissing every inch of. Her warm hazel eyes were inviting, as if they were telling Logan to explore her; her body was out of this world.

Logan loved thick women and Amaris looked like she could wind those hips nice and slow on her. If she didn't know any better, she would think it was love at first sight.

"What's your name?" she asked instead.

"Amaris." Amaris tried to get her heart to stop beating so quickly. "What's yours?"

"Logan. Nice to meet you, Amaris." Logan grazed her lips across Amaris's hand.

Xavier and Mrs. Maddox stood back, watching the exchange between Logan and Amaris in amusement. They were both surprised that Logan had taken an interest in someone. They both knew Logan's view on love for herself; it was slim to none.

"Nice to meet you as well."

"Sis, are you going to release my photographer's hand? She kind of needs that for the next few days." Xavier joked.

Logan laughed while releasing Amaris's hand. She then peeled her eyes away from Amaris and back to her mother. "You look amazing, mom."

"Thank you, darling. So do you two know each other?"

"Maybe in a past life." Amaris joked.

Logan's eyes went back to Amaris as a smile spread across her face. "Yes, maybe in another life."

The sparks flying between the two could be seen by a blind man. Mrs. Maddox tried to hide her smile. She wanted Logan to find someone to spend her life with, but Logan had other plans for herself. Mrs. Maddox tried her best to respect that, but as a mother, of course she wanted her children to find love.

"Amaris, are you hungry?"

"No, thank you, Mrs. Maddox, but I'd love to look around the property to see where I can get some really good pictures."

"I'll take you." Logan chimed in.

"No, you need to eat, Logan. I can tell you haven't today," Mrs. Maddox said sternly. She turned to Amaris and continued. "I'll have one of the workers take you around, Amaris."

"Mom, it's cool. I'll take her. I'll eat when we get back." Logan protested. Before Mrs. Maddox could object, she grabbed Amaris's hand and whisked her outside. She didn't want her mother breathing down her neck as if she was ten.

"So you're going to show me around in a suit?"

Logan laughed while grabbing the keys to one of the golf carts. "Yes, I am. Unless you want to go with someone else."

"Well, I don't know you."

"But maybe you do, remember?" Logan flashed her a playful smile.

Amaris didn't know why Logan's smile sent chills through her. "Yeah, maybe."

"Besides, I'd rather show you around, so my mother will leave me alone about eating."

They hopped on one of the golf carts. "Your mother will always worry about you. Don't take her for granted."

Logan didn't respond, knowing Amaris was right. But she hated the fact that her mother was always so worried about her. She didn't want her to live like that.

Logan started the golf cart and headed around the property so Amaris could get a good look. She loved growing up on their estate. There was always something to do. Every summer her father would fill their pond with fish just so she and Xavier could fish whenever they wanted. They would spend hours at the pond or riding around the property on their quads. It was some of her best childhood memories.

The sun was out, but it wasn't as hot as it could be, and Logan was thankful for that; the sun usually drained her energy fast. Today was a good day for her.

———— ·•●•· ————

Mrs. Maddox and Xavier sat out on the terrace, both baffled with Logan's behavior.

"Are you sure they don't know each other, Xavier?" Mrs. Maddox asked Xavier, uncertainty clearly written across her face.

"If they do, Lo didn't meet her with me. Did you see how Lo looked at Amaris? I've never seen her look at anyone like that."

Mrs. Maddox smiled. She knew her daughter had been bit by the love bug. "She's found the one." She knew from her husband and from Xavier that when a Maddox found the one, that was it. Mr. Maddox pursued her until she finally gave in. It was something she would never regret.

"How do you know that mom?"

"A mother knows. Just like I knew once you got your act together that you and Taylor would be together."

Xavier chuckled, shaking his head. He couldn't remember how many times his mother had hit him upside the head, warning him to get his act together before he lost Taylor. Thank God he finally listened or he wouldn't have been here, about to get married to the love of his life.

"You know how Logan feels with everything mom," he replied.

"I know, but she just needs the right person to change her mind. Maybe Amaris is that person."

"Well, I need her to take these pictures now and worry about Logan later. Taylor will kill her if they don't come out right." They both laughed, knowing how anal Taylor had been during the wedding planning. She wanted everything to be perfect and if the pictures came out bad, there would be hell to pay.

"I want Logan to be happy," Xavier said with all seriousness. He loved his sister with all his heart. He wanted her to experience what he shared with Taylor and what their parents had.

Mrs. Maddox placed her hand on Xavier's. "Me too, X. She deserves it."

2

"So where are you from, Amaris?" Logan asked, unable to take her eyes off Amaris.

Amaris took pictures of the property, which she was absolutely in love with. There was so much greenery, beautiful trees, and lush-green landscapes, which was weird to see in Las Vegas because it was a desert landscape state.

"I was born and raised in California." Amaris replied.

"Do you still live there?"

"Yes." Amaris saw a beautiful rose garden that she just had to get pictures of. "Stop!" she shrieked suddenly.

Logan slammed on the brakes, thinking something was in front of their cart. "What? What's wrong?"

"I have to see this garden," Amaris said excitedly, jumping off the cart and leaving a dumbfounded Logan behind. There were so many different colored roses; pink, yellow, white, and red. Amaris was in heaven as she took photos. Images of Taylor and Xavier in this garden flashed in her head. She was getting so many ideas as she snapped away. She was so deep in her own world that she didn't realize she was being watched.

Logan stood there with her hands in her pockets as she watched Amaris's face light up as she took pictures. She'd never seen someone so excited in her life. Logan could tell nature and photography were Amaris's natural habitat.

Logan was invisible at this point, so she took the time to admire the beauty in front of her. She didn't know what it was about Amaris; she was usually standoffish when it came to people, but as soon as she saw Amaris, she felt a pull toward her. That's why she was outside in her $2000 suit, standing in her mother's garden.

Amaris was saying something to Logan, but all Logan could focus on were her beautiful, full lips. She imagined tugging on Amaris's bottom lip with her teeth before kissing her.

"If you're going to stare at me like that, give me a compliment," Amaris said with amusement dancing in her eyes.

Logan's eyes locked with Amaris's, feeling totally embarrassed. "I'm sorry."

"It's okay." Amaris raised her camera and took a shot of Logan in the garden. She looked so out of place in her suit amongst nature, but there was a sexiness about her as well. She exuded confidence without even trying. Logan's aura was intense, but calm at the same time. She could see a light in Logan, but it was dim.

"I'm going to make you pay for my pictures," Logan joked.

"Would you really let me shoot you?"

"Sure, go ahead." Logan struck a pose.

"Not that type of picture." Amaris made her way over to Logan, took her fingers, and traced the outline of Logan's beautiful face. She had such strong features; her high cheek bones were gorgeous and her eyes looked like they wanted to tell a story. She didn't know why she was so comfortable around Logan.

Amaris's touch was like fire against Logan's skin. Logan's heart sped up as Amaris traced her lips.

"I mean an intimate shot. I'd love to shoot you naked, watch the sun shine on your beautiful chocolate skin as it lightens your dark eyes. I think it'd be one of my best shots."

Logan gulped, thinking about the way the shoot would end, hopefully with them both naked getting lost in one another.

"You don't hold anything back, huh?"

Amaris shrugged. "I don't believe in doing that." Amaris was all about energy. She felt like it was dumb to waste energy holding onto things, when she could express her feelings and let it go. "So would you let me?"

"I'd have to think about it. I mean, the least you could do is take me to dinner if you want to see me naked." They stared at each other before laughing.

"Maybe we can arrange that."

The energy between the two felt as though they were surrounded by a glass dome, both not knowing what their feelings were, but not caring at the same time. Logan wanted to pull Amaris closer, to feel her soft skin against hers, but she refrained from doing so. *Who are you and why do I feel so close to you?* Logan thought.

As if Amaris could read her mind, she asked, "Do you believe in love at first sight?"

Logan traced every inch of Amaris's face before speaking. "Maybe." Before Amaris could respond, Logan's ringing phone interrupted them.

Logan reached into her pocket and grabbed the phone. "Yes, mother?"

"Hey, Taylor is here and she wants to speak with Amaris about tonight."

"Okay, we'll be on our way." Logan ended the call. "The bride-to-be is here and she's requesting your presence."

"Okay." Amaris replied. They got back into the golf cart and headed back to the house, which kind of relieved Logan. She couldn't explain how she felt around Amaris, but she felt like she needed to get away from her and get herself together. This wasn't her and it wasn't what she did. She didn't want to feel like she was leading Amaris on.

Taylor's bubbly, smiling self was waiting for them outside, when they pulled up.

"And there is the beautiful bride." Logan gushed about her soon-to-be sister-in-law. She loved Taylor as her sister because of the love Taylor had for Xavier. She knew it wasn't easy loving Xavier at first, with his Casanova ways, but Taylor had stuck with him.

Taylor met Logan down the stairs and wrapped her arms around her, hugging her tight. "Hey, Sis."

Logan smiled, kissing Taylor on the cheek. "Someone's in a good mood today," she joked.

"Of course, I am."

Amaris stood back, watching Logan and Taylor. It was as if her family members couldn't help but smile when they were around her. Amaris took that as a good sign. She felt like it meant Logan's heart was good.

"From what I've heard, you've been a bridezilla."

Taylor looked appalled. "What? Who told you that?"

"I have my sources."

"I'm going to kill your brother."

Taylor couldn't even keep a straight face as the words came from her mouth. She was grateful for Xavier, because he had been so understanding during their wedding planning.

Taylor's eyes finally landed on Amaris. "Amaris, it's so nice to see you again." Amaris and Taylor embraced. Amaris liked Taylor from the moment they met. Taylor was so down to Earth and gorgeous, she knew she'd love shooting their wedding pictures.

"How was your flight?" Taylor asked.

"My flight was great, thank you."

"Oh, no problem. So did my sis show you around?"

"Just a little. I saw the rose garden and thought of so many ideas for you and Xavier."

Taylor clapped excitedly. "Oh yeah?" She intertwined their arms. "Let's talk about them." With that, she swooshed Amaris away. Amaris took one last look at Logan who was smiling from ear to ear before they disappeared into the house.

Logan gave herself a few minutes to collect her thoughts. She couldn't understand what it was about Amaris that kept her heart beating out of her chest. She found it hard to keep her cool around her and for her, that was rare. She thought of her touch that had set every piece of her body on fire. No woman had ever had that effect on her before. She knew then and there that she would have to stay away from Amaris. She had no time to fall for her when it could possibly end in heartbreak as she had vowed not to do that to anyone.

Her mother was waiting for her when she walked into the house. The look of concern on her face made Logan feel bad. "Are you okay, sweetie?"

"Yeah, I'm good mom."

"Are you up for a walk with your old mom?"

Logan wanted to tell her mom that she was exhausted and wanted to take a nap, but the hope in her mother's eyes made her suck it up. "For you mom, anything."

Logan followed her mother back outside; she was thankful the sun was starting to go down. "How are you feeling?"

"I'm good. A little tired, but I'll make it."

Mrs. Maddox intertwined their hands. "Your strength amazes me."

Logan smiled, she loved her mother so dearly. The days she couldn't get out of bed, her mother was right there taking care of her with no complaints.

"So do you actually know Amaris?" her mother asked, getting right to the point.

"No, it's the first time I've met her. But it doesn't feel like it. Have you ever felt that way?"

Mrs. Maddox thought about the only time she's ever felt like that. "Yes, with your father."

"It's a crazy feeling." Logan still felt the butterflies filling her stomach. There was a familiarity when it came to Amaris, like her soul had instantly recognized her. She felt calm, yet antsy around Amaris. It was a feeling she wasn't familiar with; a feeling she didn't know what to do with.

"Yes, it is, but it's a beautiful feeling when embraced."

For a split second, Logan thought about embracing that feeling with Amaris, but quickly shook the thought. "It seemed to have worked out for you and dad."

Her parents had been together for fifty-one years. They married right out of high school and never looked back. It warmed Logan's heart to see them still so madly in love.

"Yes, it did work for us. It could for you too." Mrs. Maddox gently pushed.

"You know it can't."

"It could, if you allowed it."

"It wouldn't be right, mom."

"How do you know what's right?"

"Mom …" Logan said, slightly irritated. She didn't want to upset her mother, but she also didn't want to have the conversation.

"I don't mean to push, I just want you to be happy."

"I am happy."

"I just—"

"Hey mom, I think it'll be better if we head in. I think I need to take a nap before the party. I'm pretty pooped."

Mrs. Maddox knew that that was the end of the conversation and she accepted it. "Okay sweetie, let's head back."

Logan knew her mother meant well and, in another life, she would have gone after Amaris, but it wouldn't happen in this one. Whatever she was feeling needed to subside, but for now, she knew she needed to stay away from Amaris.

By seven o'clock, the Maddox's estate was packed with Xavier and Taylor's 250 guests. Logan had taken some time before the guests started arriving and the party began to take a nap and it really helped her.

"What's up, sis?" Xavier wrapped his arm around Logan's shoulder.

"Hey bro, this is really nice. I didn't know you guys had so many damn people coming to the wedding," she replied.

"More than half these people are business clients."

Logan looked around the room. She knew she wouldn't want her wedding to be full of clients. To her, a wedding was supposed to be a day filled with love and joy, not a networking event. "You have a room full of clients here, Xavier?"

"Hey, these are people Taylor and I have worked with and a few we're trying to close a deal with. It's all in the business, little sis."

Watching everyone made Logan realize she made the right choice to do her own thing with her publishing company instead of following in her parents' and Xavier's footsteps. Even though Xavier was an architect, he spent about forty percent of his time with the real estate business as well, when he wasn't caught up in a project.

"Just sad."

Xavier laughed. "Shut up."

Amaris looked herself over in the mirror, making sure everything was in place. She'd had a great time talking to Taylor earlier, but she couldn't get her mind off Logan; just the thought of her sent a sensation she couldn't fathom, running through her veins. She thought about their time in her mother's garden and the way Logan quivered as she ran her finger over her face. She wondered if Logan knew she caught that. She wanted to ask Taylor what Logan's deal was, but thought it would be unprofessional, since she was technically there on business.

Speaking of business, Amaris felt her anxiety kicking in as she thought about being around all those people. She didn't do well in big crowds and from the number Taylor gave her tonight, this was definitely a big crowd. She made sure she took one of her pills before grabbing her camera and heading downstairs.

She stopped at the staircase as soon as she saw the room. Her palms began to sweat instantly and her heartbeat sped up. She closed her eyes, taking deep breaths as she tried to get herself together. She wanted to run back upstairs and forget the job, but she knew she couldn't do that to Taylor and Xavier. Besides, her reputation was on the line. She had to do a good job.

"When does the next book drop, sis?" Xavier asked, engaging his sister.

"I'm in the middle of …" Logan trailed off as her eyes landed on Amaris at the top of the staircase, looking like a true goddess. Her curly afro seemed even more puffed out and beautiful. Her beautiful purple and yellow dashiki dress made her seem like she came from a line of royalty. Then there was her favorite thing in her hand—her Canon camera—but Logan could see a pained expression on her face. She wanted to go to her and ask her if she was okay, but she knew it wasn't her place and would only complicate the feelings she was trying to bury.

Xavier's eyes followed Logan's to see what had stopped his sister mid-sentence and his eyes landed on Amaris. "She is stunning, little sis, isn't she?"

"Indeed, brother."

"So what are you doing over here with me?" Xavier had to confirm his mother was absolutely right about Logan being struck by the love bug. It was an interesting thing to see his sister like that. Usually, Logan would shoo a woman off with ease, but Amaris had her stopping mid-sentence, transfixed.

"I'm over here because we're talking and she's not my woman." Logan didn't want her brother to get any ideas like their mother. There was no future for herself and Amaris, so she didn't want to tease herself with the thought. Even saying this to herself, she still hadn't taken her eyes off Amaris. Something was wrong, it looked like Amaris was going to hyperventilate.

"Do me a favor though, go check on her. She doesn't look too hot."

"Why don't you do it? I mean, this is my party, I'm supposed to be mingling with my guest." Logan gave Xavier a deathly stare, one he knew all too well. "Alright, alright, I'll go." Xavier raised his hands in surrender and headed up the stairs.

"Sweet pea." Logan was wrapped in her father's arms from behind. She turned around and hugged her father tight. "Hey old man, where have you been all day?"

"Work. You know someone has to hold the fort down while all of you play with this wedding." Mr. Maddox joked.

"Oh, is that what we were doing?" Logan didn't care how much of a stud she was or what type of clothes she wore, she would always be a daddy's girl at heart. He was the only man who held her heart and would never lose it.

"How are you, sweetheart?"

"I'm hanging in there, daddy, you know, taking it day by day."

"That's good. I heard you had a doctor's appointment."

"Yes, but like I told mom, it was nothing different. If anything changes, you know you two will be the first to know."

Logan could see a sadness cross her father's face, but he immediately fixed it. She was just like him, able to quickly erase her feelings. Logan didn't want to have a somber mood when the night was supposed to be a night of celebration, so she changed the subject. "So how are things with the properties, dad?"

"Things are great, we are truly blessed to be in the position we're in."

"Indeed."

———— • •●• • ————

"Hey woman, are you okay?" Xavier had finally made his way to Amaris. He could tell that Logan was right; Amaris didn't look so good. She was sweating and her hands were shaking badly. Xavier pulled her away from the crowd. "What's wrong?"

Amaris felt so embarrassed to be standing in front of Xavier like this. She was supposed to be doing a job for him; she knew this didn't look good. "I have really bad anxiety." Amaris wrapped her hands behind her back, taking deep breaths to calm her nerves.

"You have anxiety around big crowds?"

"Yes."

Xavier sighed. "Amaris, you knew this would be a big wedding. Why would you not disclose this before we hired you?" Xavier didn't want to sound like a dick, but her main job was to take pictures of the wedding which meant she would have to be around a big group the whole weekend.

"I just need a moment. I took my medication. I should be fine in a minute."

Xavier knew he couldn't sit up here with Amaris, but he didn't want to leave her either. "I'll be back," he said and headed downstairs. He knew Logan was going to hate him for this, but he felt like he was helping her in the long run. He also knew Logan would be able to help Amaris because she dealt with anxiety as well.

"Hey Pops, can I steal Lo from you for a second?"

Logan's eyebrow peaked, wondering what her brother needed. "For what?"

"Just come on." He grabbed her by her elbow, leading her away from their father.

When Logan saw they were heading upstairs she pulled her arm away. "What the hell, X?"

"She's having a damn anxiety attack. I don't know what to do."

Logan felt like God was trying to play a trick on her. He knew she wouldn't leave Amaris alone. Logan knew how anxiety could cripple a person especially if it was really bad. "Alright, I got her bro."

Xavier looked relieved. "Thanks."

Logan headed upstairs to see Amaris sitting on the floor with her head between her legs. The sight tugged on her heart strings.

Amaris felt a soft hand touch the back of her neck making her jump, she then heard Logan's soothing voice in her ear.

"We'll get through this together."

Amaris couldn't speak, she just shook her head as she felt herself being lifted from the floor and carried somewhere.

Logan took Amaris into her old bedroom and closed the door behind them. She didn't need her meddling mother to wonder what was going on. She also didn't want Amaris to be seen like this, she knew how embarrassing it was. She set Amaris down on her bed.

"I want you to take a deep breath and hold it as long as you can."

Amaris did as she was told, she took a deep breath and held it for as long as she could, she then exhaled, trying to get her heart to stop beating so quickly.

"It feels like someone is sitting on my chest." She barely spoke. Her eyes were filling with tears as she tried to catch her breath. She felt like her own body was suffocating her. She hadn't had a bad attack like this in months.

Logan got on her knees so she was eye level with Amaris. "You have to try to calm your breathing sweetheart. Tell me how you got into photography."

"Wh-what?"

"Distract yourself from this. How did you get into photography?"

"I, um, I took it in high school and realized I was actually good at it."

"What do you like to shoot?"

"Anything that's beautiful." Amaris started to feel the tremble in her body slow down.

"Is that why you want to shoot me because you think I'm beautiful?"

Amaris looked into Logan's eyes. "You're the most beautiful woman I've ever laid eyes on, Logan." She meant every word. She'd been around plenty of beautiful people, but none compared to Logan; she was like a work of art.

Amaris could hear Logan's intake of air from her statement; she didn't know if it was a good or bad thing. For a moment, they both sat there staring at each other; Logan lost for words and Amaris waiting for a response. It was then she realized her panic attack had passed and she was breathing normally.

"I don't do relationships." The words were the first thing out of Logan's mouth before she could even think about it.

"That's funny. I don't remember asking you for one." Amaris could see the turmoil in Logan's eyes and she wanted so bad to know where it was coming from. It was as if it pained Logan to be around her or speak of love.

"I can't." Logan choked while standing up. Just being close to Amaris sent her senses into overdrive. She wanted to take this woman into her arms and taste her lips; to feel her body against hers, but it was like opening Pandora's box to Logan.

Amaris stood gently, grabbing Logan's arm. She was happy that Logan didn't pull away. "I believe in the universe. I believe that you're always right where you should be. I believe things are unexpected like love. I believe in soul mates. Ever since I saw you this afternoon, it was as if I recognized you, Logan. I don't know what this is, but I never run away from what the universe presents me."

Logan's eyes closed, allowing Amaris's words to sink into her body and mind. No one had ever spoken to her like that and she was a writer. "Your touch is like liquid fire against my skin. It's like you touch every part of my soul because I've felt it too—that feeling of belonging to you—but that's the part that scares me. I cannot give you what you want, Amaris. So please, forget me." Logan pulled away from Amaris and walked out of the room.

She took a moment to recover before walking downstairs to join the party. She was glad that Amaris didn't follow her out or grab her again, because she knew she would surely take Amaris into her arms if she did.

Her mother caught her by the arm seeing something was wrong. "Are you alright, sweetheart?"

Logan didn't know how to answer her mother; her emotions were everywhere and totally uncontrolled. She knew she couldn't be in the same place as Amaris, at least not tonight. She needed time to regroup and mask any emotions she could have shown to Amaris.

"You know what mom? I'm not feeling too well. I think I should head home and get some rest. I want to be my best for the wedding tomorrow."

"What's wrong? Should I come with you? Maybe you should stay here."

"No, it's fine. I'm going to just go home and go to sleep." She was trying to make her escape before Amaris came out of the room.

"Okay, will you call me when you get home?"

"Of course." Logan kissed her mother's cheek. "I love you, mother."

"I love you too."

Logan said her goodbyes and made a quick exit.

Amaris felt so rejected by Logan it took her a moment to collect her thoughts. She wasn't the type to hide her feelings, but she was affected by what Logan said. She couldn't understand what Logan's issue was. She felt like she was unlovable. She knew she couldn't dwell on the situation right now because she had a job to do, so she grabbed her camera and headed out of the room to do what she loved to do.

Logan loosened her tie as she heard her door bell ring. The whole ride home she felt like she was in a daze; she knew she had to get her mind off Amaris.

She walked to her door and opened it, smiling at the beauty that stood in front of her. "Chandra, it's so nice to see you again." Logan turned on her charm. Like always, Chandra gave Logan the biggest smile.

"Logan Maddox, it's been too long." Logan pulled Chandra into her arms and slid her tongue into her mouth, needing to erase her conversation with Amaris from her mind. Chandra was always a good distraction.

Chandra wrapped her arms around Logan's neck, returning the kiss with just as much passion as Logan was giving her. Logan picked her up, allowing her to wrap her legs around her.

"Somebody missed me," Chandra said in a seductive purr.

Logan chuckled. "Just a little bit," Logan responded as she climbed the steps to her bedroom. Chandra nuzzled her neck before biting her, eliciting a moan from her. Chandra knew exactly how to turn Logan on.

"You really are trying to get fucked doing all that," Logan remarked, as though in a threat.

Chandra laughed as Logan threw her on the bed. She spread out across Logan's king-sized bed like a cat. Logan's eyes traveled across Chandra's body. She was a sight to behold as she untied her trench coat to expose nothing but her chocolate skin. Logan licked her lips in anticipation.

"Come show me just how much you miss me." She pulled Logan down onto the bed.

* * *

"Hey girl, are you enjoying yourself?" Taylor walked over to Amaris like the gushing bride that she was.

"Yeah, of course. This is so nice, Taylor." Amaris hadn't seen Logan all night and she wondered if she was keeping clear of her. She wondered if it really pained her that much to be around her.

"How are the pictures coming along?"

"Oh, I've gotten tons of pictures of your guests, but …" Amaris acted like she was looking around for someone. "I wanted to get pictures of the siblings together, but I haven't seen Logan around here."

"Oh, Lo wasn't feeling good, so she went home to get some rest."

Wow, she really left her own brother's rehearsal dinner just to avoid me? Amaris felt a tinge of hurt from that. "Oh, no. What happened? She seemed fine when she helped me a little while ago."

Taylor looked at Amaris puzzled. "Helped with what?"

"I, um, had a bit of an anxiety attack and Logan helped me through it."

"Oh my God, why didn't you come to me? Are you okay now?" Taylor asked, concerned.

"Yes, I am. Once they're over, I'm good."

"Okay, good."

"So, what's up with Logan?" Amaris asked nonchalantly.

"What do you mean?"

"Does she have a girlfriend?"

Taylor smiled from ear to ear. "Let me guess, you're crushing on my sister."

"Not crushing, just a little curious."

Taylor knew she couldn't tell Amaris too much, so she gave her what she could. "Logan doesn't do the relationship thing."

"Really? Why not? I'm sure she has women falling all over her." Amaris needed to know what was up with Logan. She didn't want to seem like she was prying, but she just didn't understand it. Logan was sexy, successful, and from what she could tell, kind. Why wouldn't she want to spend her life with someone?

Taylor shrugged, not wanting to get into it. "I think she's in love with her career right now. I mean, everything is going well with Maddox Publishing Inc. and she's about to start production for one of her books, so she's pretty busy."

"Her book? What is it called?"

"Temptation. My sis has skills. You should check out her work."

Taylor studied Amaris for a second. "You must have had one hell of a ride with Logan." Amaris's head tilted down so Taylor wouldn't see her smile. "So, are you feeling my sis?"

"Maybe a little," Amaris admitted.

Taylor wanted to jump up and down in excitement, but she knew it wouldn't be any good. Ever since she'd known Xavier and the Maddox's family, she'd never seen Logan with a girlfriend, so she figured Amaris didn't have a chance.

"I don't chase after anyone, so if Logan wants to talk to me, I'm right here." Amaris didn't know who she was trying to convince; herself or Taylor.

"I would love to see my sis happy and in a relationship with someone special, but honestly, when Logan has her mind set, it's pretty hard to change it. If you're the one to change that, I'll bow down to you."

They shared a laugh before being interrupted by Xavier. He wrapped his arms around Taylors waist. "We have to talk to Kenneth about the proposal."

"Oh, right. Amaris, we'll talk later."

"Sure, but first let me get a picture of the beautiful couple." Xavier and Taylor posed for the camera, smiling as bright as ever as Amaris took the photo. "Such a beautiful couple. I can't wait to take pictures of you guys tomorrow, it's going to be amazing." Amaris thought of all the places she could take pictures of Taylor and Xavier and she knew it would be some of her best work.

"Doesn't matter how the pictures come out, as long as I get to marry this beauty."

Taylor gushed like a little school girl. "You're such a charmer." They shared a kiss, it was intimate and soft, making Amaris turn away. She felt like it wasn't something she should be sharing with them. Amaris had seen couples in love, but Taylor and Xavier were a scene of beautiful moments. She knew they would last.

"Alright you two love birds, I'll let you have your moment," Amaris said and slipped away.

— • ● • • —

Chandra laid on top of Logan, hot, sweaty, and out of breath. "Damn Logan, are you sure that thing isn't real?"

Logan laughed as her strap-on dildo stayed planted inside of Chandra. She remembered why she only took Chandra in doses; they always fucked for hours, leaving Logan exhausted. Even now, she could barely keep her eyes open. "I'm just that good."

"Hmm, whatever." Chandra slid off Logan, lying beside her instead.

Logan loved her sex afterglow. "Are you staying the night?"

"No, I have a meeting in the morning."

"On a Saturday?"

"Hey, money never sleeps."

That was one thing that attracted Logan to Chandra, she was a go-getter and she didn't allow anyone to give her anything. Logan had watched her build her modeling agency from the ground up.

"I guess it doesn't, Boss Lady," Logan said with a small smile. She loved how easy their relationship was. Chandra didn't expect anything from Logan.

There was no commitment pressure, they just enjoyed fucking each other and an occasional date night. "What time is your meeting, hun?"

"Early."

"Want to be my date for my brother's wedding tomorrow?" Logan knew she would need a distraction from Amaris and Chandra would be the perfect distraction.

"You want to take little ole me to the big Maddox wedding?"

Logan rolled her eyes. Her brother's wedding was a big event; it was even announced in multiple states as if everyone would be coming. "I mean, if you don't want to come—"

"Oh, I do!" Chandra said excitedly. Of course, Chandra did. She knew the Maddox wedding would not only be a wedding, but the network event of the year.

"I'll have my driver pick you up around two. Is that enough time for you?"

"I'll be ready then."

———— · ·●· · ————

Amaris's phone vibrated, breaking her from her sleep. She looked at the phone before answering. "Darling," she said sleepily.

"Hi sweetie, did I wake you?"

Amaris looked at the time, it was a little after three in the morning. "Yes, but it's okay. Is everything okay?"

"Yes, I just miss you, that's all."

Amaris smiled, Quelm was so sweet. "I miss you too, how are you calling me?"

Quelm should have been in bed with her husband. "Terry is dead to the world right now."

Amaris laid on her back so she could fully wake herself. "What are you wearing?" Her voice went from sleepy to seductive and Quelm caught on quickly.

"Just a shirt."

"Panties?" Amaris inquired.

"No."

Amaris imagined Quelm in her shirt, she knew the touch and taste of Quelm's pussy so it made her wet to think of Quelm in just a shirt with nothing underneath. "Where are you now?"

"Terry's office."

"Sit on his desk."

"Okay." Quelm stood from her chair and sat on top of her husband's desk.

"I'm going to fuck you on top of this desk so every time you see him sitting here, you'll think about how I made you come right here," Amaris said as if she was standing in front of Quelm.

Quelm moaned at the thought. She loved when Amaris role-played with her during phone sex, it was one of the sexiest experiences.

"Slide your hand in your panties and rub your clit," Amaris commanded as her own fingers found her nipples. She tugged on them gently before squeezing.

"Oh, Amaris, I'm so wet," Quelm cooed into the phone.

"I know, baby. I can feel your wetness all on my fingers as I slide my finger in your pussy, stroking you."

"Oh, baby," Quelm moaned.

"Honey where are you?" Amaris heard Quelm's husband's voice before the line went dead. Amaris couldn't help but laugh as she set her phone down. She didn't know how Quelm stayed somewhere she wasn't happy. Amaris felt like it was a waste of her life. She knew her and Quelm would never be anything more, but she wanted Quelm to be happy. Five minutes later she got a text.

"I'm sorry, my love."

"It's okay, fuck your husband. I'll text you later."

"Are you mad?"

"No. Lol. I don't want him to think anything. I'll text you later."

"Okay :(."

CHAPTER

3

"Are you ready for this brother?" Logan fixed Xavier's tie and looked him over to make sure everything was in place.

"Yes, I'm ready," Xavier said, his eyes sparkling with excitement. Logan had never seen Xavier so excited; it was contagious. "What happened to you last night? Mom said you weren't feeling good."

"Oh yeah, I was tired. You know how that is for me."

Xavier studied his sister for a second. He knew it was complete bullshit. "She has you that off balance you had to leave my party early?"

Logan didn't say anything, but the silence said it all. Chandra was a good distraction, but as soon as she left, Logan's mind went back to Amaris. She wondered if she had a good time at the party. She couldn't get Amaris off her mind.

Xavier continued. "You have—" someone knocked on the door, interrupting their conversation. "Come in," Xavier called out.

Amaris walked into the room and immediately took Logan's breath away. She looked amazing in her navy-blue dress. Logan's eyes went to the v neck on her dress; it showed enough cleavage, but not too much to be disrespectful. Logan thought Amaris was beautiful last night, but today was a whole different story. She was still natural which Logan could appreciate. Her curls seemed to be extra bouncy as she walked toward them. She wore light make up and eye shadow that blended in with her skin. Her lips looked sexy with the navy-blue lipstick she was wearing. On any other woman Logan probably wouldn't have liked it but she would give anything to be that lipstick right now.

Logan thought everything matched her skin tone so well. She could appreciate Amaris sticking with the theme color for the wedding. Her eyes went down to Amaris's calves which had her sexy navy-blue high heels laced around them. Logan pictured Amaris in nothing but those heels with her legs wrapped around her waist as she stroked her with her strap. The thought made her want to take Amaris right there.

"Don't stare too hard, sis," Xavier whispered a little too loudly into Logan's ears and she peeled her eyes away from Amaris to scold him.

Amaris ignored the comment and Logan's intense stare. "I came for prep pictures, so ignore me and do your thing guys."

Logan continued helping Xavier get ready. She heard the sound of Amaris's camera shutter and tried to ignore it as best as possible. She got a whiff of her perfume and almost lost all her will.

Xavier chuckled as he watched his sister's nostrils flare. Logan had it bad and didn't even know it. "Are you enjoying Vegas, Amaris?" he asked, not taking his eyes off his sister.

"Yes, I am. Thanks for the opportunity." Amaris made sure to get every angle she could as she tried to ignore the tension between Logan and herself. She wanted to ask why it was so hard for her to stay last night. She hated the very fact that Logan's presence was throwing her off.

Logan looked handsome in her navy blue, Hugo Boss tuxedo. Her dreads were twisted and pulled back into a fishtail. Her line-up was fresh, which brought her complexion out more. She was sexy in every way. Amaris zoomed in on her cuff links, which were silver L's laced in diamonds and took a picture of it. She thought of all the sexy pictures she could take of Logan; she would be an amazing model for Amaris's event which she was having in a few months.

"So Logan, are you feeling better? Taylor told me you left early."

"Yeah, I was feeling a little tired."

"Was that before or after you saw me?"

Logan stopped what she was doing to look at Amaris. "Are you my woman?"

Amaris tried to hide her surprise. "No."

"Then stop questioning me like you are." Logan snapped, her rudeness taking Amaris by surprise.

"Sis …" Xavier cut his eyes at Logan, even he felt like Logan was being rude. He'd never seen her behave like that.

"Xavier, will you excuse us?" Xavier looked at Amaris, asking her if she was sure with his eyes. When she nodded her head, he made his exit.

Amaris wanted to get down to the bottom of things with Logan. No, they weren't a couple, hell they didn't even know each other, but she wouldn't take the disrespect. Whatever was between them they needed to fix it.

She stood in front of Logan, taking up her personal space. She studied her trying to sense any trace of anger she could have caused in order for her to speak to her like that. She could feel the nervousness radiating from Logan, so she placed her hand on her cheek, trying to hide her hand which was shaking.

"I see you," she whispered. She needed Logan to know she saw her inner self—the girl who was scared to show her feelings for whatever reason, who made sure to keep Amaris at arm's length.

Logan's heart rate sped up from Amaris's words. She felt her words sink into her body and it hit her like a ton of bricks. She knew exactly what Amaris meant. Logan felt her heart opening to Amaris and she wanted to stop it so bad, but she felt herself reaching for Amaris, wrapping her arm around her waist and pulling her into a kiss.

Amaris didn't hesitate, she didn't hold back, instead she embraced Logan. Logan's tongue invaded Amaris's mouth, the taste of her almost too intoxicating. She'd wanted to kiss Amaris since the moment she laid eyes on her, but the kiss was nothing like she'd expected; it was far better. Her hands slid down to Amaris's ass, squeezing it while pulling her closer. It was as if there was too much space between them.

Amaris knew no matter what, no matter the time, the place, or the earth, she would belong to Logan. Their kiss was enough to send every feeling in her into overdrive. She felt dizzy as their kiss intensified, if Logan wasn't holding her up, she knew she would slide to the floor. Her legs were like jelly and her heart felt like it was beating too fast, but she couldn't and didn't want to stop it.

"Hey sis, everything okay in there?" Xavier asked through the door, making Logan break their kiss.

Amaris sucked in the much-needed air as Logan placed her forehead against hers, while still holding Amaris tightly in her arms.

"Yeah bro, everything's fine." Logan barely got the words out. She looked at Amaris and cupped her chin, not knowing what to do with her feelings. Whenever she was close to Amaris, she felt like everything was okay and she didn't know how to deal with that. Her heart had been closed off for so long and it wasn't in her cards to open it, but she couldn't hide what she was feeling.

"Do I know you?" Logan asked seriously.

Amaris smiled, rubbing her cheek against Logan's. Her skin was so smooth she didn't want to disconnect from her. "Maybe. Maybe we were lovers, soul mates perhaps. Maybe we traveled the world and made love and shared our lives together. Maybe we had a cottage in the forest and lived off the land making love wherever we wanted. I see you Logan, I recognize you and I think you feel the same," Amaris spoke genuinely. She'd never felt an instant connection to anyone the way she had with Logan and she wasn't afraid to embrace it.

Logan knew she would never find another like Amaris. She came straight from Mother Earth and God. Logan knew Amaris was right; she recognized her—she didn't know how, but she did. Amaris felt like home to her.

"Amaris …" Logan sighed.

Amaris placed her finger on Logan's lips, stopping her from saying what she knew she didn't want to hear. "Why are you so scared of this, Logan? Why can't you let this just flow? See where it goes?"

Logan closed her eyes trying to collect her thoughts. "There's so much Amaris, so much you don't know." She opened her eyes and saw something she'd never seen in another female's eyes…there was hope of a future, a future Logan couldn't give her.

"Sis, we have to finish getting ready, it's kind of my wedding." Xavier's voice impatiently rang in through the closed door again.

Logan smiled, kissing Amaris's forehead. "I'll see you in a bit."

Amaris took a step back, disconnecting from Logan. "I should go get pictures of Taylor. You look nice by the way."

"Thank you." Logan pulled Amaris back into her arms and pecked her on the lips. "You look amazing as well."

"Thank you, finish getting ready." Amaris grabbed her camera, walked to the door, and opened it. "I'm sorry, Xavier," she said to him.

"Everything cool?"

"Yes, we're cool." She smiled as she slid past Xavier.

Xavier closed the door behind him as he entered the room, looking at Logan for answers. Logan was looking in the mirror while fixing her bow tie, ignoring Xavier. Her thoughts were on the explosive kiss she'd just shared with Amaris. She still felt the butterflies in her stomach from Amaris's touch.

"So, you're just going to stand your ass there and not say what just happened?"

"We kissed," Logan said nonchalantly but her insides were tingling. She wanted nothing more than to go back to Amaris and taste her lips again.

Xavier clapped loudly while smiling. "Finally, you asshole! So what's up, are you going to pursue her?"

"I didn't say all that. It was just a kiss Xavier; nothing has changed on my side."

Xavier rolled his eyes. "Well, maybe it's time it does."

"We're not talking about this today, let's enjoy your wedding."

Xavier placed his hand on Logan's shoulder, he could feel her trembling. "She's the one sis and I'm telling you this because I love you and I see it.

You've never been this way and it's amazing, because it's literally only been a day. You won't come across this again. Please, take it, sister."

Logan allowed Xavier's words to sink in, but remained silent.

Two hours later, Logan and half of the wedding party cried as Xavier and Taylor shared their vows. Logan had never seen anything so beautiful as her brother pouring his heart out to Taylor. She found herself sneaking glimpses at Amaris, but Amaris was so in her zone taking pictures it was as though nobody but Xavier and Taylor existed in her eyes. She was as cool as a cucumber, as if they hadn't shared an explosive kiss just a while ago. Logan laughed at herself for pining over this woman.

Logan was walking through the reception when someone caught her hand, she turned around thinking it was Amaris, but it was Chandra.

"Hey lover," she cooed in her ear. Logan had completely forgotten that she'd invited Chandra.

"Chandra." She forced a smile. "You look amazing." She kissed Chandra on the cheek. Chandra did look amazing in her little black dress, but she didn't compare to Amaris.

"Thank you, you look dashing yourself." Chandra tugged on Logan's tux.

"Thank you."

"So are you sitting with me?"

"I have to sit with—"

"Logan ..."

Logan heard Amaris call her over her shoulder. Perfect timing, Logan thought sarcastically as she turned around facing Amaris. "Yes?"

"I'm trying to get pictures of the family, are you free?"

"Yes, I'm free." Chandra slid her hand into Logan's making Logan flinch. Amaris's eyes went to both of their hands and then Logan's face. Logan felt like she should explain herself, but she still kept quiet.

"Is this your date?"

"Yes." Chandra spoke up, taking her place beside Logan. It was primal, as if she needed Amaris to know she and Logan were together. Chandra could see the desire in Amaris's eyes and she didn't like it, not one bit.

Amaris didn't say anything, but she was fuming. She couldn't believe Logan had kissed her a few hours ago knowing she would have a date coming to the wedding. "Well, let me take a picture of the lovely couple." Amaris could have cussed Logan out, but she was better than that. She was there for a job, not for Logan, so she raised her camera and snapped a picture of Logan and Chandra. She ignored the smirk on Chandra's face as she took the picture. It was clear that Logan was either entertaining her or fucking her, there were no feelings involved.

Logan turned to Chandra. "I'll catch up with you in a bit, let me take these pictures. Go mingle. I know you came for the business connections as well." Chandra's shocked look confirmed what Logan already knew. "It's okay, I'll catch up with you a little later." She kissed Chandra on the cheek and led Amaris away.

"She's cute," Amaris said sarcastically.

Logan rolled her eyes. "I forgot I invited her and let's not get snippy. I didn't know we were going to kiss this morning." Logan felt bad for Chandra already, she didn't need Amaris to throw anything in her face. She felt like they were a couple and she got caught cheating.

"All I said was she was cute, I didn't say anything else."

Logan rolled her eyes. This was exactly why she didn't do relationships. She didn't like answering to people and having to deal with their feelings. "Okay, Amaris."

"Let's hurry and get these pictures done so you can get back to your girlfriend."

Logan grabbed Amaris under arm and damn near dragged her out of the reception hall. "If you don't let me go, Logan …" Logan pulled her into a side room pushing her against the wall and kissing her forcefully.

Amaris was mad at herself for the way her body sunk into Logan and her arms automatically wrapped around her neck. Logan moaned into Amaris's mouth as she invaded her mouth with her tongue. She'd wanted to kiss Amaris ever since their lips departed the first time.

Amaris broke the kiss, slapping Logan on the chest. "I'm not that damn easy. You have another woman here as your date."

"She's not my woman, I don't belong to anyone."

Amaris frowned. She didn't like the fact that was her excuse. "You don't belong to anyone? So that gives you the right to kiss me and then invite someone to your brother's wedding?"

Logan ran her hands over her face, she felt like anything she said wouldn't sound right. All she wanted to do right now was continue to kiss Amaris, but she could see that wasn't happening. "I'm sorry, Amaris, honestly I invited her last night. I didn't expect this to happen," she said, pointing at the both of them. She didn't want Amaris to look at her in a bad light. For some reason, she really cared what she thought of her.

Amaris sighed while looking at Logan. She could see that she was genuine, so she accepted the apology. She ran her hands down Logan's torso. "What are we doing here?"

Logan honestly didn't know, she just knew she wanted to be around Amaris. "We're doing this …" Logan took Amaris into her arms, kissing her again. It was like her taste was addicting and Logan was hooked. Amaris moaned as Logan's hands slid down to her ass, squeezing it possessively.

I'm hers, Amaris thought to herself. She knew she would always belong to Logan even if their lives took them in different directions. She'd never had these types of feelings with anyone else and she knew she wouldn't ever after this. This feeling coursing through her body was rare; something a person only experienced once in their lifetime with that special person.

"You just let anybody kiss you like this?" Logan joked.

Amaris tilted her head, looking at Logan while smiling. Logan knew she could see that smile every day of her life and die happy knowing she came across it. "You must have forgotten I was yours in a past life so you're not just anybody. You could have been my husband or wife, so in actuality, I belong to you."

Logan was silent for a moment as she stared at Amaris. She knew she was in trouble because she knew her heart wouldn't allow her to forget about Amaris when she left. She knew she would long to be in Amaris's presence and would feel her absence.

"What are you staring at?"

"You."

"Why?"

Logan sighed, keeping it real with Amaris. "When you leave, I'll want you here."

Amaris felt butterflies fill her stomach. She thought maybe Taylor was wrong, maybe there was a chance for them. "Then I'll come back to you," she said with no hesitation, which made Logan's heart open even more.

"You are like a moth to a flame."

Amaris hand traced over Logan's torso sending sensations straight to Logan's pussy. "Why are you fighting this?"

Before Logan could answer Amaris, her phone rang. "Shit." It was Xavier's ringtone. "They're probably looking for you." She answered her phone. "Yo."

"Are you with Amaris?"

"Yeah."

"You think you could give her back so she can do her job?"

Logan chuckled. "Yeah, sure bro, anything you want." She pressed end on her phone.

"Was she with her?" Taylor asked over Xavier's shoulder.

"Yeah, they're headed back now."

Taylor smiled, clapping her hands. "Could Amaris actually be the one to break Logan?"

"Logan's just having fun. You know she doesn't do relationships, honey."

"You didn't do relationships until you met me. Now, look at you."

Xavier chuckled while wrapping Taylor in his arms. "You're right, Mrs. Maddox. I love you."

"I love you, baby."

Logan kissed Amaris's hands. "My life is very complicated, Amaris. You don't want this life; you don't want me in your world."

"Why don't you let me be the judge of that?"

Logan wanted to, for the first time she really did want to. She'd never wanted to let anyone in her life as much as she wanted to with Amaris, which was crazy to her because she knew nothing about her. It had only been a day and she was already having all these feelings for her.

"I don't want to hurt you." Logan should have been honest, but she couldn't tell Amaris anything about herself, at least, not right now. "Maybe I'll tell you one day, but for now, you have to get back." Logan shut the conversation down by opening the door and walking out of the room, leaving Amaris standing there, dumbfounded.

She didn't get Logan at all, one minute she was kissing her and the next she was ice cold and shut off. She stayed in the room for a few moments to collect her thoughts. Logan had her emotions everywhere and that wasn't good for her anxiety. She felt like she wasn't in control around her, like her emotions weren't her own. The people she had dated for years didn't even have the type of pull Logan was having on her this weekend. After collecting her thoughts, she headed back to the wedding.

Logan knew she had to cut whatever she was doing with Amaris off. She thought it wouldn't be fair to entertain a life with her when she would potentially hurt her in the long run, so she pushed any potential feelings she had in the back of her head and went to find Chandra.

Logan found Chandra speaking with one of Xavier's clients and wrapped her arms around Chandra's waist, making her jump.

"I didn't see you," Chandra said startled.

"I know." Logan smiled.

"Logan, how are you?" The client asked her.

Logan shook the client's hand. "I'm good, thank you. If you would excuse us, we're going to take our seats."

"Sure, sure," he responded.

Logan escorted Chandra toward their table while Chandra looked at her in concern. "Are you okay?" Chandra asked.

"Yeah, I'm good, why?" Logan asked back.

Chandra ran her fingers across Logan's lips. "You have lipstick on your lips," she said, annoyed.

Logan ignored her, pulling her chair out for her before sitting herself. "Are you coming home with me tonight?" Logan needed another distraction. She needed to stop thinking about Amaris the way she was.

"If you want me to," Chandra responded nonchalantly even though she was burning with excitement inside; Logan never spent more than one night at a time with her.

"I want you to."

"Okay, I'll come home with you."

Logan leaned over and kissed Chandra briefly, but it was enough for Chandra to know what she wanted.

• —— • • ● • • —— •

By the end of the night, Amaris was fuming. Logan's blatant disrespect toward her had Amaris ready to fight. She watched Logan all night with Chandra, stealing kisses, touching her intimately and whispering in her ear. Amaris thought about the kiss they shared just hours ago; it was as if what they had experienced meant nothing to Logan. If anyone would have been paying attention to them, they would have thought Logan and Chandra were a beautiful couple.

She was glad when the reception ended and she was able to retreat to her room. She didn't say goodnight to anyone because she didn't have the energy to, she needed peace and quiet. She needed to take a shower and then cleanse her aura so she would feel better.

As the water ran down her back, Amaris closed her eyes and succumbed to her emotions. Tears sprang to her eyes and she allowed them to fall freely. She wasn't one to hold her emotions in; she felt like it did nothing for the soul. She would have her moment and then pick herself up and continue with life, knowing that tomorrow, when she returned to Los Angeles, this would be a distant memory.

She was surprised when she heard a knock on her door. She looked at the time and it was well past midnight. She had thought everyone would be asleep by now. She pulled herself out of bed to answer the door, to her surprise, it was Mrs. Maddox.

"Hi Mrs. Maddox, is everything okay?"

"May I come in?"

"Of course, this is your home." Amaris moved to the side to allow Mrs. Maddox into the room.

"I came to check on you. You disappeared so suddenly after the reception."

"Oh yeah, I'm sorry. I was really tired and just needed to recharge my batteries."

Mrs. Maddox smiled. She'd watched how Amaris watched Logan with her date. She knew it was uncomfortable for Amaris. She could also tell it hurt her to see Logan with someone else. "You know, my daughter is a very smart woman, but when it comes to love, she isn't so smart."

Amaris stared at Mrs. Maddox, puzzled. "I'm sorry?"

"I saw the way you and Logan stared at each other. It was something magical to see. Logan hasn't shown interest and I mean, no real interest in anyone in a very long time. So, when I saw you two together, I thought maybe things could change. So, I want to apologize for my daughter's coldness. I think once she sees she can get close to someone, the only thing she can do is turn them away. She doesn't want to let anyone in, I told her that's no way to live."

Amaris allowed her shoulders to sink. It did hurt her to see Logan with her date. It hurt her that for the rest of the night, Logan acted like she didn't exist. "I thought maybe there was something there but …"

"There is something there. My daughter is just too scared to admit it. You two reminded me of my husband and I."

"What do I do?"

"Keep trying. Before you leave, I'll have Logan come over if you want."

Amaris didn't want to look like a fool, but she did want to see Logan before she left. "Okay."

Mrs. Maddox pulled Amaris into a motherly hug and Amaris sank into her arms, needing comfort. *"I could love her."* Amaris admitted, which sounded crazy to her, but she knew it was the truth. Logan had made an impact on her life in such a short amount of time.

"God, I hope she gets her shit together," Mrs. Maddox said and they both laughed. "I'll see you in the morning, sweetheart."

"Thank you for coming to check on me."

"You're welcome."

———— · •◉• · ————

Someone banging loudly on the door woke Logan up the next morning. She reached for her phone and saw that it was a little past seven o clock. Her bed was empty, indicating that Chandra had already made her exit. The banging got louder, annoying her.

"Alright, I'm coming. God damn." She pulled the covers back, hopping out of bed. She smacked her lips when she saw her brother's face through the peephole. "What the hell are you doing here? Shouldn't you be on your honeymoon?" She could tell by Xavier's face that he wasn't happy and the look on her face morphed into one of concern. "What happened, bro?"

"You happened." Xavier walked in, closing the door behind him.

"What do you mean?"

"What the hell was that last night?"

"What?"

"You and your date? I mean, did I miss something?"

Logan rolled her eyes walking into the kitchen. Of course, she knew what Xavier was talking about with all the dirty looks she was getting from him and Taylor last night. "No, you didn't miss anything."

"Then what was that?"

"Look, Amaris is not my woman and I invited Chandra. What was I supposed to do? Ignore her?"

"So you kiss on Amaris and then go back to Chandra?"

"Why do you care? I mean, this was one fluke ass weekend! Did you think I would stop what I was doing and be with Amaris? She means nothing to me! I don't know her!" Even as the words came from her mouth, she didn't believe it. She knew Amaris had made her way into her heart and now it was time to shut her out.

"Who are you trying to convince, me or you?" Xavier saw right through his sister's bullshit. He was witness to the spark between the two and that wasn't a fluke.

"It doesn't matter, because whatever that was, is over."

"You're sorry for this one, man." Xavier headed to the door, disappointed in Logan's behavior.

"Fuck you, Xavier! What do you want me to do, be like you? Live happily ever after like you?"

"What's wrong with that?"

"It's not in my future! You know this!"

"You don't know anything, Logan! You're assuming. You're not even giving yourself a chance!"

"I'm done with this conversation." Logan didn't want to keep having the same conversation with her brother. No one was able to decide her fate, but she wouldn't make anyone suffer because of her.

"Of course you are, you're always done with the conversation."

Logan walked over to her door and opened it for Xavier. "Your ass shouldn't even be here. Get out and go on your honeymoon. Don't worry about me." Xavier shook his head and walked out the door.

• ——— • • ● • • ——— •

Logan walked into her parent's house after damn near being summoned by her mother. She didn't know what it was about, but her mother told her to meet her in her office. "Hey mom, what was so important …" She stopped mid-sentence when she opened her mother's office door and saw Amaris standing there, waiting for her. "Amaris?"

"Could this be something, Logan?"

The question caught Logan off guard, she actually looked around for her mother, knowing she wouldn't spot her anywhere. Mrs. Maddox had set her up. "What?"

"You and I?" Amaris drew closer to Logan, needing to be close. All day, she had waited for the time she would see Logan again. "Could we be something or am I imagining what I felt?"

Logan wanted to tell Amaris she wasn't imagining anything, she wanted to tell her she'd thought about her all night even though she was with Chandra. She also thought about the conversation she'd had with Xavier this morning all day. Logan felt like for the first time, she wanted to let someone in, she wanted to let Amaris in. They were like magnets; even now, the distance between them was killing Logan.

"You're a stranger," Logan blurted out.

Amaris threw her hands in the air laughing. "Yes, and so are you, but here I am, wondering if the universe has brought my soul mate to me. I have never felt anything like this which is so crazy, but I work off of vibes I work off of connection and you and I had an instant connection, I believe. Please, don't tell me I'm alone in thinking that."

Logan's heart was in turmoil, she wanted to confess her sudden feelings to Amaris, she wanted to pull Amaris into her arms and tell her to stay a little longer, but that little part of her that didn't want to break Amaris's heart kept her silent.

Amaris felt her heart rip a little as she waited for Logan to answer her. She'd never been so vulnerable with someone, but she felt like she needed to be vulnerable with Logan. She was giving it her all with the possibility of leaving Las Vegas hurt.

She closed the gap between them, grabbed Logan gently by the back of her head, and pulled her into a kiss. Logan gripped her tightly in her arms as she allowed Amaris's tongue to invade her mouth.

Logan inhaled her scent; she smelled like sweet honey. She wanted to remember what this woman smelled like. Amaris put every ounce of passion into that kiss so Logan could know she was serious. When they both broke away from the kiss, they stared at each other, breathing hard, wanting to take each other.

"Logan, tell me to stay," Amaris said, almost pleading.

Logan traced her lips over Amaris's, pondering her request. She wanted her to stay, she wanted to see where this was going, but that small part of her still told her it wasn't right.

"I can't tell you that. I'm sorry." Logan kissed her forehead, breaking their embrace and headed out of the office, her heart ripping with every step she took.

"Logan!" Amaris yelled from the room. Logan stopped in her tracks, but didn't turn around to face Amaris. She knew if she did, she would go back to her and never allow her to leave. "I see you." Amaris's voice broke as she tried to hold back her tears. She'd never been so emotional over someone. She felt stupid, but she was willing to feel stupid for Logan because she felt like she would be worth it.

Logan felt the sting of Amaris's words. She felt a sense of loss. "I'm sorry, Amaris." Logan forced herself to walk out of her parents' house and out of Amaris's life.

CHAPTER

4

THREE MONTHS LATER

"Action!"

Logan watched in amazement as the actors acted out a scene from her book. Her film had been in production for two months and she was overly excited about it. She couldn't believe her book had come this far. To have it adapted into a film was one of her biggest accomplishments.

"And cut!" the director yelled and everything stopped. "Alright folks, that's a wrap for today. I'll see everyone at five am and not a minute later." Everyone dispersed as did Logan. She grabbed her bag and headed for the door. She was physically exhausted and was ready to hit the bed.

"So how are you liking it so far?" Logan's lead actress stopped her before she could reach the door. Logan tried to stay away from her because she was bad and she knew it. Since day one she played the flirting game with Logan and hadn't stopped.

"I think it's going well. You're doing an amazing job," she responded with a forced smile.

"Thank you. You should take me out for drinks tonight." Reign said with a sly smile.

Logan eyed her down, studying her for a second. She was a gorgeous, chocolate skinned lady and if she was anyone else, Logan probably would have taken her up on her offer, but Logan didn't mix business with pleasure. She wouldn't allow her film to be affected if Reign felt some way when their relationship didn't go anywhere. She knew Reign was used to getting what she wanted, but she didn't plan to be one of them.

"I don't think that's a good idea."

"Why not?" She pouted.

"I don't mix business with pleasure."

"Oh, so this would be pleasure?" she said, licking her lips.

Logan smirked. "Let's be honest, Reign, if I take you for drinks, you'll end up asking me to fuck you and I will, which could fuck up the movie. So, I rather not. I'll see you tomorrow morning." Logan left Reign there looking dumbfounded. If she was any other girl, Logan probably would have taken her home, but she was the lead actress in her movie.

Her driver opened her door seeing her approach slid into her seat and leaned her head against the backrest of the seat. Her body was exhausted, but her mind was racing. She closed her eyes to get a moment of peace and as always, *she* appeared. Amaris's beautiful face had plagued Logan ever since their first and last encounter.

After the wedding, Amaris left before Logan could attempt to change her mind and at the moment, she thought it was for the best, but she couldn't get her off her mind ever since. She even thought about reaching out to her, but after the way she treated her at the wedding, she felt like she had no right, so she sat there with her eyes closed and enjoyed the vision.

Amaris laid exhausted in Quelm's arms. They'd spent hours fucking until Quelm finally tapped out. Amaris had a high sex drive, especially when she had a strong connection to that person; she could go for hours and hours, which was one of the things Quelm loved about her. But, even Quelm couldn't keep up.

"You're too much for me," Quelm said, breathing hard.

Amaris smiled as she played with Quelm's nipple ring, something they'd gotten together. She could hear Quelm hiss under her breath. Although she was exhausted, it still sent a tingly sensation throughout her body.

"You did fine darling," Amaris complimented her.

Quelm ran her hands through Amaris's afro. "I have a question for you."

"Okay."

"If I left my husband, would we be together honestly?"

Amaris's fingers stopped playing with her nipple ring. The question caught her off guard. They'd never talked about anything besides what they were now. Amaris didn't expect anything more and that's what she thought Quelm wanted too. "I don't know, to be honest. I thought we were just having fun."

"Fun for two years now? Do you not have any other feelings for me, Amaris?" This was supposed to be fun for Quelm, an escape from her boring husband, but she had fallen in love with Amaris.

Amaris heard the hurt in Quelm's voice. She sat up in bed so that she could look at her. "That's not what I said. Your question just threw me in a loop. Are you thinking about leaving him?"

Quelm shrugged her shoulders. "It's been on my mind lately. I don't know how much longer I can pretend to be happy."

Amaris didn't know if she'd want an actual relationship with Quelm. It was too easy for Quelm to cheat on her husband, what would stop her from doing the same thing to her if she got bored? "You need to do whatever makes you happy. Life's too short to settle." Amaris was big on not wasting time. Whenever she felt like a relationship had taken its course, she would be grateful for the moment, but would not dwell on losing Quelm.

"But would we be together?" Quelm asked again.

Amaris didn't want Quelm to base her marriage off of their relationship. She needed to leave her husband on her own free will not because she wants them to be together. "If you leave your husband, let it be for you, not the potential of us. If you did leave him, you need time to yourself, time to heal from everything and to figure out if you're gay or if I'm just a fling."

Amaris was the first woman Quelm had ever been with. She knew what the first experience of being with a woman felt like; there was a connection, so she knew they would always have a bond, but she also knew how it felt to get over it. She wouldn't go all in with Quelm only for Quelm to realize she wasn't what she wanted full time.

Quelm held Amaris's hands, kissing her fingers one by one. "I love you. I'm in love with you. I know this was supposed to be us having fun, but I've fallen for you."

Amaris heard the love and sincerity in her voice. It touched her, but it reminded her of herself with Logan; she heard herself in Quelm. It had been a long three months and she still hadn't heard a word from Logan. She knew she wasn't the only one who felt the chemistry between them, but she guessed she was the only one who wanted to reciprocate the feelings. She felt like a fool every time she thought about Logan.

She and Taylor had become great friends and anytime she spoke with her, she had to stop herself from asking how Logan was. She felt like a fool for even having any type of feelings after the way Logan acted at the wedding with her date.

"Are you listening to me?"

Quelm snapped Amaris out of her thoughts. "Yes, I'm listening, but I stand where—" Quelm's phone interrupted them. Amaris knew it was her husband calling, because it was his ring tone, but Quelm didn't move to answer it.

"Go ahead and answer."

"We're talking."

"Answer the phone!" Amaris snapped. She could see Quelm's shoulder sag in defeat as she grabbed her phone and answered it.

"Hi sweetie … yes, I'm on my way home now. Do you need anything …? Okay, I love you too." She pressed end on the phone.

Amaris knew the routine and she was perfectly okay with it. "I'll see you later darling, go ahead and get dressed." She stood up and left Quelm in her bed to give her space.

When Logan made it home, she had a surprise visitor waiting for her. "Daddy, what are you doing here?" She gave him a hug and a kiss wondering how he'd gotten into her penthouse.

"I just came to check on you. You've been so busy with the movie we haven't seen much of you. How are you?"

Logan grabbed a bottle of water from the fridge before joining her dad on the couch. "Everything's good. I'll be going to Cali to film next week."

"How long will you be gone for?" Mr. Maddox asked, concerned.

"Should take only a few weeks, two months at the most. We have to get a few scenes in Los Angeles."

"And you cleared that with Doc?"

Logan could see the worry on her dad's face. She knew everyone in her family was worried about her being alone in another state even though it was only four hours away. She was actually looking forward to getting away and not being under her parents' thumb. "I'll be fine dad. Don't worry, the Doc cleared it."

"Maybe I should send your mother with you."

Logan chuckled, because she knew her father wasn't playing. But, she wouldn't be a burden to her mother. "Dad, I'll hire someone to help me if I have to, but mom isn't coming with me. You need her here."

"Are you sure, sweet pea? I know she wouldn't mind."

Logan wouldn't take her mother away from her father. He needed her just as much as he thought Logan needed her. Logan could only imagine how her dad would get along without her mother. "I'm sure dad, don't worry."

Since Logan's family had property set up in different cities, it was easy for her to rent out a condo in one of her father's buildings. Her dad told her she didn't need to pay rent, but there was no way Logan would stay there and not pay her dad. Her assistant, Lani, would be joining her, so she made sure Lani had the condo a few doors down from her; she wanted her close, but also wanted some space between them.

Mr. Maddox grabbed his hat and stood up. "Well, it looks like you've made your mind up."

"Don't go dad, why don't I order us some food? We can eat and catch up a bit."

Mr. Maddox smiled. He would never give up time to spend with Logan, especially since she was leaving. He sat back down getting comfortable. "Sounds like a date."

———— • • ● • • ————

Three days later, Logan and Lani were in California, settling into their condos. "This is going to be so much fun," Lani chirped, excited.

"Lani, we're here to work and I need a favor from you."

Lani plopped down on the bar stool; the move had them both drained. "What's that boss?"

"I need you to keep Reign away from me. She's already shown interest and I'm not trying to go that route."

Logan was all about her business, she wanted to get these scenes done and go back home. She knew her family would be worried about her until she made it back to Vegas.

"Okay, I'll run interference."

"Good. Now let's go eat. I'm starving."

"Can we stay in? I'm tired and I don't want to have to get all dolled up to keep up with you."

Logan chuckled while spinning Lani around on the barstool so she could face her. "Whatever you want. For the next two months, you'll be my partner in crime."

Lani smiled, trying not to blush. She longed to be more than just Logan's assistant, but Logan really meant what she said when she said she didn't mix business with pleasure. Lani remembered how stupid she felt when she made an advance on Logan and she shut her down. They'd remained good friends and colleagues since then, but that was all they were and that crushed Lani. For three years, she bottled her feelings up and put them in the back of her mind.

"Lani," Logan called.

"Yes?"

"Why are you looking at me like that?" Logan knew the look and she wished Lani didn't look at her like that. There was always a sense of want written in her eyes, which made Logan feel bad. If things weren't the way they were, with Lani being her assistant and a few other things, Logan might have given her a chance, but at this point in her life, she knew she couldn't.

"No reason. I was just thinking about something."

Logan scooped her up from the chair and started to walk her toward the couch, trying to lighten the mood. "Let's find something to watch and then something to eat."

"Sounds like a plan. Now, put me down. You shouldn—"

"Don't Lani." Logan sighed as she set her down on the couch. She hated when her friends and family treated her like she was a handicap.

"Sorry."

"I'll let it slide this time." Logan plopped down on the couch. "Let's see what we got."

<hr>

"Are you sitting down, Amaris?"

Amaris could hear the excitement in her agent and best friend, Tasha's voice. "Yes I'm sitting down. What's up?"

"So, I got a call from Scott Easton who runs The Galley. He wants to give you the opportunity to display your photos in your own gallery!" she screamed through the phone.

Amaris couldn't believe it. She'd been trying to get into The Galley for months, but it was always so hard to get in touch with Scott. The Galley was one of the biggest art galleries in Los Angeles. "Shut up!" she screamed right back with shock and excitement.

"Yes, girl! He's thinking a few weeks. You have to bring your best work, because this is it, big time. There will be cameras and editors for the LA Times. Amaris, this is it. This is what you've been waiting for, your big break! Let's do this girl."

Amaris's heart started to race, thinking about what it really meant. "Shit," she whispered. Her hand became clammy and sweat started to form on her forehead. She could feel her heartbeat start to speed up as she went into a full anxiety attack. She found herself on the floor, taking deep breaths as she tried to calm herself down. Just the thought of everything Tasha shared had Amaris mind going a mile a minute. She was thinking about what pictures to use, how people would react to her photos, blah blah blah.

Oh my god! What if they hate them? What if I get bad reviews? Oh my God. She could hear Tasha yelling her name through the phone, but there was nothing she could do; she couldn't reach for the phone as she was frozen in her own attack—her body was attacking her.

"Control it, Amaris." Logan's face popped in her head suddenly. She remembered when Logan helped her through her anxiety attack at the wedding rehearsal. She could hear how gentle her voice was as she coached her through it.

"Deep breaths." She imagined Logan sitting with her, breathing with her, and rubbing her back. She remembered how calm she felt with her at that moment. The last thing she heard was her name being called before her world went black.

———— · •●• · ————

"Amaris!" Amaris heard Tasha's voice as she felt her shaking her.

"Hmm."

"Can you open your eyes for me, sis?" Amaris could hear the concern in Tasha's voice and realized she passed out on the floor. She opened her eyes and felt bad for the look Tasha was giving her. "You scared the shit out of me. When you didn't answer, I got nervous and rushed over here," Tasha said, worry lacing her words.

Amaris sat up, feeling a little weak. She hadn't had a bad anxiety attack like that for months. "Yeah, I think I just became overwhelmed." She got up from the floor, wiping herself off.

"It's been over an hour since you were out. With all the traffic, it took me a while to get here. I thought you'd be up by the time I made it to you. Have you been taking your medicine?" Tasha asked while grabbing Amaris a bottle of water out of her fridge. She felt like she could finally breathe again seeing that Amaris was okay now; she didn't know how many traffic laws she broke trying to get to her.

Amaris took a long swig of her water. "Yes I have. It was just a bad episode." Her hand was still shaking, so she decided to take another long swig of the water.

Tasha wrapped her hands around Amaris shoulders. "Will you be able to do this, sis? I mean, I know we both want this, but if it fucks with your anxiety, then it's not worth it."

Amaris wouldn't allow her anxiety to mess with her career. This was her time; this is what she'd been waiting for. She knew she would come with her best and finally make a name for herself at The Galley. "I can do this. I'm just going to have to stick to my meds and make sure I'm good." Amaris hugged her best friend, loving her even more.

Tasha had always believed in her and her dream and she did everything possible to get her exposure including getting her the gig for Xavier's wedding.

"I love you, Tasha. Thank you for this. I will not let you down, I promise."

Tasha smiled, hugging Amaris. "I know you won't, because if you do, imma kick your ass."

Amaris giggled. "We should go out and celebrate this is huge!"

"We'll go out tomorrow, have a few drinks and dance the night away at Rage."

"Sounds like a date."

Logan enjoyed her day on the set with everyone, she loved how professional everyone was. Reign was ruthless in her pursuit any time she got to speak to Logan and she made the effort to speak to her often. But, Logan remained professional and thanked Lani silently when she interrupted them.

"We're going out tonight, chica, and I'm not taking no for an answer." Lani said to Logan with a smile.

"Oh. Where ya going? I want to go too." Reign inquired without being invited in the conversation.

Lani rolled her eyes looking at Logan. "Logan and I are going to the nightclub."

Logan had other plans. She wasn't going anywhere, she was exhausted and just wanted to climb into bed and call it a night. Lani knew her situation and knew she needed her rest. "Lani, I'm beat. I can't do it tonight."

Lani rolled her eyes. She always thought Logan was such a party pooper, it was like pulling teeth to get her to go out. "Come on, Logan, we always go to Rage when we're in town. It's like a tradition."

Logan shook her head. "I know and I love you, but I can't do it tonight. Take Reign and show her a good time."

"Yes, please take me, I'm dying to get out. I've been stuck in the hotel and I don't know anyone else here."

Lani didn't want to hang out with Reign, especially when she knew Reign had a thing for Logan.

"You ladies have a good time for me. Let me know when you make it home safely," Logan said, directing the last part to Lani.

Lani smacked her lips. "Really Logan, you're not going to come?"

"I need my rest. See you ladies later." Logan kissed Lani on the cheek and headed home.

As if on cue, her phone vibrated and her mother's picture flashed across the screen. "Well, hello there mom." Logan said smiling. She always loved to talk to her mother; she had a way of brightening her day.

"Hey, sweetheart. I was just calling to check on you."

"I'm good, we just wrapped up the day, so I'm going home to lay it down."

"Good, you need to make sure you get enough rest. I don't want you to get sick."

"I'll be fine mother. I'll grab something to eat and head home like an old prude."

Mrs. Maddox giggled. "There's nothing wrong with being an old prude."

"There is, when you're only twenty seven." There were days when Logan loved her life because she'd had a blessed life, but there were days she felt so handicapped. Normal things like just going to the club could have her down for two or three days.

"You have to be thankful for each year you get to spend on earth." Mrs. Maddox knew each day wasn't promised to anyone, but it wasn't for Logan especially. She always made sure she threw a big birthday party because she was thankful for the years she got to spend with her precious daughter.

Logan was thankful as well, she just wished she could be healthy sometimes. She wanted to have a normal life; no running to the doctors, no waking up at night sometimes not unable to breathe, no worrying about her health all the time.

"You know, Logan, you are out in California, why don't you get in contact with Amaris?" Mrs. Maddox gently pushed.

Logan groaned inwardly. She tried to block all thoughts of Amaris from her mind. So, just knowing she was in the same city as Amaris was torture. Logan thought about what Amaris said the day of the wedding about how she would come to Logan if Logan called her and she knew she was telling the truth. She wanted to call her, to reach out and tell her to come to her, but she knew she couldn't and she knew she wouldn't.

"Mom ..."

"I'm just saying. You know Amaris and I have grown close since the wedding and she's a really good girl. It just seemed like there was something between you two the weekend of the wedding."

"What?" Logan asked shocked. In the three months since the wedding, neither Mrs. Maddox nor Taylor had ever said anything to Logan about keeping in contact with Amaris. "Grown close? You didn't even tell me you kept in touch."

"I didn't have to, but she calls me every other week to see how I am. Taylor and I have gone down there a few times and we've all gone shopping and out to dinner."

Logan was appalled. "Mom, I feel betrayed. Wow."

"Girl, shut up. What would it have mattered to you? She's not an ex of yours. Just because you're blind doesn't mean Taylor and I can't have a relationship with her. Amaris is great."

Each word was like a punch to Logan's gut. She didn't need her mother throwing anything in her face. She of all people knew why she didn't believe in falling in love with anyone. "Mother, you know the deal."

"Yes, I know your deal, but it doesn't mean I agree with it. I think you and Amaris would make a great couple."

Logan remained silent as she toyed with the idea, but just as quick as the thought came, it left. She wouldn't hurt Amaris. "I have to go, mom."

"Do you want her number?"

"No, I'm good. I love you."

"I love you too, darling," Mrs. Maddox said, disappointed. She wished Logan would see her stance on love; no one knew how long they had here. She wished Logan would give herself a chance at love. She felt like Logan's life would be so much better if she had love in it.

Logan ended the call, feeling down. She wanted to take the number, to hear Amaris's voice, but what good would any of it be if Logan wouldn't be around to share her life with Amaris?

Amaris and Tasha pulled up to Rage and the line was already long. She was glad she knew the bouncer because with the shoes she was wearing, there was no way she would have stood in line to get in. Her eyes scanned the crowd to see if there were any women she was interested in. She saw a few and knew it would be a good night.

They skipped the line and walked up to the bouncer. "Hey, Julio."

Julio, the cute bouncer who had a crush on her, smiled upon seeing her.

"What's up gorgeous? When are you going to let me take you on a date? You're killing me with that dress."

Amaris smiled, doing a twirl for Julio just to give him a peek. Her little red dress showed just enough to catch the eye, but not enough to be considered a hoe. Amaris was proud of her body and embraced her curves. "Thank you, Julio. Now are you going to let me and my girl in or what?"

"Of course, of course. Get yo sexy ass in here." He unhooked the rope and Amaris grabbed Tasha's hand, pulling her inside.

The club was packed and the music was blasting; it was just what Amaris needed. She was ready to have a good time with her girl.

"Tash, I'll get us drinks. What are you drinking?"

"A Long Island." Tasha yelled in her ear.

I'll be back." Amaris headed for the bar. She danced her way over there as *Get Low* by the Ying Yang twins blasted throughout the club. The bar was full like always; it took a minute for Amaris to squeeze her way in.

"Excuse me!" Amaris yelled for the bartender.

"I've been trying for the past five minutes, there's no use," a voice said behind Amaris.

She turned to look at the person who spoke and smiled. "You're gorgeous," she blurted out. The woman dropped her head trying to hide her smile. Amaris's eyes scanned over the woman, taking in her beauty. Her chocolate complexion was flawless and her dimples made her look innocent. She was rocking the hell out of her black dress. Every piece of her hair was laid and Amaris thought she was absolutely beautiful.

"Thank you," the lady said with a smile.

"What's your name?"

"Lani." She stuck her hand out for Amaris to shake. Amaris took it, allowing her hand to linger.

"Lani, forgive me for staring, but goodness, girl."

Lani tucked her hair behind her ear, blushing. "Oh my God, you're embarrassing me. Stop it."

Amaris was never one to hold her tongue. Anytime she saw beauty, she embraced it and enjoyed it. Beauty in women was no different. "I'm sorry, I just had to compliment you. I've never seen you around here. Is this your first time?"

"No, I've been here a few times."

"I have to call bullshit on that, I would have noticed you by now."

"I live in Vegas, but I'm out here working for a little while."

"How long will you be here?"

"A month or two."

"Oh good, that gives me enough time to spend with you."

Lani shook her head and burst into a laugh. She thought Amaris was cute and bold as hell. "Spend time with me? You don't even know me."

"Right, that's why we should spend time together, so we can get to know each other."

"You don't hold back, huh?"

Amaris smiled. That wasn't the first time she'd heard that and no, she didn't hold back; she always felt like life was too short to sugarcoat shit. If she was interested in someone, she let them know, if she didn't like someone, she let them know they were not good for her energy.

"No, I don't," she blurted out confidently.

"I don't even know your name."

"Ask me my name."

"Why should I?"

"Because you want to know."

Amaris was right, she had Lani intrigued. Lani thought Amaris was beautiful and she felt some attraction to her. "What's your name?"

"Amaris. It's nice to meet you, Lani."

"Nice to meet you as well, Amaris."

Her smile is pretty, Amaris thought. She could feel the vibe between them and knew she would have to exchange numbers with Lani. "Come dance with me."

"What about your drinks?"

Amaris pulled her toward the dance floor. "I'll get it later. There's someone more important in front of me now."

Lani was taken aback. She was instantly drawn to Amaris. Her energy was contagious, her confidence, a turn on. She was used to studs being the aggressor and hitting on her the way Amaris was, but coming from Amaris, it was sexy. If Amaris wanted to get to know her, she would surely allow it. She felt like it would be good to have some company while in California; it would distract her from Logan and she had to admit, Amaris was a beautiful distraction. She allowed Amaris to pull her further onto the dance floor as a slow reggae song started to blare through the speakers.

Tasha caught Amaris attention. She gestured for her drink, but Amaris pointed to Lani and shrugged while smiling. Tasha would have to get her own drink. Lani started to grind on Amaris to the beat of the reggae song. Even though they were both in a dress, they didn't act like it, both grinding on the other and dipping low. It was as if it was just them on the dance floor enjoying each other.

Lani felt her panties moisten as Amaris's hands traced her body. Her touch was so light that she could barely feel it, but when she did, it felt like a zap of electricity coursing through her body. Lani felt like Amaris was putting her under a spell.

The two women danced to a few songs before they needed a drink.

"Come on. Who are you here with tonight" Amaris asked Lani as they left the dance floor.

"Nobody. I came by myself."

Amaris looked at her like she was crazy. She felt like you had to always have at least one person with you when you went out, just in case something popped off and you needed back up. "You're hanging with me and my friend tonight, you shouldn't be out here by yourself. Cool?"

"Cool."

Amaris grabbed Lani's hand and led her toward Tasha who was sitting at the bar. By the time they got to the bar, Tasha was there with two drinks for them.

"Damn girls. I thought y'all would never get off the floor." Tasha handed Amaris then Lani a drink each.

"Tasha, this is Lani, Lani this is Tasha, my agent and best friend in the world."

Tasha smiled. "Nice to meet you, Lani. I see Amaris has brought you into her web."

"Maybe just a little." It was a web Lani wasn't complaining about being trapped in.

"Escape! This girl will have you selling your soul to be with her."

Amaris cut her eyes at Tasha playfully. "Shut up, you're going to run her off. She's going to hang with us tonight. She's new in LA and came by herself."

"By yourself? Girl you should always have someone."

"I was going to come with my friend, but she was too tired to come and I still wanted to go out, so I decided to go solo." Even though Logan told Lani to take Reign, Lani opted out of it. She got fake vibes from Reign and didn't want to be bothered with her. Besides, she was never one to need people with her; she enjoyed her own company. Either way, she was going to come out and have a good time.

"Well my dear, you're in luck, because Amaris and I will take you under our wing tonight. So, let's toast to a good night ladies, shall we?" Tasha said raising her glass. They all clinked their shot glass together and downed it in one swallow.

The burn felt so good to Amaris, she closed her eyes and savored it. "Let's get another, shall we?"

"Let's," Lani responded eagerly.

CHAPTER

5

Amaris and Lani danced the night away and by the end of the night when Amaris asked Lani to go home with her, Lani was so turned on she didn't even second-guess it.

"Do you bring every girl you meet at the club home?" Lani asked, looking around Amaris's loft. She loved the artistic feel of it. There were big canvas pictures of beautiful women hung up around her place. "Are these your exes?"

Amaris smirked while removing her shoes; her feet were killing her and she embraced the relief from her feet being free. "No, they're just my subjects. I love beautiful people. You should let me shoot you." Amaris picked up her camera as her mind started thinking about a whole photo shoot with Lani; she would love to photograph her.

"I look a mess right now." Lani shied away from the camera. Her hair felt like it was everywhere, and her makeup was smeared from sweating so hard from all the dancing.

"You are beautiful." Amaris focused on Lani's eyes and snapped the picture.

"And you're a charmer," Lani retorted.

"I'm not a charmer, I just speak the truth. People always hold back on what they want to say. They see someone attractive and they don't want to come off as aggressive. Why not enjoy beauty when it's in front of you? I speak my mind because I want the person to know how I feel," Amaris said with conviction.

She had spent much of her early teens and twenties trying to please people and hold her tongue. After discovering herself, she told herself she would never hold back—good or bad.

"So why are you single?" Lani asked again.

Amaris pulled Lani's hair back so she could see her face fully. She was in full photographer mode. "I haven't found someone I've connected with spiritually." She was lying, she did find someone or so she thought. Her mind drifted to Logan and what they'd shared in that short amount of time. She felt like with time, they could have been something amazing—a love story for the ages—but Logan had made herself clear that they would never be anything.

"Why not?" Lani couldn't pinpoint why she was so intrigued by Amaris. She usually went for studs, never a femme, but there was something about Amaris that made Lani really want to get to know her.

"I don't know. Maybe I'll ask the universe to bring me someone or maybe I'll be patient and let them come to me. What about you, are you single?"

Lani wished she wasn't. She wished Logan could see that they could be something more than just coworkers. "Yes, I'm single. I mean, I have a crush on someone, but they don't feel the same way."

"What a shame." Amaris snapped another picture before setting her camera down.

"Well, the thing is, she's my boss and she doesn't date her workers."

"Quit."

Lani laughed. "It's a good paying job. I don't think I'll find another job like it and my boss treats me very well. We're actually good friends outside of work."

"But no play?"

"No play at all."

"Damn." Amaris led her out to her balcony; she wanted to feel the cool night breeze against her skin. They were silent for a moment, enjoying the night air. Amaris was thinking about her show, which was coming up. She had such a good time tonight celebrating with Lani and Tasha.

"When you say you haven't found someone to connect with spiritually, what did you mean by that?"

"Well, I'm all about spirituality and vibes. So when I meet someone, first our vibes have to be right with each other. I pick up on a person's aura right away and I know if I want to converse with them or keep it pushing. Take you for instance, your aura was positive, which made me talk to you. If I meet someone, we're going to have to have a deeper connection than just looks and things in common. That person needs to nourish my soul."

"Have you been close to that?"

Amaris smiled, her thoughts immediately going to Logan. "I think I have."

"What happened?"

"Well, first it was crazy because I hadn't even spent twenty-four hours with this person, but it felt like the moment I met her, my soul recognized her as mine. We were like magnets."

Lani smiled. "So why isn't she here?"

"Because she was too scared to believe in it like I did, so I moved on with life."

"Would you go back to her if she changed her mind?"

Amaris thought about Lani's question for a second. It had been three months since the wedding with not a word from Logan. Even with her time with Mrs. Maddox and Taylor, her name wasn't brought up. However, she knew she would go to Logan if she called and said she wanted to see her. She knew she would go with no questions asked because she still felt that connection even though they were miles apart.

"Yes, I would," she replied.

"You must have really liked her."

"I did. I still do, but if someone doesn't want you, what can you do, ya know?"

"Trust me, I understand entirely."

"You should ask your boss out on a date."

Lani giggled. "No, I think I'll let it be. I don't want things to be awkward and complicated for us. Especially since we're the only ones here."

"So what exactly are you doing here?"

"I'm an assistant. My boss is here looking over her first movie that's being filmed."

"Oh really? That's cool. Is it a legit movie or is it a low budget movie?"

Lani giggled, shaking her head. Clearly, Amaris didn't know Logan because nothing Logan did was low budget. "Nah, this is the real deal. There will be a premier here when everything is done."

"Well, that's really good. Where is she going to film the rest of the movie?"

"Las Vegas."

"Oh. You live in Vegas?"

"Yeah."

"I was just out there a few months ago for a photo gig."

"Oh yeah? How was it?"

"It was so beautiful. That's where I actually met the person I was talking about. The family was beautiful. I still keep in touch with the bride and mother in law; they've both become really good people in my life."

"So do you see this person a lot then?"

"No, I haven't heard from her since the wedding. She made it very clear that we wouldn't be anything. I don't know why it hurt more coming from her than any of my exes."

"Seems like you have it bad."

"Maybe just a little."

"Then why am I here?" Lani was a bit jealous of a person she didn't even know. She could see in Amaris's eyes that she cared for the girl just by the way she spoke about her. There was something there.

Amaris slid closer to Lani. "You're here because I asked you to come home with me tonight. Have you changed your mind?"

"No," Lani said quickly. She wanted to be there with Amaris, but she didn't want to play second to a ghost.

Amaris scooted closer, tucking Lani's hair behind her ear. "Good." She pulled Lani closer as she captured her lips. She could feel Lani hesitate for a moment from the shock, but she quickly recovered and started kissing Amaris back. Amaris savored the taste of Lani's lips.

Lani's hands traveled down to Amaris's ass, giving it a soft squeeze. Amaris giggled as she pulled away from the kiss. "Let's go inside."

"Okay." She allowed herself to be led into Amaris's room.

— · •●• · —

Logan's eyebrow rose as she watched Lani walk into the studio. She was worried sick when Lani hadn't called her to let her know she made it home. After she didn't answer her phone, Logan used her spare key to get into Lani's condo. When she saw that it was empty, she blew her phone up with calls, but there was no answer. She spoke with Reign when she got into the studio and was surprised to hear Lani never even took Reign to the club with her.

Suddenly, Lani walked into the studio smiling from ear to ear in a sweat suit Logan knew wasn't hers and it pissed Logan off. Logan got out of her chair, grabbed Lani by the arm and pulled her out of the studio.

"Logan what the hell?" Lani cried out.

"Where the hell have you been? I was worried sick." Logan barked. She was relieved to see that Lani was okay, but she was also pissed. She felt like she had a sense of responsibility over Lani since they came to California together.

Lani snatched her arm away. "I was hanging with someone I met at the club. I spent the night at their house, daddy." Lani was pissed that Logan was checking her like she was her girl.

"You couldn't answer your phone or return my calls? I thought you were taking Reign with you."

"I decided not to take her. I don't know that girl." Lani tried to hide her irritation. She was a grown woman and she didn't have to answer to anyone.

"I was worried about you."

"Well, as you can see, I'm okay. Are we going to get to work?" Lani had woken up next to Amaris in a good mood. After a round of amazing morning sex, she had to pull herself away to get to the studio. Amaris told her to just shower and borrow some of her clothes so she wouldn't be even more late.

"Yeah, we can get to work, but if you're going to be late, I would appreciate a text or phone call."

"Fine, boss." Lani stormed past Logan causing her to get a whiff of the perfume she was wearing.

That little whiff took Logan back to the memory she tried to bury away. She felt her lips on hers and her hand around her neck as they kissed. Amaris. Her thoughts circled around that scent—Amaris's scent, the scent that plagued her thoughts on a daily basis. "What are you wearing?"

Lani stopped, looking at Logan puzzled. "What?"

"I've never smelled that scent on you. Is it new?"

Lani smelled herself and smelled Amaris on her. Just the thought made her smile. "Yeah, it's something new. I got ready at my friend's house. It's her lotion."

"I see. What's your new friend's name?" Logan knew it was maybe one in a million chance that it was Amaris, but the thought of Lani with Amaris made her stomach turn.

Lani didn't know why Logan was so interested in her love life all of a sudden. After wanting nothing to do with her romantically, she was now concerned about who she'd spent the night with? "It doesn't matter and it's none of your business."

Lani walked away from Logan leaving her dumb founded. Lani had never spoken to Logan that way and her first thought was to drag her ass back outside and cuss her out, but she didn't want to bring bad vibes to the set. She would be there with Lani for a few months and she didn't need them beefing.

Logan took a moment to get herself together before walking back into the studio where Lani was already at her laptop in her own world working. Logan walked past her and sat in her chair. She closed her eyes as her mind traveled to a happy place. Amaris's beautiful face filled her mind and she couldn't help but smile. She wondered what she was doing right now and if Amaris thought about her the way she did her.

She sighed, opening her eyes and bringing herself back to reality. It was easy to reach out, but she knew she wouldn't. She couldn't allow herself to go there, to think of her that way. She needed to stop torturing herself.

Amaris sat there as she clicked through the thousands of pictures she had on her computer. She knew she needed to make this project something dear to her heart. Then her eyes scanned over the pictures Lani allowed her to take of them during their sexcapade last night. She had to admit, the sex between Lani and herself was amazing. Lani was wild and free and was willing to explore the different toys Amaris wanted to try on her.

After hours of sex, they both finally succumbed to exhaustion and fell asleep. When Lani jumped up saying she was late for work this morning, Amaris told her to just shower and dress there so she wouldn't be even more late and after a quick kiss goodbye, she sent her on her way.

Now here she was, hours into pictures and she finally knew what she would do for her show. It would be filled with love and light. She felt like with everything going on in the world today, she wanted to make everyone see that love always won and choosing light over darkness was always the answer.

She clapped excitedly as her vision came to her. "This is going to be great." She flipped through more pictures, studying each picture and choosing the ones she thought would get her point across.

She stopped when she came across Logan's pictures, she wanted to tell herself that she didn't know why she kept the pictures she snapped of her, but she knew that would be a lie; she wanted to be able to see her face whenever she thought of her, which was often.

Her finger outlined Logan's face, but she stopped at her eyes. Logan's eyes said so much and so little at the same time. She remembered capturing the image when they were in Mrs. Maddox's rose garden talking. Logan had stared straight at the camera as Amaris took the picture. She wanted so badly to ask Logan what her eyes wanted to tell her that her mouth couldn't. She replayed their conversation when Logan had pulled her into a room and kissed her senseless. She'd told Amaris more than once that she couldn't hurt her, that she didn't need her in her life and Amaris just wished she knew why. Even Mrs. Maddox didn't want to share what the big secret was.

The whole situation depressed Amaris. Yes, she had Quelm who was now willing to leave her husband, she also possibly had Lani whom she was still getting to know, but her thoughts always went back to Logan. Logan had a pull on her that she didn't even know she had. Amaris sighed, closing her laptop. She still had it bad for a stranger—a stranger who wanted nothing to do with her.

"Get a grip, Amaris," she whispered to herself as she reopened her laptop. She skipped past all of Logan's pictures; she would not allow her to ruin what she had planned. She needed to stop thinking of her and focus on her show.

Quelm's ringtone went off, taking Amaris away from work. "Hello, darling," Amaris cooed into the phone.

"Well, someone sounds like they're in a good mood. Where were you? I called you a few times last night but you didn't answer."

"I went out. I didn't get home till late."

"Oh. Did you have a good time?"

"Yes, I had a great time. I was celebrating."

"Celebrating what?"

"Let's go to lunch and I'll tell you about it. Are you free right now?"

"For you, always."

Not exactly, Amaris thought, but kept it to herself. She couldn't call or see Quelm when she wanted, but she was okay with that because she didn't expect anything more from her. "Meet me at the cafe in twenty minutes."

"I'll be there."

Amaris ended the call while grabbing her things. Twenty minutes later, she was walking into Cafe Dejon, the same cafe she met Quelm at, two years ago. She smirked as she walked up to Quelm. She looked so pretty in a yellow sundress.

Amaris's eyes went to her glistening legs; she was doing extra today with the baby oil. Once she stood up, Amaris placed her hand over her heart dramatically. She had her red 'fuck me' heels on and Amaris tried to figure out what the occasion was for Quelm to be looking so delicious, so much that she wanted to skip lunch and take her back home.

"You're trying to kill me," Amaris said as she wrapped Quelm in her arms, kissing her cheek.

"What do you mean?"

"You look absolutely amazing."

Quelm hid her smile as Amaris held her hand so she could twirl. Her plan worked perfectly. She wanted Amaris to see what she was holding onto. Quelm wasn't stupid, she knew Amaris entertained different women and she knew she was entertaining last night. Even if she was out at the club, she would text Quelm to let her know she was out and couldn't talk, but for her to ignore her completely, she knew she was with someone else. The thought made Quelm's blood boil.

"Thank you, baby. So what's the big news you wanted to share?"

"Well, Tasha booked me my very own show at The Galley!"

Quelm clapped her hands excitedly. "Oh my God, are you serious? Baby, that's wonderful!" Quelm jumped up, giving Amaris a big hug. She knew what this meant for Amaris and she also knew how hard she worked to get to this moment. "You are so amazing, darling."

"Thank you, baby," Amaris said with a broad smile.

• — • • ● • • — •

Logan checked her watch. It was a little after one and she was starving. Once they called for lunch break she decided to head to the little cafe around the corner from the studio. Normally, she would wait for Lani, but because Lani was on her shit list at the moment, she decided to leave without her.

She headed around the corner enjoying the Cali breeze against her cheek. She actually liked being in California, but she couldn't see herself living there, the smoggy air was killing her lungs. Besides that, it was a nice place to visit.

Logan walked into the cafe, glad there weren't a lot of people. When she usually came around this time, the cafe would be packed. After tasting their food the first day on set, Logan knew why. She looked around the room at the people who filled the tables; she wanted to sit and eat and was hoping for a window seat. She spotted a familiar face sitting in the corner and was going to walk back out, but she was already spotted. So, she smiled and made her way over to the table.

"Hey Reign, how did you get here so fast?"

"Oh, my scene was over, so I dipped out a little early. Would you like to join me for lunch?"

Logan knew she shouldn't have, but she didn't want to be rude. She had done a good job of keeping her distance from Reign on set, only talking to her when necessary. She didn't have anything against her, she just didn't want to get caught up. Even now, Reign was looking too good for her own good. Her shorts were riding up her thighs begging Logan to explore the treasure between them, and her shirt was cut just enough in the center to tease anybody who was interested enough to walk by.

"Sure. Let me order my food, I'll be right back." Logan could see the look of glee come over Reign's face.

"Okay."

Logan walked up to the counter to order her food. She told herself she would keep the conversation friendly and chuckled to herself for having to give herself a pep talk. Once she got to the table she noticed Reign had pulled her shirt down, giving her a little more cleavage. *Man, this girl is a savage. If she only knew, Jesus!*

"So where are you from, Reign?"

"I was born and raised in ATL. I just moved down here to LA about six months ago to pursue my acting career, you know how that goes?"

Logan smiled. "Well hell, you scored your first gig and I'm happy to have you here. You're doing an amazing job and I don't regret my decision to cast you as the lead character."

Reign's didn't attempt to hide her smile, this was a dream come true for her. She'd left everything in Atlanta to follow her dreams. She still couldn't believe she landed the leading role. "I really appreciate this opportunity, Logan. I know you think I just want to jump your bones, but I'm thankful for this opportunity. My friends were so jealous when they found out I would be starring in your movie."

"Well, you earned it."

"So what's your story?"

"My story?"

"Yes. How did you know you wanted to be an author?"

"Well I've been writing since I was young. I received my first book deal at eighteen and the rest is history. I knew I wanted to own my own company and give back to other authors."

"Did you ever think your book would be adapted into a movie?"

Now, that did surprise Logan. She wrote because she loved it and there was nothing else in the world she ever wanted to do more than that, so when a movie deal was presented to her, it was mind blowing.

"No, I feel very blessed. This isn't something I'm taking lightly." Logan knew how blessed she was, but she had also been dealt a shitty hand.

"Good. Tell me something else." Reign rested her face in her hands, really looking intrigued.

Logan shrugged her shoulders while stuffing her mouth full of her pasta salad. She didn't know what Reign wanted, she wasn't about to pour her life story out to her. "There's nothing much to tell mah. I grew up in Vegas, I live there now and I have my business there too. That's about it."

"Why don't you have a girlfriend? What's wrong with you?"

"Why does something have be wrong with me? I don't have a girlfriend because I don't want one right now. My life is pretty busy running my company. I don't have time to entertain a girlfriend."

"It has to get lonely sometimes," Reign said sincerely. She could never understand Logan's demeanor. When they were at the studio, she wasn't rude, but she only interacted with everybody when she needed to. She was such a mystery to Reign, one that she wanted to solve.

"Sometimes," Logan admitted. Whenever Logan did get lonely, she had her set of women she could call over, but because she was in California, she had no one and she wasn't going to fly anyone out; she didn't want them to think their relationship status had changed.

Reign slid her hand on top of Logan's. "Well, if you ever get lonely, I'm here," she said seductively and Logan knew she was in trouble.

———— ·•●•· ————

"Oh my God." Reign moaned as she felt all eight inches of Logan's strap stroke her pussy. Logan watched as Reign's ass smacked against her pussy. She was so turned on it was hard for her to focus. All thoughts of her not fucking Reign was out the window. She knew at the cafe she was going to bring her home.

"Throw that ass back, girl." She smacked Reigns ass making her yelp.

"Logan, you're killing my pussy, baby." Reign's nectar coated Logan's strap as she thrust deeper into her. She threw her ass back on her, feeling herself about to climax. "It's so close, oh yes!"

Logan grabbed her hips, pounding her pussy harder. Their skin smacked against each other as she slammed herself into Reign. She knew her heart was beating too fast, but she didn't want to stop. It had been a long time since she had someone and the ecstasy she felt just by pleasuring Reign made her want to cum.

"Oh yes, baby here it comes! Here it is!" Reign moaned in ecstasy as she squirted all over Logan's strap, her body spasming as she rode the wave of bliss.

Logan chuckled as she fell onto her bed, panting and exhausted. "Shit girl, you squirted all on me."

"I'm sorry, I couldn't help it. You were tearing my shit up. So is that what you've been hiding from me?" Reign spread her body across Logan's, getting comfortable. She could already feel her eyes getting heavy.

"I wasn't hiding it, I just didn't want you to get hooked," Logan said cockily.

"Wow, that's such a stud thing to say."

"I know, right."

Reign traced the scar that started from Logan's chest and stopped just above her stomach causing Logan to flinch from her touch. It surprised her because she was used to the women she dealt with knowing to keep their hands off of her scar.

"What happened here?"

"Nothing serious. I had surgery," Logan said flatly.

"On your heart?"

Logan suddenly flipped them over so that she was laying on top of Reign. Even with her make up smeared and her hair wild and all over her face from sex, one could not deny Reign's beauty.

"You always ask these many questions?"

"Only when someone is so secretive."

Logan chuckled before covering Reign's lips with hers, sending them into another blissful intercourse.

• ● • •

"I want to ask you something, Amaris."

Amaris caressed Quelm's hair as she laid in her lap. After eating lunch they decided to go back to Amaris's place to celebrate. "Okay, go ahead."

"Were you with someone last night?"

Amaris's hand stopped between Quelm's hair. She was surprised by the question. They'd been seeing each other for a while and Quelm had never asked her anything like that. "Why?"

"I texted you, but you didn't respond, so I was wondering if you were busy with someone." Quelm knew she had no business asking Amaris the question.

They weren't exclusive and she went home to her husband every night.

"I was at the club."

"That's not what I asked."

Amaris rolled her eyes. She didn't like being questioned by someone who had no claim on her. It was like asking Quelm if she fuck her husband. Amaris knew it happened and she didn't care that it did, but she didn't need Quelm's confirmation either.

"Yes, I was with someone." Amaris felt like she had no reason to lie, but it did affect her when she saw the look of hurt on Quelm's face. "Since when did we start asking about each other's lives in that way?"

Quelm's eyes dropped, ashamed. "Because I wanted to know."

"All this time we've been doing this, why now?"

Quelm knew why. She'd fallen too hard for Amaris. She knew she shouldn't have caught feelings, but it was hard not to because she felt like Amaris was such a great person and had become a big part of her life. "Because I'm in love with you and the thought of you with someone else breaks my heart."

Amaris knew right then and there that she had to end what they had. Quelm was too deep into something she shouldn't have been in. She had a family—one that she knew she couldn't break away from. The plan wasn't for them to fall in love, they were supposed to be having fun. She was supposed to come to Amaris when she needed to blow off some steam from dealing with her husband.

"I care for you, Quelm. I really do, but I thought this was supposed to be something light."

"It was, but it's been a while. Can you honestly say you're not in love with me?"

Amaris wasn't in love with her. Love was a strong word, being in love was a strong emotion, one she knew she didn't feel towards her. There was only one person she felt like she was in love with and that person didn't love her back.

"I'm not," she said honestly.

Quelm sat up, completely heart broken. She thought that over time,

Amaris would grow to love her. She thought about leaving her husband so they could actually have a future together. She'd felt stupid for having those thoughts seeing that this was only a fling for Amaris.

"I think I should go."

Amaris didn't object to Quelm leaving like she usually would. She thought it was for the best that Quelm went home, if not, they would be in an awkward spot and Amaris wasn't up for that. "Okay, I'll walk you out."

They both got dressed in silence. Amaris walked her to her car, opening the door for her. "I'll see you later."

Quelm didn't respond, instead she drove off, leaving Amaris there. Amaris rolled her eyes as she took her phone out of her pocket and dialed her mother's number.

"Hello, sweetie pie, is everything okay?" It was like her mother was a psychic, she always knew when Amaris was off. When she came back from Vegas and saw her mother for the first time, she pulled Amaris into a motherly hug and told her that they should talk about it.

Amaris felt crazy pouring her heart out to her mother about Logan, but she sat there and listened without judgment or speaking and it was what Amaris needed. She needed to get everything out in the open, to release the energy from her spirit. Amaris knew she wouldn't be able to hold onto those types of emotions or it would consume her.

"I don't know, mama."

Ms. Cole could hear the stress in her daughter's voice. "Come over, we can talk about it."

Amaris had so much work to do for her show, but she also knew she needed to be in the presence of her mother. "I'm on my way."

"Okay."

Amaris dropped the call and headed for her mother's. It was a short drive to her mother's house.

Ms. Cole was waiting for her on the front porch when she pulled into the driveway. "Hey, sweetheart."

"Hi, mama." Amaris walked into her mother's waiting arms.

Ms. Cole could feel the tension in her daughter's body as she hugged her tight. She could also hear the anxiety in her daughter's voice when they were on the phone, so she knew Amaris needed to make her way over to the house.

"Let's sit, I made us some lemonade." Ms. Cole said as Amaris followed her to the backyard. Once they were settled, Ms. Cole wasted no time. "So what's wrong baby?"

Amaris let out an exasperated sigh. "Quelm told me she's in love with me."

Ms. Cole remained quiet waiting for Amaris to go on, but when she didn't, she realized Amaris was waiting for her to respond. "Okay, she told you she loves you. You don't feel the same way?" Ms. Cole liked Amaris and Quelm together, she knew Quelm was a wonderful woman.

"No, I don't. We have fun, but love? Mom ..." Amaris wasn't going to tell her mother that Quelm had a whole family waiting for her at home. She didn't want to look like a home wrecker in her mother's eyes. She knew if her mother knew about Quelm being married she would get a long lecture about karma, something she wasn't trying to hear.

"After all this time, Amaris? I mean, it's been a couple of years. You're still just having fun?" Ms. Cole asked, confused. She knew Amaris was a free-spirited little bird like herself, but she did want her to settle down and be happy with someone. She also knew Amaris had more than one friend, but she had told her at some point she needed to be with one person and build something special.

"Yes, I'm just having fun. Quelm and I had an agreement from the start and falling in love wasn't part of that agreement."

"Come on, Amaris, when you spend time with a person, feelings grow."

Amaris thought about Lani, she knew she could fall for her, but she didn't have those same feelings for Quelm. She thought it was because she had already set boundaries with Quelm, but with Lani there were no boundaries. "Mom, I can keep my feelings in check."

"Well, if you're thinking like that, sweetheart, then let Quelm go. Please, don't string her along, if you don't see a future with her, let her be. Let her find someone who is willing to give her the love she's ready to give. Would you want someone to play with your emotions? Better yet, would you want to be in love with someone, confess your feelings, and not get the same thing in return?"

Amaris felt like her mother had punched her in the gut. Feelings she tried to block out came crashing in on her as she thought about the day Logan walked out on her after the wedding. The feeling of rejection was something she'd never forget. Thinking about the way she felt made her feel bad for turning Quelm away the way she did, but she couldn't help the way her heart felt. She never hid anything from Quelm, she never asked for them to have a full-blown relationship. She had thought they were on the same page; they'd been on the same page for two years, now she wondered what had changed. Then there was Logan. Her heart still ached for her and a part of her still had a glimpse of hope that they would end up together.

"I have felt that, I still feel that sting."

"So why do it to Quelm?"

"Mom, she understood everything."

"Well, now she doesn't, so you need to decide what you're going to do for the both of you."

Amaris didn't want to decide, she shouldn't have had to decide. They had an agreement, Amaris was okay with being Quelm's side piece. "I'm in love with someone who isn't in love with me," she confessed.

"Honey, I thought we were past that person, how are you still speaking about her?"

"Because it was a great experience. Hell, I feel crazy right now for having all these emotions over someone. I didn't even spend twenty-four hours with her and I'm in love with her."

Ms. Cole could see the sparkle and turmoil in her daughter's eyes as she spoke. It was something she'd never seen in her eyes before. Amaris was usually so positive and upbeat, but somehow, this had really affected her. It broke her heart when Amaris came home and broke down in her arms. As a mother she wanted to find whoever had hurt her daughter and give them a piece of her mind.

"Like seriously who is she to really have you like this?"

"I told you her name is Logan Maddox."

"No, that's not what I asked. I asked who she is. What has she done to make you feel this way? What has she said to make you feel this way? Are you sure you're just not lusting over her? Love is a strong word."

Amaris thought about her feelings for Logan. Even she thought she was a fool, but her feelings were like nothing she'd ever felt when she was in Logan's presence. "Mom, the moment I saw her it was love at first sight. It was like I recognized her, like I knew her before and my heart wanted her. Even months later, I still have that aching feeling in my heart for her. I long for her, I've never longed for anyone the way I long for this woman."

Ms. Cole intertwined her fingers with her daughter's, giving her a gentle squeeze. "Then what is it sweetheart? Why are we here talking about her like this? You've never been one to give up so easily. Why aren't you guys sharing your life together?"

Amaris sighed, wanting to know the same thing. "Something is holding her back. I don't know what it is, but I can tell it's hard on her. When she left, I knew she didn't want to, but it was like she had to."

"Have you talked to her since the wedding?"

"No." Amaris felt like it would be too painful to hear Logan's voice after how they left. She was hoping that over time she would forget about her. Quelm and now Lani was helping with that, but it still didn't feel like it was enough. Anything would trigger a thought or hope with Logan.

"Why not?"

"Because I don't know what to say, mom."

"If anything, get your feelings out because baby girl, this is affecting you and once things start to affect you it sends your anxiety into a frenzy. Write everything out and then let it go and give it up to God."

"I hear you mom."

"I love you."

"I love you as well."

Ms. Cole pulled Amaris into a big bear hug. Amaris allowed herself to sink into her mother's embrace; she didn't care how old she was, there was nothing like the hug from her mother. Her mother always had a way of soothing her and she knew it was what she needed.

She knew her mother was right; she needed to let things go with Logan. Three months had passed and she hadn't heard anything from her, that was a clear indication nothing was going to happen. So she would write to her, get her feelings out and let it go like her mother suggested, even if her heart didn't want to.

Logan's finger moved across her keyboard with ease as she typed her new story. Reign was in her bed, naked and sleeping peacefully. After going two more rounds, she finally tapped out. Logan should have been exhausted, but she actually felt refreshed. Sex always made her feel human, like she could actually be normal. It took a lot out of her, but it gave her energy all in the same breath.

She couldn't sleep, so she decided to bust out some words on her laptop while she had it in her.

As she typed, an instant message from one of her social media pages popped up on her screen. She froze when she saw the name behind the message. Memories of Xavier's wedding flashed in her mind as she read Amaris's name on the top of the username. Logan couldn't believe Amaris had found her on social media. Months had passed between them, and she'd heard nothing from Amaris. It wasn't like she wanted to, because it would only make things harder, but it didn't mean she didn't think about her.

She clicked on the message, taking a deep breath before she started to read.

"You know, I've been torturing myself the past few months wondering if I should even contact you. I feel like you've made it clear that you wanted nothing to do with me, yet here I am. Logan, I can't stop thinking about you. There isn't a day that goes by that you don't cross my mind at least once. I can't understand why I can't let the thought of you go.

"I hope life has been treating you kindly. If you want me, I will come to you in a heartbeat, I will come to you with open arms and an open heart. The universe is telling me

you might be my soul mate, but that doesn't mean we'll end up together. A part of me knows that while another part doesn't want to believe it.

"I will end this with; I'm yours. As sad as that sounds to me, I can't deny the truth.

"Peace and Blessings. Amaris."

Logan sat there for what seemed like forever with her fingers on her keyboard. She wanted to respond back, but didn't know what to say. Amaris was raw with her emotions knowing Logan could throw them away with no regards to her. She felt Amaris's words and knew they were genuine.

She thought Amaris was a brave woman. Not once, but twice she had poured her heart out to her not knowing what the outcome would be.

Her fingers tapped on the keys, but she still didn't write anything. She was a writer, but she was at a loss for words right now. There was so much she wanted to say to Amaris, but she knew she wouldn't be able to do so over social media.

Amaris waited on the other end of her phone, wondering if Logan would message her back. She told herself to find peace in the situation either way.

A short message saying *call me* with a number at the end of it set butterflies free in her stomach. She took a moment to ease her anxiety before calling.

"Amaris?" Logan's voice was like silk through the phone.

"Hello, Logan."

A smile crept across Logan's lips, but she recovered quickly. "How are you?"

"I'm doing well and yourself?"

"I'm good."

There was an awkward pause between them, both not knowing what to say. Logan ran her hands through her dreads, sighing in frustration. This was the reason she didn't get her feelings involved with anyone; it was all too much. Caring about someone else's emotions wasn't what Logan needed in her life. "I don't want to break your heart," she blurted out.

"Then don't, Logan."

"There's things I can't control that could leave you heart broken."

"Explain it to me." Amaris was tired of Logan beating around the bush. She wanted to know what the big secret was, what was keeping them from pursuing each other?

"I'm no good for you, Amaris. I could never give you what you want." Logan knew she couldn't give anyone what they actually wanted. She made a vow to herself to not hurt anyone in her process.

"You haven't asked me what I want, Logan. I don't like people making decisions for me."

"I'm trying to protect you."

"From what?" Amaris threw her hands up in frustration like Logan could see her from the other end. She needed answers, she needed for there to be a good reason. She thought to ask Mrs. Maddox, but she didn't want to put her in an awkward situation.

"Me." Logan could see Reign stirring in bed and decided to cut the conversation short. "I gotta go, I'll call you …"

"Ask me to come to you, Logan."

Logan's heart felt like it would rip into shreds. This was a feeling she wasn't used to, she was able to keep her feelings in check, but with Amaris, there was no control. Amaris had a grip on her like no other and she didn't like it one bit.

"Amaris …" she said in a strained voice. Logan knew she had no right to give into Amaris's request. She was a ticking time bomb that might explode at any minute. Logan knew if she told Amaris to come to her and their chemistry happened to be the way it was at the wedding, she would ask Amaris to stay.

"Have a goodnight, Amaris." Logan reluctantly ended the call.

Amaris screamed in agony. She couldn't understand how Logan could keep denying her when she wanted the same thing. She didn't know how many times she could keep pouring her heart out to Logan and getting nothing in return. She'd never been this open, this vulnerable and she knew why she couldn't be. She was giving Logan too much power over her and Logan didn't deserve that power.

She grabbed her pills on her nightstand, needing to feel the numbness they provided. She felt like she would drown in her own misery. She popped the top off the bottle and swallowed two pills. She allowed her body to sink onto her bed and waited for the pills to take effect.

Logan closed her laptop as Reign sat up in bed. She got up from her seat and walked back into her room. "Hey, sleepy head." Logan sat on the bed while looking at the time. It was a little past nine at night.

"Hey, how long was I asleep?"

"A few hours. Are you hungry? I can order something." Logan really wanted to send Reign on her way, but she didn't want to be rude. Her thoughts were on Amaris and the ache she felt for her. She wanted to see her, she wanted to feel Amaris in her arms again. She didn't want to feel like this anymore, having so much longing for someone.

She allowed her thoughts to travel to a life with Amaris. She saw glimpses of how happy Amaris might have made her. She wanted that so bad, she knew she had to be truthful with those feelings, but realizing it made her want to vomit.

"Earth to Logan."

Logan brought herself back from her thoughts. "What was that?"

"I was saying I'm going to decline dinner and get out of here. I have an early call tomorrow and I need to get some rest." Logan was relieved as she watched Reign get dressed. She loved a woman who knew when it was time to go. She had to train the girls she dealt with to not get comfortable and think they were going to cuddle after having sex. All her partners knew unless she invited them to stay, they would not be staying the night with her.

"Okay. I'll have my driver drop you off."

"Thanks, I appreciate that."

After Reign got dressed, Logan walked her to the door.

At the door, Reign leaned in, giving Logan a small peck. "We should do this again sometime."

Logan forced a smile. Even though the sex was good, she knew she couldn't have sex with Reign anymore. She'd broken her own rule and she would have to check herself for it. "Have a goodnight, mah."

"You too."

CHAPTER

6

ONE MONTH LATER

Lani's eyes traced every aspect of Amaris's face as they laid in bed. She felt like there was never enough time with Amaris. She felt like she could lay with her forever like that and be perfectly fine with life.

Lani knew she had fallen hard for Amaris, she knew she was a goner the night she'd met her in the club, but she didn't know how to express her feelings because she didn't want to feel rejected if Amaris didn't feel the same way about her. She didn't want another episode of Logan happening, not when she liked Amaris so much.

Amaris felt Lani staring at her as she kept her eyes closed. She had a nervous energy about her all night and Amaris was trying to figure out what it was.

She opened her eyes, giving Lani a tight smile. "Lani, are you going to tell me what's going on? Or are you going to keep me in my misery?"

Lani giggled as she leaned over and kissed her. "What do you mean?"

"You've been nervous all night. All antsy. Is everything okay?"

"Yes, everything is okay."

"Then what is it love?" Amaris could really see that something was bothering Lani and she had no clue what it could be. The past month had been amazing between them. They'd gotten to spend the time getting to know each other and Amaris thought that Lani was someone she really wanted in her life.

After her conversation with Logan, she hadn't heard from her again and she had to tell herself to let it go. She couldn't make someone have interest in her, she couldn't make someone see that she was worth it, so she did what was right for her spirit and walked away from it.

She also had to walk away from Quelm, things had gotten too awkward with them after Quelm's confession and Amaris thought it was best. It gave her the opportunity to be vested in Lani and she was glad for that.

"I think I'm falling for you, Amaris."

Amaris watched as Lani's shoulders sank as if she was relieved to get her feelings out. "You're falling for me?" Amaris tried to hide her smile.

"Yes and I know we haven't been dating long, but it's just something about you." Lani's fingers outlined Amaris's face and she sunk into her hand in response. "There's something about you that drives me crazy. I enjoy our time together. I'm drowning in your energy and I don't want to come up for air. I've never felt like this about anyone I've dated. I know your show is tomorrow, which I'm so excited about, but I leave at the end of this week. My boss's job is done and we are going back to Vegas. Is this just a temporary thing or can you see more? Can you see us trying to make this work long distance?"

Amaris appreciated Lani's candor. She always told Lani that she liked to be open, she didn't like to hold her feelings back, so she expected nothing less of Lani. "Well, I'd like to see where we can take this." Amaris didn't want to hurt Lani's feelings, but she thought to be honest on where she stood. "Let's not add pressure to anything, let's see what happens. Take it one day at a time and see where this crazy thing takes us."

She pulled Lani under her, allowing her lips to trace over Lani's. She could feel her tremble under her, which turned her on. Lani never shied away from letting Amaris know how her touch affected her.

"We'll make this work?" Lani questioned Amaris one more time. She really didn't want to lose Amaris. For the first time, she felt like she had something real.

Amaris smiled, knowing she deserved a chance to be happy. She deserved to be with someone who wanted to be with her and make her happy. "Yes, we'll make this work." She covered Lani's lips with hers.

Logan watched as Lani basically pranced herself into the studio early in the morning. Logan couldn't help but to smile. Lani had a glow about her and she'd had it since she started dating her mystery woman. Logan tried to pry more than once to get the name of the person who kept a smile on her assistant and friend's face, but even after a month, Lani didn't give a name. She kept telling her she didn't know how serious it was so she didn't want to share anything yet. Logan respected her wishes as long as she was happy.

"Well, somebody must have gotten some last night," Logan joked.

"Matter of fact, I did." Lani plopped down in one of the chairs. She had an amazing night with Amaris that went into the morning.

"Well, look at you. So, we're leaving soon, when do I get to meet your girl?" Logan inquired, hoping to get a different answer.

"Well, she's having an exhibit tomorrow. You want to come?"

"Yeah, that'll be cool. You know I like stuff like that."

"Okay, I'll text you the information. I look forward to you guys meeting."

Logan raised her eyebrow in suspicion. "Oh yeah? Because it hasn't seemed that way since you've been dating her."

"I just wanted to make sure things were cool first before I went introducing her to people. She's different Logan, I can see a future with her."

Logan could see the twinkle in Lani's eye as she spoke about her girlfriend. She was happy that Lani was happy.

When Lani came to her and told her the feelings she had for her, Logan was honored and surprised that her friend and assistant felt that way about her and in another life, she probably would have given them a chance, but not this time. Even though Lani knew about Logan's health condition, she still wanted to be with her. Logan knew she couldn't put that on Lani; she couldn't put it on anyone. It was the same reason she wouldn't be with Amaris. It was the reason she decided to be alone.

Lani tried to convince her to give them a chance, but to no avail, this was something Logan wouldn't budge on. So, she was genuinely happy that Lani found someone and if they ended up spending their lives together, that would be even better.

"Well my dear, if she has you smiling like this every time I see you, then enjoy this, live in it. Did you guys discuss you going back to Vegas?"

"Yes and we're going to try to make it work. We'll switch on and off visiting each other. It's a good thing we're only a few hours away. I couldn't imagine living on the east coast and trying to do something like this."

"Well, if it's meant to happen, it will happen, just go with the flow. You know, Lani, all I've ever wanted was for you to be happy. You're an amazing woman and you deserve to be happy with someone."

Lani was touched by Logan's words. She remembered feeling so crushed when Logan didn't share her thoughts of them being together. They spent long nights together and she'd done so much for Logan that she thought they'd be great together.

She thought knowing about Logan's condition would get Logan to see that she could still be with someone and share a happy life, but Logan put all thoughts of that to bed. So, Lani was stuck with her feelings for Logan while working beside her every day, but since she'd met Amaris, it wasn't as hard as it used to be for her. She found herself slowly being able to let Logan go.

"Thanks, Lo." Lani hugged Logan while kissing her cheek. "Now, I think I have some emails I need to get to so if you don't need anything right now, I shall get to work."

"I'm good right now—" Logan stopped mid-sentence as Reign walked into the building. She looked at her watch and saw that Reign was thirty minutes late. "I'll be right back." Before Lani could respond, Logan was making her way over to Reign. She put on her charming smile as soon as she got to her. "Hey Reign, let's go outside and talk for a second."

"Well, I'm already running late, so I don't have time for this."

"Oh, it's okay. You've already cost me money, a little more won't hurt me." Logan grabbed her by her arm, escorting her out of the building. She tried not to laugh thinking about doing the same thing to Lani just a while ago.

"Damn, Logan, what's up?"

"Do you want this job?"

"What?"

"I didn't stutter. Do you want this fucking job?"

"Of course, I do." Reign didn't know where Logan was coming from. She showed in her work how much she wanted this role. It was her first big role and she was proud of it.

"Well, I need your ass to act like it. This is the third day this week that you've been late. We have a role call for a reason and if you can't get with that then maybe I need to switch my leading lady."

Logan knew she'd fucked up after having sex with Reign. Reign instantly thought something was going to happen between them and Logan had to shut it down. She broke her own rule by mixing business with pleasure. She knew what was done was done, but she wouldn't allow Reign to disrespect her or her crew with her tardiness. It would cost her time and money to find someone and re-shoot everything, but she would do it to prove a point.

"We're about to wrap, Logan, you can't be serious." Reign knew that she had been pushing Logan's buttons by being late, but she felt a little burned at Logan's rejection. She was hoping to bag Logan during their time filming together, but that proved to be harder than expected.

Since the night they slept together, Logan had rejected all of her advances to sleep together again and when she told her they needed to keep their relationship on a professional level, it was something Reign wasn't used to. Even with that, she didn't want to push Logan to find someone else to play in her movie. This was her big break and she didn't want to lose it.

Logan smirked concededly. "Reign, I'm a millionaire. I can afford it, so would you like to try me?"

Reign gawked at Logan, not believing her words. She knew she had pushed a little too hard, but she didn't expect this reaction. "It won't happen again, I promise."

"Good, now let's get to work."

— · ·●· · —

Amaris smiled as she saw Mrs. Maddox's name pop up on her phone. Mrs. Maddox had grown to be a very important person to her in such a short amount of time.

"Mrs. Maddox." she said, putting the phone to her ear.

"Kayman. Please, call me Kayman dear."

Amaris giggled while sliding her laptop to the side. "Hello Kayman, how are you today?"

"I'm doing well. I just wanted to confirm with you that Taylor and I will be down there for your show. The husbands want to come to support, will that be okay?"

Amaris thought it was more than okay. She loved the support everyone was showing her with her show. Her anxiety was through the roof knowing she would have to present her work to the photography world in a few days, even though she was ready. When she invited Mrs. Maddox to her show, she really didn't expect for her to accept, but Mrs. Maddox was just as excited as her own mother when she told her the news.

"Yes, that would be great." She wanted to ask if Logan was going to join them, but she knew that was a joke. Logan made it clear by not calling or messaging her after their talk that there was something eating at her, and Amaris didn't know if she wanted to be a part of something she couldn't share.

"Okay, so we will see you at the show. Maybe Taylor and I can stay out there for a day or so and we can catch up with a girls' day." Amaris had become like another daughter to Mrs. Maddox, so she wanted to spend a little more time. Besides, she wanted to make sure Amaris was really okay. She wanted to ask Amaris if she'd run into Logan while she was there, but she thought she would bring it up like she brought up their conversation. Amaris had finally broke down and begged Mrs. Maddox to tell her what was going on with Logan after they'd finally spoke, but she had to tell Amaris it was up to Logan to tell her. She wished she could, but she knew it wasn't her place.

"That would be fun. How are the newlyweds doing?" Usually, when Amaris did a job she did the job and went home. Her friendship with Taylor and Mrs. Maddox was unexpected, but welcomed.

Mrs. Maddox gushed. "Oh you know, being newlyweds. I wouldn't be surprised if we had a little Maddox in the oven soon."

"That's good, love is so beautiful especially when it's with the right person," Amaris said, thinking about Lani; she could be her right person.

"Yes, it is, sweetie. So any lucky lady in your life?" She held her breath for the answer.

"Well, I am seeing someone and she's great, Kayman. I think we have a chance."

"Oh really? That's wonderful, dear." Mrs. Maddox wanted to beat some sense into Logan's head at this point. She felt like she was going to miss out on a wonderful woman over fear.

"Yes, we've kind of just made it official. She'll be at my show, so you guys can meet her."

"I look forward to it. But I'm going to let you go, sweetheart. I just wanted to let you know that we were coming."

"Okay. I will see you guys in a few days."

"Yes, you will. Have a good day."

"You as well." Amaris ended the call. Not even five seconds later, Tasha was calling her. "Hey, Tasha."

"Hey, where are you girl?"

"What?" Amaris asked, confused.

"Amaris, you're supposed to be at The Galley, we're going over placements today. Did you seriously forget?"

Amaris spun around looking at her calendar on the wall. "Oh shit! I'm on my way." She jumped up, throwing on whatever was in front of her.

"Hurry up, you're late."

"I'm coming." She ended the call and rushed out of her house. She couldn't believe she'd forgotten about the meeting. She knew Tasha was going to talk so much shit to her.

When she made it to the gallery, Tasha's face said it all. "I'm sorry, I don't know how this slipped my mind," she apologized profusely.

"Let's go, we only have thirty minutes now. You're over an hour late, girl."

"I said, sorry."

"Come on, they're going to be closing up in a bit."

Amaris followed Tasha into the room that her show would take place in. Right now it was bare, but in a few days it would have her work on their walls. It was still an amazing thing to think about.

"So, you'll give a little speech on the stage in the front and then everyone will come in here and see your work. So, let's see what you want to do." Tasha looked at Amaris with a smile spreading across her face. "Let's see your vision come to life, sis."

Amaris looked at the empty room and realized her dream was about to come true. "Let's do it."

———— · • ● • · ————

Lani walked up behind Amaris, pressing her body into hers. Amaris was so lost in her thoughts she didn't hear Lani come into the house.

"Are you ready for this?" Lani asked her over her shoulder.

Amaris leaned back, allowing herself to sink into Lani. She welcomed the warm contact after such a long day. No, she wasn't ready for this, her show was in two hours and she was freaking out on the inside; she'd had two anxiety attacks that morning thinking about her show. It was all on her, she knew this could make or break her.

"You know you deserve this, baby, this is your time to shine. You're going to do great, Amaris, and I'm so glad to be the one on your arm tonight as you present your work. I'm excited to see it," Lani assured her.

Amaris smiled while turning in Lani's arms. She wrapped her arm around her neck and kissed her. Lani's words were exactly what she needed to hear right now. "Thank you, mah."

"Now, are you ready to go? You don't want to be late to your own show."

Amaris took a moment to look at Lani, she looked absolutely beautiful in her dress. "Yes, we should, but first, let me get a look at you." She twirled Lani around, taking a look at every inch of her dress. Her dress hugged her curves, but her breasts were the star of the show. Her fire red dress matched the colors in Amaris dress. She had to admit they complimented each other very well. "You, my dear, look amazing. Now if this wasn't my show, I would take you to bed and fuck your brains out."

Lani wished Amaris knew what her words did to her. Just that one sentence sent chills down her spine and made her panties moist. She wanted Amaris to take her right there on her balcony. "You know you can't talk to me like that."

The air around them became thick as Amaris pressed into Lani. Their sexual chemistry was out of this world; the energy between them just meshed. "Oh yeah? Why not?"

"Because ..." Lani kissed Amaris, not wanting to say anything else. She wanted her hands on her and inside her.

Amaris's hands were all over Lani as Lani's tongue invaded her mouth. She moaned, sucking her tongue deeper into her mouth as their kiss grew stronger.

Lani grabbed Amaris hand, sliding it up her dress. "Touch me," Lani begged. Her pussy was so wet there was no way she could leave feeling like that.

"Why?"

"Because I want you to make me cum."

Amaris wanted to, she wanted to play and eat Lani's pussy so badly, but she knew they had to leave in order to beat traffic. She could see Lani had other plans though and they would be stuck in that same traffic.

"Yeah, I guess I should do that," Amaris said just as Lani pulled her towards the bedroom.

— • • ● • • • —

Logan looked herself over in the mirror, checking to see if her suit was intact. Lani had told her to dress up because there would be press there and Logan wanted to tell her she didn't have to tell her to dress up because she always dressed to the tee when it came to events.

Her phone rang, displaying her brother's name. "What's up, X?"

"Hey, mom wanted me to tell you we're out here and she wants to see you."

"Who is we? And why are you guys out here?" Logan grabbed her jacket and headed out her building.

"Me, mom, dad, and Taylor. We're here for Amaris's show."

Logan hopped in her car and gave her driver the address. "What show?"

"I don't know, she's having some sort of show, but mom said it's uber important so she wanted to come out and support her."

Logan frowned at the thought of her family seeing Amaris. She still couldn't believe they had actually formed a relationship with her, but then again, she could because Amaris had that type of personality. "Oh, that's cool," she said dryly.

Xavier laughed, shaking his head. "Mom says she has a girlfriend now. You missed out, little sis."

Logan tried to ignore that ping of pain she felt from her brother's words. Amaris had found someone; someone was spending time with her. The thought of that sent a wave of jealousy through Logan's body, but she wouldn't give her brother the satisfaction of knowing it bothered her. "Oh yeah? Well, that's good for her."

Xavier rolled his eyes. He knew his sister enough to know she was fronting. "What are you doing? You should come."

"That's a negative." Logan wouldn't go to Amaris's show knowing she had a girlfriend. She couldn't be in her face and see her hanging on somebody else's arm. "Besides, Lani invited me to her girlfriend's show, so I'm on my way there."

"Lani has a girlfriend?"

"Yeah, some girl she met when we came down here."

"Okay. Well, we're pulling in, but we are all getting together tomorrow and don't try to get out of it."

Logan chuckled, she'd actually missed her family so she was looking forward to seeing them. "I'll come see you guys at the house. Tell mom I want breakfast."

"You know she'll be happy to do anything for her princess," Xavier teased.

"Nigga, shut up. I'll see you tomorrow."

"Mom wants to take Amaris to dinner after her show, you should join us. Bring Lani and her girl."

Logan rolled her eyes, she wished everybody would stop trying to play matchmaker. "No, I think I'm okay. I don't think I want to be around Amaris." She also didn't want to be the fifth wheel to all the couples.

"Why not?"

"Because there's nothing there, bro, so please, stop trying to make something there."

Xavier knew when to back off. He wanted to give one last ditch effort because they were all in the same city again, but he knew not to push his little sister. Logan could shut down on a person with such urgency and that's the last thing Xavier wanted. "Okay "I'm sorry. I'll see you in the morning?"

"Yes. I love you. Tell everyone I love them and I'll see them in the morning."

"Okay, little sis, I love you as well." They ended their call just in time as Logan's driver pulled into the venue.

"We're here ma'am," he called out.

"Thank you, Thomas. I'll see you in a few hours. Give it about two hours."

"Yes, ma'am."

Logan hopped out of the car and was accosted by the press. She took a deep breath and put on a smile before the questions started coming at her.

"Five minutes until showtime, Amaris." Tasha warned Amaris as she stood backstage. She peeked behind the curtains and was amazed at how many people had actually showed up.

"Okay, I got you." Amaris shook her hands, trying to get the jitters out. Her heart was beating so fast she felt like she couldn't breathe. She felt an anxiety attack coming on and she was trying to stop it. She closed her eyes, taking deep breaths. Amaris tried to block out all the people she saw in the audience. She tried to remember that she wanted this.

Tasha saw Amaris's body language and grabbed her gently by the arms. "Hey, you are amazing. This is what you are meant to do. This is your time. You are my best friend and I believe in you. You can do this, Amaris, calm yourself down. Don't lose your shit, this is your time."

Amaris shook her head, loving Tasha for being there for her. They had been friends for over ten years and business partners for eight. She loved Tasha for believing in her and never giving up on her. "Thank you so much, sis. Thank you for all of this. I love you so much."

"I love you too. Now, let's do this."

Lani waved Logan over as she walked into the venue. Logan smiled as she made her way over to her. "Hey, mami," she said with a smile.

"Hey, it's about time you got here. The show's about to start." They hugged and kissed each other's cheeks.

Logan looked Lani over. "Look at you, mah, looking all good."

Lani twirled for Logan so she could get a good look. "You know how I do."

Logan smirked, she had to admit Lani looked damn good tonight. "If you weren't taken I would have to take you home tonight," Logan teased.

Lani playfully slapped Logan. "Girl, shut up." They laughed together.

"Logan?" Logan jumped, hearing a familiar voice behind her. When she turned around, her whole family was standing there. "Mom? What are you doing here?" She hugged and kissed her mom.

"We're here for Amaris's show. What are you doing here?"

"You guys know Amaris?" Lani asked, surprised.

"Yes, she was the photographer for Taylor and Xavier's wedding."

Logan was confused. "Amaris's show?" The last thing she saw was Taylor and Xavier exchanging looks before the lights went out and a spotlight came up on the stage. Logan felt like her heart stopped as Amaris walked out onto the stage.

Mrs. Maddox placed her hand on Logan's arm trying to give her some type of support. Logan looked at her mother with pain in her eyes before looking back at Amaris. She looked absolutely stunning. She literally took Logan's breath away. Amaris wore a beautiful, yellow lace dress. The top wrapped around her neck, but showed off her beautiful shoulders and collar bone. There were red roses sewn into the lace which wrapped around her breast, down to her waist and across her thighs. Her dress hugged her body, showing off her hips and breasts. Beautiful, gold-beaded jewelry wrapped around both of her arms giving her a goddess-like look. Instead of her afro, she'd pressed her hair which framed her face perfectly.

Logan liked the fact that she didn't wear much makeup; she liked her natural look. Her eyes traveled down to the sexy, red 'come fuck me' pumps that graced her feet. Logan wanted to kiss the fucking ground Amaris walked on. She would gladly grovel at her feet. Amaris exuded such confidence up there on stage that Logan wanted her bad.

She had to plant her feet onto the floor because she felt like her body was going to move on its own. She hadn't seen Amaris in months and she felt the distance as she watched her on the stage. She thought about their last conversation which didn't end on a good note. She'd told Amaris she would call her back and never did.

Taylor's mouth dropped. "She looks fucking amazing," she whispered to her husband.

Xavier looked at his sister from his peripheral vision, prepared for whatever was about to happen. "Logan looks like she's about to be sick," he whispered back.

"Good, she's dumb for the way she treated Amaris." Taylor was on Amaris's side and she wasn't hiding it. She loved Amaris and couldn't believe the way Logan had treated her at the wedding. She loved Logan too, but she felt like she could have handled the situation better.

"This is bad," Xavier whispered to Taylor as he watched Logan's reaction.

"Why?" Taylor asked, confused.

Xavier pulled Taylor away from everyone so they couldn't hear him. "Logan told me Lani invited her to her girlfriend's show."

"Okay?"

Xavier waved his arms around. "This is Amaris's show. Amaris and Lani are together."

Taylor's eyes grew big realizing the truth. "Oh, shit." She looked at Logan. "We need to get her out of here."

Xavier shook his head. "This needs to happen, baby, but this isn't going to be pretty."

Amaris couldn't see anyone in the audience and it made it easier for her to speak. "Good evening everyone, I want to welcome and thank everyone for coming tonight. This show means everything to me. The images I hand selected are of people who have made some type of impact on my life. I believe in connections, I believe in multiple soul mates, I believe in love, the universe, and beautiful people. I believe people come into your life for reasons even though you might not understand some.

"I've had the chance to meet some very beautiful people and I hope you enjoy a view of them just as much as I have. They say the eyes are the mirror to your soul and I'd like to think I've captured that. I hope you all enjoy the show." Everyone clapped as the room went dark and two doors opened.

Logan didn't know what to do. She had put everything together realizing this whole time Lani had been dating Amaris. She'd felt a jealousy she'd never felt before, that little twinge of pain in her heart was now a gaping hole. It hurt her to think of Amaris sharing her life with someone, but it was with someone she knew, someone close to her.

Even though she knew the answer, she found herself turning toward Lani. "Is that her? Your mystery woman?"

"Yes."

Logan saw the twinkle in Lani's eyes, she was happy. Amaris was the one making Lani happy. All the times Lani had come in smiling and happy, it was because of Amaris. Lani and Amaris were fucking. Just the thought made Logan's stomach turn. "That's great." She forced out with a tight smile.

"Yeah, I can't wait for you to meet her, but it'll have to be after the show. Let's go inside and look at her work."

"Give me a second, imma go to the bar really quick."

"Okay."

Logan walked away from her family and Lani and headed to the bar. She felt like the world was spinning at the news she'd just found out. She loosened her tie so she could breathe better. "Can I get a shot of Patron please?"

"Logan." She felt a pair of hands on her back and she turned to see her brother. "Are you okay?" he asked, concern showing on his face.

"My fucking assistant." Logan could barely get the words out. She couldn't believe Amaris would do that to her. Thoughts of them laughing in bed plagued her mind and it pissed her off.

"Sis, she doesn't know. Do you think Lani would have invited you here if she knew you and Amaris knew each other?"

Logan downed her shot and signaled for another one. "How could she not? We've been here for over a month. They've been together since we got here. Are you telling me my name never came up? Or that Amaris never asked Lani why she was here or who her boss was? I can't believe that."

Xavier thought it would be good for Logan to see Amaris, but now he thought it was a bad idea. Logan was livid, he saw it in her eyes. Xavier didn't want Logan to blow up and ruin Amaris's night. "Maybe we should get out of here. We can go grab something to eat."

Logan shook her head. "Naw, I'm here, I'm staying. I want to see Amaris's face when she sees me, when she realizes what the fuck she's been doing." Logan downed the second shot and headed toward the room Amaris's photos were in.

Xavier grabbed her arm. "Sis, this is her big night, don't ruin this for her."

"I know how to conduct myself. Besides, I have way more to lose here." Logan snatched her arm from her brother's grip and walked away from him.

He followed behind her and almost bumped into her back when she stopped abruptly.

"Dammit, Logan, what the hell?" When Xavier looked up, he knew why she'd stopped.

Logan's eyes went around the room staring at the pictures. She recognized the eyes staring back at her, she recognized the lips—her lips. Her mind took her back to the moment those photos were taken. Her mother's rose garden appeared. She remembered why she smiled so hard. Amaris's face, her beautiful face, the way she held her camera, and the way she looked at her, that was why she smiled so hard. Amaris had taken pieces of her face and used them for her show. No one knew it was her, but she knew her own face.

She thought about Amaris's dress and it came to her. "She has roses on her fucking dress."

"What?" Xavier asked, confused.

"The dress, the pictures, mom's rose garden." Logan didn't know if she should cuss Amaris out for a few things. One, using her pictures without her permission and two, fucking her assistant. But she also thought she wanted to kiss her, she wanted to go to her and confess how much she missed her. Her heart was so conflicted. *She wore roses without even knowing I would be here tonight. Does this mean she still thinks of me and our time in the garden? Does she care for me the way I care for her?*

"Logan, I'm so lost."

"The first day I met Amaris, she made me stop at mom's rose garden. We had a moment there, it was the moment I knew I was in trouble." A sly smile crossed Logan's lips as the memory replayed in her mind. It felt like they were back in the rose garden. "What has this woman done to me?" Logan thought aloud.

They both heard a gasp behind them. "Logan?"

7

Amaris felt like she was going to lose her shit when she saw Logan walk into the room. She wanted to know what she was doing there. She knew Mrs. Maddox wouldn't invite Logan, not when they weren't speaking. But here she was, in the flesh. After months of not seeing each other, Logan was standing right in front of her and she looked heavenly.

She hated to admit that her first thought was to walk into Logan's arms. Here she was on the most important night of her life and all thoughts of where she was went out the window the moment she saw Logan.

"Hello, Amaris," Logan said coldly. She swallowed any emotion she had on seeing Amaris in person. She was pissed, she was jealous.

"What are you doing here?" Amaris asked, unable to hide the shock on her face.

Xavier saw Lani heading their way and knew it was about to get messy. The look on her face indicated she had no clue what was going on. "Lani is on her way over here," he whispered to Logan.

"My fucking assistant, Amaris," Logan spat before Lani got there. Logan's face recovered after seeing Lani wrap her arm around Amaris's waist.

"Babe, you met my boss!" Lani said enthused.

Amaris turned to look at Lani, confused. "Your boss?" *No. No. No. This can't be happening, not now, not here. Logan can't be the same person.*

"Yes, this is Logan Maddox. Logan, this is my girl, Amaris."

Logan and Amaris locked eyes. Logan locked her jaws, trying to hide her anger. She wondered how Amaris didn't know that she was Lani's boss. The only thing that stopped Logan from going off was Lani. The look of pure happiness on Lani's face made Logan keep her shit together. It wasn't Lani's fault and she wouldn't hurt her friend. So, she swallowed her anger and smiled while sticking her hand out.

"Amaris, so you're the one who's keeping a smile on Lani's face. This is such a small world, the last time I saw you, you were snapping pictures at my brother's wedding." Logan put on her charming smile.

Amaris wanted to throw up. A part of her wanted to jump into Logan's arms and tell her how much she missed her, but the other part of her felt Lani's arms around her. She was with Lani and Logan wasn't going to make any indication that they knew each other. So, she played the part and stuck her hand out. "Hello Logan, it's nice to finally meet you. The wedding was so fast-paced I didn't get to meet everyone fully."

Logan smirked as she took Amaris's hand into hers. She gritted her teeth feeling that energy between them that she'd felt at Xavier's wedding. She wanted Amaris, her heart ached for her. "It's such a small world."

Xavier's eyes went to his family and Taylor who were looking on with worry in their eyes. Xavier put his hand up letting them know he wouldn't allow things to get out of hand. "Well guys, I think we should enjoy these amazing photos Amaris took. Amaris, it's nice to see you by the way. The family is waiting for you when you have a chance."

Amaris nodded her head. "Okay, I'll be there in a second."

"Babe, you know the Maddox family?"

Amaris took a long deep breath. She couldn't believe Lani hadn't put two and two together after their conversation on her balcony. "Yes. After the wedding, Taylor, Mrs. Maddox and I grew close. I talk to them on the regular."

Lani laughed. "This is so crazy, this whole damn time we all kind of knew each other. The Maddox's are like family to me as well. This is so great."

Logan wanted to slap Lani, only because she didn't know the hell that she was going through standing in front of Amaris. "Hey ladies, will you excuse me for a second? I need to go to the restroom," she said, trying to spare herself the torture.

"Okay, Lo," Lani replied, ignorant to the look on her boss's face.

Logan had to get out of there, she couldn't watch them together. She made a dash for the restroom and was relieved when she saw that it was empty. She looked at herself in the mirror and took a deep breath. "Fuck."

"This is so bad," Taylor said, watching Logan walk away.

"How could Logan not know that Lani and Amaris were dating?" Mrs. Maddox asked, confused. Speaking with Logan, Logan had never mentioned anything about Lani and Amaris dating.

"Logan didn't know and hell Amaris didn't know either."

"How could they not know? Lani and Logan are together every damn day. They work together." Mrs. Maddox could only imagine what Logan was going through. She could only imagine what Amaris was feeling right now. Mrs. Maddox never thought in all her wildest dreams that the girl Amaris was going to introduce them to was Lani. She didn't know what to think because Lani was family as well. This was a messy situation.

"Amaris loves Logan," she said with a sigh.

"Yeah, well mom, it doesn't look like that means anything if Logan doesn't get her head out of her ass."

In the bathroom, Logan sighed as she heard the door open and close. She didn't have to open her eyes to know that it was Amaris; her scent filled the bathroom.

"Are you trying to torture me?" Amaris asked, her eyes filled with pain and her voice cracking.

Logan opened her eyes as she heard the crack in Amaris's voice and turned to look at her. Her chest was heaving up and down and she looked distraught. Logan's heart broke seeing her like that. "Torture you?"

"I don't hear from you in a month, I haven't seen you in months and then all of a sudden, you're here at my show. The biggest night of my life, the one night I have to keep my shit together."

"Amaris, I didn't know this was your show or I wouldn't be here. What are you doing with Lani?"

"We're dating, but I didn't know she was your assistant." Amaris saw how this all looked and she wanted to clear things up. If only she had known…

"This whole time, my name didn't come up?"

"No. Lani just said she was here with her boss working. She never gave a name."

"This is fucking crazy." Logan ran her hands over her dreads.

So many emotions were running through Amaris's head. She hated herself for missing Logan and for being glad to see her after all this time. Lani was out there waiting for her, but Amaris had to see Logan alone, she had to breathe in the essence of her.

They were silent as they stared at each other. Logan knew she would regret it, she knew she was making a mistake, but she couldn't stop her legs from moving toward Amaris. Amaris backed up. She was barely keeping her shit together and she knew if Logan took another step she would lose it.

"Don't," she said in a whisper, even though she meant for her voice to come out firm and commanding.

Logan didn't listen, she kept coming and in one swift move, she had Amaris in her arms, claiming her lips. Amaris collapsed into Logan as she felt what she'd been missing since the wedding. Logan's touch was like fire, but her lips were like ice. She kissed Amaris with passion and anger.

Jealousy plagued Logan's thoughts as she thought about Lani and Amaris together, so she pulled back enough for them to lock eyes. Amaris looked as if she was in a daze.

"Amaris, you are mines. What the fuck are you doing here with Lani?" Logan growled.

Amaris was taken aback. She tried to get out of Logan's hold, but Logan held her in place. "I am not yours, Logan. You didn't want me. Did you really expect me to just keep waiting for you?"

"Last time we spoke, you said you were mines."

"Logan, stop playing these mind games with me." Amaris wiggled out of Logan's grip. "How many times do you want me to beg you?"

"I'm not asking you to beg me."

"What do you want Logan? Because I'm not into childish games. Lani is a really good woman, she actually likes me, she actually wants to be with me."

Logan finally released Amaris, backing away. The thought of Amaris spending the rest of her life with Lani was heartbreaking, but she didn't want to break Lani's heart. She felt like she was stuck between a rock and a hard place.

"What do you want?" Amaris asked again, feeling like she was holding her breath as she waited for Logan's answer. All she wanted right now was for Logan to pull her into her arms and kiss her again, tell her that she missed her, and it was her that she wanted. She knew that no matter how bad she would feel, she would break up with Lani that night if Logan said they had a chance together, but she needed Logan to throw her a bone.

She could see the turmoil in Logan's eyes and it almost broke her. She knew she would have to return to her show soon, she couldn't stay in the bathroom forever. "Logan ..."

"Will you come see me tonight?"

"Tonight? I can't." Amaris knew Lani would want to celebrate her big night.

"Please. I'll explain everything and then you can decide." Logan thought about what her family said, she needed to tell Amaris the truth. She needed to tell her why they couldn't be together even though they had these unknown feelings for each other.

Logan took her business card out of her pocket and wrote the address to her condo on it. "I'm going to leave now because I really don't want to ruin your night. I'm happy for you and your accomplishment. I will wait for you, Amaris, and if you don't come, I understand." Logan extended her card hoping Amaris would take it.

Amaris's eyes zoomed in on the card. Her hand itched to take it, but she didn't know what it would mean if she did.

"Amaris, please." This time, Logan begged.

Logan wrapped Amaris in her arms, nuzzling her neck. It felt so good to be close to her again. It was crazy how her body reacted to Amaris, it was as if they'd known each other their whole lives. "Do I know you?" She repeated the same question she'd asked Amaris the night of her brother's party.

Amaris pulled back so that she could see Logan's face, the face that plagued her thoughts and dreams on a daily basis. "Maybe. Maybe we met in college and knew we were meant to be together. Maybe we shared a big house and had kids together. Maybe we traveled the world together. Maybe—"

Logan hugged her again, cutting her off. She inhaled her scent. If she didn't show tonight, she would accept that. She had ample time to tell Amaris the truth, but in case she didn't, she wanted to remember what Amaris smelled like. It was the same as the last time—her natural scent was like an aphrodisiac.

"I've missed you, Amaris."

It was everything Amaris wanted to hear. She'd waited so long for Logan to come to her, to say those words, and hold her the way she was holding her. It felt so right and so wrong all at the same time. She'd just told Lani they would make it work once she went back to Vegas and here she was, getting lost in Logan's arms inside the ladies' room.

"I've missed you as well, Logan, very much," she replied.

"I'll go now. See you later, hopefully." Logan reluctantly let Amaris go and made her exit from the bathroom.

Amaris took a moment to get herself together. She knew she couldn't go back out there in the state she was in. She closed her eyes, taking in a few breaths in order to get her emotions under control. She couldn't have Lani thinking something was wrong.

When she opened the door, her mother was standing there waiting for her. "What's going on?" Her mother had watched everything play out, but said nothing. But as soon as she saw Amaris follow Logan to the bathroom, she knew something was up. She knew her child enough to know when something was wrong.

Amaris sunk back into the bathroom, waiting for her mother to follow her. She was happy when she did. Her mother closed the door, locking it so they had some privacy. "That's the woman I told you about."

"The woman?"

"The one I met at the wedding in Las Vegas."

Ms. Cole replayed the conversation they had a month ago. "The one who didn't want to pursue you?"

"It's not like that mom."

"But it is. And what is she doing here?"

Amaris sighed, rubbing her temple. "She's Lani's boss."

"Her boss! Are you serious?"

"Yes, I didn't know that or I wouldn't have pursued Lani. It's too close and now I'm stuck."

"Stuck, why? The girl didn't want you. You have Lani out there waiting for you, she wants to be with you. She didn't play games with you, so why the hell are you stuck on someone who doesn't know how to be an adult?" Ms. Cole didn't want Amaris to play with people's hearts. She liked Lani and she thought Lani was good for Amaris. She could tell that Lani was very fond of her daughter. She didn't want Amaris to miss out on happiness because she was stuck on a 'what if'.

Amaris knew where her mother was going, but she couldn't explain the pull Logan had on her. She wished it was that easy to say 'fuck Logan' and go back to Lani, but she knew she couldn't. It was as if their souls were connected and anytime they were close, it felt right; it felt like Amaris was home.

"She is like fire, mom, she is like light. I'm completely drawn to her," she said, feeling conflicted.

"It doesn't mean she's right for you."

"Mom, I can't do this right now, I need to get out there." Amaris walked past her mother and went back to her show. This was her night and no one would take this night from her. She'd waited for an opportunity like this and she wasn't going to fuck it up.

Tasha stood inside the gallery with her hands on her hips and a face Amaris knew all too well.

Amaris put her hands up. "I know, I know," she said in mock surrender, watching as Tasha's face turned from a scowl to a smile, then to a big cheese. Amaris looked at her like she was crazy. "What's going on?" she asked with a small frown.

"Look." Tasha handed Amaris a piece of paper. Amaris opened it and realized it was a check, but it was not just any check, it was a check for a hundred thousand dollars.

"Wh-wh-what is this?" Amaris said with a shaky voice.

"Sis, somebody bought all of your work, every last piece of it."

"What? Are you serious? This is way over the asking price." Amaris ran her hands across the check to see if it was a real check.

"I'm serious, girl! Congrats sis, you did it!" Tasha and Amaris hugged while jumping up and down. She didn't expect to sell any work tonight; she just wanted to share her art with everyone. This was just icing on the cake.

"Who is it? I want to thank them."

"They want to remain anonymous, but who the fuck cares? They're paying you a hundred thousand dollars! You're in the big leagues, sis."

"Congrats baby," Ms. Cole said, hugging her daughter tight. "You deserve this."

"Thanks mama."

• •●• • ———

Amaris wanted to cry from the success of her show. Her night was filled with so much love and support it was overwhelming. She spent the night speaking with other photographers and local artists as well as the Maddox family, her mother, and Lani. It was more than she could ever ask for.

Despite that, her anxiety was through the roof because she had to make the decision of whether she was going to see Logan or not. However, Lani expected them to go home together and she knew she would be disappointed if she sent her home, but that part of her that ached for Logan wanted to take Logan up on her offer.

Mrs. Maddox made her way to the bar, seeing that Amaris was finally alone. "Are you enjoying your night, dear?"

Amaris smiled. "Yes, I am. This was an amazing night."

"Good. I'm so proud of you, Amaris. You have such a gift. I wanted to offer you an opportunity."

"What kind of opportunity?"

"Mr. Maddox and I need a landscaping photographer. Do you do landscaping?"

"I've done it in the past, but my forte is people. I love to capture people."

Mrs. Maddox nodded her head, knowing Amaris did have an eye for capturing beauty in a person. Her photos displayed that tonight, as well as the photos she took at the wedding. "The job would be for three months, room and board paid for with a compensation of twenty thousand dollars. Ten thousand initial payment and ten when the job is done."

Amaris was stunned to silence. She felt like the universe blessed her twice in a matter of hours. "Are you sure you want me Mrs. Maddox? I can recommend a great landscaping photographer."

Mrs. Maddox smiled uneasily. "We were hoping we could have you for the job."

"Well of course, I'll take the job. I'll just have to square some things out. When does the gig start and what exactly is it?"

"Let's do lunch tomorrow with Taylor and I'll tell you all about it."

"Okay, sounds like a plan."

Mrs. Maddox hugged Amaris tight. "You are an amazing artist," she said and slid Amaris an envelope. "See you tomorrow."

Amaris waited for Mrs. Maddox to leave before opening the envelope. She pulled the letter out and began to read.

Amaris,

Thank you so much for inviting us to your show, we all enjoyed ourselves so much. I'm sorry for how things turned out with Logan. I wish Logan would open her heart to you. So much time is wasted not spending the time with the people you love or could love. I've witnessed the spark between you and Logan. Don't let that spark die, fight for it. The world has made Logan cold, I hope you're the one to melt the ice around her heart. I know the life of a starving artist, so I hope this helps. From Mr. Maddox and I, see you soon."

With Love,

Kayman

Amaris flipped the letter over, wondering what Mrs. Maddox meant. There was nothing there, she looked into the envelope and pulled a piece of paper out. But it wasn't just a paper, it was a check for $50,000. Amaris wanted to jump up and down and scream for joy, but she kept herself composed. In one night, she had accumulated $150,000. She was set for a while.

"Hey baby, are you ready to leave?" Lani wrapped her arms around Amaris from behind.

Amaris thought about what Mrs. Maddox wrote in her note and replied, "About that …"

— • ● • • —

Logan was almost in a deep sleep when she heard the knock on her door. She looked at the time and saw that it was after midnight. When she opened the door and saw Amaris, she couldn't hide her smile. She honestly didn't think Amaris would show up.

"I sat in my car for an hour wondering if I should come up here." Amaris said as though she was trying to explain it.

Logan stepped to the side, allowing space for Amaris to come in. "Have you made your decision?" She really thought she would stay with Lani tonight so she went to bed when she got home.

Amaris knew she was kidding herself the whole night. She knew in her heart she would go to Logan after her show. She had to block out the hurt look on Lani's face when she told her she was going to see her tomorrow.

She walked inside Logan's door knowing there was no turning back now. "Would you like something to drink?"

Amaris looked around Logan's condo, not knowing what to expect. It felt more like a hotel room instead of her home. The walls were bare, no pictures of family, no art, no color. There was a couch and a TV in the living room. That was it, nothing to show that the place was lived in. Amaris thought it was sad that the house was almost cold.

"You don't like to decorate?"

Logan shrugged. "My parents own this building. I'm just here until the end of the week. It's not my home, so there's no reason to decorate."

Logan's eyes traveled down Amaris's dress as she walked further into the room. Even after a long night, she still looked amazing. Amaris had great legs, Logan could only imagine what they looked like resting against her shoulders as she fucked her. She straightened up knowing she shouldn't have been thinking like that. She knew why Amaris was here; she wanted answers, answers Logan was finally prepared to give her.

"How was your show?" she asked Amaris without once taking her eyes off her.

Amaris's face lit up. It was so full of excitement, it was infectious. "Somebody bought all of my work for $100,000! Can you believe that, Logan?"

Logan chuckled while sitting at her bar. "Your work is great, so yeah, I believe it. Congratulations on your success, Amaris."

"And then your parents shocked me by gifting me $50,000 . You guys sure are generous with your money."

Logan shrugged. "My family has more money than they can spend in three lifetimes. It didn't hurt their pockets. They love to give back and from what I heard, they really like you."

"Well, it blessed me and I'm grateful for them. I don't have to worry about rent or bills for a while now."

Logan wanted to tell Amaris that she would take care of her. That if they were together, she wouldn't have a care in the world; she could just focus on her photography and be happy and carefree. "I'm glad to hear that."

Amaris's demeanor changed, ready to get down to business. "So Logan, why am I here? Are you finally going to tell me your secret?"

Logan sat there in silence for what seemed like forever. The wheels in her head were turning. She didn't know if she should tell Amaris everything or just a little to gauge her reaction. She knew if Amaris took this wrongly, it would close her off to everybody.

Amaris walked over to Logan and stood between her legs. She could feel Logan stiffen around her. It scared her to think whatever was eating at Logan was so bad that Logan really didn't want to tell her. "Talk to me. Don't make me feel like I'm crazy, please," she said in a soft, soothing tone.

Logan wrapped her arms around Amaris's waist, drawing her closer. "You are crazy, but I'm crazy as well because I feel our connection."

Amaris giggled while resting her forehead on Logan's. There it was, that feeling of being whole, that feeling of being at peace—true peace. "Good, that's really good." She was relieved to hear Logan confirm something. She needed to know she wasn't in this alone.

"Can you be happy with the fact that I want you to have a happy life even if it's not with me?" Happiness was all Logan could imagine for Amaris. Her heart was too beautiful to not live a happy life.

"No, I can't. If there's some chance that you're my soulmate, you would be asking me to roam this earth without you."

Logan chuckled, shaking her head. Amaris had a response for everything. "Amaris, your—" she gasped suddenly as a sharp pain pierced her heart, stopping her mid-sentence.

Amaris knew something was wrong the moment Logan clutched her chest, she would never forget the look of pain on Logan's face.

"Amaris …" Logan stared at her with fear in her eyes. Her chest tightened as she tried to take another breath. She'd never felt pain like that in her life and it made her panic.

"Logan, what is it?" Amaris asked, frantically.

Logan tried to grab her chest, trying to make the pain stop even though she knew she couldn't. "Call 911," she choked out as she fell off the barstool. Logan thought this was it, she thought she was going to die and she'd never get to say goodbye to her family or tell Amaris how she felt.

Amaris ran to the couch and grabbed her cell phone from her purse. She tried not to let her fear cripple her, because she knew Logan needed her at that moment and if she had an anxiety attack, it would be all over.

The last thing Logan heard was Amaris frantically speaking to the 911 operator before her world went black.

CHAPTER

8

When Logan stopped breathing, Amaris felt like she did as well. She'd never been so afraid and as the time passed slowly, she felt like the ambulance would never get there. She cradled Logan's head in her lap as tears cascaded down her eyes.

"Logan, please don't do this to me, baby. Please don't leave me." She lost count of how many prayers she'd sent to God as she held Logan's lifeless hand in the back of the ambulance. She was trying not to be consumed by her anxiety and she thanked God that she was winning the battle.

The Maddox family was already at the hospital by the time the ambulance pulled up. Amaris didn't know how they'd gotten there before them. Mrs. Maddox looked like she aged ten times over as she waited for them to take Logan out of the ambulance.

"Logan, stay with me!" the paramedics yelled as they continued CPR on Logan.

Amaris felt like she was watching a movie as one of the paramedics jumped on top of Logan pumping her chest while the other pushed Logan through the hospital doors. Logan's face began to turn blue, a clear sign that things were definitely wrong. Amaris's hands began to shake as she felt herself losing her shit.

Xavier grabbed Amaris by the shoulders, she looked like she was in shock and Xavier needed her to focus. "What happened?"

"We were just talking and she grabbed her chest, she told me to call 911. What is this Xavier? She's too young to be having a heart attack."

None of it made sense to Amaris. Logan was healthy, she was only twenty seven, she couldn't be having a heart attack. Amaris wondered if she was working too hard or if she was too stressed. "Did she seem sleepy? Did she look sick?" Xavier asked so calmly, it scared Amaris. It was as if it was normal, like he was expecting it.

"No, we were just talking and it came out of nowhere. Xavier, what's going on?"

Taylor placed her hand on Xavier's arm, Xavier looked at Taylor and smiled uneasily. He wanted to tell Amaris, but now wasn't the right time. "We'll talk later," he said instead and ran into the hospital after his parents leaving Amaris standing there at the entrance stuck on.

Taylor looked at her with pity and wrapped her arm around her shoulder. "She's going to be okay. My sis is a fighter. Come on," she said leading Amaris into the hospital.

• —— • •●• • —— •

"Logan, stay with me!" Logan could hear someone yelling, but they sounded so far away. Her body felt so heavy and weak. She felt a sense of calmness rush over her.

"Logan."

Logan turned around and saw Amaris. A smile crept across her face. "Amaris." Amaris ran and jumped into her arms. She held her tight, inhaling her scent. When they broke their embrace she could see that Amaris was crying.

"Hey, what's the matter?" she asked with a frown.

"You can't die, Logan, I need you to fight, baby."

"What?" Logan asked, confused.

Amaris just took the palms of her hands and pressed it down on her chest. "Logan, fight!"

Logan felt a shock to her system making her yell, "Amaris!"

"Fight!" Amaris pressed down on Logan's chest again.

• • ● • • —————— •

Hours had passed and there still was no news on Logan. Amaris was a nervous wreck as she sat there and waited. She didn't even want to look at Logan's parents because the look on their faces broke her heart. She wanted answers, hell, she needed answers. Everyone was so wrapped up in their own thoughts that she knew it wasn't the time to ask.

"Amaris?"

Amaris looked up and saw Lani staring down at her with a puzzled expression. She knew she had some explaining to do.

"Amaris, what the hell are you doing here?"

Amaris stood up, taking Lani's hand. She wasn't going to do this in front of Logan's family, so she led Lani outside so they could have some privacy.

As soon as they got to the lobby, Lani crossed her arms defensively. When she got the call from Mrs. Maddox that something was wrong with Logan, she'd rushed over immediately, but she never expected to see Amaris there.

"Why are you here?" she asked, already suspicious.

"I was with Logan tonight." Amaris knew there was no other way to say it. Any way she spun it, it wouldn't sound good. Lani smacked her lips as she started to walk away.

Amaris followed behind Lani. "Lani, Lani hold on." she grabbed Lani's arm, turning her around. Tears were cascading down her cheeks and it broke her heart. She wasn't in the business of hurting people, she knew it wasn't good energy to do so.

"My boss, Amaris." Lani felt betrayed by Amaris, but even more betrayed by Logan. Yes, she was her assistant, but they were friends before anything.

"Do you remember the night on my balcony when I told you about the girl I had a connection with?"

"Yes."

"It was Logan. We met at Xavier and Taylor's wedding. Lani, I didn't know Logan was your boss until tonight at my show."

"And you just couldn't wait to get back in her bed huh?" Lani asked with spite. Here she was professing her love to Amaris, yet she turned her back on her the first chance she got.

"Logan and I never had sex. I came to see her so we could talk and then this happened."

Lani shook her head, feeling the sting of Amaris's betrayal. She knew then that she had already lost Amaris. Right when she thought she'd found someone who she could love besides Logan and she just happened to have fallen for Logan as well even before she had a chance with her.

She thought about tonight, the way they acted like they didn't know each other. They had made a fool of her; she was just a joke to them. "You two are so cruel. To stand there tonight like you were complete strangers and all the while you two knew each other."

"I took Logan's lead, but I was going to tell you."

"What were you going to talk about? Being together?! To tell me to go fuck myself, right? To you, it's fuck my feelings, right?!" Lani wanted to keep crying, but she refused to give Amaris the satisfaction. She thought Amaris was different; the way she spoke, she thought she really cared about her. But it was all a lie.

"No, it's not like that Lani! I care about you." Even Amaris felt like those words weren't enough. The hurt in Lani's eyes was crushing her. She felt so bad that she was with Logan, but then she thought if she wasn't with her what would have happened? Who would have found Logan? Would they find her dead?

"But not enough to choose me over her," Lani said hurt. She felt pieces of her heart shattering. She knew the pull Logan had on people. There was something about her that made women lose their minds.

Amaris remained quiet wanting to say the right things. She didn't want to hurt Lani any more than she already had, but she knew Lani was right. If Logan asked to be with her, she would drop everyone she was dating and take the chance with Logan.

"It's okay, you don't have to answer that. I know the effect Logan has on people. She's a wonderful woman, but there's no future with Logan. Trust me, I know," Lani said matter-of-factly. "Amaris, we can be good together. You make me feel so alive, baby." She caressed Amaris's cheek, needing to feel any type of contact. "I can make you happy. I don't have as much money as Logan, but I have a big heart, a heart that I'm ready to give to you."

Lani's words touched Amaris's soul. It was like watching herself in the mirror. She pulled Lani into her arms and kissed her. Lani was a good woman and Amaris knew there could be a future for them. She just didn't know if she could set her feelings for Logan aside to give them that chance.

Once she broke their kiss, she smiled, staring at Lani. "You are an amazing woman, Lani."

"And so are you, so be amazing with me."

Amaris kissed Lani's hand, she wanted to talk more, but now wasn't the time, especially when Logan was fighting for her life. "We'll finish this later, let's go back inside."

Lani didn't want to drop the subject, but she knew she wasn't going to get anything else from Amaris. "Okay, fine."

Amaris led them back into the hospital.

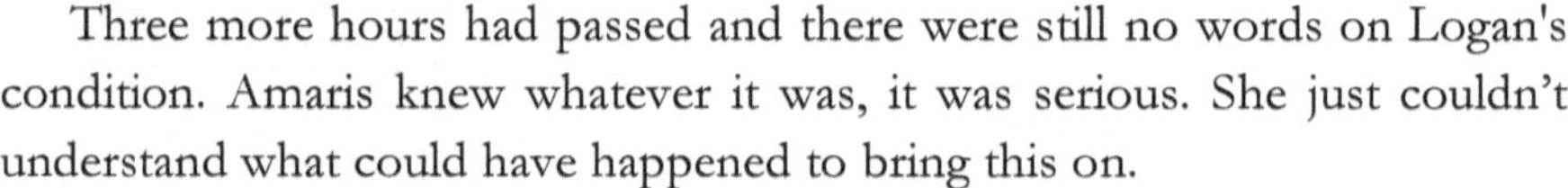

Three more hours had passed and there were still no words on Logan's condition. Amaris knew whatever it was, it was serious. She just couldn't understand what could have happened to bring this on.

Amaris turned to Lani. "Lani, is there something wrong with Logan? Like is she sick?"

"Baby, it's not my place to tell."

Amaris frowned at Lani's answer. It seemed like it was nobody's place to fucking tell, so when would she finally get her answer? She was about to get up and ask Mrs. Maddox, but the doctor burst through the doors looking exhausted. Logan's family was out of their seats in a flash.

"How is she?" Mrs. Maddox said with fear in her voice.

The doctor's eyes were weary, a clear sign that he put in some work. "Logan's heart stopped three times during the operation, we had to resuscitate her. Mr. and Mrs. Maddox, Logan had a heart attack."

Mrs. Maddox collapsed into her husband's arms as tears sprang to her eyes. "Is she okay?"

It didn't make sense to Amaris. How could Logan have a heart attack at such a young age? She was healthy wasn't she?

"She's not breathing on her own right now. We're going to keep her on the respirator overnight and see how she's doing in the morning. Now, you said her doctor is on the way down from Vegas?"

"Yes, she should be here in a few hours."

"When she gets here, I'll speak with her. I'm going to be honest with you, it's touch and go. Logan is going to have to fight if she wants to come back from this."

Amaris's head started to spin on hearing the doctor. She couldn't understand what the doctor meant. She couldn't understand what had happened in this short amount of time for Logan to be fighting for her life. It just didn't make sense.

"Mrs. Maddox, what's going on? How could this be happening?" Amaris felt so out of the loop. She knew now wasn't the time to ask, but she thought she deserved to know.

Xavier stepped in. "Hey, Amaris, why don't you come with us and we'll explain everything." Xavier escorted Taylor and Amaris to the cafeteria. He knew Logan wanted to be the one to tell Amaris, but he wanted to put Amaris out of her misery.

"What's going on?"

Xavier and Taylor exchanged uneasy glances before he spoke up. "My sister has severe congestive heart failure. Her heart is very weak." Amaris fell back into the chair, feeling like she'd been hit by a ton of bricks.

"She's been on the heart transplant list for two years now."

Everything started piecing itself together in Amaris's head and she finally realized why Logan kept running away from her. She didn't want to ask the question, but she needed to know even if she wasn't ready for the answer.

"Is Logan dying?" she asked in a small voice.

Xavier ground his teeth so obviously that Amaris noticed. "If she doesn't get a new heart in time, her heart will eventually give out."

Amaris laid her face on the table as she clutched her chest. She felt like her heart was going to explode from the ache that rocked her body.

"I just found her," she cried as her anxiety took over. She felt her body begin to shake and there was no breathing to stop it. The thought of Logan dying was too much to handle.

Taylor walked around the table and sat next to Amaris. She was trying to hold back her tears as well. Everyone knew Logan was sick, but when something like this happened, they all really realized just how sick Logan was.

"Logan is going to be okay," she said as she wrapped her arm around Amaris, hugging her tight. "I've known Logan for a while now and what I do know about her is that she's tough. She's going to get through this and we will find her a heart."

Amaris wanted to believe Taylor, but from what she heard, it had already been two years and Logan hadn't found a heart. How much longer would she be able to live without a new one?

"This is why she doesn't want to be with me?" she couldn't help but voice out the question that had been plaguing her since hearing about Logan's condition. Everything made sense now.

"Yes, this is why she doesn't want to be with anyone. In case she died, she didn't want to leave anyone behind."

Amaris became mad at Logan because she didn't give her a choice in the matter; she made the choice for her. Amaris would have spent any amount of time with her and would have cherished it.

She shook her head slowly. "That's so sad."

"After we saw you guys at the wedding, we were hoping Logan would open her heart to love someone, but she's still as stubborn as they come and now you're with Lani, which is tough, because we love Lani as well. We just want everyone to be happy." Xavier clarified.

Amaris closed her eyes, trying to block any image of Logan not being in this world; she hadn't spent enough time with her. She needed more time to fully love her, to get to know her, to be with her. Amaris had experienced some heart breaking things in her life, but she felt like this one cut the cake.

"I need more time," she whispered.

"So she has a bad heart?" Ms. Cole reiterated as Amaris laid her head in her lap, allowing the tears to fall freely.

"Yes, she's been waiting for a heart for two years now."

"With all that damn money they can't buy her a heart?"

"It doesn't work that way, mama."

After hours of sitting at the hospital, Mr. Maddox sent everyone home promising he would call them if anything changed. Logan was in an induced coma at the moment, so he felt like there was no need for everyone to sit in the hospital. Lani had asked Amaris to come home with her, but Amaris couldn't. She was mentally and physically drained and the only person who could help her through it was her mother.

"You do know why she did what she did by staying away from you right?"

Amaris rolled her eyes. "Mom, I understand, but it doesn't mean I like it. She should have been honest with me from the start. She should have given me the choice to walk away from her. This whole time, she had me thinking she was an asshole."

Ms. Cole knew Amaris wasn't going to like what she had to say, but she felt like she needed to say it. "Maybe this is for the best, Amaris."

Amaris sat up, feeling like her mother had slapped her in the face. "For the best?"

"Could you really handle that, Amaris? Could you handle loving someone and then losing them like that? The heartbreak is unbearable, trust me, I know."

Amaris cringed, forgetting for a moment that her mother had experienced death with her father. "Mom, I'm sorry, I forgot."

"It's fine, sweetie. I'm just telling you it's nothing you get over, it stays with you for the rest of your life. I don't want you to go through that Amaris. Have you thought about your anxiety? Have you thought about watching Logan slowly die? Could you handle that seriously?"

Amaris didn't have an answer for her mother. She was lost in her emotions. She needed to speak with Logan. She wanted an explanation as to why she waited so long to tell her. She wanted to know where she was with them, if she was going to give them a chance no matter what the outcome could be.

She knew one thing for sure, she was in love with Logan. She realized she knew nothing about Logan, but she was going off of pure energy and energy meant everything to her.

"No, probably not, but would I for the right person? Absolutely, mom."

Ms. Cole sighed, knowing how her daughter was. "Pray for her while you also pray for yourself, because if you do decide to go on this journey with Logan, you guys are going to need all the prayers you can get."

Mrs. Maddox was a wreck as she waited for Logan's doctor to give her any news. She sat by Logan's bed, holding her hand tight and praying to God to let her be okay. Even when Mr. Maddox asked her if she wanted to go get some rest, she refused to leave Logan's side. She wanted to be there if she woke up.

"Kayman." Mrs. Maddox heard the familiar voice of Logan's doctor.

"Hi, Dr. Stein."

"Please, you know you can call me Stacy." Dr. Stein hugged Mrs. Maddox tight. She was Logan's doctor, but they'd grown a friendship over the years between the doctor's visits.

"Your husband is coming up so we can talk, but how are you holding up?"

Kayman's eyes went to Logan who was hooked up to multiple machines. The thought of her daughter not being able to breathe on her own made her heart ache. "I just need her to be okay, I need her to wake up. My baby is still so young, she has so much to give this world."

"And she will, we just have to have faith. Logan is one of my strongest patients."

Mr. Maddox walked into the room looking just as tired as his wife. "Hey, Doc." He sat next to Kayman and grabbed her hand. "So how's our baby girl?" he asked with reluctance in his voice. He didn't really want to hear the answer, but it was something that couldn't be avoided.

Dr. Stein sighed. She hated to be the bearer of bad news. "It's not good news guys. Logan's heart is enlarged." Dr. Stein grabbed her x-rays before shutting the lights off. "If you look here, this was Logan's heart a few months ago. And this is her heart now," she said, pointing to the respective images.

Mr. and Mrs. Maddox stared at the x-rays in horror. They both saw that Logan's heart was bigger than it should have been.

"It's enlarged?" Mrs. Maddox asked in a small voice that she herself could not believe was hers.

"Yes. Logan needs a new heart and she needs one fast. Because of this new development, she will jump to the top of the donor list, but it's still a waiting game."

Mr. Maddox asked the question he knew his wife couldn't, because it was hard for her to ask. "How long if she doesn't get a new heart?" Mrs. Maddox squeezed her husband's hand as she held her breath.

"A month to three months."

"Oh my God." Mrs. Maddox's grief took over as she broke down in her husband's arms. "My baby," she cried.

Mr. Maddox held his wife tight as his own tears surfaced. "It's okay, baby, she's going to be okay. Come on now, you know our baby girl, she's a fighter."

"Thomas, I can't lose her, I can't lose my daughter." The thought was too much to bear.

"You won't baby, we'll make sure she gets a heart," he assured his wife and himself as well.

"We need to get her back to Vegas, I'll see if we can transport her."

"Thank you, Doc." Dr. Stein gave them both a sympathetic smile before leaving the room. "Logan will be okay." Mr. Maddox tried to reassure his wife and himself again.

———————— · • ● • · ————————

Amaris sunk into her seat as she heard the news of Logan. Mr. And Mrs. Maddox had called everyone back to the hospital so they could tell everyone together. The thought of Logan only living for a month—three if she was lucky—sounded foreign to her, but when they showed everyone the x-ray and she saw the size of Logan's heart, she knew it was true. A month was all they were giving Logan to live. That was all Logan was given on this earth— three if they were lucky.

It made Amaris mad at Logan, mad for being stupid and wasting time they could have spent together. Now their time was dropped down to 30 to 90 days. As she looked at Logan laying in the bed motionless, she wanted to yell at her. Her feelings were hurt, her heart was broken. She felt like her future was taken from her. The news was all too much for her to handle right now, so she collected her things and headed out the door.

"Amaris …"

She heard Mrs. Maddox call after her. She stopped in her tracks, not wanting to turn around to face Kayman. "Yes?"

"We're transporting Logan back to Las Vegas tomorrow and I know you have your thing going on with Lani, but would you like to come up for a few days?"

Amaris hadn't even thought about Lani which she felt bad for. Her thoughts and emotions were everywhere and she didn't want to say or do anything she'd regret with Lani. So instead of being around her, she took the time she needed to have her space. She slowly turned around to face Kayman with a sigh. "I don't know, Kayman, I mean …" Amaris stopped as she felt a lump in her throat.

Kayman walked over to Amaris and pulled her into her arms, she could feel Amaris trembling against her. "Logan would want to see you when she wakes up. I won't force you and I won't ask you again, but please, think about it. We're leaving at eight, we have a room ready for you at our estate if you want to come."

Logan could hear her brother and father talking as she started to become more conscious. Her body felt so heavy and weak it was a challenge to open her eyes. She could feel the tubes and wires connected to her. Her throat felt like someone had tossed an iron down it, the tube made it uncomfortable to take a breath. She kept fighting to open her eyes or move her hand, but nothing was working; her body was too weak.

Logan come the fuck on. Open your damn eyes! You can do this.

Taylor's eyes went to Logan's hand as she saw it twitch. "Guys, I think she's waking up!" she squealed.

Mr. Maddox and Xavier's eyes went to Logan to get any sign of life. "Baby, I think you're tripping."

She's not tripping, my damn hand is moving. Logan tried to get her hand to move again, but couldn't. However, she was able to dart her eyes from side to side.

"See? Her eyes are moving. I'm not tripping," Taylor said as she gripped Logan's hand. "Logan, can you hear me? Open your eyes, sis." Taylor felt Logan squeeze her hand so softly it was barely there. "Oh my God."

"I'll go get the doctor," Xavier said as he hurried out of the room.

Kayman was startled by Xavier swinging the door open. "What's wrong?" She asked, fear lacing her voice.

"Logan is waking up. I'm going to go get Dr. Stein."

Kayman and Amaris rushed into the room. Amaris could see Logan's eyes fluttering and she was at Logan's bedside quicker than her mind could register. She took Logan's hand and wrapped it in hers.

"Logan," she whispered.

She's here. Oh my God, she stayed. Logan fought to open her eyes until she felt like she peeled them open her damn self. The fighting was all worth it when she saw Amaris's face smiling at her.

Amaris felt like her heart leaped out of her chest seeing Logan's beautiful eyes. "Hi, love."

CHAPTER

9

Logan squeezed Amaris's hand as her way of saying hi back. Logan's heart felt so happy to see Amaris, she didn't expect her to be there when she woke up. Then she noticed that Amaris looked tired and worried. She felt bad for making everyone worry, especially Amaris, knowing how bad her anxiety got to her and she didn't want to be the cause of any harm on her.

She pointed to the tube in her mouth, wanting it out, just as Xavier came back into the room with Dr. Stein in tow. She wanted to be able to talk to Amaris and her family

"Well, hello there sleeping beauty, it's nice to see you're finally awake." Dr. Stein smiled while examining Logan. "I know you want this tube out, so brace yourself, it might be a little raw."

Logan nodded her head slowly as Dr. Stein started to pull the tube out of her throat. Logan squeezed Amaris's hand feeling the burn of bile following the tube. She took a deep breath being freed of the tube.

"Hey, everybody," she said with a scratchy voice.

Kayman walked over to Logan and kissed the top of her forehead. "My sweet baby girl. How are you feeling? Do you need anything?"

"Maybe just some water."

"Coming right up."

Dr. Stein looked over Logan's vitals as everyone said their hellos to her. No one really wanted to talk about the elephant in the room, but they all knew Logan would have to know. Dr. Stein glanced at everyone, kind of asking if it was okay to speak. Mr. Maddox nodded his head, giving her the okay signal.

"Logan, do you think you're up for a talk right now?"

Logan could hear the hesitation in her doctor's voice, which alerted her. Her eyes went to Amaris and by the looks of it, Amaris already knew what was going on so there was no reason to send her out. "Yes, we can talk, Doc."

Amaris squeezed Logan's hand as she sat next to her. She wanted her to know that she would be there for moral support.

"Logan, you had a heart attack which for your age, we all know is very serious. The hospital didn't know your condition at the time, but they ran some tests to see what the issue was," Dr. Stein explained.

"Well, we already know what the issue is, right Doc? I'm waiting on a new heart." When Logan was first told that her heart was bad, she'd cursed God. She wondered what she did to deserve a bad heart, but she also told herself she just needed to hold on until she was able to get a good heart.

Dr. Stein nodded her head. "Yes, we're waiting for a heart, but we don't have as much time as we had."

Logan felt the tension in the room thicken and she was afraid to ask. "Be real with me, Doc. Give it to me straight."

"A month, three if we're lucky. Your heart is enlarged, it's working too hard. If we don't get a heart, it's going to give out."

Amaris felt herself holding her breath as she waited for Logan's response. Hearing the news again crushed her more.

Logan wanted to scream, cry, and break down, but she took a deep breath and held her composure. She looked around the room at her family, it was as if they were all waiting for her to break, but she wouldn't do it. She wouldn't let her mother see her hurting because she knew how much her mother was hurting from the news. This wasn't what she was expecting at all. She knew she needed a new heart, but she thought she would have time, not a month, a month wasn't shit! Four weeks; thirty days. She couldn't fathom not being alive after thirty days. Everything she wanted to do with her life felt like it had died with the news the doctor had just shared.

"Well, okay," Logan said in a hoarse voice. "We knew this day was going to come, it just came sooner than we thought." The fake confidence she tried to wear on her voice didn't sound convincing at all.

"Logan, we already got you to the top of the list. Your parents are flying you back tomorrow where we'll keep you in the hospital and keep you healthy."

"No." If this was it for Logan, she wouldn't spend the little life that she had left stuck in a hospital. "I won't be this helpless victim."

"Logan, as time progresses you'll get worse. Your body will start to shut down, it would be better—"

"Doc, I appreciate what you're saying, but I won't spend my time in the hospital. I have so much to do. My movie is in production. I have a business to run. People are counting on me."

"Fuck the business, Logan! You are dying! Don't you see that?" Mrs. Maddox snapped causing everyone to turn to her in shock. No one was used to her speaking like that, especially to Logan.

"Mom—" Logan started to speak again.

"Lo, your heart is weak. You can't do things you used to do anymore. You're dying." Mrs. Maddox finally cracked as the tears started pouring down her eyes. "I'm sorry, I can't," she muttered and walked out of the room with Mr. Maddox following behind her.

It hurt Logan to her core to see her mother like that, but this was her life and she wouldn't change what she was doing. She knew if she had to sit in the hospital for months she would start to give up. If she was up and moving and living her everyday life, she felt like she had a better chance of getting through this.

"Guys, I need a minute. X, go check on mom and dad please."

"Will do, sis."

Everyone started to head out, but Logan stopped Amaris. "Amaris, please stay."

Amaris stopped in her tracks as everyone else walked out. Just looking at Logan made her want to cry. She didn't know what to say to her; she didn't know how she could comfort her.

Logan sat up in bed even though it was painful. She stared at Amaris for what seemed like forever before speaking, "The night I laid eyes on you I thought God had played some sick joke on me. To have an instant connection with a total stranger. I felt like I've known you my whole life, but I know nothing about you. When I was diagnosed, I told myself that I wouldn't fall for anyone and I wouldn't allow anyone to fall for me knowing I could die. Yet, you came bursting into my life like a damn freight train. You're a stubborn woman, Amaris. You just couldn't leave my head and my heart. I don't want this for you, I don't want you to feel the pain of loss if I die. You get that, right? I'm trying to protect you from feeling this."

Amaris shook her head while throwing her hand up; she was mad and hurt. "You're too late, Logan! I already feel this. Thirty days, that's all they're giving you. I thought I would have the rest of my life with you somehow and now it's been reduced to thirty, measly ass days. You should have told me, you should have given me the choice of being here or not. You are so fucking selfish!"

"I didn't want this! You think I want to die? You think I want to leave my family, leave you? I haven't lived. There's so much I want to do, but you don't need this shit. You can be happy with Lani. You two can live a happy life together."

"Lani isn't you!" Amaris walked over to Logan and bent towards her propped up body so that they were looking straight into each other's face. "She isn't you, Logan. I don't feel complete with anyone the way I feel any time I'm in your presence. This world is crazy, this life is crazy. I am in love with a stranger, you can be a serial killer for all I know."

Logan chuckled while shaking her head. "You're in love with me?"

Amaris sighed, sitting on the bed. Her hand went to Logan's cheek, caressing it so gently. She tried to fight that part of her that didn't want to admit the truth because it was so crazy to think. "Yes, Logan, I am in love with you. Maybe we were together in another life."

"Maybe on a different planet I'm yours and you're mine and we have children together. Maybe in another life I met you at a coffee shop and we connected like this. Maybe you were mine over and over and over again," Logan said.

Amaris smiled as she laid her forehead against Logan's. There it was, that feeling of being home. The feeling of her soul recognizing its other half.

Logan's hand went to Amaris's cheek as she sighed. She had longed for Amaris over the past months and now she was here. "I've missed you so much, Amaris. My heart has missed you so, so much," she confessed. If this was it, if she only had a few months on this earth, she had to make it count.

"I love you," Amaris said with no hesitation.

"As crazy as it sounds, as crazy as we are, my God, I love you, woman." Logan hadn't said those words to any woman who wasn't in her family, but it flowed so easily from her lips, saying it to Amaris. When she opened her eyes, she realized that Amaris was crying silently.

"Amaris, please don't cry, please."

"You can't die, Logan. I just found you, do you hear me?"

Logan gently pulled Amaris into her arms, kissing and hugging her. She allowed her own tears to finally surface. "I hear you baby, I hear you."

"You have to promise me you'll fight. You have to promise me you won't give up."

"I promise, I'll fight to the very end. I won't give up."

"I can't do life without you anymore, Logan."

"You won't have to, I won't stay away from you anymore. I love you."

Amaris's hand went under Logan's chin and brought her lips to hers. Logan immediately responded, kissing Amaris back with just as much passion. Amaris knew she would take Kayman up on the offer to go to Las Vegas. She knew she would stay there as long as Logan was there. She also knew she had to have a conversation with Lani. In the end, she knew Logan was her soul mate.

• ——————— • • ● • • ——————— •

"I didn't have to come here for this, Amaris, you could have told me this shit over the phone. It's not like I didn't know your choice." Lani's heart ached. She knew when Amaris called that it was to break her heart.

"Lani, I'm so sorry. I just—"

"You just love her." Lani finished her sentence for her. It hurt coming out of her mouth, but she wasn't going to fight the truth. She knew when she didn't hear from Amaris for days that Amaris had made her decision.

Amaris held Lani's hand, feeling horrible. "Yes, I do."

Lani wasn't upset with Amaris; she was hurt because again, she wasn't good enough to be chosen. Logan had turned her down and now Amaris had basically told her, her love wasn't enough.

"I'm going to go," she said, trying not to let her emotions overwhelm her.

Amaris stood up and wrapped Lani in her arms. She wasn't one to toy with anyone's feelings and she didn't want Lani to think her feelings meant nothing to her, because they did.

"Lani, you have a beautiful soul and if I had met you before I met Logan—"

Lani put her hand up, stopping Amaris. She didn't want to hear the excuse, nothing Amaris could say would make her feel better. "You two be happy for however long you guys have. There's no hard feelings. I'm just sad I won't get to love you," Lani said resolutely and kissed Amaris's cheek before walking out of the house.

Amaris wanted to follow Lani, but she knew it would do no good. Her heart was still with Logan at the end of the day. "Lord, please forgive me."

Logan was surprised when Lani walked into her room. Amaris had already told her she was going to speak with her and Logan knew Lani enough to know she wasn't going to let it ride. Right now, she could tell that she'd been crying.

136

"Come here, Lani." She extended her arm hoping Lani would come to her. Lani was her friend, her family and knowing she'd hurt her made her feel ten times worse.

Lani just stood there with her arms crossed. She wanted to say so much to Logan, but couldn't form a sentence. As soon as she saw Logan, her anger turned into sorrow.

"Lani, please come here, mah."

Lani didn't know why, but she found herself making her way over to Logan. Logan scooted over, allowing Lani to lay in bed with her. She then wrapped her arms around Lani, pulling her closer.

"Lani, you're my friend and I love you so much. The last thing I wanted to do was hurt you, but I can't explain this thing with Amaris and I. I'm so sorry that she was the person that you fell for. I'm sorry that this played out like this. Please, forgive me."

"The first night I met Amaris she told me about someone who she'd had a connection with. She said she couldn't explain the connection, but it was something she'd never experienced before, but that person didn't see anything with her. I asked her if that person told her they wanted to be with her would she go to them and she said yes without hesitation. I think she loved you before she even gave me a chance. I can't compete with that, I can't compete with those feelings."

It warmed Logan's heart to know that. All along, Amaris really wanted her and she'd stayed away from her all this time. Thinking about it, Logan didn't know what she was thinking to have denied them both of the happiness they both deserved.

"I love you, Lani, you are my family. I don't want to lose you as an assistant nor a friend." Logan meant every word she spoke. On the days she could barely move, Lani would come to her place with manuscripts and food and they would work from her house. When no one got what she was going through, Lani did, so knowing she was bringing harm to Lani made Logan feel some type of way.

"I love you too, Lo, you know that, but I think imma have to take a step back for a while. My feelings for Amaris aren't going anywhere, so seeing you two together isn't something I want right now."

Logan nodded her head in understanding. "Why don't you go on a vacation anywhere you like, for however long you need, and I'll pay for it."

Lani looked up at Logan. "You'd do that for me?"

"Lani, you should know I'd do anything for you. Come back to work when you're ready."

"Thanks, Lo." Lani intertwined their fingers. "Are you scared?"

Logan tried to hide the look of shock on her face. She wasn't expecting the question. "I don't know, it hasn't registered yet. When it does, I might break down," she joked.

"I don't want you to die," Lani whispered as her voice cracked. She was hurt that Amaris chose Logan over her, but she and Logan had worked side by side for years, their connection and friendship was timeless.

Logan hugged Lani as tight as her weak body could allow, kissing her forehead. "I'll tell you what I told everyone else, imma fight till my very last breath. I hope and pray I get a heart in time."

"You have all this money, can't you just buy one?"

Logan chuckled while shaking her head. "It's not that easy, Lani. The sad part is someone has to die in order for me to live. Ain't that some fucked up shit?" That was the part that ate at Logan so much. Of course, she wanted a heart, but to think she got one because someone else lost their life was a bizarre feeling. She knew someone else's tragedy would be her blessing, she really didn't know how she would live with that.

"I know it sounds fucked up, but I hope someone who has a match for you dies." Lani gave a slanted smile. They both knew it was a messed up thought, but it was Logan's reality. "You just hold tight, Lo. God's got you." Lani hugged Logan tight, but careful not to hurt her while Logan prayed that Lani was right.

CHAPTER

10

Kayman fluffed Logan's pillows for the tenth time trying to make her comfortable in bed.

"Mom, mom, I'm good." Logan chuckled while shaking her head. Her mother was beyond smothering her, but she didn't say anything because she knew her mom wouldn't listen anyway. She'd been home for a week and her mother hadn't left her side. She had told her to go home to her father, but she wasn't hearing it.

Logan really did want her to go home, she wanted to be alone and get back to her life, but her mother was hindering her from that. Even though her doctor had told her to take it easy, Logan wasn't going to put her life on hold. She had a movie that was in production, she had manuscripts that needed to be read and because Lani had gone on an extended vacation, Logan had to run her publishing company by herself; something she wasn't used to. It made her appreciate Lani even more, but she knew she would give Lani her space to get through everything.

"Are you sure?"

"Yes, sit down. I want to talk to you." Kayman sat on the bed with Logan. "Mom, I'm going to go back to work."

"What? Logan you can't—"

Logan put her hand up silencing her mom. If it was up to her mother, she would be in the hospital right now. Logan meant what she said about living her life to the fullest. "Mom, if these are my last months to live, I need to leave a legacy. I want my movie to get done and I want to help as many authors as possible. Please, understand that. I feel fine, mom and as long as I do, I'm going to work. I've already spoken to the studio and they're willing to get the ball really rolling with production so we can get the movie done early. I love you mom, but for real, go home to dad. He needs you as well. I'm sure he'll appreciate having his wife back home."

Kayman didn't want to leave her daughter alone, the thought of something happening to her and her being alone didn't sit well with her. "You need someone here."

"Mom, I'm fine, I promise. I want you to go home to dad. You can't smother me, I still want to have my independence." Logan knew if she allowed it, her mother would move in with her for these next few months and that couldn't happen. She loved her mother, but she would drive her crazy if she stayed.

"Amaris is coming tomorrow. Will you come meet her at the house?"

"I'm going to pick her up from the airport and she will stay with me." Logan had made the decision. She wouldn't be away from Amaris, especially if they were in the same city.

"Oh okay. So her flight gets—"

Logan put her hand up again, laughing. "Mom, I know. We've talked."

Kayman put her hands up playfully. "Well, excuse me, darling." Kayman wasn't used to seeing her daughter so open when it came to a relationship. "So you guys are doing good?"

"We're seeing where it goes. I mean we still have this looming monster over our heads."

The moment Logan allowed the words to come out of her mouth, she regretted it. The sadness that crossed her mother's face was heartbreaking. She knew that her mother was suffering even though she herself was so light-hearted about it. She also knew that if she allowed herself to sink into darkness, she wouldn't get out of it and she couldn't allow herself to go there. The situation was dire, but she had to be optimistic. That was something she was learning from Amaris. Amaris was all about positivity and Logan was trying to stay on her level.

"Well, I think it's great that you guys are giving it a shot." Kayman hoped that Amaris and Logan brought some type of joy to each other's lives no matter how short it was. She was trying to cope with the idea of her daughter dying, which was still something hard to acknowledge. She had to tell herself that if Logan really had only three months to live, then she hoped the rest of her life would be filled with love.

"Yeah, me too."

Tasha sipped her wine as she and Amaris sat out on the balcony. "I can't believe you're up and leaving me."

"I have to."

"You don't. Amaris, we have something so good here. I have clients talking about you. This is not the right time to leave."

"Tasha, time is not on my side. Time is not on Logan's side. She is where I need to be."

"Why?" Tasha couldn't understand it. She'd never seen Amaris like this. Willing to give everything up, willing to give herself up for someone else.

Amaris knew her mom and Tasha were on the fence with Logan, but as long as she knew in her heart that Logan was the one, she would walk to the end of the earth for her. "Because she asked me to and that's all I've wanted for months now. So, I will go to her because I love her." It was that simple to Amaris.

The finality of Amaris's words stopped Tasha from pushing any further. She knew her friend enough to not waste her breath. "I wish you happiness, sis. I love you."

"I love you too, always."

Amaris stared out the window as her plane started to land. It was the hardest thing to say goodbye to her mom that afternoon, but she felt good knowing her mom supported her. She made sure she took her anxiety pill before hopping on the plane because she knew she would need it to deal with Logan.

Since the hospital, it felt like everything was moving so fast, but she was okay with it. She was moving as the universe was moving her. She wanted to be by Logan's side during this time. When Logan asked her to stay with her at her place, it shocked her to say the least. She was planning on staying at the Maddox's estate, but Logan had other plans.

Amaris prayed every night for God to bless Logan with a heart. They were finally where she wanted to be; she just needed Logan to stick around.

She tried calling Lani to see how she was doing, but wasn't surprised when she didn't get an answer. She sent her countless texts, apologizing for how everything went down, but didn't receive a response. Logan told her to let Lani be, but it still didn't sit right with her spirit. She wished things could have turned out differently and she tried not to beat herself up about it.

Amaris sat back as the plane finally landed on the tarmac. She inhaled and exhaled, getting herself ready. She didn't know where this journey was going to take her, but she had to tell herself if this was it for her and Logan, she wanted to enjoy as much time with her as possible.

"Here we go," she whispered.

Logan paced back and forth as she waited in the baggage claim area for Amaris. She tried to stop her heart from beating so quickly, but she couldn't help it. She was a nervous wreck. She barely slept the night before in anticipation of Amaris's arrival. Her mother wanted to come with her to the airport, but Logan sent her home. She needed her mom to know she could still do things on her own like driving to an airport. But she still felt like her mom would pop up any minute as she waited for Amaris to land.

She stopped pacing as she saw Amaris descend the escalator. She couldn't help the smile that crept across her lips. It was evening, yet Amaris was a breath of fresh air to Logan. She wore gray sweats and a shirt. Her afro bounced as she walked down the escalator, not waiting for it to go down itself. Her smile was infectious and Logan thought she was absolutely beautiful.

Logan made her way to Amaris, taking two strides at a time wanting to get to her. Once they reached each other, they both stood there for a moment taking each other in. Logan had never been so excited to see a woman, but she knew Amaris wasn't just any woman. She felt so goofy because it felt like she was in a movie. She felt like everyone at the airport disappeared and it was only them standing there, taking each other in.

Without a second thought, Amaris wrapped her arms around Logan's neck pulling her into a hug and Logan scooped her into her arms, hugging her tight.

"Hi, mah," Logan said softly.

"Hi," Amaris responded breathlessly. She didn't expect to feel as happy as she did being in Logan's arms like that. "Did you miss me?" she joked.

"Yes, I did. How was your flight?"

"It was good, thanks for the first class ticket."

"No problem," Logan said, finally releasing Amaris. "Let's get your bags and get out of here."

"Okay."

Logan extended her hand for Amaris to take, which Amaris gladly took as she slid her hand into Logan's. They made small talk while they waited for Amaris's bags. Both trying to hide their nervousness, they just looked at each other and laughed.

"So, mom said that you're going to work on a project for her and dad?"

"Yeah, we haven't really gone into much details about it, but I'm stoked to help the parents out in any way I can."

Logan wondered if it was really a job or if her mother just wanted a reason to get Amaris out there; the later sounded more like something her mother would do. "Well, we can get you all settled in and then if you like, you can go talk to my mom to see what it's about."

Amaris grabbed her bags off the belt as soon as they reached where they were standing. She didn't respond immediately because she wasn't really worried about the job, she just wanted to put her things away and enjoy Logan's company; she'd been so worried about Logan since Logan left the hospital. Although any time they talked, Logan would say she was doing fine, but Amaris needed to see her face when she said it. She didn't know her enough to gauge the emotions in her voice to see if she was lying.

Even though it took almost all of Logan's energy, she managed to put Amaris's suitcases in her truck without any help from Amaris. Amaris protested knowing Logan shouldn't exert herself, but Logan insisted on doing it. That was one thing Amaris had picked up on; Logan was a very stubborn female. She took the role of stud very seriously. She could also tell that Logan hated to appear weak, but Amaris didn't want Logan to hurt herself.

Logan reclaimed Amaris's hand as they sat in the car. It felt so weird to her because she really wasn't used to showing affection especially in public, but it felt nice with Amaris.

"Are you hungry?" she asked looking at their intertwined hands before looking at Amaris's face.

"Um, a little. But we don't have to get food now. I'd like to see my quarters, Ms. Maddox." Amaris teased. She was starving, but she was too nervous to eat anything at the moment.

Logan chuckled, bringing her engine to life. "As you wish."

Amaris's eyes went to their connected hands. If someone had told her a month ago that she would be picking up to move to Las Vegas, she would have looked at them crazy. Tasha's face appeared in her mind as she thought about it.

When she first told Tasha she was moving to Las Vegas, she literally had a fit. She knew nothing about Logan and now her best friend was proclaiming her love for her. They had just had the best show of Amaris's career and now she was leaving. Tasha couldn't understand it. Amaris had to sit her down and explain the situation to her in detail. Although she still didn't take it well, she told Amaris to follow her heart.

When they pulled into Logan's penthouse, Amaris had no words to describe the building. It was simply amazing and it was interesting to see the staff kind of jump up when Logan walked in. You would have thought Logan owned the place.

"Ms. Maddox, how are you?" the concierge greeted Logan with a cheery smile.

"Kenneth, this is Ms. Cole, my guest. She will need a key to my penthouse and access to the garage. Make sure she gets everything she needs," Logan said, addressing the cheery concierge.

"Yes ma'am, right away."

"Thank you." Logan led Amaris to her private elevator, allowing the doors to close behind them.

Amaris couldn't help but feel intimidated by Logan. People jumped when she spoke. It was so beyond what she was used to. She didn't grow up in luxury, it was just her and her mom and they lived a simple life. She didn't know how it felt to boss people around the way Logan had just done.

"Damn! They treat you like you own the place." Amaris joked.

Logan looked down at Amaris with a sly grin. "I do," she said matter-of-factly.

Amaris's mouth fell open. She was completely dumbfounded. "What?"

Logan shrugged like it was no big deal. Her family owned multiple properties in different parts of the country. With Vegas being their home, they owned properties all around the valley, so it was nothing new to Logan. "You know my family is in the real estate business."

"How many properties does your family own?"

Logan shrugged while shaking her head. "Too many to count, this is their business. This is how my parents made their fortune, they've been very blessed and in return, I've been very blessed. This is nothing new to me, but I have to remember it's new to you," Logan said apologetically. She grew up knowing she was privileged; her family gave her everything she asked for within reason. It was nothing for her and her brother to be able to go to any house their parents owned and stay for a while, but she had to remember that not everyone grew up like her and her rich kid syndrome showed at times.

Amaris shrugged, brushing it off. "Like you said, you've been blessed." The elevator doors opened and Amaris had to keep her mouth from falling open in amazement. Logan's penthouse was nothing like the condo in LA. Amaris felt like she was in a movie as she looked around. The living room was as big as her loft in LA. There was a big white beautiful sectional in the middle of the room with a 70 inch TV mounted on the wall. But what got Amaris was the artwork on the walls. She was absolutely stunned silent.

Logan stood back as she watched Amaris's reaction to the photos on the wall. The moment she saw Amaris's photos she knew she had to have them. She didn't think she'd see Amaris again, so she wanted a piece of her. She knew that Amaris took pride in her photos so she thought it would be amazing to have them in her home.

"I thought they would look good in my house and I wanted a piece of you with me."

Amaris didn't know what to say or do. She wanted to smile, laugh, and cry all at the same time. When she'd found out someone had bought her collection, it was an amazing feeling, but knowing it was Logan was overwhelming. She was sure that Logan didn't know what it meant to her for her to be the one to have her work and that to actually see them hung up in her home was unreal.

Without thinking, she jumped into Logan's arms, nearly knocking them both down. Logan chuckled while lifting Amaris into a big bear hug. She couldn't remember the last time she'd felt so happy; she didn't want this moment to end.

"Lo, this is so amazing. Thank you so much for this."

"You don't have to thank me, sweetheart. Your work is amazing. I can't wait to see more of it."

Amaris's heart was filled with so much joy. She was so nervous to move down to Vegas with Logan because they knew nothing about eachother, but she told herself to listen to her heart. She knew the universe wouldn't guide her in the wrong direction.

Logan kissed her forehead, allowing her lips to linger for a moment. She'd gone years without a significant other, but she didn't want to think about going another hour without Amaris; the things love could do to a person. She knew in her heart that she would do anything to make Amaris happy, even if it was only for three months. "Would you like to see more of the place?"

"Yeah, sure."

Logan took her hand and showed her around the penthouse. She'd lived there for five years and found it very comfortable. It was a six thousand square foot, five bedroom, six bathroom penthouse, which included an indoor pool and library. The moment Logan saw the penthouse, she knew she wanted it, it had everything she needed.

Amaris felt like each room was better than the next. Logan's library was extensive. She could see herself getting lost in a book on the sofa for hours.

Logan stopped at a door to the room she had prepared for Amaris. "This is your room, you can decorate it however you'd like. My mom put the essentials on the bed, sheets, covers, and pillows. We can get anything else you need."

Amaris opened the door and peeked inside. The room was literally a blank canvas. There was a bed and exactly what Logan had said. The walls were bare and to the right was a dresser. The room didn't look like it even belonged in the elegant house.

Logan could see the disappointment on Amaris's face and spoke up. "We can paint the walls, get pictures, put anything anywhere you want. I just want you to be comfortable and I didn't know what you liked." Logan didn't know why she was babbling, she wanted to laugh at how nervous she sounded.

"This is nice, I appreciate it." Amaris wanted to tell Logan she had no problem sleeping with her in her room, but she knew it had to do with respect; Logan wanted her to have her own space. They were technically strangers so Amaris knew it might be strange for the both of them to be sleeping in the same bed.

"This is your home, anything in here is yours. I'm glad you're here Amaris. It feels unreal, but I'm happy."

Amaris brought Logan's hand to her lips and kissed it. "Me too."

"You want to eat?"

"Yes, I can eat now," Amaris replied and Logan led them to the kitchen to find some grub.

———— ··•●•·· ————

"So, what made you want to write instead of going into the family business?" Amaris asked, taking a sip of her wine as she stretched out on Logan's bear skin rug. After realizing Logan didn't have any food in her fridge, they opted for takeout. Then Logan added grocery shopping to her to-do list.

"I loved writing ever since I was a teenager. I loved creating these characters and story lines. From then, I knew it was something that I wanted to do for the rest of my life."

"So you knew you wanted to have your own publishing company?"

Logan thought about it for a second. Honestly, all she wanted to do was write. Her publishing company just came with it because she wanted to write whatever genre she wanted. "I wanted to be my own boss, I wanted to be able to write what I wanted when I wanted. I mean, I give myself deadlines, but I didn't want anyone else giving me a deadline. I didn't want to be at the mercy of anyone else. So, my company was the next step."

Amaris could get where Logan was coming from. Ever since she was a little girl, she didn't see herself working a nine-to-five. The moment she picked up her first camera, she knew it was something she wanted to do. She had an eye for it, so she was able to book jobs. She loved being a freelance photographer and even though she struggled sometimes, there was nothing else she would rather do.

"And you have authors on your roster right?"

"Yes, I love all of my authors. They were handpicked by Lani and I and they're hungry and grateful. I'd do anything for any of them."

Amaris could see the pride in Logan's eyes as she spoke about her authors. "So what happens now? What happens to your authors? What happens to your movie?" Amaris wanted to tread lightly on the subject. She didn't want to upset Logan, but she thought it was a question that Logan should think about.

Logan saw the hesitation in Amaris's eyes as she asked the question. She knew that Amaris wasn't aware that she wasn't going to allow her condition stop her from her dreams, she was going to finish her movie. "The movie will still be done. The crew will just have to work overtime, but I plan to compensate them well. I need to get this done." It was Logan's goal to see her book become a movie. She'd worked on the deal for over a year, she couldn't just let it go to waste.

"But your doctor said—"

"I know what my doctor said," Logan cut Amaris off, "but I'm not going to let that define my life. If I listen to my doctor, I'm going to die in three months and I'm not ready for that." Logan wasn't one to give up easily, so she damn sure wasn't going to give up on her own life.

Amaris caressed Logan's cheek, listening to every word she uttered. If it were to be her, she would have the same mentality. She believed in speaking positivity into the universe and she prayed that the Lord and the universe heard Logan's prayers. However, before coming to Vegas, she had to mentally prepare herself for the fact that Logan might die. She had had endless conversations with her mother about what she was doing and her mother allowed her to make her own decision.

"You will get a new heart, my love, and we will spend this life together. Now, I just need to get to know you and we'll be good."

They both laughed as Logan wrapped her arms around Amaris's waist. She took a moment to look at Amaris, she thought Amaris was absolutely beautiful. "It's crazy how we vibe, Amaris. This whole thing is so crazy."

"It will be our crazy love story."

"Maybe we've had plenty of love stories," Logan joked.

"Maybe in another life you were a secret agent and I was a fugitive and we fell in love."

Logan's laughter came from the base of her throat as Amaris joined in the laughter. "You should write a damn book with your ideas."

"Will you sign me?"

"Of course."

"Bullshit." They shared another laugh. Amaris wanted things to be light, she didn't want their time to be gloomy; she didn't want Logan's condition to define how they spent their time together.

"Amaris …"

A chill went through Amaris's body from the way Logan had said her name. She knew it wasn't in a playing anymore. She could hear the lust in her voice. "Yes?"

"Can I kiss you?"

"I told you I am yours whenever you wanted me, Logan, and that hasn't changed. If you want to kiss me, just do it, don't ask. I am yours," Amaris reiterated. She meant every word she spoke. If Logan wanted to bend her over right now and fuck her brains out, she would gladly oblige.

Logan hissed under her breath. The energy shifted in the room and she felt the sexual tension between them. Logan thought about multiple things she wanted to do to Amaris. She now felt their closeness and smelled her scent—that same scent that plagued her senses since they last saw each other. Her eyes went to Amaris's lips— the lips she'd dreamt about several nights. She still couldn't believe that they were sharing the same space, breathing the same air.

Amaris licked her lips, waiting for Logan to kiss her. She could hear her heartbeat in her ears. "Logan …"

"Yes?"

"What are you waiting for?"

Logan sunk her hands into Amaris's hair while pulling her into a kiss. She couldn't stop the moan that escaped her mouth as their lips met. Amaris's taste was so intoxicating that Logan couldn't get enough of her. Their kiss deepened as Amaris crushed her breasts against Logan's, wanting to be as close to her as she could. She'd longed to feel Logan like this.

Logan's hands slid down to Amaris's ass, cupping her ass cheeks in her hand. She was a sucker for thick women and she would be a sucker for Amaris any day of the week.

Amaris's clit began to throb as Logan deepened their kiss. This was the kiss she'd remembered at the wedding; the want, the passion, the longing, only this time, she wouldn't have to say goodbye to Logan; they could take this as far as they liked.

Amaris broke the kiss, trailing down to Logan's neck with her tongue. Then, she planted soft kisses across Logan's neck.

"Bite me," Logan growled in her ear. Without hesitation, Amaris sunk her teeth into Logan's neck, biting her hard before sucking. Logan moaned as she gripped Amaris's hips. She wanted to take her right there on her couch, but she knew they had to wait. She knew she couldn't fuck Amaris the same night she got there. She knew the responsible thing would be to get to know Amaris a little longer before taking it there with her. She was trying hard to hold onto the logical side of her brain and she knew if she kept allowing Amaris to suck on her neck like that, it would be a wrap.

She reluctantly pulled Amaris away from her causing Amaris to look at her with confusion on her face and lips swollen from their kiss. Logan's eyes went to her hardened nipples and noticed that Amaris had nipple rings, she could see them poking out of her shirt.

This fucking girl is going to drive me insane. Oh how she wanted to taste Amaris's nipples.

"What's wrong?" Amaris asked, the look of rejection written all over her face. "You don't want me?"

"Oh, I want you. I want every part of you, but I think we should wait. You should know my likes and dislikes, my favorite color and food before we take it there. But girl, please believe that it's taking the will of God for me to not take you right now."

Amaris didn't want to wait. She felt like she'd waited too long for Logan. She wanted her now. "Seriously, Logan?"

Logan chuckled. "Yeah, I'm trying to be respectful."

Amaris was appreciative of that, but they were both adults. Without warning, she pushed Logan back onto the couch.

"Whoa girl, what are you doing?" Logan asked shocked, but loving it at the same time.

"Listen, I understand all that respect stuff, but baby I've waited months for you to get your shit together." Amaris said and pulled Logan's sweats down. "I'm not waiting any longer. My pussy is wet, Logan. I want you," she said as she pulled Logan's briefs down.

Logan laughed, feeling like a bitch. Amaris was topping her, something she'd never allowed anyone to do to her. "Like that mah?"

"Yes, like that."

From the distance, they heard the ping of Logan's elevator opening. "Oh shit, someone's here." Logan and Amaris jumped up trying to fix their clothes.

"Hey lil sis, are you home?" Xavier's voice echoed throughout the house.

"God dammit," Logan grumbled as she ran to the foyer. She wanted to give Amaris a little more time to look presentable. She met Xavier and Taylor before they could make it into the living room. "X, Taylor what are you guys doing here? I thought we had an agreement to call before we just showed up." Logan cut her eyes at Xavier.

"Sis, I told him we should have called, but you know how your brother is." Taylor rolled her eyes annoyed at Xavier as well. She tried to talk Xavier out of coming the whole ride to Logan's house, but he waved her off. They both knew Amaris would be there and Xavier wanted to give them a hard time. He also wanted to be nosy and see what they were doing with their time.

Amaris ran from around the corner, fully dressed. "Hey guys!" She wrapped herself under Logan. Logan smiled while kissing the top of her forehead.

Xavier and Taylor exchanged glances, both trying to hide their smiles. They'd never seen Logan show any type of affection with a woman. Hell, Xavier couldn't remember seeing a woman at Logan's house. He knew his sister was getting some, but hell, the other women might as well have been ghosts.

"Amaris! You made it!" Taylor said excitedly as she and Amaris hugged. "How are you liking the place? Has Logan showed you around this monstrous place she calls home?"

"Yeah, she did, I can't believe there's a pool inside here."

"I know girl, it's a trip."

Xavier and Logan watched as Taylor pulled Amaris further into the house, leaving them alone. Logan knew any hopes of them having sex just went out the window. When they got to talking, they would be talking for a while.

As soon as the two ladies were out of ear shot, Logan slapped the hell out of Xavier. "Nigga, what are you doing here? You know this is Amaris's first night here."

"I know, we just wanted to see how you guys were doing. You haven't had a woman here with you and I know you like your space, so how's it going?"

"Well, you just interrupted me about to fuck so how do you think I'm doing?"

Xavier chuckled while shaking his head. He didn't think his sister would be attempting to sleep with Amaris on the first night. "Well, I apologize. I thought you guys would just be chilling."

Taylor and Amaris plopped down on a couch in the living room. "So how are you really feeling? Is my sister treating you okay?"

Amaris nodded her head. "Yes, we're getting along, but it's only been a few hours so check with me within a week. She did let me know I could always stay on her parents estate if things got too hectic," Amaris told her. She didn't expect for things to get bad with them, but she didn't know what they were going to go through either. She didn't know if Logan was going to let her in or shut her out during this process. They were literally walking on faith and their emotions.

"I think you guys will be okay."

"Why do you say that?"

Taylor had noticed Logan's demeanor when she came strolling up to her husband and her as they entered the foyer. There was an aura about her that she'd never seen her have before. "Because Logan hasn't stopped smiling since we've walked in. Logan has been so shut off from love, so seeing her open up is such a beautiful thing. It takes that special someone to be able to do that and I know that person is you. Please, be patient with her, she's stubborn, but she means well."

"Damn, is she really that bad? I'm getting warnings from everywhere."

Taylor giggled. "No, she's not bad at all, she just likes what she likes and she's stubborn in her ways. I think you can keep up with her. Hell, I think you can even give her a run for her money."

Speaking of the devil, Xavier and Logan came walking into the living room. Amaris and Logan locked eyes and Logan couldn't stop herself from smiling. Maybe Taylor was on to something.

"Hey Tay, let's go ahead and get out of here, I think the two lovebirds would like to be alone."

Logan wrapped her arms around Amaris as she sat beside her on the couch's arm. "Yes, we would like to be right now. But let's have dinner this week."

Xavier and Taylor looked at Logan like she'd lost her mind. They'd never gone on a double date before.

"Like a double date?" Xavier joked.

Logan rolled her eyes. "Yes punk, a double date. I want to show Amaris around a bit."

"Okay, just let us know," Taylor replied before they headed for the elevator.

"See you guys later," Logan called after them as both she and Amaris waved just as the elevator doors closed.

Logan wanted to continue where they left off, but she thought it would be smart of her to call it a night. She didn't want them to regret anything because they were in a rush. Looking into Amaris's eyes, she knew that she was ready to get back to where they had left off.

"I think we should call it a night. I need to rest."

Amaris couldn't help but pout her lips. "Sleep?"

Logan chuckled, kissing her forehead. "Yes, sleep. We have all of our lives for sex. I want to do this the right way. Okay?" Logan never wanted to do anything so right in her life, she's never cared so much about a relationship.

Amaris wanted to say no, that it wasn't okay, but she had to respect Logan's wishes. "Okay. Well I guess I'll bid you goodnight, Madame."

"I'll walk you to your room."

"I'd like that."

Logan interlocked their fingers and headed toward Amaris's room. She didn't want to say goodnight, but if she stayed in Amaris's presence for a moment longer, she would take her to bed. She also wanted to ask Amaris to sleep in her bed, but thought that would be too much, too soon.

Amaris leaned against her door staring at Logan. She wanted her to make a move, she was giving her one last chance to take her. She couldn't read her, but she could see her thoughts were running. "A penny for your thoughts?"

"I'm glad that you're here."

"I'm glad that I'm here as well, love."

Logan gave Amaris a quick peck on the lips. "I'll see you in the morning. Sleep well."

"Goodnight." Amaris slid into her room, closing the door behind her. She looked around the empty room and reality hit her that she was actually in Vegas with Logan. Not only that, they were under the same roof! It wasn't the way she would prefer it, but it was a start.

"Well, alright," she whispered to herself as she started to get ready for bed.

Logan laid out in bed letting out a long sigh. Her bed had never felt so empty and it was because she had a gorgeous woman down the hall from her that she would love to fill it with. She didn't know what her problem was, she wasn't shy to have a rendezvous with someone, but with Amaris, she was hesitant. She didn't know what it was about that woman that rocked her soul.

Her phone vibrated on her nightstand, breaking her from her thoughts. She picked up the vibrating phone, swiped her finger across the screen, and placed it on her ear. "Hello?"

"Hey doll, how are you?"

Logan sat up hearing Chandra's voice on the other end. "Hey Chandra, I'm good, how are you?"

"I heard that you were in the hospital. Are you okay?" she asked sincerely. Chandra, like most people, didn't know about Logan's heart condition, so it came as a shock to her that Logan was in the hospital.

"Yes, I'm good. I just fell under the weather from working so hard. You know I'm trying to be on your level," Logan joked. She wasn't going to tell Chandra the reason she was there. She never wanted anyone to pity her.

"Well, don't ever go that hard. I need you strong and ready for our session, doll. I was in the neighborhood and I'm downstairs. Can I come up for a night cap?" Chandra's voice was hopeful. Logan would like nothing more than to have a night cap, but Chandra wasn't the person on her radar.

"You know what Chandra? I would love for you to come up, but I'm still recovering and I have a guest staying with me for a while. So, I'm going to take a rain check, I'm sorry." She should have said her girlfriend was here, but because they hadn't establish things yet, Logan didn't want to jump to conclusions.

"It's okay," Chandra replied, sounding disappointed. Her thoughts went to Logan having a woman living with her. Logan had a rule, no woman stayed the night. It was very rare when she allowed her to stay after one of their sessions. She wondered who was upstairs with her. "Call me when your guest leaves."

"Will do," Logan lied.

"Have a good night."

"You as well." Logan pressed end on her phone.

• —— • •● • • —— •

Amaris knew she wouldn't be able to sleep being in a new place, so she decided to change into her bathing suit and check out Logan's pool. It wasn't everyday she stayed in a penthouse and had access to an inside pool. Her eyes darted to Logan's bedroom door, the light was still on. She thought to invite her swimming, but decided to let her rest. She didn't need Mrs. Maddox coming after her because Logan wasn't getting enough rest.

She tiptoed down the hallway in order not to disturb Logan. The scenic view from the pool was amazing. Amaris was in total awe as she sat down and took a look at the view. The strip was so bright she felt like she was actually on Las Vegas boulevard. She thought how lucky Logan was to be surrounded by such beauty every day. She wondered if Logan took the time to appreciate it.

She dived into the pool and started making her way to the other end. She took a deep breath, gasping for air as she finally made it to the surface. She hadn't swam since she was a kid and her lungs felt it as they burned and screamed for oxygen. She rested her arms against the wall, inhaling and exhaling slowly.

She thought about Logan for a moment and was disappointed that she'd cut the night short. She was used to being up late, working on edits for her pictures, she didn't expect for Logan to go to sleep on her on their first night together. She had actually hoped that they would be rolling around in the covers right now, but Logan shut that down.

Amaris thought to go out and explore Vegas since she didn't get to do so the last time she was there, but she didn't want Logan to worry if she woke up and looked for her. Then she wondered what Lani was doing right now. Lani would literally fight sleep to stay up with her on her late nights. She'd always tell Amaris she liked going to sleep with her so she would wait. She couldn't lie, she missed Lani. She didn't regret her decision, but she hated how quickly everything played out. She'd broken up with Lani and Lani was gone on her mysterious trip. She'd asked Logan where Lani was, but Logan told her to give her space for the moment. She didn't like the response, but she let it go. She was hoping that once Lani came back to Vegas, they would be able to talk.

Logan watched Amaris from a distance, she seemed so deep in thought she didn't know if she should interrupt her. When she heard the splash of water she decided to investigate. She didn't expect to find Amaris in a bathing suit looking every ounce of sexy. Logan wanted to tell her to step out of the pool so that she could get a better look at her, but she held back, but her tingling pussy agreed with her thoughts.

Logan wondered what Amaris was thinking about. She seemed so deep in thought she would give anything to know what was giving her such a troubled look. She had hoped that Amaris would be happy with her; it had been a while since she had been in a relationship, so she was a bit rusty.

She wanted Amaris to be happy in Vegas with her, she didn't want her to regret her decision to give them a shot. She was so used to being confident in a relationship, hell, with women, period, but she knew Amaris was like no other woman she'd been with. She spoke what she felt, she wasn't afraid of her love for her and she also wasn't afraid to display it.

Logan admired how strong Amaris was. She admired the fact that Amaris knew there was a chance that she would die, but she still dropped everything in California to come be with her, to spend whatever time they had together.

"Logan?" Logan jumped on hearing her name causing Amaris to snicker, seeing that Logan had clearly been thinking about something deep in order for her to not hear her climb out of the pool. "What are you doing out of bed? I thought you were asleep. Did I wake you?"

So many questions in one breath, but all Logan could focus on was Amaris standing in front of her with water cascading down her body. She got a better look of Amaris curves, thighs, and ass. She couldn't help but bite her lip at the goddess standing in front of her. She knew she would have to thank the Lord every day for blessing her with such a beauty.

She took a step forward, ready to attack Amaris. Any thought she had of them waiting to be intimate went out the window. She wanted Amaris and she wanted her now.

Amaris saw the predatory stare in Logan's eyes and was amused. She couldn't understand why Logan was trying to hold out on sex. Whenever she wanted to have sex and if she felt safe with the person she just let it flow. She didn't believe in torturing herself like Logan was doing to the both of them.

She placed her hand on Logan's arm. "Are you okay?"

Logan's eyes finally left Amaris's body and went to meet her eyes. "Yes, I'm fine."

"What are you doing out here? I thought you were asleep."

"I heard water, so I wanted to see what was going on, but I didn't expect to find you looking like you are in your bathing suit."

Amaris looked down at her bathing suit. "Like what?"

"Fucking sexy," Logan said with no apologies.

A smile spread across Amaris's lips in response. "Thank you, baby. Would you like to join me?"

"I'm not wearing a swimsuit."

Amaris rolled her eyes at Logan's bullshit excuse. "It's fine, dress down to your briefs. This is your place you can get naked if you like."

Logan smirked. "You'd like that wouldn't you?"

"Quite frankly, yes, I would. Now the question is are you going to do it for me?"

"Maybe another time." Logan was holding onto the last piece of control she had. She knew if she did get naked, that would be the end of her will power.

Amaris rolled her eyes. Logan wasn't as adventurous as she thought she would be. "Well, okay. I'm going to get back in the pool, feel free to join me if you'd like. If not, have a goodnight and I'll see you in the morning." Without saying another word, Amaris dove into the pool. She was hoping Logan would join her, but she wasn't going to hold her breath. As she swam underwater she wondered if Logan was already feeling overwhelmed. She'd hope she would tell her if she was. Amaris had no issue going to Logan's parents' estate and staying there.

Logan thought for a split second to go back to her room, but she thought she'd be a fool to leave Amaris alone when the invitation to join was so open. Logan stripped down to her briefs and bra and jumped into the pool. She'd actually never used the pool in the five years she'd lived at her penthouse, she just had it cleaned from time to time. As she entered the water, she was surprised that it was actually heated, she was ready for the cold that would shock her system.

Amaris clapped as she watched Logan swim to her. She thought there was hope for them yet, because she really didn't expect for Logan to take the bait. She thought she would come up from the water and be alone.

"Well, hello there," Amaris said, unable to hide her smile as Logan crushed her against the wall, surprising her. "Oh," Amaris moaned from the sudden impact and wrapped her legs around Logan's waist.

"You're trying to kill me with your bathing suit."

Amaris giggled. "You're going to make me blush."

Logan caressed Amaris's cheek. "You are absolutely beautiful, Amaris."

"Logan …"

"You are and I want you so bad."

"Take me, baby. I'm yours, take me." Amaris didn't know how many ways she could say it to Logan. She'd flown there, moved there, confessed that she loved Logan; she didn't know what more Logan wanted.

"You are so willing to give yourself to me. You're so willing to love me, why?"

"Do you really want to know?"

"Yes, please."

"Logan, you are my soulmate, plain and simple. I've longed for you since the moment you walked away from me. My heart feels so full when I'm around you, you feel like home. So, all I can do is show you that I love you. Show you that I'm yours. My heart is so open to you Logan, can't you see that?"

"Yes, I do." Logan's heart swelled with so much love for Amaris it felt like her heart would explode. If she could pour her love over Amaris, she would. "Amaris, please be patient with me on our journey. I want this to work so bad, but I haven't had a girlfriend in a very long time. It's been years and sometimes I might still act like it's just me, but all you have to do is put me in check. I want you, I've longed for you and I hope you know that I'm so happy to have you here with me."

Amaris placed her forehead against Logan's. "I'm so glad to hear that."

Logan kissed Amaris gently, so gently that Amaris barely felt it on her. "Will you sleep in my bed tonight with me?" Logan wanted to feel her warmth. She hadn't slept with anyone for months and the thought of having Amaris next to her in her bed was a warm thought.

"I would like nothing more, love."

Logan smiled as she led them to the end of the pool and to her room.

CHAPTER

11

Amaris's eyes traced every inch of Logan's face as she waited for her to wake up. Logan had her wrapped in her arms so tight she could barely move, but she was okay with it. She was right where she wanted to be—with her love. Logan's face looked so pained she wondered what she was dreaming of or if she was in pain.

She laid her head on Logan's chest and listened to her heart. It sounded strong, but it was a hoax. Logan's heart was very weak, it had betrayed her body and was now killing her. Amaris still couldn't wrap that idea around her head.

On the outside, Logan looked very healthy, but she wasn't. Ninety days wasn't enough time to spend with her. Amaris felt like there was so much she wanted to do with her, but she didn't want to push her. Any future she thought of having with Logan was hanging in the balance, so she couldn't live life thinking about what their future would hold anymore. She had to tell herself to literally live every day to the fullest with Logan.

Amaris closed her eyes and bit her bottom lip to keep herself from breaking down. She didn't want Logan to wake up to her crying, but any time she thought of Logan dying, her heart hurt so bad.

"Amaris …" Logan's husky voice made Amaris jump.

When she looked up, Logan was staring down at her with a concerned look on her face. Logan had been up for ten minutes now, but she hadn't moved. She knew Amaris was up as well, but she was enjoying having her in her arms so she didn't want to ruin the moment. When she felt Amaris's body tense up she became alert.

"Yes?"

"What's wrong?"

"Nothing." Amaris wiped the tear that tried to escape the side of her eye. This wasn't how she wanted to start her first morning waking up with Logan. They'd talked almost all night until sleep had finally won. She didn't want to ruin it by having Logan wake up to her tears.

Logan placed her finger under her chin so she could look into her eyes. "What is it, babe?"

Amaris kissed Logan's finger. "I don't think there will ever be enough time with you, Logan."

Logan's hand went to Amaris's cheek, stroking it gently. This is why Logan didn't want to be in a relationship. She didn't want to put her spouse through what Amaris was already going through. She didn't want to have anyone worrying about her 24/7. She didn't want to leave anyone behind broken-hearted if she didn't make it. Amaris reminded Logan why she had chosen to face her illness alone.

"I don't want you to dwell on this, mah. I'm going to be fine, haven't you seen how strong I am? I'm going to make it until I get a heart because I refuse to leave this earth right now. I refuse for our time to be cut short. I need you to promise me something."

"Okay?"

"It might get bad as time progresses, if things get too hard for you or if it starts really messing with your anxiety, I want you to promise me you'll tell me you have to leave."

Amaris gawked at Logan, appalled she would request something like that. It didn't matter to her how bad things got or how bad her anxiety got, she wasn't leaving Logan's side. "No, I won't promise you that."

Logan laughed at how headstrong Amaris could be. It was something she was learning about her as they shared conversations. "I don't want my health to start affecting yours—"

Amaris placed her finger on Logan's lips, silencing her. "Shh. I'm not going to listen to you, I'm here and that's it."

Logan kissed Amaris's lips and agreed with her. It was their first full day together and Logan didn't want them to have a dark cloud above them. Today, she actually felt good and she wanted them to enjoy their day together. "I was thinking we'd start the day off with having breakfast at my parents' house. Is that cool?" Logan knew her mother was dying to see her and Amaris together, so she would entertain her for now.

"Yes, that's fine. I love being around your parents."

"And why is that?"

"Because their love radiates from them. It's quite nice to see."

"You're such a lover, huh?"

Amaris shrugged. "I guess you can say that. I just think everyone is so focused on themselves and everything else that doesn't mean shit, we've lost the love aspect. So when I see it, I enjoy it. Your parents are great."

Logan kissed Amaris's forehead. She made her look at the world so differently. She was used to seeing her parents every day, so she stopped paying attention to them fully. They'd been together her whole life so it was normal to her. "Yeah, they are."

"So I was thinking about something …" Amaris began, hesitating a little bit.

"What?"

"Would you let me take pictures of you?"

"Pictures?"

"Yes. Just random pictures of you in your everyday routine." Amaris wanted Logan's family to have something of her, just in case Logan didn't get a heart in time. If it got to the point where Logan got really sick, Amaris wanted her family to have pictures of Logan as her normal self.

Logan thought it would be a little weird to have Amaris snapping pictures, but she knew how much she loved her camera. She also thought it would be neat to see Amaris in action. "Okay, that's fine, but I want you to live your normal life even though you'll be here. Like if you get photography job offers, I want you to take them. I don't want you to stop doing what you love to do because you're here with me."

"I hear you. I won't put things to the side, but I do plan on spending as much time with you as possible. So, Ms. Maddox, will you take me to your office and let me see you in action one day?"

Logan chuckled, surprised at her request. She'd never brought anyone to her job before, so it was an unexpected request. "You want to go to my office?"

"Yeah, I mean it's your baby. I want to see your baby and how you do your thing."

"Yeah, we can make that work."

"When do you resume production?"

"On Monday, everyone will be back out here, but tomorrow, I'm going to look at some of the tapings from Cali. Do you want to tag along with me?"

Amaris felt honored that Logan wanted her to go with her to the studio. "Yeah, I'd love that."

"Cool. So let's get dressed and then head to my parents' house."

"Okay, I'll meet you in the living room."

"Alright." Logan watched Amaris walk out of the room. She laid back in bed and couldn't help but smile. It felt good to have Amaris lay next to her last night. She'd gotten the best sleep she'd ever gotten in a long time. There was something about Amaris's energy that calmed Logan. She was looking forward to seeing where they would go.

Her mother's ringtone broke her from her thoughts. "This woman must have a damn sensor on me," she muttered as she grabbed her phone from the dresser. "Hey mama."

"Hey sweetie pie, how are you feeling today? How are things going?"

"I'm feeling good and things are good. Amaris and I are going to come over for breakfast. Is that okay?"

"You know I'm okay with that, there's plenty of food for everyone. Did you girls have a good first night?"

"Yeah, it was good. Just trying to get used to it, you know."

"Yes, I know."

"But we'll be there in a little bit, mom. I love you."

"I love you too."

Logan ended the call and sighed. "Another day." She hopped out of the bed and headed for the shower.

Thirty minutes later, she met Amaris in the living room all dressed and ready to go. She was dressed in a beautiful yellow and green sundress. Logan loved how she always dressed; it was never too much nor too little. Everything always looked just right to her.

Amaris raised her camera and snapped a picture of Logan as she walked toward her. Even going to breakfast with her family, Logan was dressed in a suit. Amaris wondered why all business people did that, always feeling the need to be dressed in business attire. "Are we going somewhere fancy?" Amaris said as she snapped another picture.

"No, why?"

"Because you're dressed in a suit. I thought we were going to breakfast at your parents'."

"We are." Logan said, looking down at her suit. She thought she looked good, but she was used to wearing her suit. She never knew who she could run into and she always felt the need to look her best. "This is what I mostly dress in, I like feeling nice."

"Well, Miss. Nice, strike a pose for me and let me capture you in all of your glory."

Logan gave Amaris her best boss woman pose and laughed before she could snap the picture. Amaris smiled behind the lens, snapping random pictures of Logan.

"Are you ready to get out of here, woman? I'm starving." Logan said with a mock frown.

"Yes, lead the way," Amaris answered and followed Logan to the elevator. She admired Logan as they went down the elevator. She thought Logan was such a beautiful human being. She enjoyed the fact that Logan was all hers.

"Damn. I wish you had pants on, I would take you on my motorcycle."

"You have a motorcycle?" Amaris asked and clapped excitedly. She'd never been on the back of a motorcycle, but she always wanted to. She wondered what it would be like to fuck Logan on her motorcycle. The thought made a sly grin cross her face.

"Yes, have you driven one?"

"No, maybe you can teach me."

"Oh, that's going to be fun experiencing that with you. We'll definitely have to take Red out."

"Red?"

The doors to the parking garage opened. Logan led Amaris to her cherry red 2018 YZF-R1. Amaris's mouth literally dropped. It was one of the most beautiful things Amaris had ever laid eyes on. She circled the bike, snapping pictures of its beauty.

"My God, she's beautiful," she said in wonder.

"How do you know it's a she? It could be a he."

"No, no, no, this is definitely a sexy woman. This isn't a boy."

Logan smirked. She never thought of her motorcycle being a he or she, but now, really looking at Red, she could understand why Amaris would think it was a girl. Her bike did have a bit of femininity to it.

"You're right, Red is a girl and I can't wait to take you for a ride. Right now, I'm hungry, so we'll take a regular old car. Let's go." Logan gently pulled Amaris toward her car.

When they made it to the Maddox's estate, Logan wasn't surprised when she saw Xavier's car in the driveway. She knew her mother would call him and Taylor when she found out Logan and Amaris were coming over for breakfast.

"It looks like X and Taylor are here." Logan pulled into her spot in the driveway. Amaris was about to open the door, but Logan grabbed her hand, stopping her. "I got you."

She hopped out of the car, running across her car to open the door for Amaris. Amaris stared at her woman, smiling at how chivalrous she was. Logan seemed to take her stud status seriously. She hoped that Logan wasn't a 'touch-me-not'. It would be such a deal breaker if Amaris wasn't able to please her sexually. That was something they would have to talk about at a later time.

She stepped out of the car taking Logan's awaiting hand. "You're such a studband," Amaris joked.

"I just want to treat my lady right."

"Oh, is that right?" Amaris liked the sound of being called Logan's lady. She wanted to be more than that. She wanted to be Logan's everything.

"Yes."

Logan engulfed Amaris in her arms, kissing her senseless. Amaris moaned in satisfaction. How could something so simple feel so right? Logan's tongue asked for entrance into Amaris's mouth, which she gladly obliged. She grabbed the back of Logan's head, sucking her bottom lips into her mouth. Amaris could feel her pussy getting wet. She wanted Logan to touch her, she wanted her to taste her.

Logan wanted to take Amaris right there. She had it in her right mind to push her back into the car and eat her pussy. She was about to say fuck breakfast and go back home, when someone cleared their throat behind them, interrupting their moment.

Logan broke their kiss and buried her face in the side of Amaris neck, embarrassed and slightly annoyed. She knew it was her mother without even looking.

"Hello mother."

Amaris wanted to hide behind Logan as she tried not to laugh. She felt like a teenager getting caught by their parents. "Oh my God," she whispered.

Mrs. Maddox stared at the doorway with her arms crossed. "Are you two finished or should I go back inside and give you time?" she asked playfully.

She didn't want to watch her daughter make out with her partner, but it was refreshing to see Logan show affection toward someone.

"No, we're done mother." Logan grabbed Amaris's hand as they walked up the steps towards Mrs. Maddox. "Hello mom." Logan hugged and kissed her mother's cheek.

"Hey baby girl, how are you feeling today?"

Logan's eyes darted toward Amaris. "I'm great."

Amaris squeezed Logan's hand. Mrs. Maddox watched the exchange between the two love birds, it made her heart swell with happiness. If Logan did pass away—she prayed to God she didn't—at least, her daughter would have experienced love all the way till the end.

"Well, that's good. Amaris, it's so good to have you here with us."

"It feels nice to be here with everyone, thanks for the invite, Mrs. Maddox."

"Oh child, no need to thank me. Come on in ladies, everyone's here." They followed Mrs. Maddox into the house and then into the dining room.

"Hey guys." Logan chirped as Amaris and she went around the table, hugging and greeting everyone before taking their seats.

"So how was the first night? " Xavier asked with a devilish smile.

"Yeah, it was good. Amaris found the pool and took a night dip."

"Oh yeah?" Mrs. Maddox asked, surprised. "Have you even used the pool, Lo?"

"Nope, last night was the first night." Logan was usually too busy with work to enjoy her penthouse. She usually only used her living room, office, and bedroom.

"It was your first time?" Amaris asked, shocked. Logan's pool was beautiful, she planned on enjoying every part of it every day.

"Amaris, you'll soon realize that Logan is a workaholic. I don't think she's seen half of her penthouse," Xavier teased.

Logan rolled her eyes. It sucked that her brother was right. Last night was the first time she actually remembered she had an indoor pool and a nice one at that. It was nice to experience that with Amaris. she thought about all the time she wasted with work; she loved what she did, but now that she might die, it didn't seem as important.

Logan felt Amaris's hand slide across her neck. She caressed it lovingly. "Well, I plan on Logan enjoying every bit of what she has. She's not going to be a workaholic with me around."

Logan thought of the ways Amaris could keep her busy. She hoped it involved her tasting Amaris's pussy or watching her strap slide in and out of her pussy. She chuckled to herself as the image played in her head. She was pining for this woman bad. She didn't want Amaris to think that was all she wanted even though she was aware that she was fully ready.

"Well, I just hope that Logan takes it easy, we need to preserve her strength," Mrs. Maddox chimed in.

"Well, mother if it was up to you, I would live in a bubble for the rest of my life," Logan said annoyed.

"Lo, you know I just want you to stick around. In order to do that, you can't exert your body," Mrs. Maddox said gently.

"Mom, I know that I'm sick. I don't need a constant reminder, jeez. I need you to realize that I might die." Logan snapped. She knew her mother meant well, but it was too much sometimes. She wanted to be treated like she was normal.

"Logan," Amaris gasped, appalled. She'd never heard Logan speak so harshly to her mother.

Logan sighed, seeing the hurt on her mother's face. She didn't mean to say it the way she did. "Excuse me, I think I need some air." She got up, leaving everyone at the table as her mother wiped the tears that formed in her eyes.

"I'll go speak to her. I'm sorry, Mrs. Maddox," Amaris said with pity.

Amaris got up from the table and headed outside in search of Logan. She was leaning against the railing when Amaris walked outside. She pressed her breast against Logan's back while massaging the nape of her neck. Logan's eyes closed as she relaxed under Amaris's touch.

"Imagine carrying your child in your womb for nine months, nurturing him or her for nine whole months. Imagine going through labor for hours to bring your creation to this world. Imagine watching your child growing for twenty plus years and now, imagine how you would feel as a mother to know that the same child you nurtured and loved might die before you. Imagine as a mother how you would feel knowing there was a possibility you might bury your child instead of the other way around, as it should be. How do you think you would treat that child?"

Logan choked on her tears as Amaris's words settled over her. She closed her eyes not wanting her tears to fall. She knew if she cried, she would break and it was too early to break. She still needed to keep herself together to continue to live every day. She took a long, deep breath getting her emotions in check before opening her eyes.

Amaris knew she'd gotten through to Logan even if it was just a little bit. Logan turned around and wrapped Amaris in her arms, hugging her tight. "Thank you."

"You don't have to thank me, love."

"I can be a hothead at times."

"I see," Amaris joked. This just showed her that they still had to get to know each other.

"I know my mother means well, I just get so frustrated with her at times. I don't like being looked at as weak and my mom treats me like I'm a baby."

"When you start to feel that way, baby, remember what I said. This is hard on your mom. Be patient with her. Understand where she's coming from. Try talking to her and not at her."

"She tries to run things sometimes, there's no getting through to her."

"Oh, that reminds me of someone."

Logan rolled her eyes, but laughed at herself. Amaris knew firsthand just how stubborn Logan could be. They'd spent months apart because of it.

"Whatever, girl. Do you want to finish breakfast?"

"Yes."

•———— ·•●•· ————•

After breakfast, Logan pulled her mother to the side to speak with her. "I know you love me, so I'm sorry for snapping at you. It's just that sometimes I feel like you treat me like a child, like a baby, and I'm a grown woman."

Mrs. Maddox caressed Logan's cheek. "I know that you're a grown woman, but you will always be my child and I will always worry about you, Lo."

Logan hugged her mother tight. She was thankful for her; she just wanted her to ease up some. "I love you, mom."

"I love you too, sweetie. Go enjoy your day." Mrs. Maddox blew Amaris and Logan a kiss as they hopped into the car and drove off.

"So where are you taking me?"

"Well I thought to give you the cheesy Vegas tour of the strip. Are you down?"

"I'm down for anything as long as it's with you Lo."

Logan kissed Amaris hand as she jumped on the I15 toward the strip. "First stop will be the Bellagio. We'll watch the water show and then we'll go to the Bellagio Gardens. They change the theme every few months and I'm dying to see what the theme is right now."

"Well ma'am lets do it." Amaris was excited to see Logans stomping grounds. She'd never been to Vegas besides the time she photographed Xavier and Taylors wedding. She wasn't drawn to it like most tourists, but she found it quite cute to be a tourist with Logan.

The day did not disappoint. Amaris enjoyed the water show immensely but the gardens were a whole other experience. It was decorated for the Chinese New Year which was the year of the rabbit and Amaris had to admit the designers had gone all out. Her eyes jumped to the beautiful gold coin tree, then the huge red and gold rabbit that was in the center of the garden. What took Amaris' breath away was the Jade emperor who sat in all his glory. Amaris wished she could meet the designers just to compliment them on the amazing work they had done. The display was truly a work of art. She was in awe of everything. She'd lost count of how many pictures she took of the beautiful flowers and different statues.

Logan stood back as she watched Amaris take her pictures. The huge smile plastered on Amaris' face showed Logan it was a great call to start their tour at the Bellagio.

Amaris laid her camera against her stomach no longer feeling Logans presence beside her. When she turned around, she found Logan leaning against the railing staring back at her. God, she looked good in her suit as she blended in with the colorful flowers. Amaris raised her camera and snapped a picture of her woman. Logan smiled and she snapped another before joining her. "So, you like it?"

"Oh, I love it Lo, thank you for bringing me here."

"No need for thanks baby." Logan kissed Amaris' forehead allowing her lips to linger. At that moment she realized how happy she was. She couldn't remember the last time she allowed herself to do something so simple. She was always buried in her work or being smothered by her family. Amaris just let her be and she loved her for it. "Are you ready for our next stop?"

"Yup."

"Alright let's go." They intertwined their hands and headed for the exit. Amaris stopped in front of a beautiful bronze ding pot. Incense was strategically placed around the ding pot.

"Look at this baby." Amaris bent down to read the description. "It says the pot represents a ritualistic offering to the heavens as a sign of gratitude and hopes of a fruitful new year." Amaris liked the sound of that. They could use some good luck right about now. "Do you have cash?"

"I do," Logan reached into her pocket and pulled out a few dollar bills.

"Let's make an offering." Amaris folded the bills and set it on the dish. She then closed her eyes and whispered how grateful she was to the universe for bringing her and Logan together. She then said a short prayer for Logans new heart to come. She faced Logan who had a questionable look on her face.

"What did you wish for?"

"It was more of a prayer." She kissed Logans hand. "For your new heart." Logan hoped that Amaris prayer was answered.

The rest of the day was smooth sailing. They went across the street to the Eiffel Tower and road up the elevator to have a look at the beautiful Las Vegas strip. After hearing all the facts about the hotel Logan treated Amaris to the best gelato, she'd ever had at Café Belle Madeleine. Next was the Gondola ride at the Venetian. Logan made sure to pay for a private boat ride. Amaris scooted closer to Logan as they glided across the water. "Lo this has been an amazing day."

Logan wrapped her arm around Amaris shoulder drawing her as close as they could be. "I have one more spot we can go after this."

"Really? You're up for more?" Amaris didn't want to push Logan too much. Their day had already been so full which she wasn't complaining about but she didn't want Logan to pay for it tomorrow. She wondered if she was in pain, if she was, she had a great way of hiding it.

"Yes, just one more stop, it's somewhere special for me and I'd like to share it with you."

"Really?" Amaris said touched by the gesture.

"Yes."

"Ok baby."

"It's tradition for the lovely couple to kiss under the bridge," their gondolier suggested.

Amaris eyes locked in on Logans lips before Logan took the lead and captured her lips. The kiss was brief and left Amaris wanting more. She had to stop herself from sharing her sexual thoughts with Logan but as if Logan could read her mind she said, "In due time my love, in due time."

Their last stop was the High Point Overlook, one of Logans favorite places in the city. Amaris was amazed at the view as she got out of the car with her camera in hand. The mountains looked unreal; Amaris felt like she was standing in front of a good green screen. It amazed her just how beautiful nature was.

Logan walked up behind Amaris engulfing her from behind. "I come here when I need to shut the world out. It always calms me."

Amaris laid her head against Logans chest. "I can see why, it's so beautiful baby."

"I've never brought anyone here," Logan confessed.

"So why am I here?"

"Because you're the love of my life and I want to share everything with you."

Amaris flipped around in Logans arms as her words engulfed her. "Say that again."

"Which part?"

"You know."

"You're the love of my life."

Amaris stood on her tippy toes kissing Logan. This was it, this is what she wanted with Logan for the rest of her life. She knew their love would carry them until Logan received her heart, it had to because she wouldn't live the rest of her life without her.

Logan ran her fingers through Amaris's hair as they laid on the couch, watching TV. It was so crazy how normal it felt for the both of them. It was like they'd been dating for years; they survived a whole week together without killing each other. Logan couldn't believe how natural it was for her to come home to Amaris. She actually looked forward to it.

Against everyone's better judgment, Logan went back to work. She couldn't let her authors down, hell she couldn't let herself down. She promised Amaris she would be careful and not over exert herself. Even though sitting there and going through manuscripts still exhausted her, she got up every morning, got dressed and went to work.

Amaris also started her project with Logan's parents which was keeping her pretty busy. She loved it and the building they were working on was amazing. She loved waking up to Logan, but the 'no sex' was killing her. They'd had some hot and heavy make out sessions, but then, Logan would stop them and tell her she thought they should wait. Amaris had it in her mind to take Logan, but she wanted it to be a mutual thing. She wanted Logan to want her just as much as she wanted her.

"Do you want kids?"

"I never thought about it because I always considered my photography as my baby, but honestly, I wouldn't be opposed to kids. What about you?"

"Yup, two," Logan said with no hesitation.

"Two?" Amaris cocked her eyebrow. "Who would carry?"

"Both, one and one." Logan always wanted children. She's never been afraid to remember that she was still a woman and she could carry a child.

"No shit," Amaris said, intrigued. Most studs she knew wouldn't dare think about being pregnant.

"Yeah, for real. I would have loved to experience pregnancy." Amaris pictured Logan walking around in her suit with a pregnant belly. The thought made her laugh.

"What's so funny?"

"I just thought about you in a suit walking around pregnant."

Logan smirked, thinking about what kind of mind fuck that would be for people. "Hey, I'd look sexy."

Amaris rubbed Logan's stomach imagining a baby there. "You'd look beautiful," she said honestly.

Logan had given up that dream when she got the news she had a bad heart. "Maybe in my next life."

"Don't give up hope, Logan. We still have time." Amaris didn't want Logan to fall into the negative hole about her condition. As long as her heart continued to beat, they still had time.

Logan switched positions so that she was on top of Amaris. "Why am I waiting?"

"What?"

"Why am I waiting to do the things I want with you?" If ninety days was all she would possibly have, she didn't want to waste it living in fear or with regret. She'd already wasted months away from Amaris.

"So what are you saying?"

Logan didn't say anything else, instead she swooped down and captured Amaris's lips taking her breath away. Amaris recovered quickly as she caught on to the rhythm of their kiss. The hunger in Logan's kiss almost made Amaris crème in her panties. Her lips were soft, but forceful.

Logan's phone rang on the dresser and she tried to break away from the kiss, but Amaris grabbed her cheeks keeping her there. Logan tried to ignore her phone and be in the moment, but the ringing didn't stop.

"Dammit. Hold on, love," she said.

"Seriously?" Amaris asked, out of breath. She was about to rip Logan's dress shirt off and fuck the shit out of her. She was done with the heavy teasing and kissing. She needed Logan to make her cum. She would take her time, so they didn't overdo it, but she couldn't wait any longer.

"It could be my mom or work and trust me, they won't stop calling." Logan rolled off Amaris and grabbed her phone. "Hello?"

"Logan, we have a problem."

"What?"

Amaris watched as Logan's facial expression changed from serene to strained. She knew that their intimate time was over. Logan sat up in bed as she listened to one of her editors tell her about a massive printer screw up.

"I'm on my way," she growled into the phone before hanging up. She didn't want to look at Amaris, but she had to get to her office. "I have an emergency at the office. I'm sorry, I need to go."

"What's going on?"

"Something with the printers. We had a major deadline to get my books out to distributors, if I don't get this fixed tonight, we're not going to reach our deadline."

"Okay. Do you want me to go with you?"

"No, it's okay. Who knows how long I'll be there." Logan leaned on the bed and gave Amaris a quick peck. "I'll be back as soon as I can. I'm sorry."

Amaris gave her a half smile. "It's okay." She watched as Logan slid into some shoes and dashed out the door.

CHAPTER

12

Amaris didn't know what time Logan made it back home, but when she woke, Logan was fast asleep beside her. Her clothes were still on, so Amaris figured she really had a long night.

She didn't want to wake her, so she tiptoed out of the room and headed to her own. Things weren't going as she thought they would. She thought they'd spend the first few days tangled in the sheets, but that hadn't been the case.

When she got to her room, she noticed she had missed calls from her mom. Amaris stepped outside onto the balcony while dialing her mother back.

"Hi." Her mother's sweet voice came flowing through the phone, instantly putting a smile on her face.

"Hi mom."

"You can't even give me a call to tell me you made it safely?"

"I'm sorry mom. I made it safely," Amaris joked.

"How are you, sweetheart?"

"I'm good, just settling in."

"And Logan?"

"I'm trying to keep her spirits up, but she seems okay. She's sleeping now."

"I've been praying for her." Ms. Cole wanted to add *'and you'* , but she knew she didn't have to, Amaris already knew.

"Thank you, mom. I'm sure Logan appreciates that."

By the time Amaris got off the phone with her mother, three hours had passed. She loved that they had a relationship where they could joke and talk about anything.

She realized it was well past two o'clock and Logan was still asleep. She wanted to wake her, but she wanted her to get her rest. She was exploring Logan's penthouse when a ping of the elevator went off. Amaris heard the clicking heels and thought it was Taylor. She ran to greet her, but stopped dead in her tracks when she realized it wasn't her.

She was met by Chandra, whom she remembered from the wedding. Her eyes went from Chandra's long sexy legs, her fire red skirt suit, to her laid press. Just from her outfit, Amaris knew she was trying to make a statement.

"Hello," Amaris said, trying to be as welcoming as possible. There was no threat in her voice.

Chandra looked Amaris up and down. "You look familiar," were her first words—no hi, no introduction of names.

"Yes, I know we've seen each other before." Amaris tried to remain neutral.

"Are you Logan's maid?" Chandra knew Amaris wasn't the maid, but her presence had thrown her off. She was hoping to have Logan alone, it had been a few months since their last rendezvous.

"No, I'm not the maid, sweetheart, I'm Logan's girlfriend." Amaris said matter of fact. All courtesy was out the window. Amaris hated disrespect and she didn't appreciate Chandra's comment.

"Girlfriend?" Chandra clucked. "Logan doesn't do those."

"I do now." Logan walked down the hallway and straight to Amaris, she didn't even look at Chandra, her eyes stayed on Amaris's beautiful face. She wrapped her in her arms lovingly before planting a kiss on her lips. Amaris held onto Logan thinking she couldn't have loved her any more than she did now.

When Logan's eyes met Chandra's, the warmth in them were gone. They were ice-cold. She heard the little comment Chandra had made to Amaris and she didn't appreciate it one bit. "I think you owe my lady an apology, first for showing up to our home unannounced, second for disrespecting her in our home."

Chandra's jaw was on the ground, she stammered as she tried to find her words. "I-I didn't know …"

"Of course you didn't, we haven't spoken in a while, so how could you?" Logan didn't count their small conversation they'd had a week ago. She didn't expect for Chandra to just pop up at her place, that was unlike her.

Amaris could see how each word Logan spoke sliced through Chandra. She registered the hurt in her eyes, she would have felt sorry for her if she hadn't come off so rude. Their eyes locked as Chandra swallowed her pride. "I'm sorry …"

"Amaris …" Logan spoke up, reminding her to address Amaris properly.

"I'm sorry, Amaris."

"If you knew better, you would know Amaris is an amazing photographer. She was the photographer at Xavier and Taylor's wedding, not the maid."

"And now she's your girlfriend?"

Logan smiled as she and Amaris locked eyes. "And now she's my girlfriend." They hadn't discussed making things official, but now was as good a time as any.

"I thought you didn't do girlfriends, Logan." Chandra was trying to hold back tears. For years she'd asked Logan to take their relationship to the next level, to be exclusive with each other, but Logan had always told her she didn't want a girlfriend, now here she was, claiming Amaris and sharing a home with her.

"When the right person comes along, sometimes it just happens."

Chandra had heard enough. She couldn't take the way Logan looked at Amaris or spoke about her. It was a way Logan had never looked at her. "I think I'm going to go."

"I think that would be best."

She scurried to the elevator wanting to get out of there. She was embarrassed and hurt.

Amaris didn't even wait for the elevator doors to close before she jumped on Logan. Her tongue slid into Logan's mouth and she wrapped her legs around Logan's waist. Logan met her with just as much intensity. It was like they continued from last night. Logan carried Amaris to her room and laid her down without breaking their kiss. Amaris didn't care that there wasn't going to be any more interruptions between them.

She pulled Logan's shirt from over her head trailing soft kisses across her stomach. Logan hissed under her breath. She thought about this moment since she'd met Amaris, wondering how she would feel against her, it was even more amazing than what she thought. Amaris's eyes caught the scar that ran down Logan's chest. She traced the line with her finger, making Logan flinch. "Does it hurt?" she asked, concerned.

Logan took her finger and kissed it. "No, it doesn't." She pulled Amaris's dress over her body only to find that Amaris was completely naked underneath her dress. "No panties?" Logan joked.

Amaris shied away. The truth was that she'd hoped Logan came home last night and they continued where they left off, she wanted to be completely ready for her. "I wanted to be ready to receive you."

"And are you ready to receive me, Amaris?" Logan's voice was husky from want. Amaris's words had a way of doing things to her.

"Logan, I am yours." Amaris's heart was beating so quickly she felt like it was going to explode. She had sexual partners in the past, but not with the kind of connection she had with Logan. She knew their chemistry was on a soul mate level. Logan was her person; she'd been her person from the moment she laid eyes on her.

Logan spread her body on Amaris's, claiming her lips again. Amaris moaned into Logan's mouth as Logan's fingers found her clit. "You're so wet," she muttered against her lips.

"Yes," was all Amaris could say as she felt Logan's fingers getting lost in her creaminess. Logan inserted another finger inside Amaris and slowly began to stroke her pussy.

"Oh, Logan." Amaris bit her bottom lip as her hips started to move against Logan's fingers.

"That's right, baby, ride my fingers, " Logan whispered in Amaris's ear. Amaris was so hot and wet, Logan thought she would lose her mind. She tried to stop her heart from racing because she wanted to enjoy this moment with Amaris. There would be no more interruptions for them. The only way she wasn't going to make love to Amaris was if the world was ending.

"Logan, it feels so good," Amaris moaned and Logan couldn't take it anymore. She moved her fingers and started grinding against Amaris, which made Amaris moan even louder. To be connected with Logan that way was more than she could ever expect. She felt like her head was spinning from the passion between them. She knew from then that she would never be able to be with another person. Logan would always be it.

Amaris's nipples protruded, begging Logan to suck them. Her nipple rings made them even more enticing. Logan took one of Amaris's nipples into her mouth, biting it. Amaris bucked and hissed underneath her.

"Oh, Logan, you're driving me crazy," Amaris moaned. She could die a happy woman right now. The way Logan's tongue teased her nipples made her head spin. How she was so good with both her tongue and fingers was beyond Amaris's comprehension.

Logan's fingers sunk into Amaris's fro as her grind became desperate. She was so wet and turned on by Amaris. No woman had ever had this type of effect on her. "I love you," she said breathlessly as she tried to kiss Amaris. Her heart thumped in her ear, telling her she was over doing it, but Logan didn't care. If she died right there she would die happy, making love to the woman she loved.

Amaris's body tensed underneath her. "Logan!" she cried out as she came undone. Her body shook underneath Logan uncontrollably. Logan started to slow down but Amaris kept grinding against her.

"Don't stop, cum with me this time," Amaris told her breathlessly and they began to grind against each other bringing one another closer to their peak.

"That's right, baby, grind against me," Amaris cooed in Logan's ear. She was close to cumming again, but she wanted Logan to cum first.

Logan's body bucked as she felt herself cum. She moaned into Amaris's neck as she felt her body sink into Amaris. Amaris came again right after her. They laid there afterwards, both gasping for air.

"Shit," Logan whispered.

Amaris wrapped her legs around Logan not wanting them to disconnect. She could feel Logan's heart pounding on top of hers. "Are you okay?"

"Yes," Logan lied. She was dizzy and felt like she couldn't catch her breath, but she didn't want to end this. She wanted to always remember this moment with Amaris.

After a few minutes, Amaris rolled them over so Logan could lay on the bed so that she could get a good look at her. Her complexion was ashen, not the normal beautiful chocolate Amaris was used to. Amaris sat up, alarmed.

"Logan, you don't look so good," she said afraid.

"Just give me a few more minutes. I promise, I'll be okay."

"I'm going to get you some water."

"Okay." Logan told herself not to pass out as Amaris rushed out of the room. Her heartbeat was hammering in her ears and the room was spinning. She closed her eyes and counted to ten. She needed to calm her heart down before Amaris came back, she didn't want her to rush them to the hospital.

Amaris headed for the kitchen, after grabbing two bottles of water, she scurried back to the room. "Here, drink up."

Logan grabbed the bottle of water and guzzled it down. "Thank you, baby."

"You're welcome."

Amaris grabbed her camera after she felt like Logan was okay. Logan's body was spread out across the bed, she looked spent, but in a good way. "Look at me." Logan smiled as she directed her attention towards Amaris and she snapped the picture. "I think you promised me a photoshoot, you remember?"

Logan flipped on her stomach remembering their time in the rose garden. "Yeah, I remember."

"Are you up for it?" Logan looked so deliciously sexy that Amaris wanted to catch this raw moment.

"Whatever you want. I'm your canvas."

The high Logan was on from their love making was coming down and she felt the ache in her body start to return, but when she saw the hope in Amaris's eyes she couldn't turn her down. She would muster up some energy to do the photoshoot for Amaris. It would be something Amaris could keep forever.

Those were the magical words Amaris wanted to hear. "Okay. Well, while you're lying on your stomach can you raise your legs and cross them?"

Logan laughed, thinking Amaris was joking, but she kept a straight face. "Are you serious?"

"Yes, humor me." Amaris tried not to laugh. Logan put on the most girly demeanor she could muster as she crisscrossed her legs and planted her chin in the palm of her hands. Amaris giggled like a teenager, but snapped the picture anyways. "Oh, this is classic! I'm going to print these. Give me a big smile." Logan gave Amaris her biggest smile causing her to smile as well. "Thank you for playing along with me, your smile is everything love."

Logan's smile dropped to a much normal one and Amaris zoomed in on her face, capturing her smile. "You're always complimenting me."

"It's so easy to. Now, lay your head flat on your hands and look at me."

Logan did as she was told. It amused her to no end to see Amaris in her zone. Amaris grabbed the sheets and folded it over the half of Logan's ass. She moved her hair to the side so she could get the indent of Logan's spine leading down to her ass. She made sure to plant a soft kiss on one of her ass cheeks.

"Sorry, I couldn't help it."

"Umm hmm," Logan hummed.

Amaris grabbed a few of Logan's locs, framing her face with it. "My God, you're gorgeous." There was something innocent in Logan's face, it was almost childlike.

"Stop, you're making me blush."

Logan was used to compliments from women, but it hit different coming from Amaris. She felt every emotion in Amaris's words, she felt her love wrap around her each time like a warm blanket.

"I love you, Amaris," she said with all seriousness.

"And I love you, Logan, forever." Amaris raised her camera and snapped a full body length picture of Logan. She checked out the picture. "Oh, yeah this is going to be black and white."

"Let me see," Logan said with a girly smile. Amaris sat on the bed showing Logan her picture. Logan was in awe at what Amaris was able to capture. She wasn't looking her best, her weight was declining and she didn't see the light in her eyes, but Amaris was able to capture what Logan was used to seeing whenever she looked in the mirror.

"This is beautiful, baby. I love it," she said in a soft voice.

"I'm glad you do."

"Now, set that camera down and come join me in bed."

"Oh, photoshoot is over?"

"Yes, I have something else in mind."

Logan pulled Amaris back into bed, so that she could nestle into her arms. Amaris caressed Logan's cheek, sensing a bit of sadness from her. She wished she could take it away. All she wanted to do was see Logan smile.

"Do I know you?" Logan asked the same question for the umpteenth time.

A smile spread on Amaris's lips. "Maybe in a past life. Maybe we married. Maybe you were a guy and you gave me lots of babies. Maybe we lived in a treehouse in the middle of the forest. I think I was yours, regardless"

Logan chuckled. "Maybe I was your mistress and we fucked each other senseless any time your husband was away."

Amaris thought about Quelm and instantly laughed. If Logan knew that was actually her life at one point. "Yeah, maybe."

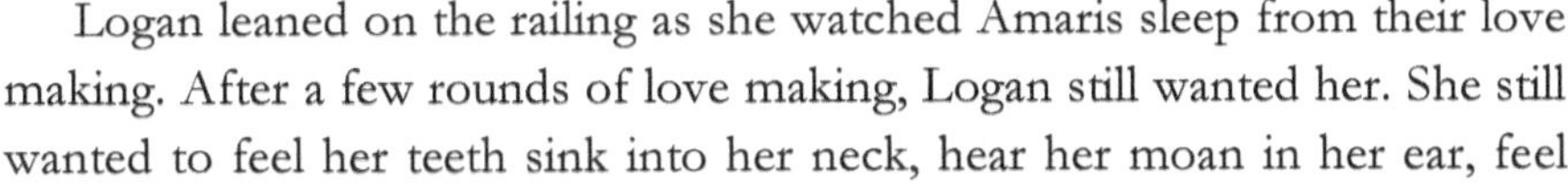

Logan leaned on the railing as she watched Amaris sleep from their love making. After a few rounds of love making, Logan still wanted her. She still wanted to feel her teeth sink into her neck, hear her moan in her ear, feel their breasts pressed together. Just the thought made Logan's clit tingle. She couldn't get enough of her. Logan knew she was over doing it, but she didn't care. She was going to enjoy Amaris for as long as she could. She knew as time went on, as her heart grew weaker, so would she. She would be bed-ridden, unable to enjoy life anymore. The thought of it made her head hurt.

She looked up in the sky. "God, I know I don't call on you often, but I need to ask you this one favor. Please, give me a new heart. I can't leave Amaris when you just gave her to me. Please Lord, don't take me away from her. I want to live, I want to enjoy life, I want to enjoy life with her." Logan kept her eyes to the sky as if God was really going to answer her. After a moment of silence, Logan plopped down in one of her chairs. She took her phone out and called her mom.

"Is everything okay?" Mrs. Maddox asked, alarmed and sleepy.

Logan didn't say anything at first. She was sad that even in her sleep, her mother was on edge. "I think I loved her the moment I laid eyes on her."

Mrs. Maddox relaxed in bed. "I know you did, baby. Amaris gives you that sparkle that your father gives me."

"I don't want to die mom, I don't want to leave her." Logan choked as tears began to fall. She'd never really thought about dying until now, when the thought of leaving Amaris nearly suffocated her.

Mrs. Maddox tried to hold it together without crying. "You're not going to die, you hear me? You're strong, we're Maddox women and we come from a long line of strong women. You'll just have to hold on until a new heart comes and it will come, you hear me?" Mrs. Maddox hoped she was right, she prayed so hard that she was right. She couldn't say goodbye to one of her children.

"Yes, I hear you. I love you mom."

"I love you, Logan, so very much."

Logan talked to her mother until she calmed down. When she felt like she had herself together, she went back into her room and slid in the bed.

Amaris draped her arm around Logan and snuggled into her. "You okay, baby?"

"I'm okay." Logan pulled Amaris closer, hoping sleep would come easy.

CHAPTER

13

Amaris couldn't believe she was actually on the set of a movie. She snapped pictures of the crew in action and whatever scenes they allowed her to get. She was in awe of Logan as she watched her give direction to the actors. She had a director, but she might as well have been the one directing, because they all listened to her. Amaris quickly realized that Logan commanded attention without even trying. People just took direction from her with ease. She loved every minute of it.

She tried to give Logan her space because she knew she was working, but every now and then, their eyes would meet and Logan would give her a wink, making her blush.

The sexual tension between them built up. Amaris could feel it, hell, even Logan could. So, when the *actual* director called for a lunch break, Amaris was dripping onto her panties from all the sexual tension that had been building up between Logan and she.

Logan walked to her and gave her a sound kiss, not caring that they were in public; she just couldn't get enough of her. "Let's go get something to eat.

We can have lunch in my trailer, just the two of us." she murmured against Amaris's lips.

Amaris was a little disappointed that they had to break off their session, but she knew they needed to eat. Plus, she couldn't pass up any opportunity of spending some alone time with her woman—the word sounded kind of good to her. She nodded her head while looking into Logan's eyes. She caught a glimpse of mischief in those eyes, but it was gone as quickly as it came and she wondered what that could mean.

Half an hour later, Amaris finally understood what that look had meant. "Fuck." Amaris tossed her head back as Logan teased her clit with her tongue. She thought they would be eating in Logan's trailer for lunch; she just didn't expect to be the meal. Now here she was, three orgasms in and grinding into Logan's face for a fourth one. "Oh my God, my clit is so sensitive, I can't take it."

"Yes, you can." Logan lapped Amaris's juices up. Amaris had to be a goddess because everything about her was on another level.

"Here it comes, here it comes. Oh shit." Logan felt Amaris's juices squirt into her mouth. Her body shook as she fell back onto the counter. She was spent, she could crash right there.

Logan chuckled as she stood up. "You can't keep up with me, girl." She scooped Amaris into her arms and carried her to the back bedroom. Amaris had no energy, so she didn't fight Logan when she laid her in the bed. "I love you, baby. Get some rest." Amaris didn't respond; she was already half asleep.

After cleaning herself up, Logan headed back to set. "Hey lover." Reign ran her hand across Logan's stomach.

"What's up, Reign?"

"So, you have your own photographer now, superstar?" Reign flashed her million dollar smile. Staring at Logan brought back memories of how good she felt inside her.

"Something like that."

"So when are we going to hook up again? We enjoyed our time together last time."

Logan felt like the moment she made a commitment to Amaris was the moment the flood gates opened for everyone she fucked with. "I can't. I have a girlfriend."

"A girlfriend?"

"Yes, that lovely photographer that you were speaking of is my girlfriend." Obviously, Reign must have missed her kissing Amaris publicly or she would have known.

"Girlfriend?" Reign repeated.

"Yes, now let's get back to work. Time is money." Logan didn't entertain any other conversation with Reign. She got everyone together and they continued filming.

It was a long fourteen-hour day, but Logan was able to get through it. Having Amaris there, encouraging her, helped her out, but by the time they got home, the bed was calling her name.

"You know you're overworking yourself," Amaris said, a little sternly.

"I know, but I need to get this done, baby, and I'm so close." Logan laid her head in Amaris's lap. This film might be her legacy to the world besides her books and she wanted it to be beautiful.

"I start my project tomorrow with Xavier, can I trust you to take it easy?"

"I'll take it easy."

"I'm serious."

"I know. I'll take it easy."

Amaris bent down and gave Logan a quick peck. "This is so natural."

"Us?"

"Yes. It feels like we've been together for years."

Logan thought she was the only one who felt that way. Granted, they'd only spent a few days together, but they just meshed so well. "I get what you mean."

"I think I can do this forever with you," Amaris said as Logan played with one of her curls. "Do I know you?"

Logan laughed because it was her turn. "Yes, I am yours. In a past life you found me wounded, you took me back to your village and nursed me back to health. We ended up falling in love with each other. We married and spent our lives in that same village you grew up in."

Amaris giggled. "We should really write a book together."

"I know," Logan said as they both laughed. She pictured them sitting at the table or at her desk writing their story. "In this life, do you believe in marriage?" she suddenly asked.

Amaris honestly never thought about marriage. She loved coming and going as she pleased. She loved the freedom of being able to sleep with who she wanted, no strings attached, but it was different with Logan. She wanted everything with her. "Uhm, I was more of an 'if it happens, it happens' type of person."

"And are you still that way?"

"Not with you."

"So, you'd marry me?"

"Tonight, tomorrow, the next day, whenever."

"Why, because I'm dying?" Logan really wanted to know where Amaris's head was. She didn't want Amaris to pity her.

"How many times do I have to tell you that I am yours, Logan? I was a goner the moment you walked into my life. My soul recognized its other half. When we were apart it felt incomplete. When I was with Lani, it was nice, but I still longed for you."

"But you didn't know me. We still don't know each other."

"And if you asked me to marry you right now, I wouldn't hesitate to say yes. There are just some things the soul knows, some things the heart knows, and they both know that we belong together in this life and in the next."

Logan just stared at Amaris. She knew Amaris was never one to hide her feelings; she said what was on her mind without fear of rejection or the repercussions. "So, marry me." Logan was done wasting time with Amaris. She was going to have whatever little bit of life she had left with Amaris as her wife.

"Are you serious?"

"Yes, marry me this weekend."

"Okay." Amaris said with no hesitation.

"Okay?" Logan sat up making sure she heard Amaris correctly.

"Okay." Amaris confirmed.

Logan jumped up pulling Amaris from the couch with her. "I love you so much, Amaris." She swung Amaris around as they both laughed in glee.

"Are we crazy for this?" Amaris said out of breath.

"Probably, but I don't care." Logan had never been so happy in her life. "I'll be right back."

"Where are you going?"

"Give me just a second."

Amaris flopped back on the couch as Logan disappeared into the room. Her head was spinning, she felt like people would think they were losing their minds, yet she didn't care. She knew that they had always been in sync and they would make their marriage work no matter what. Her mom was probably going to freak out.

Logan walked back into the room as the elevator doors opened. A large white man stepped into the room holding a briefcase. "Evening, Ms. Maddox."

"Hey Chris, thank you for coming on such short notice."

Chris waved Logan off. "Anything for the Maddox's family. I'm just so excited to be a part of this special occasion."

Logan joined Amaris on the couch, intertwining their hands as Chris set the briefcase down. Once he opened it and revealed all the beautiful engagement rings, Amaris's mouth dropped. There were so many to choose from, it slightly overwhelmed her.

"Chris owns the jewelry store downstairs. So, if we're going to do this, we should do it right. We need engagement rings."

Amaris felt like she was legit living a different life. A few months ago, she was living the bachelorette life in California and now, here she was with the love of her life, picking out engagement rings.

They spent the next few hours choosing engagement rings for each other. Amaris was surprised when Logan didn't choose a wedding band, but an actual girly engagement ring. It looked so dainty on her finger. She couldn't wait to take pictures. After Chris left, they spent the rest of the night in bed, celebrating their engagement.

• ——— • •●• • ——— •

"Hey Sweetie, is everything okay? You're calling so early." Ms. Cole sat up in bed. Amaris eyed her engagement ring as she sat in the back of the car.

"Hey mom, everything is fine. I just need you to come to Vegas this weekend."

"Why?"

"Because I'm getting married." Amaris held her breath waiting for the hammer. She knew her mother was used to her doing crazy things, but nothing like this. For the longest moment there was silence between them as Ms. Cole tried to process the news.

"Mom, are you still there?"

"Yes, I'm here sweetie, I'm just at a loss for words. Married? You guys just started dating." Ms. Cole was afraid that Amaris would have a mental breakdown if Logan died.

"I know it sounds crazy mom, but you know I never jump into anything unless I'm one hundred percent positive. I have no doubt in my mind about Logan and I."

"Amaris, what if she—"

"She won't, mom. She's going to get a new heart."

"Can't you guys just wait a second, get to know each other?" Ms. Cole knew she was pleading on deaf ears. She knew her daughter well enough.

"Mom, I need you here this weekend."

"I will be there." Ms. Cole sighed. She wasn't going to fight Amaris. It was her life and she would be there to support her. "I'll be there with bells on."

Amaris sighed in relief. "I love you, mama. I'll book the flight."

"Okay, see you at the end of the week." Amaris ended the call.

Logan squeezed her hand. "How did she take it?"

"Better than expected."

"You still want to get married?"

"Yes."

"Let's see if you feel the same way after we break the news to my family," Logan joked.

— · • ● · · —

"What do you think it is?" Taylor sat in Xavier's lap as they all waited for Logan and Amaris.

Mrs. Maddox played with her wedding band nervously. "I don't know, I just hope it isn't anything bad." Mrs. Maddox answered instead. She was hoping Logan didn't have bad news about her heart. She didn't know if she could take any more bad news.

Everyone stood as they heard the car pull up. Mrs. Maddox was relieved when she saw Logan and Amaris smiling as they walked into the house.

"Hey family!" Logan gave everyone hugs before sitting down. Logan pulled Amaris down onto her lap. Everyone stared at them with anticipation. Logan could see her mother holding her breath, so she decided to put them out of their misery. "I asked Amaris to marry me." Everyone surprisingly clapped with excitement.

"Congrats sis." Taylor jumped up to give Logan and Amaris a hug.

"I knew this would be a short courtship but dang, I didn't know you'll jump the gun the first week," Xavier joked while hugging Logan. "I'm happy for you, sis. I'm happy for both of you." He hugged Amaris. Anyone that could get Logan out of her love drought was someone special.

Amaris felt her anxiety start to go down as she received hugs from Logan's family. The last person was Mrs. Maddox. She stood there with tears in her eyes. The joy in her heart was something she couldn't explain. She took

Amaris's hands into hers, squeezing them.

"Amaris, since my daughter was diagnosed with her condition she has sworn off allowing herself to love someone. The first time Logan met you, I knew you would be the one if she let you in. I'm so grateful for you Amaris. So grateful that you opened Logan's heart to love again." After Mrs. Maddox was finished, there wasn't a dry eye in the room. "I love you, and I welcome you into my family."

"Thank you, Mrs. Maddox, it means so much to me."

Logan's mother pulled Amaris into a loving hug. "Thank you so much, Amaris," She whispered in Amaris's ear, causing her to feel like her heart would explode from all the love they were receiving.

With tears brimming in his eyes, Mr. Maddox gave Amaris a hug as well. "Welcome to the family."

"Thank you, Mr. Maddox."

"So family, don't kill me, but we have another announcement."

"What?" Mrs. Maddox and Taylor asked together.

Logan intertwined her hand with Amaris. "I don't want to wait to marry this lovely woman. I've spent way too much time without her already. So I asked her to marry me this weekend."

"What?" Everyone said in unison.

"Sis, it took me a whole year to plan Xavier and my wedding, it's already Wednesday, that's a couple of days away!"

"Yes, I know, but with all of our connections, you're telling me we can't pull this off?"

"Sweetie, what about invitations, the food, the reverend, Amaris's dress, the venue?" Mrs. Maddox asked. She wanted Logan and Amaris to have the best wedding day, she didn't want it to seem rushed.

"Mom, it could be simple, we don't want the bells and whistles. We want to get married in your rose garden and we want it to be small. Family only, no business partners or clients. No offense, bro." Xavier put his hands up while laughing.

The panicked look on Taylor and Mrs. Maddox's face made Amaris feel bad. She didn't want anyone stressed on their accord. "Baby, maybe we should wait, give enough time to plan."

Logan shook her head no, she knew her family could pull it off. "Mom, I want to make this happen this weekend. I will pay whatever it costs to expedite everything. Let's make it happen," she pleaded with her mother with her eyes.

Mrs. Maddox couldn't say no. "Okay, let's start planning a wedding," She said and clapped her hands.

—— · · ● · · ——

It was a stressful few days, but in the end, Logan's mother used her Maddox magic and planned their wedding in less than 72 hours. Logan spent a pretty penny getting the wedding together, but she didn't care. Seeing Amaris walk down the aisle would be payment enough.

"You know you look fly as fuck right?" Xavier told her and she couldn't hold in her laugh as Xavier peeked over her shoulder. They looked at each other in the mirror sharing another laugh.

"Thank you, brother." She was sporting a custom-made Armani periwinkle suit.

Xavier straightened her bowtie for her. "Just a while ago, it was you in this position, now the roles are reversed."

"Yeah I know, it's crazy."

"I'm so…" Xavier trailed off. Logan saw the tears spring to her brother's eyes.

"Do not become a sissy on me," She teased and Xavier choked back his tears. He never thought he would be able to experience this moment with his sister.

"I'm just happy, sis, that's all."

A soft knock on the door interrupted them. "Come in." Mr. and Mrs. Maddox walked into the room, beaming with joy.

"You look beautiful, sweetheart," Mrs. Maddox said as she kissed Logan on the cheek.

"Thanks, mom. Thank you for everything that you've done." Logan said and Mr. Maddox cleared his throat, making everyone giggle. "You too, dad."

Mr. Maddox took Logan's hands in his. "Baby girl, I never thought I would see this day …" He cleared his throat as it got choked with tears.

"Oh, daddy." Logan couldn't help but become emotional as well. She knew what her wedding meant for all of them.

"Amaris is a fine young lady and I wish you both years of happiness. I love you so much, sweet pea."

"I love you too, daddy." Logan held her father tight as the tears threatened to escape her eyes. Her father had always been a man of few words, but she knew how much he loved her. She was still daddy's little girl.

"Let's get you married," he said, patting her back.

Logan smiled. "Okay."

———— · •●• · ————

"Amaris, you look breathtaking." Ms. Cole stared at Amaris in awe. Amaris felt like her cheeks would fall off from how hard she was smiling. She'd been under so much stress the last few days, but it all led up to this. She was about to walk down the aisle to her soulmate. All the time they wasted didn't even matter anymore. She was going to spend the rest of her life with Logan.

"Thank you, mom," she responded.

"Only you would fall in love in an hour and get married in the next hour," Tasha joked. She'd known Amaris for ten years and watched her do some crazy things, but this was by far the craziest.

"The heart wants what the heart wants," Amaris said with a big smile.

Tasha hugged Amaris tight. "I know, sis. I'm happy if you're happy. Logan seems like a great woman and the way I've watched how she looks at you with love and adoration, I know you two will have a great marriage."

Music started to play in the background. "Well, there's our cue, you ready?" Ms. Cole asked Amaris. Amaris had never been so ready in her life. She would be starting her forever today with Logan. She knew Logan would get a heart and they could really start their lives together.

"Yes, I'm ready." Amaris intertwined her arm with her mother's and they headed for the rose garden.

Logan let out a deep breath as she waited for Amaris to pull up.

"You okay, sis?" Xavier rubbed Logan's shoulders feeling the tension.

"Yeah, just a little nervous." She felt like her heart was going to pop out of her chest. This was one of the biggest steps of her life. Everything she vowed not to do was tossed out of the window because of Amaris's persistence and now, she was about to become her wife.

Everyone stood as the golf cart carrying Amaris and her mother pulled up, the one carrying Tasha right behind it.

"Here we go," Logan whispered to herself. She knew Amaris would be beautiful, but it was nothing compared to seeing her beautiful bride in person. "My God." Logan couldn't breathe, Amaris had literally taken her breath away.

"She looks good, baby sis," Xavier whispered.

"She looks better than good, she looks amazing," Logan said breathlessly.

It felt like Amaris glided down the aisle toward her. Logan's eyes traced every inch of Amaris in her dress. The cream color went beautifully against her chocolate skin. The plunging neckline was just enough to be sinfully delicious as Logan stared at her breasts. A laced train wrapped around her waist and extended ten feet behind her, but of course, Logan zeroed in on her legs. Those beautiful, glistening legs that she couldn't wait to have in the air later tonight.

Amaris knew how much Logan loved her legs, so she didn't wear the traditional long wedding dress. She had it stop right at her thighs so her future wife could get a nice look at everything she was going to offer her and by the look on Logan's face, her mission was accomplished.

Her afro was pressed and straightened and a golden crown adorned her head, a gift from Logan for their wedding day. She had it hand-delivered this morning with a small note stating a Queen should have her crown. Amaris was amazed at the crown, it had to be worth a fortune with the diamonds that were added to it. It would probably be the most expensive thing that's ever adorned her head.

She wore little makeup, which Logan loved, because she loved her natural beauty. Logan couldn't believe this beautiful woman was hers. She silently vowed that she was going to spend the rest of her life making Amaris happy.

Amaris smiled as she walked down the aisle. She knew there were people in the aisle, but she had tunnel vision; her only focus was Logan, her awaiting bride. Logan's smile was infectious, her locs was pulled back so her big cheeks were on display. She looked amazing in her custom made periwinkle suit. It hugged her in all the right places. Her pantsuit hugged her thighs giving her a little figure. Her breasts poked out of her white crisp shirt that was tucked in. Her jacket screamed *'I am the shit!'*

Amaris licked her lips just at the sight of Logan. She was so beautiful, Amaris couldn't believe she was marrying the love of her life. She was seriously walking down the aisle to the love of her life. Life couldn't get any better than this at the moment.

This woman sure knows how to wear a suit, Amaris thought. She tried to get her mind not to go to the gutter.

"Who gives this woman away?" the officiant asked causing Amaris to look at her mother.

"I do," her mother responded.

Logan stepped down and kissed Ms. Cole's cheek. "I will take care of her. I promise." Ms. Cole smiled, hugging Logan tight. "I know you will. I love you."

"I love you too." Ms. Cole placed Amaris's hand in Logan's before taking her seat next to Mr. and Mrs. Maddox.

"You look amazing," Logan whispered so only Amaris could hear her.

"You don't look so bad yourself, stud," Amaris responded with a smile.

Logan's heart was pounding as she stared into Amaris's eyes. There was no doubt in her mind that she was going to love her forever.

Amaris squeezed Logan's hands. "Breathe, baby," she told Logan and watched as she let out a breath she didn't know she was holding in. "You sure?" Amaris asked Logan for the umpteenth time. She wanted to give Logan a final chance to change her mind.

Logan placed her hand on Amaris's cheek before leaning in to kiss her. "I've never been more sure, I love you baby." Tears threatened to spill out of Amaris's eyes at Logan's gesture. She never thought her life could feel so full.

"Shall we continue?" The officiant asked.

"Yes," Logan and Amaris said in unison. When it was time for the vows, beads of sweat formed on Logan's forehead. She was a writer, but when she thought about what she wanted to say to Amaris, her mind went blank. There were too many emotions she couldn't get out.

"Amaris, would you like to go first?"

"Sure." Amaris stepped up to Logan and ran her hand down her face. "I see you, my love." Logan smiled and she grabbed Amaris's hand and kissed it. "Logan, the first time I saw you I thought you were the most beautiful woman I ever laid eyes on. I never believed in love at first sight until I met you. God, I love you, Logan Maddox. People might think we're crazy, but a love like ours is a once in a lifetime love. I told you that I am yours, because I am. I've been yours from the moment I saw you.

"I used to say we were soul mates, but I now know you're my twin flame. My soul mirror image. Our souls have been connected over so many lifetimes and we found each other in this one. I will do everything in my power to make you happy, to keep you strong, and keep that smile on your face. Logan, in this life and in our next life, I will find you and choose you. You're my person, baby."

There wasn't a dry eye in the audience. Everyone was so happy for the couple, knowing Logan's circumstance.

Logan swallowed as she tried to hold back her tears. She felt the tingles in her heart as Amaris spoke every word.

"Logan, it's your turn," the officiant said.

Logan took a deep breath before starting. "'Do I know you?' Those were possibly the first words we spoke to each other. Maybe we lived in the forest and lived off the land. Maybe I was a wounded warrior and you brought me to your village and nursed me back to health. Maybe we fell in love and lived our lives in the village you grew up in." Everyone looked confused, but Amaris smiled with adoration in her eyes. Only they knew what Logan was talking about. "I didn't know you Amaris, but my heart did. It knew you the moment I walked through the doors that weekend, even when I tried to stay away, your persistent ass wouldn't let me. Thank you, baby. Thank you for not giving up on me, for being patient with me. I know that our love is rare and it's something to be cherished and I vow to love you till my very last breath." She felt Amaris tense at her last sentence, but Logan needed her to realize the reality in what she was saying. If she didn't get a new heart in time, she would love her till the very end.

"Now, Logan, you're going to take this ring and place it on Amaris's ring finger while repeating after me: I, Logan Maddox, take thee, Amaris Cole, to be my lawfully wedded wife, in sickness and in health, for richer or poorer, till death do us part." Logan slid Amaris's wedding band on her ring finger.

"Now, Amaris, it's your turn. Please, repeat after me: I, Amaris Cole, take you, Logan Maddox, to be my lawfully wedded wife in sickness and in health, for richer or for poorer, till death do us part." Amaris slid Logan's wedding band on her ring finger.

"I now pronounce you wife and wife, you may now kiss your bride," the officiant pronounced and Logan instantly pulled Amaris into her arms and kissed her senseless. "Ladies and gentlemen, Mrs. And Mrs. Maddox."

— • •●• • —

Logan watched Amaris dance her heart out on the dance floor. She was so happy it was radiating from her. Her happiness made Logan feel so complete. Today had been beautiful, they were surrounded by nothing but love. Logan couldn't have asked for a better day.

Amaris sashayed over to Logan who seemed deep in thought. She slid into Logan's lap, breaking her out of her thoughts. "Hi wife, are you okay?"

Logan cupped Amaris's chin, kissing her gently. "I'm more than okay. I'm just watching my beautiful wife get it on the dance floor," she said as the DJ slowed it down. "Are you up for a little slow dance?" Truth was, Logan was exhausted, but she wasn't going to ruin their wedding day.

"For you, my love, anything."

Logan led them to the dance floor. Amaris wrapped her arms around Logan as they began to slow dance. "Was today everything you dreamed it would be?" she asked. She needed to know.

Amaris smiled. "It was more, thank you for a beautiful day."

"How long before I get to take you away and ravage you?"

"Just say the word and we're out of here."

"Word."

⸻ • ● • ⸻

An hour later, they were saying their goodbyes to everyone as they headed toward McCarran Airport.

"Baby, you're not going to tell me where we're going?" Amaris asked.

"Nope, it's a surprise." Logan kissed the back of Amaris's hand.

Amaris's mouth dropped when they pulled up in front of a jet. "Love, what is all this?"

"We're going on our honeymoon. Come on." Logan led them out of the car.

"Hello Mrs. and Mrs. Maddox, welcome. Why don't you ladies get settled while we get your luggage situated?" A cheerful looking pilot asked them with a big grin.

"Thank you, Kevin." Logan mustered up all the energy she could and scooped Amaris into her arms, making Amaris giggle.

"Baby, put me down."

"Nope. I have to carry you over the threshold." Logan carried Amaris onto the plane.

"Mrs. Maddox, do you need anything?" One of the flight attendants asked.

"No, we're okay, Jess, thank you." Logan set Amaris in one of the passenger seats. "Don't get too comfortable, Mrs. Maddox, once we take off, I'm taking you to the room."

Amaris couldn't believe the jet that they were on. It was huge. It was at least twenty seats. The leather chairs felt good on her skin. She couldn't believe this was her life now. It seemed unreal. Logan sat down across from Amaris and Amaris took the time to take a look at Logan. She looked Logan over, trying not to be concerned. She didn't look good, but she knew she was trying to hold it together. Amaris told herself she would make Logan rest during the flight. She didn't know how long it would be, but Logan needed sleep. She had dark rings forming under her eyes and was looking a little pale.

Amaris ran her foot up Logan's leg to get her attention, "Wife?"

Logan smiled while grabbing Amaris's foot. "Yes, Mrs. Maddox?"

"When the flight starts, I need you to get some rest."

Logan shook her head. "Naw, I'm going to fuck you like crazy."

Amaris stood up, straddling Logan. She wanted contact with her. It was still surreal that they were married. "As much as I would like to ride your face right now you look tired baby and before you say you're not, I know you are. We have a whole week to fuck like rabbits."

Logan chuckled. "It's our wedding night, baby. I don't want to sleep." Logan lied. All she wanted to do was sleep. Her body was screaming for her to rest.

"I love you, Logan, but you're hard-headed. You can't push yourself. Let's sleep baby, we have the rest of our lives to make love."

"Okay, baby."

Amaris planted soft kisses all over Logan's face making her instantly relax. "I can't believe we're married," Amaris said, unable to stop the smile that spread across her face.

"I know, we did it." Logan kissed Amaris's wedding band. "Amaris, I'm going to make you so happy, baby."

Amaris shook her head staring into Logan's eyes. Her whole body was buzzing with happiness. "You already have, love." Amaris kissed Logan, pouring all of her love into her.

Logan parted her lips, allowing Amaris to slide her tongue in her mouth. Amaris always tasted so sweet, like something she could never get enough of. She grabbed the back of Amaris's neck, pulling her deeper into their kiss. Amaris moaned into Logan's mouth while untying her tie. All thoughts of Logan resting left her mind. She started unbuttoning Logan's shirt when they both heard someone clear their throat. Amaris broke the kiss reluctantly.

Logan looked at Kevin, annoyed. "Yes?"

"We're about to take off and need seat belts buckled."

"Okay, thank you."

Amaris slid on the seat next to Logan, exposing the spot she had left on Logan's pants.

Logan smirked. "I haven't even touched you and this is how you are?"

"Huh?" Amaris asked, confused. Logan looked at her pants, allowing Amaris to follow her eyes. Amaris laughed in embarrassment as she saw the white substance on Logan's pants.

"Oh my God," she said still laughing.

"That pussy wet, mah."

"It is. Your kisses drive me insane."

"There's more where that came from. Now buckle up, Mrs. Maddox." Twenty minutes later, they were in the air. As soon as it was safe to unbuckle, Logan unbuckled Amaris's seatbelt. "Let's go."

Amaris allowed Logan to lead her to the back of the plane, surprisingly there was a nice sized room with a queen size bed.

Logan closed the door and locked it. Lust filled her eyes as she stalked towards Amaris. Amaris knew she was in trouble and tried to reason with Logan. "You told me you would rest on the flight."

"I will after. I want my wife." Those words coming from Logan's lips was Amaris's undoing.

"Say it again."

"I want my wife."

Amaris unbuttoned the rest of Logan's dress shirt. "I am yours, Logan."

"You need to be naked now." Logan turned Amaris around unzipping her dress. She gasped as the dress fell and the most seductive red corset adorned Amaris's body.

"My God, woman, you're literally trying to give me a heart attack."

Amaris's breasts were damn near out of the corset. Her ass sat nicely in the crotchless panties. Amaris smiled, loving Logan's reaction, it was exactly what she wanted. She crawled onto the bed on all fours and bent over so that Logan could get a full view of her ass and pussy.

Logan's mouth watered at the image. "You are bad." Logan undressed quickly before making her way to the bed. She bent down behind Amaris and buried her face in Amaris's pussy. They both moaned on contact. Amaris, because of Logan's tongue and Logan because of the taste of Amaris.

Amaris's taste sent Logan's taste buds into a frenzy. She grabbed Amaris's hips and bounced her on her tongue. Amaris moaned in ecstasy as Logan's tongue assaulted her in the best way possible.

"Oh my God, Logan," she moaned into the pillow. She didn't want the flight crew to know what was going on, although she figured they might have a clue.

"You taste so fucking good." Logan lapped her juices up like it was her last meal. She thought about what Amaris said and stopped. "Didn't you say something about riding my face?"

A slick smile crossed Amaris's face. "I did say something like that, huh?"

"Uhm hmm." Logan laid on the bed and stuck her tongue out.

Amaris shivered at the view. "God, I love you." She crawled up the bed and positioned herself over Logan's face. She moaned as she slid down on her wife's tongue. "How did I get so lucky?" she whispered as she started riding Logan's face.

Logan was in heaven pleasing Amaris. Her tongue swirled over her clit, making her buck.

"Oh my God, just like that Logan," Amaris moaned out.

Logan attacked Amaris's clit. She wanted her first cum as a married woman to be something she would never forget.

"I'm cumming baby. I'm cumming." Her ride became desperate as her orgasm neared. She felt dizzy and sweat formed on her forehead. Her heart slammed in her chest as she held her breath. "Oh God!" Her body shattered into a million pieces as she squirted in Logan's mouth. Logan lapped her juices up hungrily. Amaris's body shook from the ongoing attack on her sensitive clit.

"Stop, stop, I can't take it." Amaris fell over onto the bed, so Logan didn't have access to her anymore.

Logan laughed triumphantly. She flipped over, laying on top of Amaris. "Are you okay?"

"Your tongue needs to be registered as a weapon, my God."

Logan smiled, staring at her wife. She still couldn't understand how she loved someone so much in a short amount of time.

Amaris was so beautiful laying underneath her. She had a glow about her that made Logan want to be surrounded in her presence. Her hair was a little wet with the sweat, but she was still gorgeous. Logan could tell she was tired because her eyes were hazy.

"How did I go about my life without you by my side, Amaris?" Everything before Amaris felt incomplete to Logan.

Amaris opened her eyes fully, so they could stare at each other. "That doesn't matter now, we made our way back to each other, my love." Logan pecked Amaris's lips and Amaris put her forehead against hers. "Feel me, Logan."

"Huh?"

"Concentrate on my energy, feel what your love does to me."

Logan took a deep breath and concentrated like Amaris asked. At first, she didn't feel anything, but then she felt a tingle in the middle of her forehead. The tingle spread through her body until she realized they were buzzing together; Amaris was sharing her energy with Logan.

"That's amazing," Logan said breathlessly. "It was almost overwhelming."

"I've never done this with anyone and I never will. Only you, my beautiful wife, will have access to my energy like this. I love you forever."

14

Logan was still asleep when Amaris woke. She couldn't believe Logan had planned their honeymoon in Bora Bora. The bungalow on the water was more than anything Amaris could imagine. She wanted to wake Logan, but thought to let her sleep. Even when she insisted they slept the rest of the flight, they still made love until they both passed out from exhaustion. Looking at Logan right now, she wanted to take her. Her locs were loose and fell over her face. She had the most peaceful look about her.

Amaris slid out of bed and grabbed her camera. She snapped pictures of Logan as she slept. Her phone vibrated, interrupting her secret photo shoot. "Shit." She rushed to the dresser to grab it before the vibration woke Logan up.

"Hello."

"You're married?!" Quelm screamed into the phone. Amaris looked over at Logan before she stepped outside onto their patio.

"Hello Quelm," she said quietly.

"Were you going to tell me, Amaris?" Quelm said as tears ran down her cheek.

"It was sudden, how did you even find out?"

"You don't just marry Logan Maddox and it stays a secret. It's in every magazine known to man."

Amaris wondered how the hell news got out in less than twenty four hours.

"Where did she even come from, Amaris?" Quelm continued in a broken voice.

"I met her a few months ago when I came for that wedding gig."

"So, you've been dating her? I thought we would be honest with each other."

"Quelm, we haven't fucked in months, why is this bothering you so much?" They hadn't spoken since their fall out and Amaris started dating Lani. She didn't understand why Quelm was even calling her.

"You knew I was in love with you, that I'm still in love with you. I told you I would leave my husband for you."

"I never asked you to do that, Quelm. We had a good time and you're such a beautiful soul, but I'm married now and I would never do anything to jeopardize that."

Logan reached for Amaris, but felt nothing but the sheets. She groaned while opening her eyes. She searched the room, but it was empty. She then heard her voice faintly. Logan's body felt so heavy she didn't know if she could get up. She was so tired, she just wanted to sleep. She started to drift back to sleep until she heard Amaris's voice amplify. She sprang out of bed, thinking Amaris was arguing with someone at the resort.

The room started to spin as Logan collapsed to the floor.

Amaris heard a loud thump in the room and ended the call with Quelm. She rushed into the room to find Logan trying to pick herself up off the floor. "Baby!" Amaris ran to her wildly. "What happened, love? Did you slip?" She helped Logan off the floor and back onto the bed.

"Are you okay? I heard you yelling." Logan grabbed her chest as she felt like someone was squeezing her heart.

"I'm fine, baby. Hold on." Amaris ran to her bag and grabbed Logan's pills. "Here." Logan opened her mouth so Amaris could put the pill in it. "Let me get you water." Amaris grabbed one of the water bottles from the mini bar and handed it to Logan. Logan guzzled the water down making sure the pill went down.

Amaris rubbed Logan's chest hoping her breathing would calm down. Logan closed her eyes and took deep breaths until the pain subsided.

"Okay, I think we're in the clear." Logan said as she opened her eyes. She could see the worry written over Amaris's face. "Hey, it's okay. I just jumped up too quickly."

"Are you sure?"

"Yes, I promise. I heard yelling. I thought you were in trouble."

Amaris sighed and kissed Logan's cheek. "You were coming to my rescue?" Amaris asked with a small smile. She couldn't help it.

"Of course," Logan said seriously.

"One of my exes called me because supposedly, we made the cover of some magazines. She couldn't believe I'd gotten married so we kind of had it out."

Logan tried not to let jealousy overtake her. Of course, Amaris had been with women before her, hell she was with Lani, so that meant she would have exes.

"Why does it matter?"

"She wanted to be with me, so she was shocked when she saw us."

"Do I have something to worry about?"

"Lo, I'm your wife, you have nothing to worry about."

Logan smiled, feeling the tension leave her body. "Okay."

Amaris straddled Logan and planted soft kisses all over Logan's face. Logan didn't know why she loved that gesture so much. It was something about the way Amaris took the time to kiss each of her eyes, her nose, her cheeks, forehead, and then lips. It was soft and genuine.

"Do you want breakfast, love?"

"I'm still kind of tired. Do you mind if I sleep a little longer?"

"Of course not, but I'm going to order breakfast."

"Okay, baby."

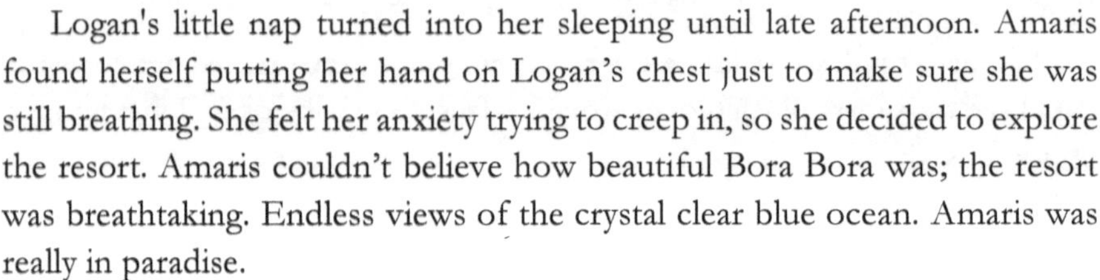

Logan's little nap turned into her sleeping until late afternoon. Amaris found herself putting her hand on Logan's chest just to make sure she was still breathing. She felt her anxiety trying to creep in, so she decided to explore the resort. Amaris couldn't believe how beautiful Bora Bora was; the resort was breathtaking. Endless views of the crystal clear blue ocean. Amaris was really in paradise.

Logan couldn't believe she'd slept all day. When she looked at the phone, she was surprised to see that it was after four in the afternoon. There was a letter on the pillow from Amaris telling her she was exploring the resort. Logan felt bad for leaving her alone on their honeymoon. She slowly eased out of bed and headed for the shower.

Amaris was in her own world when a man decided to join her at her table. "Hello beautiful, what are you doing here sitting alone?"

Amaris took a sip of her Sex On The Beach while staring at the uninvited man. He wasn't bad looking, he was actually gorgeous with his chocolate skin and bald head. He was shirtless and definitely worked out, but he wasn't Logan.

"I'm enjoying the amazing view and enjoying some peace and quiet."

"Are you here alone? I'd love to take you to dinner."

Amaris felt Logan before she even spoke. Her presence wrapped around her like a blanket. "Sorry my man, she's already taken, matter of fact, she's here on her honeymoon. Isn't that right Mrs. Maddox?"

When Amaris turned around, her breath got caught in her throat. Logan was in swim trunks and a sports bra. Her dreads were hanging and her body was glistening. Amaris could smell the coconut oil mixed with Logan's natural scent. Her nostrils flared as her hormones tried to take over.

"Yes, that's right. This is my wife, Logan Maddox."

"Logan Maddox from Maddox Publishing?" The man asked, shocked.

"Yes, that's me."

"Yo, your shit is the truth."

"Thank you." Logan was flat with him. When she found Amaris sitting at the table alone she took the opportunity to admire her wife. Amaris looked amazing, she had on a beautiful yellow flowy dress, her hair was still pressed and flat ironed, her skin looked flawless under the sun. But then, her view was ruined by the motherfucka who decided to sit with her.

"If you'll excuse us, we're going to go explore." Logan extended her hand and Amaris took it with no hesitation. Without saying anything else, Logan led her away from the table. When they were far enough to Logan's liking, Logan cornered Amaris until she backed into a tree.

Logan's eyes were shooting daggers at Amaris. "You are mine," she growled. Her jealousy had gotten the best of her. First this morning and now this, it irked the shit out of her. Amaris felt the anger radiating off of Logan.

"Hey," Amaris said as she gently grabbed Logan's face. "I am yours." Amaris confirmed.

Amaris pulled Logan down into a kiss for reassurance. She never wanted Logan to think she would entertain anyone else. She took marriage seriously and she loved Logan too much to fuck anything up. "I love you, Lo."

Logan rested her forehead against Amaris taking in the essence of her. "I love you too. I'm hungry."

Amaris giggled while connecting their hands. "Let's get you some food."

<hr>

They enjoyed the rest of the day exploring Bora Bora. They took a tour around the island and tried some of the best authentic food they'd ever had. Logan just enjoyed watching Amaris interact with the locals and take pictures of the island. When she was behind that lens you couldn't tell her anything. She loved how passionate she was about her craft. It was the same way she felt about writing.

"Favorite food?" Logan lathered Amaris's hair as they stood under the shower. Amaris had the answer, but the way Logan was working her scalp had her in ecstasy. She wondered what Logan wasn't good at. "Did you hear me, baby?"

"Yes, sorry. My favorite food is pasta, I can eat any type of pasta in any type of sauce. I'll eat it every day. What about you?"

"Asian food. Fucking love it."

"Really?"

"Yup." Their relationship was so unconventional. They were literally getting to know each other while starting their marriage. "Coke or Pepsi?"

"Pepsi all the way."

Logan smiled. "That's my girl. Lean back for me."

Amaris leaned back into the shower and allowed Logan to wash her hair. It was one of the most intimate experiences. They enjoyed the silence between them, the only sound in the room was their breathing and the shower running.

After their shower they dressed for dinner. Amaris was shocked when Logan led her to the beach where there was a candlelit dinner waiting for them.

"You've thought of everything haven't you?" Amaris stood on her tippy toes to kiss Logan.

"I wanted our trip to be perfect."

"Well, it is."

"Good." Logan pulled a chair out for Amaris to sit. Once they were seated, the waiter pulled the lids off their plates and Amaris burst into laughter.

"How the hell did you work so quickly, woman?" Amaris asked in wonder. The most delicious plate of lobster alfredo sat in front of them. Her mouth watered just thinking about tasting it.

"When you were doing your hair, I called it in. I hope you enjoy it, Mrs. Maddox."

Amaris loved when Logan called her Mrs. Maddox. It was something about the way she said it, so possessive.

"Thank you, baby." Amaris twirled a fork full of pasta around before stuffing her mouth. Her eyes rolled behind her head, the pasta had to be one of the best dishes she'd ever eaten. The lobster just melted in her mouth. "Oh my God, this is so freaking good." Amaris did her little happy dance and Logan chuckled.

"You dance when you eat?"

"Oh, yeah."

"You're so freaking cute."

"Have you talked to mom just to check in with her?"

"No."

"You should call her after dinner. Just to let her know you're okay."

"I'm grown, love."

"Yes you are, but we're still going to call." Amaris knew Kayman was probably worried about Logan. It wouldn't hurt just to ease her mind. "You're hard-headed, aren't you?" Amaris quizzed.

Logan chuckled while taking a sip of her wine. "No."

"I think you are. You don't like to take orders when it comes to yourself, but you have a wife now and I just want you to know I don't play that shit."

Logan quirked her eyebrows. "Excuse me?"

"I'd never do anything to steer you wrong or put you in harm's way. It's me and you, we're a team. So, if I ask you to do something, it will always be in your best interest, okay?"

"Okay." What else could Logan say to that. She was stunned that Amaris low key put her in her place. It was hard for her to loosen the reins on her life. It'd been just her for so long, she needed to get used to having someone there. Not only was Amaris there, she was her wife.

After dinner, Amaris grabbed her phone and called Kayman.

"Amaris, is everything okay?" Kayman asked in a panic. This was the reason Amaris wanted Logan to call home.

"Hey mom, everything is fine, it's perfect actually."

"Oh good. I thought—"

"Don't, it's okay," Amaris cut her off. "Matter of fact, someone wants to speak with you." Amaris passed her phone to Logan.

Logan grabbed the phone. "Hello mother."

"Hi sweetheart, are you okay?"

"I'm great, Amaris is taking good care of me."

"Good." Kayman responded.

Amaris signaled to Logan that she was stepping out and walked onto the patio to give them some privacy.

"Are you guys getting along?" Kayman was worried about Logan and Amaris feeling like they made a mistake. They really didn't know each other, but Kayman would never be the one to step in the way of someone being happy and she loved them together.

"We're doing well, Amaris is amazing. Bora Bora is so beautiful and peaceful too."

"Good, that's what I like to hear."

"Is everything going as planned with production?"

"Yes, your dad checked today and they're still on schedule. You know Daddy would raise hell if things are not track, so you have nothing to worry about." That put Logan at ease. She knew she couldn't stop production because of her honeymoon, so she felt good that her parents were still looking out for her.

"Thanks mom. I'm going to get off the phone now and go enjoy my wife."

Kayman smiled to that. "I love you sweetheart."

"I love you too. I'll check in again."

"Thank you." Her mother replied.

Logan ended the call and went to seek Amaris out. She found her on the patio. She was staring out at the water, lost in her own thoughts. Logan wondered what she was thinking about.

She walked up behind her and stood there. Amaris leaned against Logan as tears fell down her eyes.

"I want to travel the world with you. I want time with you." Amaris was fine until she had time to herself. Staring into the darkness of the ocean, everything suddenly hit her like a ton of bricks. Each day that passed, Logan's heart was growing weaker.

Logan turned Amaris around so she could look at her. The hurt in her eyes nearly broke Logan. Regret was starting to settle in the pit of her stomach. All those reasons not to be involved with someone were coming up. "We'll have plenty of time, baby. Don't think about the alternative. I'll be okay." Amaris hated herself for crying, but the thought of Logan dying was gut wrenching.

"I'm sorry for crying, but you've become my life so quickly. I don't know what I would do without you."

"Don't think about it Amaris. I told you I would fight and I will. Stop crying, love, it'll be okay." Logan wrapped Amaris in her arms as she cried into her chest until she had no tears left. Logan remained silent and allowed Amaris to be vulnerable. She knew this was what Amaris needed.

Once her shoulders stopped shaking, Logan scooped her up and carried her to the room. "You shouldn't be carrying me," Amaris said sleepily.

Logan smirked while laying Amaris in the bed. "I'll carry you for as long as I can, Mrs. Maddox."

Amaris's eyes were so heavy she didn't argue with Logan. Logan watched as she peacefully drifted off to sleep. Surprisingly, Logan wasn't sleepy, so she grabbed her laptop, sat on the patio and got to work.

It was the wee hours in the morning when Logan finally returned to their room. Amaris was still fast asleep. Logan took the moment to admire her wife. She was completely naked; at some point she must have woken up and undressed while Logan was on the patio working. The view of Amaris mocha chocolate body made Logans mouth salivate. Her breast slowly moved up and down from her light breathing. Her nipples were slightly erect from the fan above them. Logan wanted to tug them with her teeth. She wanted to do a lot more to her wife at that moment. Logan set her laptop down and opened her drawer. After taking a moment to slide on her strap she joined Amaris in bed. Logan gently spread Amaris legs laying between them. Amaris responded immediately wrapping her legs around Logan. "My love," she said sleepily.

"I want you Amaris."

Amaris could hear the huskiness in Logans voice causing her to open her eyes. Logans eyes were filled with want which instantly turned her on. "I am yours Logan, have me however you want me."

Just those words were almost Logans undoing. She couldn't believe she'd found a woman who so willingly gave themselves to her mentally, emotionally, and physically.

Amaris tongue traced Logans lower lips pulling her away from her thoughts. Logan sucked Amaris tongue into her mouth as she entered her at the same time. Amaris gasped feeling Logan fill her pussy with her strap. "Logan," she cried out from pure pleasure.

"This will not be quick Amaris, you're going to beg me to let you cum before we're finished." Logan pulled out of Amaris running the head of her strap up and down Amaris wet folds. Amaris quivered under her as her pussy moistened from the teasing. If this was just the beginning, she wouldn't make it to the end. A simple touch from Logan could send her body into a sex haze.

"You can't tease me like this wife."

"Oh, but I can." Logan cupped Amaris breast taking her time to run the tip of her tongue over her hardened nipples. She would never get tired of her wife's sweet taste. She sucked her nipples greedily, licking and biting them like a mad man. Amaris couldn't help herself from beginning to pant. Logan was so ruthless with her tongue. "Bite harder baby." Logan obliged Amaris and nipped her breast a little harder causing Amaris to moan louder.

Amaris bucked her hips wanting to feel Logan inside of her again. "Please," she begged.

Logan slowly entered Amaris filling her again, but just as soon as she did she slowly pulled out allowing Amaris to feel all eight inches. Before Amaris could protest Logan slammed herself back inside of her. Amaris yelped in pleasure. "Oh my God." Logan smiled as she rotated her hips slowly in and out of Amaris. She could feel how slick Amaris got by the way she easily stroked her.

"You can not fuck me like this," Amaris moaned.

"And why not?"

"It's fucking tortuous."

Logan smirked as she buried her face in the crook of Amaris' neck. Amaris wrapped her arms and legs around Logan drawing her in deeper. "I love you so much baby, I'm so happy that you're my wife," Logan whispered into Amaris' ear.

Amaris didn't know why Logans words had made her so emotional. Maybe it was the love she heard in Logans voice, or the way Logan was making love to her right now. "I love you too." Amaris began to meet Logans pace. Logan raised her head staring into Amaris' eyes as she grinded inside of her. She didn't pull out of Amaris anymore, she kept all of her strap inside of Amaris touching the deepest parts of her. They continued holding eye contact as they made love to one another. Their love spread throughout the sheets and across their bodies. Both women could feel the intensity of what they were experiencing. They both knew it was more than sex, it was a claiming of two souls becoming one.

"I am yours forever Amaris," Logan said breathlessly. Logan never wanted to be without Amaris. Amaris had consumed her entire being.

"And I am yours Logan. In this life and in our next life. I will always be yours." Amaris declared and she meant it. She never wanted to experience this with anyone else, in this life and in her next. She would do everything in her power to remember Logan and then she would find her and fall in love all over again.

"Cum for me."

"As you wish," Amaris gave Logan a sly smile before flipping them over. She straddled Logan while easily sliding down on her strap. Logan wished like hell that her strap was real. What she would give to feel Amaris for real. She watched in awe as Amaris took her in and began to wind her hips. "It feels so good baby," she moaned.

Logan palmed Amaris breast as Amaris bounced on top of her. Gone was the slowness of their love making, Amaris was now desperately fucking Logan. Logan etched the vision of Amaris breast bouncing in her face as she lost herself. "God you're fucking sexy Amaris."

Logan slid her index finger in Amaris mouth, Amaris gladly sucked it as she bounced harder and faster. She was hitting her g spot and on the brink of an explosive orgasm. "I'm so close."

Logan sat up wrapping her arms around Amaris, crushing their breast together and she started to thrust her hips upward to meet Amaris. Amaris eyes rolled behind her head as Logan hit a spot she didn't know existed. "Oh shit, oh shit, oh shit Logan!"

"Um hmm give me that cum baby."

The headboard slammed against the wall as they fucked each other harder. Sweat trickled down their bodies but neither cared, nothing was going to stop this moment, well nothing but Amaris orgasm. Logan was glad they had their own bungalow because the way Amaris screamed and moaned when her orgasm took over the neighbors would have surely called security.

"Logan! Logan! Oh God Logan!" Amaris body shook uncontrollably as she felt like her body short circuited. Her orgasm rippled through her body causing her to collapse onto Logans chest. Logan held her tight while she enjoyed the high she felt.

"Are you okay my love?"

Amaris lazily shook her head laying it on Logans shoulder. "I think I died and came back."

Logan burst into laughter. "That good huh?"

"Fucking amazing." When she gained some of her strength back, she finally rose to stare at her wife. "You should wake me up like that more often Mrs. Maddox."

"I will keep that in mind Mrs. Maddox."

CHAPTER

15

THREE WEEKS LATER

Logan put her head on her desk as she felt the tightening of her chest. Tears sprung to her eyes as she tried to take her next breath. Each time she tried to breathe, the pain intensified. She needed her pills, but she couldn't get up to grab them. "Come on Logan," she said to herself, trying to give herself a pep talk. She'd made it past a month, but still hadn't gotten the page telling her she had a new heart.

"Mrs. Maddox!" Her new temporary assistant, Kylee ran to her aid.

"Get my pills, please." Logan pulled at her tie, loosening it. She thought her heart was going to give out at any moment. Kylee frantically grabbed the pills. Usually, her isosorbide dinitrate pills would relieve the pain in her chest, she hoped they did the trick now. Logan took one and swallowed it without water. She thanked God when the pain started to subside. Logan sat back in her chair with her eyes closed trying to recover.

"Should I call Amaris?"

"No, it's fine. I just need a second." Logan wiped the tears from her eyes.

"Are you sure? You're not looking good." Kylee didn't want Amaris to rip her head off for not telling her what was going on with Logan.

"No, I'm okay. I just need a minute."

"Okay, let me know if you need anything."

"Thank you."

Amaris was in her zone as she snapped pictures of the Maddox's new building. It was coming along so well. She was so thankful Logan's parents gave her the opportunity.

It'd been three weeks since they came back from their honeymoon and she thought they were settling into married life well. It was so funny to her that she actually had to get to know her wife. She thought they were doing well and she enjoyed getting to know Logan. At times, Logan was difficult because she was so hard-headed, but then she would make it all up from her being an asshole by just kissing her. She couldn't believe Logan had her wrapped like that.

Three weeks passed and she was thankful God had given her more time with Logan. They were past the one month mark and Logan was still going strong. She prayed every day that Logan would get a new heart soon.

Amaris took her phone out to check on Logan. They promised each other they would check in every few hours and Amaris realized she hadn't heard from Logan.

"Hi wife." Logan's voice boomed through the phone.

Amaris first thought was that Logan's voice was off. It sounded strained. "Hi baby, how are you?"

"I'm good, just busy. How's work going?"

"Work is good, the building is coming along nicely. I think mom and dad will be pleased with the pictures."

"Good. Glad to hear that baby."

Amaris slid her camera behind her back as she started to head for her car. "What do you want for dinner, Lo?"

Logan sat back in her seat feeling spent, she was in so much pain she could barely think. "I don't know, baby, whatever you want to make is fine by me." She wanted to get off the phone, but she knew that would alert Amaris.

"You're no help," Amaris chided.

"Hey love, I have a meeting in a few minutes I have to get ready. I'll call you right after, okay?"

"Okay, I love you."

"I love you too." Logan ended the call and finally let out the groan she was holding in.

It was like something was sending shock waves through her body, which led straight to her heart. Logan stood up and slowly walked over to the window. She leaned her forehead against the cold glass. It felt so good at the moment.

Ten minutes later, her doors opened and she turned around and was shocked to see Amaris standing there. "Amaris? What are you doing here?"

Amaris knew something was wrong with Logan the moment she heard Logan's voice over the phone.

Amaris walked over to the window where Logan stood. Logan was drenched in sweat; she looked disheveled, nothing like she usually looked. Purple rings under her eyes looked like they didn't belong on her beautiful chocolate skin. She looked clammy.

"I'm taking you home." Amaris was pissed. She told Logan that no matter how hard things got, she would have to be honest with how she felt.

Logan could tell by the look on Amaris's face that she wasn't bullshitting. So, instead of fighting her, she grabbed her laptop and followed Amaris out of the office. The silence was killing Logan. She forgot what it felt like to be in a relationship. The thought of Amaris being mad at her sent a wave of nausea to her stomach.

"Amaris—" Logan tried to break the silence between them.

"Don't." Amaris cut her off, fighting back her tears as she drove them home.

"Amaris, I—"

"I said don't! Let me just get you home." Logan leaned back in her seat and remained quiet. If Amaris was anyone else, she would have gotten cussed out for speaking to her that way, but it was Amaris, her wife. She knew she was an asshole for breaking her promise. She was already thinking of ways to make it up to her.

Logan couldn't get out of the car quick enough when Amaris pulled into the parking lot. They rode the elevator upstairs to their penthouse in silence.

Amaris walked into the kitchen and set her camera down. Her emotions were going everywhere. She was mad and sad. Logan was so frustrating.

Logan walked into the kitchen already dreading their conversation. Amaris had her back turned from her. "I'm sorry," she said in a soft voice.

Amaris whipped around, fire blazing in her eyes. "You lied to me!"

"I didn't want you to worry, baby."

"You. Lied. To. Me." Amaris exaggerated every word. "I am your wife and you lied to me!"

"I didn't—"

"You said you would be honest no matter what. I told you that I can feel you, Logan. I see you. I knew the moment I heard your voice something was wrong."

"I'm sorry, baby."

"If this is what our marriage is going to be, I don't want it." Just hearing those words hurt Amaris, she didn't mean it.

Logan closed the space between them backing Amaris into the counter. "What did you say?"

"You heard me. I won't have a marriage where my wife can't be truthful."

The thought of Amaris not being her wife hurt more than any type of pain that she was in.

Logan leaned her forehead against Amaris's, surprising her. Their connection instantly affected Amaris.

Tears fell down her cheeks. "Amaris, I will never lie to you again. Please, don't leave me." Logan choked back tears.

Amaris wrapped her arms around Logan's neck. "Don't make me."

"It's just that I see what my condition does to my family and now it's doing it to you. You're constantly worried about me. It makes me feel like shit."

Amaris held Logan's hands bringing them to her heart. "When you asked me to marry you and I said yes, it meant I accepted everything. I can handle it, Logan, so I need you to be honest with me. We're a team. I'm your wife. I need to know what's happening."

"Okay baby, okay. I'm sorry."

Amaris ran her hand down Logan's face. "I see you."

Logan sighed. "I love you so much, Amaris. So fucking much."

Amaris pulled Logan into a hug. She held onto Logan for dear life and Logan did the same. They stood there embracing each other pouring into one another.

"Today, it felt like somebody was squeezing my chest. I couldn't catch my breath, my body is aching so bad," Logan confessed.

"Should I call your doctor? Do you think we need to go to the ER?"

Logan sat on the barstool shaking her head. "No, my heart is getting weaker. My body is going to start shutting down on me, Amaris." Finally realizing that made her condition all too real. "My heart is weak," Logan whispered.

Amaris wrapped herself around Logan as if she could shield her from the truth. "But you're strong, my love. We've made it past a month. You just have to hold on a little longer. Your new heart is coming." Amaris kissed Logan's cheeks, forehead, nose, and then lips slowly. She knew Logan liked it when she did that because her body would instantly relax.

"We'll get through this. We'll be strong together. I'll breathe for you when you feel like you can't."

Logan looked at Amaris with admiration in her eyes. She didn't realize how good it would feel to have someone fighting with her. She had already told herself she was going to do this alone, but having Amaris, having someone to come home to was worth it.

Amaris placed her hand in the center of Logan's heart. She then grabbed Logan's hand and placed it in the center of her heart. She needed them to remember their connection, remember what they were fighting for. They were a team. "It's me and you baby. We'll breathe together. Close your eyes for me."

Logan closed her eyes as she felt Amaris's heartbeat through the palm of her hand. "Let's breathe together, love, we're going to anchor in some positive vibes and picture you healthy with your new heart."

"Baby, I don't know how—"

"Nope, stop that. Just picture yourself healthy with a new heart. Now, breathe with me."

Logan followed Amaris's breathing, while trying to picture herself healthy with her new heart. She saw herself at her movie premier with Amaris on her arm. She then saw herself sitting in the sand at the beach. She was smiling, genuinely happy.

"Do you see yourself, baby?"

"Yes," Logan said breathlessly as the tears cascaded down her eyes. The peace she felt was overwhelming and the tears she didn't know she was holding onto came pouring out.

"It's okay, baby, it's okay. I got you." Amaris held Logan tight as she wailed like a baby.

"I don't want to die," Logan cried. She'd never been as scared as she was now. She always thought she would get a new heart before it came to this point, but now she felt like death would be knocking on her door soon and that terrified her. It was crippling.

"You're not going to die." Amaris let her own tears fall. "You just need to hold on a little longer, that's all."

Logan's body shook as the agony of everything suffocated her.

"Let it out, baby, it's okay. Let it out."

•———— • •●• • ———— •

Amaris stared at Logan from the doorway; she was fast asleep in bed. Amaris was finally able to calm her down enough to get pain meds in her system and to put her to sleep.

Amaris closed the door and headed to the room Logan had prepared for her when she first moved in. Her heart was hammering in her chest as her anxiety attack took over. She made it to the room and closed the door before collapsing to the floor. It felt like the walls were closing in on her as she tried to catch her breath. She tried to remember her breathing techniques, but couldn't focus.

"Come on, Amaris," she said to herself. Her vision became blurry as she spiraled. Today was too much. She'd been doing good since she moved to Vegas, but today had really challenged her. Amaris knew she was going to pass out, so she tried to brace herself as she felt her eyes roll behind her head.

Logan woke up in the middle of the night and Amaris wasn't in bed. "Baby?" she called groggily. The pain meds were still heavy in her system. "Amaris?" she called for again, but no answer. Logan looked at the clock on her dresser and saw that it was a little after one in the morning. Logan's body felt so heavy and she felt sleep trying to take over, but she needed Amaris in bed.

Logan pulled her legs over the bed so she could sit up. "Shit!" The pills were so strong she could barely focus. "Get up, Logan," she prepped herself. It took her another ten minutes to finally get out of bed. She leaned against the wall as she forced herself to walk down the hallway. Her legs felt like jelly. "Amaris?" Logan called out for her again and again.

Amaris heard her name being called, but it sounded so faint. "Amaris?" the distress in Logan's voice is what made her finally come to.

"Shit." Amaris couldn't believe she'd allowed herself to pass out. She hadn't had a bad anxiety attack like that in a while. She opened the door and caught Logan down the hallway. "What's wrong, baby?"

Logan whipped around, surprised to see Amaris. "Where did you come from?"

Amaris wrapped herself under Logan's arm to support her. "Why are you out of bed, love? Let's get you back."

Logan wanted to ask Amaris what happened to her, but the mention of bed made Logan's body feel even heavier.

"Okay."

Amaris helped Logan back to bed. "Lay with me, Mrs. Maddox." Her eyes felt so heavy she knew she was going to be out soon.

"Of course, I'm going to lay with you." Amaris stripped out of her clothes and slid under the cover with Logan. Logan scooted closer to Amaris wanting contact with her skin. She ran her hand across Amaris's stomach.

Logan didn't know why she thought about a baby growing inside of Amaris at that moment. "I want babies with you," she blurted out.

Amaris turned on her side so she could see Logan's face. "Do you?"

"Yes."

She caressed Logan's cheek. "Well, my love, lets enjoy each other a little longer before we add kids. We should be dating and married for at least a year before we add a little one." They both giggled. They'd technically been dating and married for a month.

"Yeah, I think you're right."

"You should get some rest, Lo."

"Okay, baby." Amaris leaned over and gave Logan a short peck on the lips. Logan wrapped Amaris in her arms and they both drifted off to sleep.

———— • •●• • ————

"Hey mom?" Amaris called out as she walked into the Maddox's home. She was having lunch with Kayman and Taylor and she was super excited about it. She always enjoyed spending time with her mother and sister-in-law.

"We're in here," Kayman answered.

"We?" Amaris whispered. She didn't see Taylor's car out there yet.

When she walked into the dining room and saw her mom she almost passed out. "Mom!" Ms. Cole smiled as Amaris ran into her arms. This was the longest they'd gone without seeing each other. Amaris hadn't seen her mom since her wedding. Her mom wanted to give her and Logan space to get settled.

"Hi my baby, I've missed you so much."

"I missed you too mom, you have no idea." Amaris hugged her mother tight. "How did you get here?"

"Well, Logan thought you might need some mother-daughter time so she sent a plane for me. I flew in this morning."

"Seriously?"

"Yes."

Amaris was touched by Logan's gesture. "Let me call her." Amaris took her phone out and dialed Logan's number.

"Hey Mrs. Maddox."

"I love you, you know that?"

Logan smiled as she watched the scene play out on set. "You liked your surprise?"

"Of course, I did. Thank you so much for bringing my mom out."

"No need to thank me, love. I know you missed her, but listen, I'm in the middle of this scene. Can I call you in a few?"

"Of course. Take it easy today. I love you."

"I love you too, Amaris." They ended the call.

After brunch and a little shopping, Amaris finally had some alone time with her mom. Logan had called and told her she was going to be late because she was wrapping up the final scene for her movie. Amaris was excited for her.

"So baby, how are you? How is married life treating you?" They were sitting out on the rooftop, watching the sunset.

"Married life is okay."

"Just okay?" Ms. Cole asked, concerned.

"Everything is fine, although some days it's hard with Logan's condition. I had a really bad anxiety attack a few nights ago, I passed out," Amaris said, ashamed.

"You've been stressing? You know you have to take care of yourself first, Amaris."

"I know mom. It was just a bad day."

"Have you been taking your medicine?"

"Everyday."

Ms. Cole held Amaris's hand. She was worried that Amaris was going to neglect herself trying to take care of Logan. Ms. Cole felt like this was too much for Amaris to take on, but she wouldn't butt into her life.

"If you're not okay, no one will be okay. If things get too rough I think you should hire someone to help take care of Logan."

"I'm sure Kayman has a plan set in motion if it comes to that." Amaris prayed that it didn't.

"Well, whatever you do, just make sure you're okay as well."

"I will mom."

— ·· • ·· —

"Alright everybody, that's a wrap!" Logan yelled as they shot the final scene. "We did it!" Everyone celebrated.

"Hey, listen up everyone," Logan yelled through the bullhorn quieting everyone. "I want to thank everyone who worked so hard on this project. This is my baby, but you all worked like it was yours. Now I don't know if I'll be here for the premier …" She fought back tears as some of the workers got teary eyed. "If I'm not there, I want you all to represent, be proud of the work you've done because I know that I am. I love you all so much and this has been an experience I'll never forget. So, thank you for your hard work." Everyone applauded.

Logan looked at her watch and noticed it was well past midnight. "Now, I'm going home to my wife. I will see you all at the wrap party on Friday." Logan said her goodbyes and headed home. She couldn't wait to get home to Amaris, she was so busy all day they hadn't really had the chance to talk.

Amaris was fast asleep when Logan finally made it home. She loved the fact that Amaris slept naked. The sight of her beautiful chocolate skin made

Logan's mouth water. They hadn't had sex in over a week because Logan wasn't up to it, but tonight she wanted her wife. It was a joyous night and she wanted to celebrate.

Logan looked down at her chest. "Okay, keep your shit together for at least an hour." Logan stripped out of her clothes.

Amaris almost lost her shit when she felt someone lay on top of her. She was in such a deep sleep she hadn't heard Logan come in. The panic left her body once she felt Logan's lips on hers. Fear turned into pure pleasure as Logan slid her tongue into Amaris mouth. She felt like it'd been ages since Logan touched her like this.

Amaris moaned as Logan started grinding against her. "Are you sure baby?" Amaris didn't want Logan to over exert herself.

"I want you, Mrs. Maddox." That was all Amaris needed to hear to get her pussy wet. She started to meet Logan's thrust. Their moans began to fill the air as they both got lost in one another.

Logan loved being with Amaris in this way. No strap, just their pussies grinding against each other. Amaris was always so wet and ready for her, the friction felt good against her clit. "Amaris, you feel so good, baby." Amaris flipped them over straddling Logan. She let out a soft moan as she continued their grinding.

"Logan, I've missed this so much." Sex with Logan was beyond anything she could explain. Their connection was already deep, but when they had sex, it was unearthly.

"Me too, baby." Logan almost lost her shit when Amaris slid down and covered her pussy with her mouth. "Oh my God, Amaris." Logan had never been as open with sex with anyone the way she was with Amaris. She was usually the one doing the pleasing, but Amaris gave just as much as she received.

"You taste so good, my love." Amaris twirled her tongue around Logan's clit causing Logan to moan loudly.

"Why are you teasing me, woman?" Amaris giggled mischievously. She knew exactly what she was doing. She swiped her tongue across Logan's clit again making her shake. "You're playing now."

"Just a little."

Logan wrapped her hands between Amaris's afro. "Suck it."

Amaris shuddered at Logan's command. "Say it again."

"Suck it."

Amaris made eye contact with Logan as she began to suck her clit. Logan's head spun as Amaris licked and sucked her clit. "Oh my God, baby," she moaned. Amaris gripped Logan's hips as she lap her juices up like it was her last meal.

"I'm close," Logan moaned in ecstasy. Her heart was pounding, she tried to steady her breathing as the tingling sensation ran through her body. She knew if she didn't cum quickly she might pass out from lack of oxygen.

"Are you okay, baby?"

Amaris looked up at Logan. "Yes," Logan said, breathlessly. Amaris crawled back to the top of the bed straddling Logan.

"I want to see you cum." She also wanted to make sure Logan was really okay.

"Is that right?"

"Yes." Amaris began a slow grind, allowing Logan to match her. They kissed passionately as they matched each other. Amaris connected their hands, opening herself completely to Logan. Logan felt the shift of energy in the room. It was as if everything between them intensified. Both of their hips bucked against each other.

"You're so fucking sexy, Mrs. Maddox."

"I love when you call me Mrs. Maddox," Amaris confessed

Logan bit her bottom lip as she felt her orgasm nearing. "I'm going to cum."

"Okay baby. Cum for me, baby."

Logan started to quicken her pace and Amaris matched hers. "Oh shit, Amaris." Logan bit her lip as she felt her body shudder from her orgasm.

Logan felt like her senses short circuited as Amaris's continuous grind made her cum again. "Fuck, fuck, fuck!" Her body shook under Amaris.

Amaris grabbed Logan's face and kissed her sloppily as her own orgasm took over her. Logan brought Amaris down onto her chest and they stayed like that enjoying each other.

Amaris planted soft kisses on Logan's shoulder blade as Logan caressed her back.

"I really do love being like this with you, Amaris. Being so close to you brings me so much peace."

Amaris smiled as she listened to Logan's heartbeat. "It's been a while, my love."

"I know. Let's not go that long again."

"Agreed."

"Guess what?"

"What?"

"We wrapped the movie shoot today."

Amaris sat up excitedly. "Baby, that's so fucking awesome! I'm so sorry I missed it. We have to celebrate!"

"We just did," Logan joked.

Amaris playfully smacked Logan. "I'm serious."

"We're having a wrap party this Friday. Can you take pictures?"

"Yes love, you don't even have to ask that. "This will be our first event together as a married couple."

Logan smiled at the realization. "Oh yeah, it is. I better pull out the big guns in my closet." Logan ran her hands through Amaris's hair. "Even on your worst day, no one can top you. You're so gorgeous, Amaris."

Amaris locked eyes with Logan. "I love you, Logan."

"And I love you. Always."

CHAPTER

16

You know they say you always have that one last good day before things go downhill. Logan wished she knew her last good day would come so soon, she would have tried to etch every detail into her memory, but life is unpredictable.

Amaris raised her camera and snapped a picture of Logan. She looked so good standing there in her burgundy suit while the tailor did measurements on her. Logan was getting fitted for her movie wrap party and looking how that suit fit her, Amaris knew she was going to turn heads.

"Logan, you look so damn good," Amaris complimented.

Logan blushed as she posed playfully for Amaris. "Thanks love. Your dress should be here later today. Will you have time to make sure it fits?"

"Yeah, my gig should be over around two."

"Okay, perfect. I can't wait to see you in it."

Amaris walked over to Logan and gave her a quick kiss. "I can't wait for you to see me in it and out of it. Now, I'm going to get out of here. I don't want to be late for my meeting."

Amaris tried to run off, but Logan grabbed her hand and gently pulled her back to her. "Can't be running out of here so fast, Mrs. Maddox. Give me a proper kiss goodbye."

Amaris knew Logan wouldn't let her go if she didn't, which made her blush. So, she gave Logan the proper kiss she was asking for. Logan let out a moan she didn't know she was holding onto. Amaris smirked and headed for the door.

"Next time, don't play with me." She stepped onto the elevator catching Logan's sparkling eyes.

"I love you, baby."

"I love you, Lo." Amaris blew Logan a kiss before the elevator doors closed.

Logan had a car waiting for Amaris when she made it downstairs. She shook her head while smiling. Her phone rang as she slid in the seat. She looked at her screen and saw Logan's face pop up. "I could have driven you know," she said as soon as she took the call.

"I know, but I wanted you to relax before your meeting. You're going to do great, Amaris. I'm so proud of you."

Amaris felt like her heart would explode. "You're a good wife, you know that?"

"I'm learning. Now knock them dead. Call me after."

"I will, lover." Amaris pressed end on her phone.

Amaris let out a long sigh and settled into her seat. Her hands were shaking from nervousness. Tasha had set up a meeting for her with an art gallery in Las Vegas. It was a small gallery in the art district, but Amaris didn't mind. She just loved having the opportunity to have her work displayed. Amaris didn't want to lose the artist aspect of herself because she moved to Vegas. She promised herself she wouldn't, so having this opportunity was major for her.

Before she knew it, she was downtown, pulling into the art gallery. "We're here, Mrs. Maddox," her driver, Thomas, said.

"Thank you, Thomas." Amaris grabbed her portfolio and headed inside.

"You know I've never seen you like this, Logan," Tosh, Logan's tailor acknowledged.

"Like what?"

"In love. You have it bad for that young lady." Tosh smiled while measuring Logan's arm.

"Yeah, I do have it bad for her. To think I wasted time being scared to love her because of my condition."

"I've been tailoring your suits from the beginning of your career and I've never seen the sparkle in your eye that's there now. I'm so happy for you. You deserve this."

Logan stopped Tosh from measuring and hugged him, surprising him. "Thank you, Tosh. I appreciate that." Tosh was their family tailor; she'd known him since she was a little girl. She used to watch him tailor for her father, so he was more like an uncle to her.

Tosh wiped his eyes. "You know I pray for you every day, Logan. I pray God blesses you with a heart."

"He will. I just have to hold on a little longer."

Logan smiled, feeling uneasy. "Amaris makes me want to hold on. Her love," Logan shook her head, "is unearthly, like nothing I've ever experienced before. I'm not ready to leave that."

"That's good, that'll keep you strong."

"I hope so Tosh, I hope so."

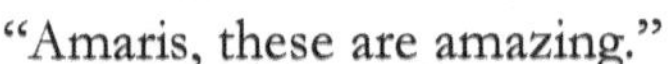

"Amaris, these are amazing."

Amaris smiled as the owner of the gallery went through her portfolio. "Thank you."

"When your manager, Tasha, reached out, I couldn't believe it. I was at your show in LA, I was surprised you'd want to display your work here. We're a small gallery."

"That doesn't bother me. I love what I do, I just want people to enjoy it as well."

"Well listen, we have a show coming up in two months. I would love for you to join the show." Amaris smiled, beaming from ear to ear.

"Awesome!"

"I'll get the paperwork to Tasha."

Amaris stood and shook Marcus's hand. "Thank you so much for the opportunity."

"Can't wait to see what you come up with."

"I can't wait to show you. Have a good day." She collected her things and headed out. Her mother was still in town because of Logan's party, so Amaris decided to head to the Maddox's estate to see what she was up to.

She found her out at the pool, soaking up the sun.

"You look comfortable," she told her mom with a small smile.

Ms. Cole pulled her glasses over her head. "Hey baby. I'm just enjoying my vacation. The Maddox's are so welcoming, I haven't had to lift a finger since I've been here."

Amaris sat next to her mom. Seeing her so relaxed made her happy. Ms. Cole had worked hard all of Amaris's life without complaining, she deserved to not have a care in the world.

"What have you been doing?" Amaris asked her mother.

"Exactly what I'm doing now, not a damn thing." They both laughed.

"So, I got into the show downtown."

"You did?! That's great. Congratulations baby."

"Thanks mom. It'll feel good to be back. I'm grateful for the job from the Maddox's, but you know I love to be free."

"I know. Here's your chance. Do you know the theme yet?"

"Not yet, Marcus is going to send the info to Tasha."

"Good. Now how is my other daughter?"

"She's good. When I left the house she was getting her suit tailored for the party."

"I'm so excited for the party, my first Hollywood event." Ms. Cole said excitedly.

"I am too. Do you need a dress? We can go shopping, I have some time to kill."

Ms. Cole jumped up with a schoolgirl smile. "You said the magic words."

Amaris laughed while standing up. "Well lady, let's go."

Logan was knee deep in work when she got an unexpected call. "Logan, you have Lani on line one," her assistant alerted her.

"Lani?"

"Yes, should I tell her to call you back?"

"No, no, it's fine." Logan didn't know why her heart sped up. She hadn't spoken to Lani since the hospital.

"Lani?"

"Hey boss, I just wanted to check in," Lani chirped through the phone. Logan sat back in her chair, relieved to hear Lani's voice.

"How are you, woman? I miss you," Logan admitted.

"I'm good. I miss you too, Lo."

"Where are you?"

"I'm in Greece."

"Greece?"

"Yes, it's beautiful here. It makes me never want to leave." She sounded happy and that made Logan's heart a little lighter. She'd been worried about Lani since she left, but knew she needed to give Lani some space.

"You are going to come back though, right?" There was silence on the phone for a bit. "Lani?"

"Yes, I'm going to come back," she finally spoke. "I saw that you guys got married." The sadness Logan didn't want to hear was there.

"Yeah, we did. About a month ago." Logan's eyes zeroed in on her wedding band. She cursed herself for not calling Lani and letting her know.

"You didn't waste any time."

"You know I have no time to waste. I love her Lani. I love her a lot," Logan confessed.

"Well, we both know she's easy to love." Logan bit her tongue to not say something slick to Lani. She didn't want to be reminded that Lani had Amaris.

"I finished the movie." Logan thought it was best to change the subject.

"You finished! That's great Logan! I'm so happy for you!"

"Thanks. I'm having a wrap party this Friday. You should come. We both worked really hard on the movie."

Lani bit her bottom lip contemplating her next words. She didn't know how to feel about the situation. Of course, she wanted to celebrate with Logan, but to be around Logan and Amaris might be too much, too soon.

"I can't," she whispered.

"Lani ..." Logan sighed. "I don't know how much time I have left. My health is getting worse. I want to see you before I die."

Lani took the phone away from her ear as her emotions took over. Hearing Logan talk about dying was something she would never get used to. After taking a moment, she put the phone to her ear again.

"You shouldn't talk like that, Lo."

"I don't have a heart, Lani. It's month two. My body aches constantly. Sometimes, I get these chest pains that I surely think is the end. I'm not getting better. So, just keep my time frame in mind, that's all I'm saying."

"Okay. Listen, I have to go. I'll talk to you later, Lo."

"I love you, Lani." Logan meant that. Lani was a good friend and she loved her dearly. "Always remember I love you." Tears fell from Lani's eyes at Logan's tenderness.

"I love you too, Logan."

"Bye Lani."

"Goodbye." Logan ended the call. She hoped that Lani would come back home, but she also understood if she didn't.

"Mrs. Maddox, I have Isis here." Logan took a moment to get herself together. "Okay, send her in." Isis was a prospective author she wanted to sign. She was a tough sell because she loved being independent, but Logan was determined.

In walked Isis in all her glory. She made sure her hips sashayed as Logan looked at her. Her locs swooshed side to side as she moved. Her caramel skin was flawless, lips luscious, smile out of this world, and a body sculpted by Zeus himself. She was bad and she knew it. The moment Logan met her, she wanted to take her to bed, but she knew it would be a mistake and now she was married, so she took herself out of her lust-filled thoughts.

"Isis, it's so nice to see you again." Logan walked around her desk and gave Isis a hug.

"Nice to see you too, Lo. How are you?"

"Oh you know, I'm breathing." She gave an uneasy smile while walking back to her desk. Standing was starting to be unbearable. "Have a seat. Can I get you anything?"

Isis sat across from Logan. "I have to confess something."

Logan's eyebrows raised in confusion. "Okay?"

"You broke my heart by getting married. I thought we had a connection. You flirted with me like crazy anytime we were in the same room and then boom, married. What's up with that?"

Logan chuckled uneasily. She wasn't expecting that. "We did have a connection, but I'm trying to sign you. I don't fuck my authors."

"And marriage?" she quizzed.

Logan's thoughts went to Amaris, she couldn't help the smile that grazed her lips. "I never thought I could feel so complete with someone until Amaris. She's my person. That's where the marriage came from."

Isis smiled. "I want to meet your wife."

"What?"

"I want to meet your wife," Isis said slowly.

"Why?"

"Because I want to meet this beautiful creature who captured the infamous Logan Maddox's heart."

Logan started to wonder if she was that bad. People were really shocked at the fact that she was married now. "Well, Amaris will be at the wrap party on Friday. You should come."

"I will."

"Now about me signing you. Are you done playing hard to get? Are you ready to sign with me?"

"Why should I?"

"Because you know you want to. It's three books, twenty city book tour to start, and an advance."

"I don't like being controlled Logan. That's why I'm independent. I get to put my own content out. I don't answer to anyone."

"Yeah that's nice, but with that you're not reaching your full potential. You're not reaching the audience you and I both know you could reach. Now what do you want? Give me a counter."

"One book, everything else stays the same."

Logan chuckled, feeling like that was a joke. "One book? You're crazy. That's not even worth my time and you want an advance?"

"I don't want to be tied down if this shit isn't what I want. One book, but it'll be the best book on your roster," Isis said confidently. Logan never signed anyone for less than three books.

"I have some heavy hitters on my roster Isis." She didn't want Isis to try to downplay her authors.

"Yeah, but I am the best you'll have."

Logan laughed, amused. She loved Isis' confidence. "One book, twenty city tour, no advance."

"One book, ten city tour, I don't give a fuck about the advance."

"Okay, deal?"

"Deal." They shook hands.

"I'll have the contract drawn up."

Logan smiled as she stared at herself in the mirror, she had to admit she looked damn good in her suit.

"So, should I fuck you now or later?" Amaris leaned against the door frame, eye-fucking Logan.

Logan smiled while putting her head down shyly. "Well, I would say now, but we really have to go."

Amaris sashayed into the room, looking every bit as sexy as Logan knew she would be. Her dress matched her suit perfectly. Her eyes zeroed in on the slits on each side of Amaris's dress. Her beautiful chocolate legs were on display, which made Logan want to feel what was between them.

"That dress looks fucking amazing on you. My God, woman." Logan wrapped Amaris in her arms giving her a quick kiss. Amaris held Logan's face staring at her for a moment. "What?"

"Give me a proper kiss."

Logan smiled, staring lovingly into Amaris's eyes. "If I do that we're going to end up fucking and Thomas has already been waiting for twenty minutes downstairs."

Amaris pouted while nuzzling Logan's neck. Her scent sent her hormones into a frenzy. She smelled so good, almost edible.

"You smell good, baby." Amaris planted soft kisses on her neck. Automatically, Logan palmed her ass.

"This has to be quick," she groaned.

Amaris smiled as Logan picked her up and sat her on the dresser. "Yeah, quick."

They finally made it downstairs an hour and a half later.

"Sorry, Thomas." Logan slid in the seat.

Amaris stared out the windows, smiling. Logan had fucked her all around their closet. Her body was still tingling from Logan's touch.

Logan slid her hand in Amaris's, bringing her attention away from the window. "You okay, babe?"

"Yeah, just thinking about how good you fucked me. I can still feel you on top of me."

Logan scooted closer to Amaris. "You taste so good, baby," Logan whispered in her ear. "So, do you and when we get home, I plan on tasting you again." Amaris slid her tongue

out and Logan took it into her mouth. If Thomas' throat clearing didn't distract them, Logan would have taken Amaris right there in the car.

"Sorry to interrupt, but we're here, Mrs. And Mrs. Maddox."

Amaris wiped Logan's lips. The paparazzi were already flashing pictures with them in the car.

Logan linked their hands. "Hey, if this becomes too much for you, let me know. I'm here for you, you can stick by my side."

"Okay love. Can you do me a favor?"

"Anything, Amaris."

"Enjoy this moment. You worked so hard on your movie and you did it while going through this. So, I want you to enjoy every moment of tonight."

Logan smiled while bringing Amaris's hands to her lips. "Okay, my love."

"Now, let's get out there so I can show my talented wife off."

After one last kiss, they exited the car.

"Logan, over here! Over here!" Paparazzi yelled.

Logan stuck her hand out for Amaris to take and Amaris slid her hand in hers, allowing her to help her out of the car. Logan wrapped Amaris under her protectively as they posed for pictures. The flashing lights were blinding, but she knew this was a part of the business. It would be great promotion for her movie.

Logan could see her family waiting at the doors along with Amaris's mother. She couldn't believe she'd pulled it off. She finished the movie on time. She thought about what Amaris said about enjoying the moment. She was going to enjoy every bit of tonight until she felt like someone squeezed her heart.

Amaris felt the moment Logan's hand slipped from hers. She was two steps ahead of her, but she saw the look of concern on Kayman's face. She turned around to see Logan clutching her chest. "Logan?"

Logan gasped for air that wouldn't come. She felt herself fall to her knees as Amaris made her way to her. "What is it, Logan?"

"I can't breathe," Logan whispered.

"Okay, okay, hold on love." Amaris loosened Logan's tie and unbuttoned the top button to her dress shirt. Tears welled up in Logan's eyes as she started to panic.

"Somebody call 911!" Amaris yelled.

Amaris wanted to cuss the people out who snapped pictures of Logan instead of helping.

"Logan, sweetie." Kayman and everyone else surrounded Logan shielding her from the paparazzi.

"I have 911 on the line and they're sending an ambulance," Xavier said while on the phone.

Amaris couldn't believe that this was happening again. She couldn't lose Logan, not now when they were in such bliss.

She held Logan's hand tight. "Logan, look at me, baby." she could already see Logan was about to lose consciousness. "Stay with me, love. Please, stay with me."

17

Logan never made it to her party. Her heart gave out as she laid there waiting for the ambulance. She could hear her mother calling her name. She could also hear Amaris calling for her, but she felt her body giving up on her. She couldn't do it anymore, the pain was too much.

Amaris sat in the waiting room with her face in her hands. This was supposed to be a night of celebration and they ended up at the hospital. Guilt started to eat away at her. She wondered if they did too much. Them having sex was too much on Logan's heart. Amaris wondered if she missed the signs. Her mind was going in every other direction trying to figure out if Logan seemed overly tired, did she look fatigued?

Tears ran down her eyes as she said a silent prayer asking the Lord to give Logan more time. She needed more time with her. Taylor sat next to Amaris, wrapping her arm around her shoulder and she leaned into her.

"How are you holding up, sis?" Taylor asked, sadness etched on her face.

"I'm not. What if this is my fault?"

"Why would it be your fault?"

"We had sex before we came, what if it was too much on her heart?"

"Hey," Taylor held her hands with Amaris. "Don't do that. Logan wouldn't want you to do that. You guys are newlyweds. Of course, you're going to have sex. Xavier and I fucked damn near every day when we got married." The girls shared a laugh.

"I can't lose her."

"You won't. We've been here before, sis."

"Do you remember what the doctor said? She gave her a month, three months tops. We're in month two, Taylor. My wife's heart is growing weaker," Amaris said, choking on tears. Taylor bit her lip to hold her tears back as Amaris broke down in her arms.

Amaris felt like someone was ripping her heart out. Her cries became deeper as pain rippled through her body. She didn't know how to survive in a world without Logan, not anymore. Ms. Cole sat on the other side of Amaris and together, she and Taylor wrapped her in a cocoon of love.

— · • ● • · —

It felt like hours before Dr. Stein finally came out from the back to speak with them. Amaris and Kayman were the first two out of their seats.

"How is she, Doctor?" Amaris asked, unable to keep the shaking out of her voice.

Dr. Stein looked exhausted and that scared Amaris to death. "She's stable now. It was very touch and go for a minute. Logan had another heart attack."

Kayman clutched her chest as Mr. Maddox held her up. "What do we do now Dr. Stein?" Mrs. Maddox asked, the pain in her voice evident. Everyone could see the sadness in Dr. Stein's eyes. They knew it wouldn't be news they wanted to hear.

"We're at the point where it's time to make Logan as comfortable as possible. She'll need to stay on oxygen. I'm sorry guys, but this is it, she won't last much longer."

Anything else Dr. Stein said, Amaris didn't hear. Everything in her went numb so the pain wouldn't take over. This was it, Logan was really dying.

Her partner and soulmate, would no longer be here with her. Amaris couldn't be there anymore, she felt like the walls were going to close in on her. All of a sudden, she couldn't breathe. She started to panic as dizziness took over.

Ms. Cole saw the signs of Amaris's panic attack, but before she could grab her, Amaris dashed out of the hospital.

She hoped the fresh air would help, but it didn't. She couldn't catch her breath. Her heart had never beat so fast in her life. She knew she was for sure going to pass out.

"Oh my God," she choked. Just when she thought she would pass out, a pair of hands grabbed her, she wasn't expecting the person behind them. "La-La-Lani," she said breathlessly.

"It's okay, Amaris, I got you," was the last thing Amaris heard.

When she came to, she was in a hospital bed, in her own room. She heard the soft beeping of the machine beside her.

"Hi sweetheart," Ms. Cole came into Amaris's view.

"Mom? What happened?"

"You passed out. How are you feeling?"

"Very tired. I thought I saw Lani."

"Hey sunshine," Lani came into view. "You did see me."

Amaris couldn't believe it, she didn't know if she would ever see Lani again. She smiled because Lani looked good, she looked healthy and it made Amaris happy. She didn't know where Lani was and she'd hoped Lani wasn't held up somewhere miserable. Lani looked the complete opposite, wherever she was, the sun was good to her, she looked beautifully tanned with a twinkle in her eyes.

"I'll go let the doctor know you're awake," Ms. Cole said and left them alone.

"You look good, Lani," Amaris said.

"You look like shit, Amaris."

They both laughed as Amaris pulled her into a hug. "I missed you," she admitted.

Lani tried to hide her feelings, it wasn't what she came for and it wasn't what Amaris needed. "I missed you too." She sat on the bed and held her hand.

"You decided to come back home?"

"I spoke with Logan earlier in the week. She invited me to the party. She also hinted that she wasn't doing so well. For Logan to say that, I knew it was time for me to come home."

Logan was never one to show weakness, but Lani caught it over the phone and it scared her. So, when she called Kayman to see where the party was and Kayman informed her they were at the hospital, Lani knew she made the right choice.

"How's Logan?" she asked.

The mention of Logan's name started the water works for Amaris. "Not good, not good at all. She's not breathing on her own. The doctor said all we can do is make her comfortable. Logan's running out of time."

The wave of sadness hit Lani hard. She took a moment before speaking. "How long?"

"I don't know, but I have an idea."

"What?"

Amaris knew Logan would kill her if she shared this thought with her. "I can give Logan my heart"

"What! What the fuck are you talking about?"

"Calm down, please."

"Amaris, what do you mean? You can't give Logan your heart, you kind of need it."

Amaris played with her fingers nervously. "I haven't told anyone, but I'm a match for Logan. "

Lani stared at Amaris, astonished. "You got tested?"

"Yes, before I moved out here. I'm a match. Maybe that's why the universe brought us together, because we're both rare."

Lani shook her head in disbelief. What Amaris was saying was crazy. "Do you hear yourself, Amaris? In order to give Logan your heart you realize you'll have to be dead?"

Amaris thought about it all before she made the move. "Lani, I've lived such an amazing life. I've lived my dreams, I found the love of my life, I married the love of my entire life. I'm not afraid of death. Logan has been cheated of life. She still has so much more life to live."

Lani grabbed Amaris's face so they could really look at each other. "Are you out of your fucking mind? You can't kill yourself, Amaris."

"Don't you get it Lani? I would die for Logan."

"Logan wouldn't want this."

"I can't live in a world without her. I can't breathe in a world where Logan doesn't exist. I've made my decision. If it comes down to it, I will give Logan my heart."

———— ·•●•· ————

The news Amaris dropped on Lani was too much for her to handle. After going off on her, she left. Amaris knew what she was saying was out of this world but love made you do crazy things.

When she finally felt like herself, she made her way to Logan's room. Logan looked so peaceful as she slept. She pulled a chair up to her bed and stared at her. If she had any tears left, she would have broken down at the sight of her. Logan looked nothing like she did earlier in the night in her amazing suit. Her skin was ashen, the circles under her eyes were the darkest she'd ever seen them. She looked so weak, nothing like the Logan she knew.

"Oh, my love." Amaris took Logan's hands into hers. Her hand was freezing. "Lo, can you hear me?"

Logan's heart leaped for joy when she finally heard Amaris's voice. She'd been waiting for her for what seemed like forever. She slowly opened her eyes and saw her beautiful wife, her Amaris. She felt bad because Amaris looked exhausted.

"Hi baby," Logan whispered.

Amaris sat up, smiling from ear to ear. "Logan, you're awake?" She leaned over and kissed Logan's forehead.

"I was waiting for you," Logan said breathlessly. Amaris placed Logan's oxygen mask back over her face.

"Catch your breath love. You don't need to talk right now."

Logan was tired. Her body was tired. She felt it this time. She knew there was no full recovery from this, so she wanted to get all the time she could with Amaris because they were definitely on a time crunch.

Logan tried to take the mask off so she could speak, but Amaris grabbed her hand. "No, you need it. I need you to rest up. We'll talk tomorrow."

Logan tried to protest, but the look Amaris gave her told her not to. Instead, she motioned for Amaris to lay down. Amaris cuddled next to Logan in the cramped bed and Logan still felt like she wasn't close enough.

Amaris placed her hand over Logan's chest. She closed her eyes and concentrated on sending loving energy to Logan's heart.

Logan pulled her mask down. "My heart is weak, baby."

"Your heart is strong, Lo. You have to speak life into your heart, life into you."

Logan placed her hand over Amaris's hand. "When I die—"

Amaris's head shot up, the daggers she threw at Logan stopped her sentence instantly. "Don't ever say those words to me."

"Baby, look where we are. Look at me."

Amaris didn't want to hear it. She tried to get up, but Logan held her in place even though it took everything out of her.

"Amaris listen to me—" Logan started coughing as she tried to breathe.

Amaris placed the mask back over Logan's face. "Breathe, baby." Logan wanted to protest, but her heart was screaming at her to take the oxygen. Logan took a few deep breaths trying to fight the dizziness. When she gained control of her body, she took the mask back off.

"The Doctor doesn't have to tell me how serious this is. I can feel it in my body. I've never felt so fucking weak. If I don't get a heart, can you promise me something?"

Amaris shook her head no. "I'm not doing this with you." She refused to think about Logan in that way. She couldn't take it.

"Amaris, please," Logan begged.

"Please what?"

"You have to promise me you'll be happy at the end. You'll find love again when the time comes for you."

As much as Logan loved Amaris, she was still young. She didn't want her to go the rest of her life alone. She wanted her to be happy with someone.

Amaris felt like Logan had just ripped her heart out. How could she ask her something like that? Amaris couldn't even think about a life without Logan. Thinking about loving someone else felt like betrayal.

Amaris ran her hand down Logan's face. Logan smiled, used to the loving gesture. "I see you, Logan,"

"And I see you, Mrs. Maddox."

Amaris placed her forehead against Logan's. "No, you don't, because if you did, you wouldn't have asked me to spend life with someone else. You are the other part of me. We share the same soul. Years could pass and no one would ever compare to you. No one's love will ever be enough. So please, don't ask me something that's impossible."

Logan couldn't stand how amazing Amaris was with her words, because how the fuck could she compete with that? How could she fight that? She pulled the mask back over her mouth while cuddling Amaris. "I love you," were the last words she uttered before falling asleep.

Dr. Stein walked in with such a somber look, Logan knew nothing she said would be good.

"Hey kiddo."

She pulled her mask down. "Hey Doc." Dr. Stein sat on the bed. "It's been a good run, huh Doc?"

"It's not over yet, Logan. You're still breathing."

"But for how long?"

"However long you hold on for."

"I want to go home, Doc."

Dr. Stein shook her head no. "You need to be here. Your condition is too critical for you to be at home. When your heart comes, we need to get you prepped right away."

"If these are my last days Doc, I won't die in a cold ass hospital room. I want to be in my home, in my bed, surrounded by my family and wife." Logan refused to stay in the hospital.

"Logan, as your Doc—"

"Doc, I'll hire a hospice nurse or whoever I have to hire, but I need you to discharge me and let me go home."

Dr. Stein knew there was no hope in fighting Logan. She was very headstrong. "Keep your pager on you at all times. You need to be ready at the drop of a dime."

"I will be, trust me."

"Fine." Dr. Stein stood up.

"I'll get your paperwork ready." As Dr. Stein left, a familiar face walked in.

Logan pulled her mask down. "Lani! You came!"

Lani smiled as she walked over to Logan, giving her a big hug. "Hey boss."

"I can't believe you actually came."

Lani shrugged while taking a seat. "Well, I came to party with you, not this, Lo. What the hell's wrong with you?"

Logan laughed while shaking her head. "It wasn't planned. Hell, I didn't even get to party," she joked. Lani stared at Logan for a moment. It hurt her so bad to see Logan like this. It was weird to see her look so weak, so helpless. "Stop looking so sad. I'm going to be okay either way." She tried to convince both of them.

"Last time I saw you, you were in the hospital and now you're here again. I should have come home sooner. I should have—"

"Stop that now. We both know I was on borrowed time."

"Yes, but to see you like this. You've always been so strong. Bigger than life to me. Seeing you like this, in a fucking hospital bed, it doesn't seem right."

"Well it's happening and I need to ask you a favor."

"What?"

"When I die, I need you to be there for Amaris."

Lani rolled her eyes as Logan took the time to put the mask over her mouth. "Don't fucking talk like that."

Logan ripped the mask off her face. "I'm fucking tired of people telling me what to do and what not to do. Listen, I know that I'm going to die, I've finally come to grips with it. Fucking look at me, Lani. I can't even breathe without this bullshit." She tossed the mask on the bed as if she didn't need it. "Amaris is going to fall apart because I know I would if she died. She needs to be surrounded in love. Can you just promise me you'll be there for her?" Logan wasn't dumb, she knew Lani's feelings for Amaris still ran deep. "Promise me that you'll do this for me, Lani."

Lani slid her face in her hands feeling the burden of Logan's words. She thought about the confession Amaris shared with her. She wondered if Amaris was serious about going through with it. She couldn't be. Lani couldn't see Amaris doing that for anyone.

"Okay, I promise." She meant it.

CHAPTER

18

Kayman burst into Logan's hospital room with fury in her eyes. "What the hell are you thinking, Logan? Dr. Stein said you've asked to be discharged! You need to be here in the hospital for when you get your heart."

Logan ignored her mother as she continued to put her shoes on. Amaris was going to be there any minute to take her home.

"Logan!"

"I'm going home, mom. There's no heart coming! Fuck, I feel like I've had this conversation four different times. We're done, mom. I'm going home and I'm going to die. I'm sorry to tell you, but you and everyone else need to come to grips with reality." Logan grabbed her oxygen mask feeling dizzy from lack of oxygen.

Kayman clutched her heart as she tried not to break down. "I'm your mother," Kayman whispered. "I will never give up hope that you'll survive this. I will never give up hope."

Amaris told herself if she wanted to survive this, she would have to go numb. Her feelings would have to be limited. She couldn't allow herself to feel everything if Logan died or she would literally die from heartbreak. But as she stood outside Logan's door, listening to the ache in Kayman's voice as she pleaded for Logan to stay in the hospital, she felt pain so bad it was as though her heart was attacking her. Logan was being her stubborn self. Amaris didn't like the way Logan had already accepted her death sentence. She didn't like how she had given up already. If Logan had given up, then what were they all fighting for?

She finally built up the courage to go in the room. Logan's eyes lit up when she saw her. "There's my beautiful wife."

Amaris forced a smile as she walked into Logan's waiting arms. "Hey, Lo."

"Hi baby." Logan captured Amaris's lips briefly since her mother was still in the room.

"Amaris, please talk some sense into Logan. Why is she leaving the hospital?"

"You know I already protested, mom and Logan doesn't want to hear it, so we have someone who will be there around the clock. I'll make sure she's okay, mom, I promise."

Kayman didn't like this not one bit. She wanted to object, but she knew there was no use. When Logan made up her mind she was set, the only time Kayman saw her change her mind was with Amaris.

"Well, expect me to check in on you around the clock, Logan, and I don't want to hear shit."

Logan chuckled while putting her hands up in surrender. If Kayman Maddox allowed a cuss word to come out of her mouth, she meant business. "I wouldn't expect anything less, mom."

Kayman hugged Logan tight. "I love you, my sweet girl."

"I love you too, mom, so much." Logan held her mother a little longer.

Amaris bit her bottom lip as she watched Logan and Kayman's exchange. They were both so sad, Amaris could feel their energy, it radiated from them. She wished she could take their pain away, but she was dealing with her own sadness.

Logan finally let her mom go and Kayman hugged Amaris before making her exit. Logan put on a smile as her eyes went to Amaris. Her energy wasn't the vibrant, carefree one she was used to. Her smile didn't reach her eyes as well.

"Are you ready to go home, Mrs. Maddox?"

Amaris walked over to Logan's bed and wrapped Logan's arms around her waist. "Yes love, I'm ready. I know you are, being in the hospital is never fun."

Logan shrugged. "I'm used to it, but I have missed sleeping with my wife."

"Well, why don't we go home, get you all set up and watch movies."

"Sounds like a great time."

"The nurse should be there when we get home."

Logan nodded her head. "Okay, let's do this."

— · •●• · —

When the elevator doors opened, they were both surprised to see Lani standing there, waiting for them.

"Lani, what are you doing here?" Logan asked, her eyes wide with surprise.

Lani hugged both of them. "Logan's my boss, I came to make sure you both didn't need anything."

Logan started to make her way to her room. Just walking from the parking lot had her winded. She found herself taking deep, long breaths into her oxygen mask trying to ease the strain of her breathing. The nurse was already setting things up when she entered her room. Logan took a deep breath as she looked at all the equipment. She had to tell herself this was her life, but it wouldn't be for long hopefully.

"Hi Mrs. Maddox, I'm Kendra and I am going to be your home nurse."

Logan sat on the bed, relieved to be off her feet. "Hi Kendra, it's nice to meet you."

Kendra helped Logan out of her jacket. "Shall we get you settled?"

"I'm going to shower first, I need to wash the stench of the hospital off me."

"Okay. Well, let's switch this out." Nurse Kendra switched Logan's full oxygen mask to just the nose. "You'll still be okay like this. Take a few breaths for me and let me know if that's comfortable for you." She looked at Logan, waiting for a response. Logan tested her breathing with the tubes in her nostrils and then gave a thumbs up. "Okay, well I'll leave you to it." Kendra left the room to give her some privacy.

"What are you doing here, Lani, for real?"

"I wanted to check on you, the last conversation we had was pretty heavy and I know with Logan coming home, it might be a lot on you"

"I'm fine, you don't have to worry about me." Amaris was about to head to the room, but Lani held her hand. Amaris inhaled from the shock of their contact.

"Amaris, I will always care. Have you forgotten that just a few months ago I was yours?"

Amaris gently pulled her hand away as she kept her back on Lani. "No, Lani, I haven't forgotten, but I also haven't forgotten the wedding band on my left ring finger. I haven't forgotten that my wife is in the other room." Amaris hoped that Lani coming back was genuine. She hoped that she didn't come back on a mission to try and win her back.

"Amaris, I know that everyone is on Logan and her being okay, but I want you to know that I'm here for you on the days you don't feel okay and I mean that as your friend. I'll see you guys later."

Logan leaned her face against the cold wall hoping her troubles would wash away. She shivered at the cold breeze as the shower glass door opened.

Amaris placed her breast on Logan's back as she wrapped her arms around her. "You okay in here?"

Logan turned around as lust filled her eyes. Amaris saw the change in Logan's eyes. The look of want made her body heat up.

"We can't, baby."

"Why not?" Logan pulled Amaris under the water and captured her lips.

Amaris melted into Logan as their kiss deepened. She wanted Logan, she always wanted her, but she remembered what happened to Logan the last time and broke their kiss. "I can't do this," Amaris reluctantly stepped out of the shower.

"Baby?"

"Clean yourself up, I'll meet you out here." Amaris closed the door while grabbing her robe.

She sat on the bed as the tears she'd been holding back spilled out. The rejection in Logan's eyes nearly killed her. It wasn't that she didn't want Logan, she just didn't want to be the cause of Logan's heart giving out completely. When Logan came out of the bathroom dripping wet with her locs loose, Amaris' mouth watered. Her eyes traced Logan from her feet to her waist where her eyes zoomed in on Logan's pussy, up to her breast, then to her lips, those beautiful, plump lips, her nose and finally to her eyes. Her eyes were blazing with fury.

"Is this how you're going to fucking treat me?"

"What?"

"Is this how you're going to treat me? Like I'm some helpless little bitch in the street?" Logan was beyond pissed off. She never wanted anyone to think she was weak, especially her wife.

"Baby, your heart…"

"Fuck my heart, Amaris! I'm going to die either way! But if this is what you're going to do, then pack your shit and fucking leave me to die alone."

Logan walked back into the bathroom slamming the door behind her. Amaris let out the breath she didn't know she was holding. Logan had never spoken to her like that, she wasn't used to the coldness. Amaris had it in her right mind to actually pack her shit and leave Logan, but then that anxiety turned to anger.

She launched off the bed and barged into the bathroom. "If you ever speak to me like that again I will fucking leave you! I am your goddamn wife, it's my job to care!"

Logan spun around, ready to attack. "You will not fucking treat me like I'm helpless, I won't let you!"

"I'm trying to keep you alive! You're the only motherfucka who's already given up!" Amaris walked over to Logan grabbing her behind the neck. "Do you want to die? Is that it? You've given up already? Let me know now so I can stop putting my fucking energy into you." Logan tried to get out of Amaris's hold, but her grip grew tighter. "Have you given up Logan?" Logan locked her jaws as she tried to burn a hole into Amaris. Amaris's eyes softened, feeling like she got her point across. "We don't talk to each other like this, it's not us and I won't allow it to become us. Do you understand me?" Logan's anger subsided as Amaris leaned her forehead against hers. "Do you understand me, Logan?"

"Yes, I understand, but stop treating me like I'm weak."

"I'm not trying to, love, I'm just trying to keep you alive until we get your heart. Can you understand that?"

"Yes and I'm sorry. I love you so much."

Amaris kissed Logan with as much passion as she could. "I love you, baby."

• • ● • • —————

Amaris slid out of the bed softly, trying not to wake Logan. Against her objection, Logan took her right in the bathroom after their argument. It was one of the best experiences Amaris had ever had. She made Logan go slow so she wouldn't tire quickly and it was slow, tortuous, and amazing. She could still feel Logan's hands on her hips gripping her as she slid her strap in and out of her pussy.

Amaris quivered just thinking about their love making. She wanted to wake Logan up and go at it again, but she knew it was best to let her rest. Amaris sat in the chair across from their bed. She listened to the heart monitor attached to Logan. The sign that she was alive, that she was still with her. Logan had stubbornly told the nurse she would stay hooked up to the monitor only when she slept.

Her eyes went to the pager that sat on the nightstand. She wanted it to go off so bad, she wanted to get the page that would save Logan's life, but the pager remained silent. Only the continuous beeping of the love of her life.

Amaris ran her hand through her hair while taking a much needed deep breath. If someone would have told her six months ago that this would be her life, she would have laughed in their face. It's crazy to think the only problem she had was not getting caught by Quelm's husband, now she was praying to God to save her wife. Life was way more complicated than what she was used to. Despite that, she would do anything to keep Logan breathing—she placed her hand over her heart—even give her own life up.

"Amaris …"

Amaris heard Logan whisper. She got up and rushed to her side. "I'm here, love. What's wrong?" She pushed Logan's locs out of her face.

"I didn't feel you. You can't sleep, baby?" Logan pulled Amaris down onto the bed staring at her as she waited for her to answer.

"I guess I can't. I was just watching you sleep."

"Creep," Logan joked.

Amaris lightly punched Logan. "Asshole." Logan brushed her lips against her forehead.

"I thought you'd be knocked out after the session we had."

"I was knocked out, but I woke up."

"Are you okay, love? You want to talk?"

"No, you need your rest. I was just up thinking a bit."

Logan was worried about Amaris. She wondered how much she was holding back because she didn't want her to worry. "Why don't you have a girls' day with Taylor and Lani. A little pampering never hurts anybody."

Amaris looked up at Logan. "Do I seem that bad?"

"I just want you to try to get back to you. Will you do that for me?" The sincerity in Logan's voice made Amaris feel bad.

"Okay, I'll call the girls up to see when they're free. You're okay with me hanging out with Lani?"

"Yeah," Logan said with no hesitation. She trusted Amaris and Lani together.

"Well, as long as you're okay with it."

"Why don't I set it up for you girls? You'll just have to show up."

"Okay, thanks baby."

"Now, close your eyes, let's get some rest."

Amaris snuggled into Logan and closed her eyes. With Logan's warmth, Amaris had no problem falling asleep.

CHAPTER

19

Amaris let out a soft moan as the masseuse worked the tension out of her neck.

"You need to relax, Mrs. Maddox, you're so tense," the masseuse told her.

"Yeah, I know, sorry."

"How's your project coming along for the art gallery?" Taylor inquired while sipping her glass of champagne. True to her word, Logan set up a spa day for Amaris, Taylor, and Lani.

"It's okay, it's hard to focus when I'm so worried about Logan."

"You can't let this consume you, Lo wouldn't want you to. She would want you to put on the best show possible," Lani said.

"Lani's right. You have to do this right."

Amaris let Lani's and Taylor's words sink in. She knew they were right, but it was better said than done.

"Are you sure about this, Lo?"

Logan looked around the empty space, there was beautiful natural light peeking through due to the big windows, the space was perfect.

"Yes, I'm sure. Draw up the paperwork for me please, X."

Xavier leaned against the wall as he eyed his sister. His baby sister, his only sister, his only sibling. Logan didn't look so good as she sat in her wheelchair. She'd survived another week, but everyone could see she was getting weaker. The rings around her eyes grew darker, her skin became more and more ashen as days passed.

"You'll get her everything she needs right, Xavier?"

"Of course, I will."

"Thanks bro."

"Lo, you know I'd do anything for you."

"I know." Logan watched Xavier intensely as he turned his back on her. She knew that something was bothering him, he only did that when he had something heavy on his mind. "Speak your peace."

Xavier chuckled, but didn't face Logan. "Taylor and I are pregnant."

"What? Brother! Congrats!"

Xavier faced Logan. "I need you to be here to meet your niece or nephew. They need to know how great of an auntie you will be."

Logan's excitement disappeared from her face. She would love to be there to meet her niece or nephew, but her chances of survival were growing slim. She felt her body weakening as the days passed and as much as she wanted her pager to go off, it hadn't.

"I will try my best, I promise, but I need you to do something for me." Logan took a moment to put her oxygen mask over her face. Xavier bit the inside of his cheek to keep his emotions in check. This wasn't the Logan he knew. This wasn't the Logan that closed business deals with their father, who started her own publishing company, who commanded attention whenever she walked in a room. This person was a shell of a person Xavier knew. It really broke his heart.

"Okay sis, what is it?"

"I need you to make sure mom is okay if I don't make it. I need you to make sure she keeps going."

"Lo—"

"Please, X. For so long, I've been on mom's mind constantly. If I don't make it and it hits her that I'm no longer here, it could destroy her. I need you to make sure she realizes she still has you. She needs to realize that it's okay to keep going."

Logan knew her death would cripple her family. She needed someone to remain strong. She knew she was asking a lot of Xavier, but somebody had to do it. "Why are you asking me to do this? You're going to get a new heart." Xavier loosened his tie as he felt his heart constrict at the thought of Logan dying.

"Bro, look at me. I can barely walk, I can barely breathe on my own. Time is running out and it's time to start having these conversations just in case. So, I need you to promise me that you'll make sure mom is okay."

Xavier let out a heavy sigh. "Okay sis, I promise I'll make sure mom is okay."

———— · •●• · ————

Logan smiled as the elevator pinged and Amaris stepped off. She looked so refreshed it was nice to see. "Well hello, Mrs. Maddox, you look relaxed."

"I am. The spa was exactly what I needed." Amaris crawled onto the couch with Logan and wrapped her arms around Logan's waist.

"I'm glad. How are Taylor and Lani?"

"They're good. Girls time was great. How was your day?"

"It was good. I got a lot of paperwork done. Spent some time with Xavier. We had a good time, but I missed you."

Amaris smiled as she leaned up to kiss Logan. She would never get used to how cold Logan's lips were from the constant oxygen.

"I missed you too, lover."

"Do you want to take a ride with me?"

"A ride where baby, shouldn't you be resting?"

"I've been resting. Let's take a ride on my motorcycle."

Amaris sat up, looking at Logan like she was crazy. "We can't, your tank—"

"I'll wear the machine like a backpack." Logan sat up excitedly. She hadn't planned to take a ride, but she wanted to do something spontaneous.

"Baby, I don't think we should." Amaris didn't want Logan to collapse somewhere, especially if they were riding.

"Come on love, it'll be okay." Logan gave Amaris her best puppy dog eyes until she finally caved in.

"Fine, but any sign of something wrong we're going to the hospital. Deal?"

"Yup, that's a deal. Now come on, let's get changed." Logan helped Amaris up and dragged her to their room. Even with Nurse Kendra's heavy protest, Logan didn't let that stop her. She was going to enjoy whatever life she had left with Amaris.

Logan revved up her engine loving the feeling of the vibration underneath her. She couldn't remember the last time she was able to ride. Even though her body protested and indicated for her to go lay down because it was in so much pain, Logan ignored it and sped out of the parking lot with Amaris's arms wrapped around her waist. The feel of the wind ripping through her leather jacket and her hair made her feel so alive.

"This is so great, baby." Amaris spoke to Logan through her microphone.

"I know, I missed this. Feeling so free, one with the elements."

"Yes, we needed this." Amaris held Logan a little tighter. She lightened her hold when she felt Logan flinch.

"Sorry baby, did I hurt you?"

"It's okay." Logan stepped on the pedal weaving in and out of traffic. She took them to her favorite spot, which overlooked the city.

Amaris smiled, remembering the place. She hopped off the bike. "I remember this place. It's so nice out here."

"Yes, it is." Logan hopped off her bike. "Do you remember when I brought you here?"

"Of course I do, it was when I first came out here."

Logan wrapped her arms around Amaris's waist from behind causing Amaris leaned her head back soaking in the moment.

"Before I proposed."

"Uhm hmm. Before our wedding. It's so funny to think, that feels so far away."

"Like a whole 'nother life," Logan admitted. Amaris faced Logan, seeing that her eyes were distant.

"Any regrets?"

Logan's eyes looked in on Amaris. "Are you kidding me? I get to do life with my soulmate. No regrets at all."

"Smooth talker." They shared a laugh before sharing a kiss.

"Lo, I would do life with you over and over and over again."

Logan nuzzled her nose to Amaris. Their powerful moment was interrupted by Logan's phone vibrating in her pocket. "Hey mom," she said as she took the call.

"Are you trying to give me a heart attack?"

"Huh?"

"Nurse Kendra called me. She said she tried to stop you, but you took a ride on your bike. Are you crazy, Logan?"

"I was safe, mom and Amaris is with me."

"Amaris let you go!"

"Would you rather I'd gone alone?"

"Logan, you need to be resting. This is crazy. Please, go home."

"Mom, I'm an adult I can—"

Amaris grabbed the phone from Logan before she could go any further. "Hey mom."

"Amaris, why would you agree to this?" The sound of disappointment from Kayman almost crushed Amaris.

"She would have gone on her own. You know Logan has a mind of her own. At least, I'm with her if anything happens."

"Please, get her home. She needs to be resting. She was out all day with Xavier, Logan knows she can't overexert herself."

"I will, we're headed back now."

"Thank you. I love you girls."

"We love you too mom." Amaris pressed end on the phone. Logan didn't look pleased when Amaris turned around to give her back her phone.

"What did mom say?"

"The usual. You need to be resting, especially since you were out with X."

Logan rolled her eyes in annoyance. She loved her mother, but she could be overbearing at times. "Five more minutes and then we can go."

"Okay, five more minutes."

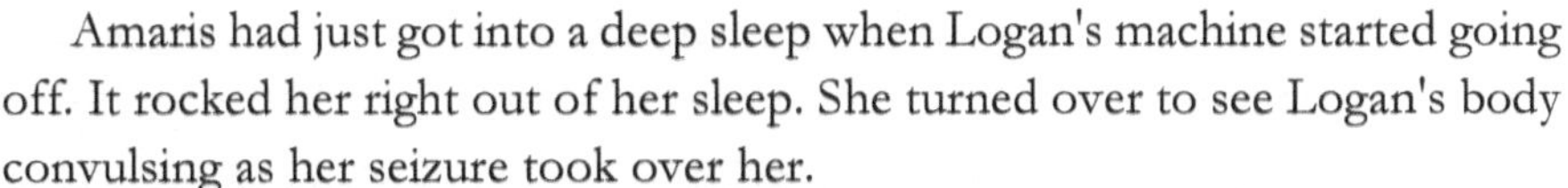

Amaris had just got into a deep sleep when Logan's machine started going off. It rocked her right out of her sleep. She turned over to see Logan's body convulsing as her seizure took over her.

"Lo!" Amaris's first thought was to hold Logan's tongue down so she wouldn't bite down on it or choke.

Nurse Kendra ran into the room and took over. Amaris watched helplessly as she tried to stop Logan's seizure. She clutched her shirt as she tried not to send herself into a panic attack. Her palms grew sweaty and her head started to spin. She leaned against the wall as she tried to inhale.

"Hold on, Lo, I got you. I got you." Nurse Kendra put medicine into Logan's IV and watched how long it took for her seizure to subside. She turned to Amaris who had a look of pure panic on her face. She rushed to her to make sure she was okay. "Hey are you alright? Have a seat." She sat Amaris down in her chair before going back to Logan. Her body had stopped shaking, but her levels were still a little high. "Come on, Lo."

Amaris couldn't help the tears from falling. Seeing Logan's body shake so violently was too much. She didn't know if she would stop breathing or not. "Is she okay?"

"The seizure seems to be subsiding."

"Amaris," Logan croaked. Amaris was at Logan's side before she even knew her feet were moving.

"I'm here, baby."

Logan sighed in relief when she felt Amaris presence. Her body felt so weak it frightened her. She kept telling herself to breathe, to stay there with Amaris, but she was so tired. She just wanted to rest. "I'm so tired, baby," Logan could barely get the words out.

"It's okay. Rest, love, I'll be here." Amaris put Logan's oxygen mask over her face seeing that she was struggling to breathe.

Nurse Kendra made sure Logan was comfortable before motioning for Amaris to follow her out the room.

"Is she going to be okay?"

"For now, yes. Amaris I highly recommend moving Logan to the hospital. I can't give her the proper care she needs from the house."

Amaris knew that if Nurse Kendra was admitting this, then it was bad. "Okay, I'll call the hospital now and set transportation up."

"I'm sorry, Amaris."

"Don't be. Thank you for all that you've done," Amaris assured her as she gave Amaris a long hug before heading back to her room.

Amaris walked back in the room and looked at Logan. She was now resting, but the rhythm of her heartbeat looked so faint. She walked over to the bed and sat down. Logan was her life and she knew she meant what she said about giving Logan her heart. At least, a piece of her would still be here in the most important person to her. She could die in peace knowing that.

She took Logan's hand into hers and brought it to her lips. Tears welled in her eyes as she felt the coldness brush against her lips. She knew she was losing Logan. "Logan, I love you so much." Logan didn't respond, so Amaris knew she was in a deep sleep. After taking one last look at Logan, she headed to her office.

She found a pen and paper and began to write.

"Dear Logan, loving you has been one of my greatest joys. I knew I loved you the moment I laid eyes on you. My soul recognized you instantly. I don't regret anything between us, even you being so stubborn. LOL.

'I'll never forget our time together. It's what brought me to this decision. I know I would never continue this life without you. I knew before we got married that I would give my life for yours. Baby, you still have so much to accomplish and I've already accomplished so much. Please, know that I'm in so much peace with this decision. Hopefully, the universe will allow me to be reincarnated and I find you again.

"I want you to promise me something, baby. I want you to love again. You deserve to love. Someone deserves to experience your love, it's such a beautiful thing. Have the babies you didn't allow yourself to think about. They'll be beautiful just like their mama. Write, never stop writing.

"God, I love you, Logan Maddox. I love you with my entire being. I'll see you in the next life, my love.

"Love, Amaris"

She wiped the tears from her eyes before they could drop on the paper and blotch it. After writing letters for her mom and Tasha, she went back in the room and set the letters next to Logan's pager. She went into the bathroom and looked at herself in the mirror. Then she smiled at herself in the mirror.

"Amaris, you have lived an extraordinary life. I'm so proud of you," she said to herself.

She opened the cabinet and reached for Logan's pain pills. She knew those would do the trick. Before she could talk herself out of it, she swallowed half the bottle. As she sat there and waited for the pills to take effect, her life flashed before her eyes. Her as a little girl dancing in the living room with her mom. Riding bikes in the neighborhood. Graduating high school. In college, snapping pictures. Her first show. Her and Quelm rumbling in the sheets and then, Logan's beautiful face, walking in the house and seeing her for the first time. Their first kiss, the first time they made love. The night on the couch when Logan asked her to marry her. Their wedding day. The honeymoon. So many good memories she would take with her till the end.

When she felt like she was about to be finally out of it, she sent her last text to Lani.

Lani was engrossed in a manuscript when her phone vibrated and Amaris's name popped up. She jumped up when she read the text. "It's time, make sure they get us both to the hospital. I love you, Lani."

"No, no, no, no, Amaris you didn't!" She called Amaris, but of course, there was no answer. She tried calling Logan, but got the voicemail. She grabbed her keys and ran out of her house, dialing 911 on her way out.

Logan stirred as she heard the loud buzzing on her dresser. She tried to fight the fog sleep she was in as the constant buzzing went off. She wondered why Amaris wouldn't grab her phone to stop it.

"Amaris, get my phone, baby," she muttered, trying to pry her eyes open, but it was like her body was fighting her. *Come on Logan,* she told herself as the buzzing started again. It felt like it took her forever to break out of her sleep. She blinked a few times, trying to clear her vision.

She reached for her phone and realized it wasn't what was buzzing. Her pager buzzed right next to her. The page she'd been waiting for. A heart! "Amaris!" Logan reached for Amaris, only to find her side of the bed empty.

Before she could react, Lani burst in her room with paramedics, scaring the shit out of her. "Lani, what the fuck?"

"Where's Amaris?" she asked, panicked.

"What?"

Lani's eyes went to the closed bathroom door. "In there!"

"What's going on?" Logan asked, fear evident in her eyes.

The paramedics bust open the door and Logan heard Lani scream for

Amaris. The shrill in her voice had Logan stumbling out of the bed.

"She's not breathing," one of the paramedics said.

Logan pushed past Lani to find Amaris's lifeless body on their bathroom floor. She would never forget that image. There was no life to her and she had white foam coming out of her mouth.

"Amaris!" Logan ran to her. "Why? Why? Why?"

"She did it for you," Lani said crying.

"What?"

"You're a match. She did it to save you."

Logan felt her chest cave in at Lani's confession. "No! No! Amaris, I have a heart, baby. I have a heart."

CHAPTER

20

Logan's family was already at the hospital when the paramedics brought her and Amaris into the hospital. Amaris was barely holding onto life.

"What happened to Amaris?" Taylor screamed.

The paramedics rushed Amaris to the back. "Follow her, I need to be with her!" Logan tried to wheel herself, but the paramedics held onto her wheelchair. "Let me the fuck go! That's my wife!"

Logan couldn't believe that Amaris tried to commit suicide to give her her heart.

"Logan, we need to get you prepped for surgery." Dr. Stein tried to speak reason into Logan.

"Fuck the heart. I need to be with my wife!" Tears cascaded down her eyes as guilt started to eat at her. It was her fault that Amaris did this.

Kayman gently gripped Logan's face. "Baby girl, this is what we've been waiting for. This is your only chance. Now, I don't know what—"

"She sacrificed herself for me, mom. She's a match. Amaris loves me so much she was going to give me her heart!" Logan wailed. Her heart was broken. If Amaris died because of her what would be the reason to have a heart?

Kayman inhaled and exhaled deeply. She needed Logan to see reason. She needed her to go into surgery. "Amaris would want you to go into surgery. Amaris would want you to get the surgery. This is why she did what she did. We need you to go into surgery because if you don't, you'll die and Amaris will still come out of this alone."

"I need to be with her, mom."

"We will be with her, we will be with the both of you."

Logan didn't want to go into surgery, she wanted to be with Amaris, but she knew her mother was right. She was torn. "Logan, we don't have a lot of time. We've waited almost 3 years for this." Dr. Stein pleaded.

"Okay, I'll go," Logan said with determination in her eyes. Everybody sighed in relief.

"Good. Let's get her back," Dr. Stein said.

Logan grabbed her mother's hand. "Take care of her, please."

"I will, I promise." Logan let go of her mother's hand and allowed the nurse to wheel her back.

Logan almost lost her shit when they wheeled her past a room and she saw them giving Amaris CPR. Dr. Stein had the nurse rush Logan past the room. "Stop!"

"Logan, we have to go. Amaris will be fine."

Logan didn't give a fuck about the heart. If she woke up and Amaris was dead she would never forgive herself. "Doc, I changed my mind. I need to be with my wife!" She didn't see Dr. Stein motion to the nurse. All of a sudden, she felt like she was on cloud nine. The nurse had stuck a needle in her IV to calm her down. She became dizzy and the world started to spin. "I need to be..." She passed out in her chair.

Dr. Stein didn't want to sedate Logan, but she knew it was the only way she would get her on that operating table. She couldn't let Logan lose this heart. They'd waited too long for this. "Let's prep her and get her to the OR."

Lani sat with her face in her hands not believing how the night had turned. She couldn't believe Amaris had actually gone through with it. She thought it was all talk.

Kayman sat next to Lani. "What happened Lani?"

"I didn't think she would actually do it."

"What?" Kayman asked, confused.

"The last time Logan was in the hospital, Amaris told me that she knew she was a match. She said if Logan didn't get a heart she would give her hers."

"What?" Kayman whispered breathlessly.

"Amaris took pills, Mrs. Maddox. She'd rather sacrifice herself and give Logan her heart than watch her die."

Kayman couldn't believe Amaris would do that for Logan. It made her happy that someone loved her daughter so much, but sad that Amaris would go to great lengths. Her thoughts went to Amaris's mother, if Amaris didn't survive this, she would lose her only child.

"We need to get Amaris's mom here ASAP, she needs to be here," Kayman said in a panic.

"I'll send the jet for her and call her mom," Xavier said while rushing off to set things up.

"Taylor, can you please call Mr. Maddox? He's in Houston for a meeting. Can you tell him what's happening?"

"Sure thing, mom."

Kayman clasped her hands together and began to pray like she's never prayed before.

— • • ● • • —

"Do I know you?" Logan flipped around to see Amaris smiling at her.

"Amaris!" Logan ran to her and scooped her in her arms. "What the hell were you thinking?" She kissed her all over her face.

"Don't be mad at me," Amaris said with a pout and Logan set Amaris down.

"You tried to kill yourself?"

"I did it for you, so you could go on with life."

Logan wrapped Amaris in her arms. "Amaris, that was the most idiotic thing you've ever done. Baby, how do you think I'm supposed to go on without you, let alone if you died because of me?"

Amaris placed her hand on Logan's chest as she stared deep into her eyes. "Because I would be with you right here. I love you so much, Logan that I would give my own life up for yours. I just couldn't live in a world you didn't exist in. I couldn't be here without you."

"Amaris, dammit." Logan captured her lips. She couldn't believe what Amaris had done. "If you would have just waited a little longer, baby. My pager went off tonight."

"What?" Amaris asked breathlessly.

"I have a heart."

"You have a heart?" Amaris said, astonished.

"Yes."

"Come on, Amaris." Amaris heard a distant voice as she felt pressure on her chest as the scene started to change into the hospital. All of a sudden she was standing over her body as the doctors performed CPR on her. "You are not going to die on us," the doctor yelled as he pressed harder on her chest, trying to get her heart going again.

"Oh my God, Logan do you see this?" The space where Logan was seconds ago was empty.

She swirled around. "Logan! Logan!" Logan was gone, it was just her watching the doctors try to bring her back. All Amaris could think about was what Logan said. She had a heart and it wasn't hers. What they'd been praying for finally happened, but here she was, dead on the table. The irony of it all made Amaris laugh hysterically. She was dead and Logan was hopefully going to live. Amaris had to be okay with that because it was what she wanted all along, for Logan to live and have a beautiful life.

She closed her eyes and took a calming deep breath. Peace washed over her, a peace *she'd never felt before. She knew that no matter what, she was going to be okay. She'd lived a beautiful life and was able to spend time with the love of her life.*

"Okay," she whispered.

Three hours later and no one had heard anything on Logan or Amaris. Everyone was on pins and needles as they waited for any type of news.

"Kayman!" Amaris's mother burst through the hospital doors. "Where is she? Where's my baby?" Ms. Cole asked frantically.

Kayman held Ms. Cole's hands trying to keep her emotions in check. "She's in the back, we don't have any answers yet. We're all waiting. Let's sit." Kayman guided Ms. Cole to a seat.

She didn't know what Ms. Cole knew. She didn't have the words to explain what and why Amaris had done what she'd done. The guilt of the situation was eating her alive. She just needed Amaris to be okay. She needed both of their children to come out of this alive.

Ms. Cole felt like she couldn't breathe. She felt that way ever since she'd gotten the dreaded phone call. "Tell me what happened, Kayman?"

"What did Xavier or Taylor tell you?"

"Just that Amaris was brought into the hospital and it was serious."

"Amaris—" before Kayman could get it out, the doctor came out.

"Amaris Maddox?" he called out, looking around the group.

Ms. Cole jumped up. "I'm her mother."

"Please, come with me."

"Is my daughter okay?"

"Please ma'am, just come with me." Everyone watched Ms. Cole disappear behind the double doors.

"Doctor, can you please tell me what happened?"

"Amaris ingested a high dosage of pain pills. Has your daughter tried to hurt herself before?"

"No! Hurt herself? Amaris would never do that," Ms. Cole said in disbelief.

"She did. Amaris was not breathing when the ambulance brought her in."

"Is—is she dead?"

The doctor sighed sadly while stopping in front of a window. Amaris was laying there lifeless with tubes everywhere.

"Amaris," Ms. Cole's knees buckled at the sight of her daughter. "Oh my baby,"

"I'm so sorry, Amaris isn't breathing on her own. We don't know if there's brain damage yet, but I'm sorry to tell you it's not looking good."

Ms. Cole couldn't believe what she was hearing. This was a nightmare she wanted to wake up from. "Not looking good?"

"Amaris was dead for almost fifteen minutes. The chances of her waking are slim."

"Oh my God." Ms. Cole lost everything she was holding onto. "Oh Amaris!"

"I'm so sorry. Are you here with someone? Please, let me get them for you." Ms. Cole could barely hear what the doctor was saying. The world was spinning.

Next thing she knew, a pair of arms was around her, multiple pairs of arms. Logan's family had wrapped her in their arms.

"We're here for you, Ms. Cole. She will pull through this. She's a strong woman," Kayman said in a soothing voice, even though she was trying to stop the tears from spilling from her eyes. She stared at Amaris through the window. She had to pull through because she didn't think Logan would survive it if she didn't.

— • •⬤• • —

Dr. Stein cut the last piece of string that attached Logan's heart to her. She let out a deep breath. "Okay everyone, this is it," she said with a shaky voice. She knew she was an amazing surgeon, but Logan was one of the special ones. She'd waited so long for a heart, it had to take.

Everyone waited for Logan's new heart to start beating. "Come on, Logan."

Logan felt a pair of arms wrap around her waist from behind. She smiled, feeling Amaris lean into her back.

"It's time for you to go back, my love," Amaris whispered. Logan shook her head as she watched herself on the operating table.

"I'm not going back without you."

"You are, baby, you have to."

Logan twisted around in Amaris's arms. "Amaris, I'm not going back without you."

"You are because you have such a beautiful life ahead of you." Amaris turned Logan's chin so she could see herself on the table. "You've waited so long for this. So many people wish to be in your spot. Don't let this go to waste, you're going to be so great, baby."

Logan felt like she was experiencing death by leaving Amaris. She felt like her heart was ripping to shreds.

"Logan Maddox, I love you so much and we've had—"

Logan cut Amaris off by kissing her. Amaris melted into Logan as they both poured their love into each other. "Come back to me Amaris. Don't leave me."

Amaris closed her eyes. "Goodbye, my love."

Everyone in the room clapped as Logan's new heart beat for the first time. "Good work, Doctor." Dr. Stein sighed in relief as she watched Logan's heartbeat grow stronger.

"Good job, Lo, good job. Alright, let's close her up."

Two hours later, Dr. Stein walked into the waiting room.

Mr. Maddox was by Mrs. Maddox's side. When they saw Dr. Stein walk out of the OR, everyone stood up on edge. "How is she?"

"The surgery went well, she's in recovery right now."

The sob Kayman was holding in finally came out. "She's okay?"

"Yes, she's okay."

Kayman hugged Dr. Stein. "Thank you so much. Oh my God, thank you."

"You're welcome, Kayman. You guys can see her in a few hours."

"Thank you." Mr. Maddox and Kayman hugged.

"Thomas, our baby girl is going to be okay."

"I know. thank you Lord." Mr. Maddox didn't realize he was crying. Taylor and Xavier hugged Kayman and Mr. Maddox. It was like everyone could breathe again, but not so clearly as they all thought about Amaris in the other room.

"Who's going to tell her when she wakes up?"

Mr. Maddox sighed. "I will."

CHAPTER

21

"Amaris," Logan whispered as she tried to open her eyes. Her body felt so heavy from all the medication. "Amaris," she croaked.

Mr. Maddox got up from his seat and sat on the bed. "Sweetheart."

Logan finally opened her eyes hearing her father's voice. "Daddy." Her throat felt like it was on fire. She tried to reach for her chest where her stitches were, but her father gently grabbed her hand, stopping her.

"Don't touch, baby girl, don't touch."

Logan's eyes searched the room for Amaris. "Where is she dad? Is Amaris okay?"

Thomas sighed, he'd been thinking about how he would tell Logan when she woke up. He knew he was about to break his baby girl's heart.

"Where is she dad?" Logan tried to remember what happened. Everything was such a blur for her. She tried to picture Amaris, but nothing came up.

"Baby girl, Amaris is in a coma, She's down the hall."

"What? No. We were just together." Logan closed her eyes trying to remember being with Amaris. She pictured her face, she pictured her arms around her waist. They were together.

"You've been in surgery, do you remember coming to the hospital?"

Flashes of Amaris on the bathroom floor crossed Logan's eyes. "No." She closed her eyes trying to remember more, instead she saw them both being rushed into the hospital, Amaris not breathing, then the doctor working on her as she was wheeled past her room.

Her eyes popped open as reality hit her. "Where's Amaris?" she screamed, but then groaned from the pain in her chest.

"Calm down, baby girl."

"Where is she Daddy? I need to be with her." Logan threw the blanket off her and tried to get up.

"Lo, Lo, you can't." Thomas tried to stop Logan from getting out of the bed.

"I need to be with her." Logan was losing her shit, her only thoughts were to get to Amaris as quickly as possible.

A few nurses ran in hearing the sudden fast beeping sound of Logan's monitor. "Mrs. Maddox, please you have to calm down."

"Fuck that! I need to be with my wife." Her body screamed for her to stop, but she didn't. It felt like her chest was ripping apart, but she still fought the nurses. She was going to get to Amaris one way or another.

"Sir we're going to have to sedate her, this isn't good for her recovery."

Thomas nodded his head in understanding. "Do it."

"Daddy, no please. I just need to see Amaris." Thomas tried to keep his emotions in check as he watched the nurse sedate Logan. He understood that she wanted to be with Amaris, but she'd just woken up from a heart surgery. She needed to put her health first.

"Da—da ..." Logan felt the medication taking effect. Her body grew heavy as she tried to fight the sleepiness that was trying to take over. "Amaris," she whispered as her eyes closed.

Thomas collapsed in his seat. "It's okay, Mr. Maddox, she'll be asleep for a few hours." All he could do was shake his head. He was mentally exhausted from not knowing if Logan would make it out of surgery, then finding out Amaris was in a coma, it was all too much.

"Let us know if you need anything."

"Thank you so much." Once the nurses left, Thomas made his way to Amaris's room. Kayman, Lani, and Ms. Cole were sitting around her bed. Xavier took Taylor home so she could get some rest. Everyone was exhausted, but no one was leaving. Kayman perked up when Thomas walked through the door.

"Is Lo awake?"

"She was. They had to sedate her after she found out about Amaris. She'll get to sleep for a while, but we need to figure out what we're going to do when she wakes back up."

"What do you suggest, baby?"

"Well…" Thomas looked at Ms. Cole. "If it's okay with you, Alisha, I'd like to move Logan and Amaris into the same room so they can be closer to each other. It might do them both some good."

Ms. Cole stared at Amaris. Her beautiful daughter showed no sign of waking up. She wanted to blame Logan for this. If it wasn't for her, Amaris would be in LA, working on her art, living life. Instead, she was in a hospital bed ready to give up her life for someone else.

She wanted to scream in agony. Amaris was her only child, the only family she had left; if she lost her she wouldn't have anyone.

"Alisha?" Thomas asked again.

She swallowed her pride because she knew it was what Amaris would want. "Yes, that would be fine."

"Okay, I'll go speak to the doctor." Thomas kissed the top of Kayman's head before walking out of the room.

Lani sat next to Alisha and held her hand. "Amaris is strong, she's going to pull through."

"I keep telling myself that, but what if she doesn't? This is my baby, Lani. My only baby."

"I know and she'll wake up. She has to." Lani wanted to shake Amaris awake. She wanted to see her beautiful eyes and smile. This had been the longest twenty-four hours of her life. The two people she cared the most about were both in the hospital; one getting a second chance at life and the other fighting for hers. A part of her wished she'd stay the hell away, but the other part of her knew this was where she was supposed to be.

"I wonder if Amaris and Logan are together right now."

Kayman smiled. "Are you kidding me? Of course they are. Those two can't stay away from each other."

When Logan woke up, she immediately felt Amaris presence. She was groggy and in pain, but when she turned her head and saw Amaris laying in the bed next to her, it broke her out of whatever haze she was in.

"Baby," she groaned as he tried to get up from bed. The pressure on her chest from sitting up made her want to scream in agony, but her only mission was to get to Amaris.

"Fuck," she held her chest as she finally made it out of the bed. She tried to take a step, but her legs were like jelly.

The door opened and Xavier stood there looking puzzled. "Sis, what the hell are you doing?" Xavier ran to Logan's aid, wrapping her arm around his shoulder.

"Get me over there, please."

"Okay, I got you." Xavier helped Logan to Amaris's bed. She took the image of her wife in.

"Amaris," she croaked as tears fell down her eyes. She couldn't believe what she was seeing. Amaris had tubes everywhere. The only reason Logan knew she was alive was because of the beeping sound from her heart monitor. "X, look at her." Logan felt like her heart was being ripped into shreds. "Look at my wife."

Xavier swallowed his own tears as he held Logan. Logan buried her face in Xavier's chest and cried her eyes out. "Why would she do this? I would never ask her to end her life to save mine." The guilt of it all was already eating away at Logan.

"Amaris loves you, that's all I can say, she loves you more than any of us were aware of. Right now, all we can do is pray she wakes up."

"What are the doctors saying?"

Xavier sat next to Logan not wanting to be the one to break the news to his sister. "You know if anyone could pull through anything, its Amaris."

"What did they say?"

"It's not good, Lo. The doctors are going to test for brain damage."

Logan gripped Amaris hand and planted a soft kiss on it, but she couldn't feel her presence. She couldn't feel her warmth or her love and that scared Logan, because if she couldn't feel those things, she didn't think her soul was there. "I can't lose her, X, I can't lose my baby."

"Sis, you won't. Just give her time. Amaris will come back to you. Keep the faith, sis."

• —— · •●• · —— •

Ms. Cole walked in as Logan laid in bed reading to Amaris. She was supposed to be recovering herself, but against the nurses' orders, Logan wouldn't stay in bed. "Logan, you should be in bed, what are you doing?"

"I'm just reading to Amaris."

"You need to be laying down, you just had a major surgery. Come on, now." Ms. Cole helped Logan back to her bed. Logan wanted to fight, but it was Amaris's mom, so she didn't.

Ms. Cole sat next to Amaris, taking her hand into hers. They sat there silent for a moment, the only sound in the room was the heart monitor telling them both that Amaris was still with them.

"Do you hate me?" Logan blurted out before she could lose her nerves.

Amaris's mother remained quiet as she pondered the question. It was a tough question to answer. She was happy for Logan because her getting a new heart was what everyone had been waiting for, but it was her baby that was laying there. "Amaris loves hard. It was one thing I feared and loved about her. My daughter loved you so much that she would give you her heart. She would take herself from this earth, from me. Do you know the magnitude of that, Logan?" When Ms. Cole turned around, tears were falling down her eyes.

Logan swallowed the tears that threatened to spill out. "Yes, I do."

"So, if she pulls through you better give her the best life possible." Ms. Cole didn't know if Logan could give Amaris everything her heart desired, she just needed her to wake up.

"She will have an amazing life, mom, I promise you. I just need you to know I would never have suggested this. Never even thought Amaris would do something like this. I would rather die than see her like this. She is the best thing that's happened to me and I pray to the universe that it gives me the chance to love her."

Ms. Cole stood up and hugged Logan. "I love you, I'm so happy for you."

"Thanks mom. I love you too."

The elevator pinged as the doors opened to Logan's penthouse. She slowly stepped out and wanted to get right back on the elevator. She felt the emptiness and coldness of her house immediately.

"Lo, are we going to go inside?" Xavier asked hesitantly.

Two weeks had gone by and Logan was finally released from the hospital. She could have left earlier, but she wanted to stay close to Amaris. The hospital literally had to kick her out. "Yeah, yeah, we're going to step inside." Logan felt herself inhale as she stepped off the elevator. A part of her waited for Amaris to come down the stairs or walk from the kitchen to meet her, but she didn't. Instead, her beautiful wife was still laying in a hospital bed, in a coma.

Logan stumbled back as the grief took over her entire body. Xavier caught her giving her the support she needed.

"It's okay, baby sis."

"I can't do this. I can't be here without her." Logan lived at her penthouse for years, Amaris had only been there for a little while and she had already made an impact there. She was everywhere Logan looked. Her paintings from her exhibition, her purse sitting on the couch. It was all too fucking much, too soon.

"Okay, okay. Do you want to go to mom and dad's house? Do you want to come to my house? Taylor and I would love to have you for however long you need."

"Thank you, brother. I just need a little more time."

"I understand, sis. I got you, I always got you."

"I'm going to get some clothes I'll be back." Logan headed to her bedroom. She didn't want to even step foot inside it, so she tried to make it quick. She grabbed her duffle bag and tossed some clothes in it. If she needed anything else, she would just buy it.

She walked into the bathroom and instantly stopped. That night played in her mind, she saw Amaris on their bathroom floor with foam coming out of her mouth. Her pill bottle sitting right next to her. There was an envelope laying on the floor. Logan grabbed the envelope, opening it, she recognized Amaris's writing immediately.

"Dear Logan, loving you has been one of my greatest joys. I knew I loved you the moment I laid eyes on you. My soul recognized you instantly. I don't regret anything between us, even you being so stubborn. LOL.

"I'll never forget our time together. It's what brought me to this decision. I know I would never continue this life without you. I knew before we got married that I would give my life for yours. Baby, you still have so much to accomplish and I've already accomplished so much. Please, know that I'm in so much peace with this decision. Hopefully, the universe will allow me to be reincarnated and I find you again.

"I want you to promise me something, baby. I want you to love again. You deserve to love. Someone deserves to experience your love, it's such a beautiful thing. Have the babies you didn't allow yourself to think about. They'll be beautiful just like their mama. Write, never stop writing.

"God, I love you, Logan Maddox. I love you with my entire being. I'll see you in the next life, my love.

"Love, Amaris"

That was Logan's undoing. Xavier ran to the room as he heard an ear piercing wail from Logan. "Lo!" Xavier found Logan on the floor in a fetal position bawling her eyes out. "Lo, was it is? Are you hurt?" Logan couldn't speak, she just lifted the hand holding Amaris letter. Xavier grabbed the paper and read it. "Oh shit," he whispered after reading it. He knew he needed to get Logan out of there immediately . "Okay sis, let's get you out of here," he said as he scooped her into his arms.

"Oh my God, Xavier, why would she do this?" Her heart hurt worse than when she had her heart attacks. This pain hit her to the core of her soul. She wouldn't recover from this if Amaris didn't make it. Reading her letter was the icing on the cake.

"Because she loves you, sis. You have to remember her love." Xavier stepped onto the elevator still cradling Logan. He'd never seen her so vulnerable. He would do anything to ease her pain. As her big brother, it hurt him to the core to see Logan like this.

Logan looked up at her brother, she reminded him of when she was a little girl. "She has to come back to me, X. This heart," Logan hit her chest, "doesn't mean shit if I don't have her. Amaris is my heart."

CHAPTER

22

TWO MONTHS LATER

L o, you have Isis here to see you." Lani buzzed through the intercom. Logan made sure she looked presentable before telling Lani to send Isis in. Isis walked into the room with a huge smile.

"And so she lives."

Logan stood up with a huge smile. "Yes, I do."

"It's so good to see you like this my friend." Isis and Logan hugged.

"Have a seat. I wasn't expecting to see you today."

"When I heard the Queen was returning to work, I had to catch a flight out."

"Well, I appreciate that."

Isis sat up in her seat and eye fucked the shit out of Logan. "All jokes aside, you look really good. Your new heart must be doing you good."

"Well, I'm still breathing, so I guess so." Logan didn't feel like her heart was hers. Yes, it was keeping her alive, yes it was inside her, but her heart was laying in the hospital bed, in a coma, for two months. Without Amaris, she felt like she could barely breathe.

"Any update on Amaris?" By the time Logan was released from the hospital, the media had found out about Amaris and then the whole world knew about her sacrifice. She had so many reporters wanting to interview her to get their love story, but Logan turned them all down. It didn't feel right telling a story without her other half.

"No update, she's taking her sweet time to come back to me," Logan joked.

Isis gave her a sad smile. "How long are you going to wait?"

"Did you come all the way from New York to ask me about Amaris or did you actually have something for me?" Logan would never give up on Amaris. In her mind, Amaris was taking a much needed rest and she would wake up when she was ready. Logan wasn't going to rush her.

Isis got the hint and pulled a manuscript from her bag. "Are you ready to sign me?"

Logan reached for the manuscript. She thumbed through the pages. "You're ready for me to sign you?" After their last conversation, Logan sent Isis the contract, but she never signed it.

"Yes."

"Your contract was sent to you, why didn't you sign it the day I sent it? I thought we had a deal."

"Lo, no one knew if you were going to be alive at the time. I didn't want to sign and then someone took over who didn't understand my vision like you. You're an author, you know how we feel about our books, they're our babies. By the grace of God, you're here, healthy and if the opportunity still stands, I'd like to sign with you."

Logan knew how great of an author Isis was. Anyone she vetted was top of the line author to her. "Isis, you should know me better than that. If I would have passed away I had things set just the way I wanted them. Everything's in writing, you would have been safe. So, what I'm going to do is read over your manuscript and I'll get back to you because honestly, I'm not accepting authors right now."

Isis smiled while standing up. She knew she deserved the hard time Logan was giving her. "Okay, well, I will be here for two more days. I look forward to hearing from you."

Logan stood up to walk Isis to the door, but was surprised when Isis gave her a big hug. "I really am happy for you Logan and I hope Amaris wakes up soon."

"Thank you, mah."

"Talk to you soon."

Logan started packing up when she saw that it was after 5 o'clock. She needed to get to the hospital before six because the nurse always tripped if she came after visiting hours.

Lani knocked on the door.

"What's up, mah?" Logan slid some manuscripts in her bag.

"On your way to the hospital?"

"You know it."

"Can I do anything for you?"

Logan stopped what she was doing and looked up at Lani. She was so grateful for her. Lani stayed by her side throughout this whole ordeal. Even with her feelings for Amaris, Logan appreciated the fact that Lani remained a good friend.

"Naw, I'm good. Do you need anything? You've been such a big help, but I want to make sure you're taking care of yourself."

"I am, don't worry about me"

"Let me get out of here, you know how those nurses are."

"Okay. I'll see you tomorrow," Lani said with a small laugh as Logan gave Lani a quick hug and dashed out of the door.

Amaris's doctor was waiting for her when she made it to her room. "Hey doc, how's it going?"

"It's going good."

"How's my wife?" Logan walked over to Amaris and kissed her forehead. "Hi baby," she whispered to her.

"I wanted to talk to you about the next step."

"Next step?" Logan quizzed.

"Yes, it's been two months and Amaris hasn't shown any progress. We need to think about taking her off the machines."

"No," Logan said without hesitation.

"Logan, I need you to get it in your mind that Amaris might not wake up."

"Doctor, are you married?"

The doctor fidgeted uncomfortably. "Yes, I am."

"Would you give up on your wife or husband?"

The doctor sighed. "No, I wouldn't. But there's a point where I would have to see reason. If my spouse was in a coma for six months I would have to at least consider it."

"It's only been two months, Doc. Talk to me if we get to six," Logan said dismissing her. She took her cue and walked out of the room. Logan sat next to Amaris, letting out an exhausted sigh.

"Hi my love." She took her hand in hers. Her hand was so cold, Logan remembered her own hand feeling like that. "I have to get someone to come fix your braids," she joked. Every two weeks, Logan would get someone to come to the hospital to do two braids for Amaris. Even though she couldn't see it, Logan didn't want her beautiful hair to suffer.

Right at this moment, she would do anything to hear Amaris's voice again, to feel her caress her cheek, or just for her to ask their infamous question, 'do I know you?' Logan knew she had a new heart and she knew it was working properly because of all of her doctor appointments, but she felt like she hadn't breathed the same since she woke up. Even her new heart knew it was missing its other half.

"You have to give me a sign, baby. I will fight for you, but you have to give me something, anything to show me you haven't left me." Logan waited for a squeeze of the hand, a flutter of the eyes, anything, but there was nothing. "It's okay, maybe not today." Logan kissed her hand before pulling Isis's manuscript out of her bag. "I have nothing but time, Mrs. Maddox," she whispered before flipping the pages.

— • •●• • —

"Mom!"

"In the kitchen, sweetie" Logan headed for her mother's kitchen.

"What are you doing, pretty lady?" Logan hugged her mother from behind.

"Making a little snack, do you want one?"

"Sure, what are you making?"

"A smoothie, something light. Have a seat." Logan sat down on the barstool. "How was work?"

"Work is good, I'm thinking about signing this new author, Isis. Her work is legit, it's a breath of fresh air actually."

"Your roster is getting bigger and bigger. I'm so proud of you, Lo."

"Thanks mom. I appreciate it."

"When's your next appointment?"

"I had one a few days ago and everything is still okay. You don't have to worry mom, the new heart is working."

Kayman walked around the island to Logan. She placed her hand over Logan's heart, surprising her. "If you could see you two months ago and see you now you would see why I still worry. To have your child so close to death, you tend to still worry."

Logan had hoped her getting a new heart would ease her mom's mind, but it hadn't. "Mom, I'm okay, you don't need to worry anymore. My heart is working just fine." Logan hugged her mother.

Kayman smiled and made her way back around the island. "Did you go see Amaris today?"

Of course."

"How is she?"

"The same. The doctor wanted to talk to me about taking her off the machines, but I wasn't having it."

"Logan—"

"Mom, I don't want to hear it. It's only been two months we have to give Amaris a chance."

Kayman knew where Logan was coming from. If it was Mr. Maddox, she wouldn't be so quick to take him off the machines. "I just want to know you're prepared for when the time comes, if it comes."

"I'm not thinking about that. Amaris is big on positive energy and speaking things into the universe, so I won't speak any negativity. I have to be her biggest supporter just like she was mine."

Kayman smiled while sliding Logan a plate of fruit. "She most definitely was your biggest supporter."

"We still have our whole lives ahead of us. I have to believe that the universe gave me this heart so that we could share our lives together. Amaris is coming back."

"I know she is because if anything, Logan, your heart is going to will her to come back to you."

Logan smiled. She hoped her mother was right.

Isis strolled into Logan's office looking every inch like the goddess she was.

"Isis." Logan stood up to greet her.

"Hey Logan." They hugged briefly.

"Have a seat, do you need anything?"

"No, I'm good. Just tell me what you thought of my book."

Logan chuckled. "Straight to business, huh?" Logan picked up the manuscript and thumbed through it. "I thought the plot was really good. Is this a sequel?"

"I left it open to be one just in case I wanted to continue the story."

"Hmm." Logan knew from the moment Isis walked in her office two days ago that she was going to sign her and after reading her manuscript, there was no way she wouldn't sign her. "You give me three books to start. I will leave it up to you if you want to make this a sequel."

"What happened to one book?"

"I'm asking for three now. Isis, you know I treat everyone fairly. I want you on my roster for the long haul. After the three books, if you're not satisfied, I promise you can do as you please and I'll give you the rights to your book."

"Are you serious?"

"Yes, because I don't think you'll leave Maddox's Publishing, not after how good I will treat you."

Isis knew Logan was cocky, it was one of the things that turned her on. A person in power was what Logan was displaying, but she was also giving her the option to say no. "Alright, three books. I want the advance this time."

Before Logan could respond, Lani's voice boomed over Logan's intercom. "Lo, it's the hospital they said they need to speak to you immediately."

"Send them through." Logan's heart sped up as she picked up the phone. "Hello?"

"Mrs. Maddox, I need you to get to the hospital right away."

"What's wrong?"

"I rather not discuss this over the phone. Please, come right away."

"Okay, I'm coming." Logan ended the phone call. "I'm sorry, I have to go. It's Amaris."

"Of course."

Logan grabbed her keys and ran out of her office. She tried to get her heart to stop beating so fast. "Please, Lord," Logan tried not to get emotional. So many thoughts were running through her mind. "Please, don't let her be dead, please Lord." Logan tried not to break every traffic law to get to the hospital. Her anxiety was so high she felt dizzy. "Please, Lord," she kept begging.

She parked in the first parking spot she could find and ran inside the hospital. Her heart dropped when she saw her parents, Xavier, and Taylor standing outside Amaris's room. She felt like her legs were now wet cement as she tried to make her way to her wife's room.

No one had an expression on their face for Logan to read. They all moved out of her way as she finally made it to Amaris's doorway. Logan felt her heart stop, she felt every cell in her body explode.

"Do I know you?" Amaris croaked with a sly smile. She was sitting up in bed, looking just as beautiful as she did when Logan first laid eyes on her.

"Maybe…" Logan choked as tears ran down her eyes. "Maybe we met at my brother's wedding."

Amaris opened her arms. "Hi baby."

Logan felt like she dashed into her arms. "You came back to me," Logan cried.

Amaris wrapped Logan in her arms, inhaling her scent. "Of course I did, my love. Of course I did." All the anxiety Logan held in for two months came pouring out as she cried like she'd never cried before. Everyone decided to give them some privacy as they shut the door. "Oh my love," Amaris tried to comfort Logan.

"I didn't know if you would wake up."

"I heard you, Logan."

"What?" Logan looked up at Amaris.

"Every day, I heard you. I heard you reading to me, talking to me, loving me. I heard you, baby," tears fell down Amaris's eyes. She tried so hard to get back to Logan, but it was like her body was fighting her, but Logan's sweet voice kept her there. "I love you so much, Logan."

"I love you too, Amaris I love you so much, baby." Logan kissed Amaris all over her face, making her laugh. She felt her heart flutter; Logan was here, she looked healthy. She looked so beautiful, her skin was glowing and she had on a little more weight. The last time she saw her, Logan was fighting for her life. She placed her hand on Logan's heart and Logan saw the realization cross her face.

"I'm okay, Amaris. The new heart is working. I'm okay, my love."

"You're okay?"

"I'm okay."

The joy that surged through Amaris's body was overwhelming. Everything she asked for, everything she prayed for had been answered. The universe had granted her her wish of living the rest of her life with Logan. She would never take this second chance for granted.

Logan stood once they wheeled Amaris back into her hospital room. "Missed me?"

"Of course." She helped Amaris into the bed. "So Doc, what's the verdict? How's my wife?"

"Well, no brain damage which is a miracle. Amaris you'll need a lot of physical therapy to get you mobile again."

"When can I take her home?" Logan hadn't stepped foot back into her house since she'd come home. She couldn't do it without Amaris, it was just too hard.

"Give it a few days, we just want to make sure she's all good before we discharge her. We'll need to set up those physical therapy sessions as well."

"Okay, gotcha."

Someone knocked on the door, interrupting their conversation. "Come in," Logan called out.

Ms. Cole walked into the room as Amaris sunk into her bed. She still hadn't had a conversation with her mom since she woke up.

"Hi mom," she whispered with emotion.

"Hi sweetie."

Logan could sense the tension and she didn't want to be a part of this conversation. "Doc, let's give them some privacy." Amaris begged Logan with her eyes to stay, but Logan discreetly shook her head no.

"You have to speak to her." Logan gave Amaris a short peck on the lips before exiting the room.

The silence between Amaris and Ms. Cole spoke volumes. Amaris wanted to crawl into a hole and die right there.

"Mom …"

"What was I supposed to do without you Amaris? Did you even stop to think of me when you decided to take your life?"

"I didn't and I'm so sorry, mom. I wish I could rewind time."

"You are my only child, the only one I have left in this world. My heart has ached so bad these last months." Ms. Cole couldn't hide her emotions. She prayed every day, all day for God to bring Amaris back to her.

"I didn't know what else to do, mom. I couldn't let Logan die."

"So you die instead! I understand that you love her—"

"No! No one understands that I love her. No one will ever understand how much I love her. I'm so sorry, mom. I'm so sorry that I would have left you, but I was at peace with my decision."

Ms. Cole shook her head. She wanted to slap some sense into her daughter. "You never love anyone more than you love yourself, Amaris."

"Logan is me mom. We are one person, she breaths, I breathe. I was okay leaving this world because I knew I would find Logan again. I'm just so sorry that I hurt you in the process. I love you so much, mom and one day I hope you forgive me for what I did."

Ms. Cole didn't know what to say to Amaris. She'd never experienced a love the way Amaris described it. So, instead of arguing with her, she walked over to her bed and cradled her daughter in her arms. She placed her nose in Amaris hair inhaling her scent. She never thought she'd be able to do this again. "I love you, my sweet girl. Always have, always will."

"I love you too, mama."

CHAPTER

23

4 MONTHS LATER

Amaris looked up at the top of the building that occupied her and Logans penthouse. After four more long months in the hospital, she finally got the okay to be released. Amaris's recovery was long and hard, but Logan was there every step of the way. She had to learn how to walk again and how to use her arms again. Logan had to feed her and dress her for months, but she didn't complain. She got her the best physical therapist and pushed her on the days she wanted to give up. They were a team and their love got them through it all.

Amaris thought she would be happy to go home but her anxiety spiked as she remembered what she did and how she'd hurt Logan. She and Logan still hadn't really talked about it. They focused on Amaris regaining her mobility.

Logan could feel the anxiety rolling off Amaris' back. She intertwined their hands, bringing it to her lips. Amaris finally pulled her eyes away from the building to stare at Logan. "Are you okay my love?"

"I think so, I don't know," Amaris confessed.

"I haven't been home since everything happened."

"What?"

Logan shrugged with an embarrassed smile. "You were everywhere I turned. I couldn't imagine being there without you."

"Oh Logan." Amaris raised up on her tippy toes wrapping her arms around Logans neck. Logan engulfed her in her arms sending comforting energy through her. She'd hope her surprise didn't backfire on her. "I'm so sorry Lo."

Logan cupped Amaris chin giving her a short peck. "We don't have to talk about it now. Let's go inside babe." Logan knew they would eventually have to have the dreaded conversation about that night but now wasn't the time. Any time Amaris tried to bring it up in the hospital Logan would deflect the conversation and tell her all she needed to do was focus on recovering.

"Okay, fine." Amaris followed Logan inside the building and onto the elevator. "It feels good to be home, maybe we can rechristen it later," Amaris said seductively. Logan hadn't touched her sexually. She wondered if Logan was still attracted to her or if she was too angry with her to touch her, but she was too chicken to ask her.

"Yeah, maybe." That didn't sound too promising, so Amaris let it go.

Amaris thought she would jump out of her skin when the elevator pinged and everyone yelled, "SURPRISE!"

She clutched her chest as she plastered a smile across her face. Logan kissed her cheek. "Welcome home baby." She pulled Amaris off the elevator as Ms. Cole, her family, and Lani embraced them.

Amaris was pulled into a hug by everyone as they all welcomed her home. She couldn't stop the tears as they overflowed. The love she felt from her family was overwhelming. "I can't believe you all did this; I so appreciate it."

"We're so happy to finally have you home," Taylor gushed while handing Amaris a champagne flute.

"Yeah, now we can get Logan out of our house," Xavier joked getting a middle finger from Logan. "You know I'm just kidding Sis."

Amaris rubbed Taylors little baby bump. "I can't wait to meet my little niece."

"And she can't wait to meet her aunt."

"Should we eat everyone," Logan suggested.

"Before we do that, I'd like to say a few things." Everyone gave Amaris their undivided attention. "I know this has been a long journey and I want to thank all of you for giving me the space I needed to heal. Thank you for all the calls, all the flowers, and all the get-well cards. I love you all so much, words can't express how much. Mom, thank you for being by my side. Mr. and Mrs. Maddox, thank you for welcoming me into your beautiful family. Thank you for all the encouraging calls. Xavier and Taylor, thank you for taking care of Logan while I was down. Lani, thank you for your genuine friendship. I love you." Amaris faced her beautiful wife. "Logan, thank you for loving me through the hard days of my recovery. Thank you for not giving up on me. I will never leave your side. This is a second chance for us, and I promise to love you to the fullest extent of my heart."

"I would do it over and over again if it meant I get to spend the rest of my life loving you Amaris." Logan leaned down kissing Amaris before the parents in the room cleared their throats playfully. Logan smiled pulling away from Amaris. "Alright everyone let's eat."

The night was simply amazing. Amaris felt so blessed to be surrounded in so much love. This was their first family get together since the wedding. After Amaris woke up, Logan asked everyone respectfully to give them space so Amaris could focus on getting better. Everyone gave them their space to take on the task as a married couple. It felt good to be back with the family.

"Lani," Amaris caught her before she could get on the elevator. "You're leaving without saying goodbye?"

"I did say goodbye to everyone."

"I mean a proper goodbye Lani." Amaris engulfed Lani in an embrace, taking her by surprise. "I will always love you for keeping my secret and getting me to the hospital. I will forever love you for continuing to be there for Logan, loving her, being her friend." Amaris would never be able to repay

Lani for all she'd done for them.

Lani knew she would always love Amaris, to have experienced her was to love her but watching the way she and Logan looked at each other tonight she realized she wanted what they had one day. "I need a favor Amaris."

"Just name it."

"I think I need to go back to Greece; you think you can hire a temporary assistant for Logan?"

"Greece," Amaris asked suspiciously. "Why?"

Lani rubbed the back of her neck hiding her smile as a memory inched to the surface. "Just something I have to do."

"Will you be safe?"

"Of course."

"Okay, well take all the time you need." Amaris wanted to pry a little more but figured Lani would tell her when she was ready.

Lani hugged Amaris one last time knowing it might be a while before she saw her again. "Take care of our girl for me."

"I will, I promise." Amaris gave one last wave as Lani hopped on the elevator.

An hour later the house was finally quiet. Amaris said her last goodbyes before she went to search for Logan. She found her staring out the window. She seemed so deep in thought Amaris thought twice about approaching her, but she needed to be close to Logan. She needed to make a new memory in their home. She didn't want Logan to think about her attempted suicide every time they were home. She wanted her to remember the love they shared, the nights wrapped in each other's arms, the nights of love making, and their talks. They'd built a sanctuary of love; Logan just needed a little reminding.

Logan felt Amaris approaching but didn't turn around. The tension in her body settled as Amaris pressed her body into her back. Tonight had been amazing, something they both needed. She too felt tension in her body being back home. She tried her hardest to forget that night but being back there she felt like the walls were closing in on her a bit. Images of Amaris lifeless body on their bathroom floor kept replaying in Logans head. She thought it would be easy being home with Amaris, but it wasn't. Her family was a welcome distraction but now alone with Amaris it was all coming back.

"Logan, make love to me," Amaris whispered.

Logan sighed, leaning her face against the window. She always liked the coldness the glass provided. "Amaris," she croaked.

Amaris turned her around dropping to her knees. "I feel you." She unbuckled Logans belt desperately wanting to erase the pain etched in her eyes. "It's over, we're here. We have to remember that." She pulled Logans pants down and then her boxer briefs. She could see Logans chest heaving up and down.

"I don't know if I can," Logan admitted.

Amaris buried her face in Logans pussy causing Logan to gasp. She needed to be connected to Logan.

"Amaris," Logan moaned as Amaris tongue found her clit. Her knees buckled as Amaris started her assault on her pussy. She tried to speak but her mouth hung open as her wife pleased her. She forgot how skilled Amaris was with her tongue.

Amaris pulled back looking up at Logan. "You taste so good baby. I miss tasting you." Amaris moaned while sucking Logans clit. It was no better feeling than making Logan feel good.

Logan wrapped her hand in Logans hair as her other hand smashed against the wall. Her legs shook as Amaris tongue applied pressure to her clit. Words she couldn't comprehend slid out of her mouth. She could hear her heart beating rapidly but this time she wasn't afraid of passing out. "Fuck Amaris, fuck," she moaned.

Amaris palmed Logans ass while her tongue slid deeper into her folds. She almost lost it when Logan started fucking her mouth. "I'm about to cum."

Amaris quickened her pace wanting Logan to cum in her mouth. She felt Logans grip in her hair tighten as she neared her released. "I'm cumming." Logan tried not to suffocate Amaris, but she couldn't help her hips from moving faster, needing to feel the release. None of them realized they were both moaning until Logans moans filled the living room as she came in Amaris mouth. Amaris lapped her juices not wanting to miss a drop.

Logan laughed as her knees gave out and she fell to the floor. "Fuck baby, that felt so good. I think I needed that."

Amaris straddled Logan before sliding her tongue in Logans mouth. Logan moaned tasting herself on Amaris tongue.

Unexpectedly Amaris stood up. "I'll be right back."

"Maybe we should take this to the room," Logan suggested.

"Or maybe we should fuck in front of the window and give whoever catches us a show. I'll be right back." Amaris disappeared down the hallway.

Logan chuckled while running her hands through her locs. She forgot how wild Amaris could be. "Logan." Logan sat up halfway and was welcomed by a naked Amaris. Her mouth instantly watered at the sight. Amaris would always be the most beautiful woman in Logans eyes. She watched her hips sway from left to right as she approached her. Her breast called her name as the bounced up and down. "We're going to make love to each other now do you hear me?" Amaris asked gently while dropping Logans strap in front of her.

"Yes," Logan could barely get out. Amaris was a seductress without even trying. "How long has it really been?"

"Too long, I want you inside of me Logan." Amaris leaned against the window. "Against this here." Amaris mind was filled with lust. The anticipation of Logan sliding her strap inside of her pussy made her wet.

Logan jumped up from the floor grabbing the strap. "We haven't really seen if this heart here is as good as gold huh?" She slid her boxers on with the strap connected. "There's a surprise for you in there that I'm going to use in a second."

Logan eyebrow rose but laughed once she felt the vibrator in the slit of her boxers. "You Mrs. Maddox is fucking naughty." Without warning Logan picked Amaris up leaning against the window.

"Will this hold?" Amaris wanted to fuck but she didn't want to go through a window in the process.

"Oh yes it will hold. Are you ready for me?"

Amaris felt Logan at her entrance as she wrapped her legs around Logans waist. "Yes." In one swift motion Logan entered her. Amaris mouth made an O as Logan filled her pussy. Logan palmed her ass as she stroked Amaris pussy. Amaris opened more for Logan sucking her in. She wanted all of Logan. "Fuck me Logan." Their bodies moved in sync against the window, Logan had all her strength so there were no holds bars when it came to her fucking.

"Fuck me harder please."

"Come here." Logan pulled them from the window walking them to the couch. She turned Amaris around and made her lean against the couch. "You want it hard?"

"Yes," Amaris cooed. Before Logan could enter her again Amaris reached around Logan and turned on the vibrator.

"Oh shit," Logan laughed as the vibrator teased her clit. "I don't know if I can focus. Her clit was already sensitive from Amaris tongue.

"You can. Now fuck me," Amaris demanded. She wanted Logan to cum as well so she thought the vibrator would be a good touch.

Logan let out a deep breath as the vibrator damn near crippled her. She moaned as she entered Amaris. Each time she stroked Amaris the vibrator rubbed against her clit. "Fuck." She laughed at herself.

"Give it to me Logan." Amaris braced her hands against the arm of their couch anticipating Logan. She had an intake of air as Logan entered her pussy from behind over and over. Logan wrapped her hand in Amaris hair as she started to pound Amaris pussy. "Yes like that. Fuck yes like that baby."

It was such a turn on for Logan to watch her strap slide in and out of Amaris. "You're so fucking wet baby."

"Only for you Lo, always for you," Amaris moaned. Her ass smacked against Logan as she threw it back on her. She was in a state of pure ecstasy. Logan had never been so rough with her, she loved it. "Yes, harder baby. Don't hold back on me. Pull my hair harder." Logan pulled her beautiful curls harder as she wrapped one arm around Amaris waist. The only sound in their home was their skin smacking against each other and their moans echoing off the walls.

"Logan! Oh fuck baby!" Amaris caressed her own nipples as her wife assaulted her pussy in the most beautiful way. She was stretching her so good. This is what she wanted, them lost in one another. Remembering how good they felt like this, together.

"Amaris I'm about to cum," Logan moaned in her ear. The harder she fucked Amaris the more she felt the sensation from the vibrator on her clit. It was pure torture.

"Cum with me Logan. Open yourself to me." Amaris threw her hips back feeling Logan touching her g spot. She felt the sensation of her own orgasm approaching.

"Oh shit Amaris. I fucking love you. God, I love you!" Logan thrust became desperate as she tried to take them both over the edge. She felt Amaris body tense and then finally release as she came.

"Logan, Logan, Logan!" Amaris shook uncontrollably as she squirted all over Logans strap. She kept grinding against Logan riding the wave of her release.

"I'm cumming Amaris, oh I'm cumming," Logan moaned. Amaris threw her ass back to keep the vibrator on Logans clit. Logans moans was music to her ears as she came hard, she could feel Logans body shaking behind her. Logan felt like all her senses went into overdrive as her orgasm took over. Her legs grew weak as she fell against Amaris.

Amaris laughed as she tried to prevent them both from falling onto the couch. "That was fucking insane." Logan said out of breath.

"It was needed, now stand so I don't fall baby."

"My bad love." Logan collected herself standing up. Amaris pulled Logan to the couch so they could lay properly. Logans laid her head on Amaris breast as she caressed her back gently.

They enjoyed the silence for a moment. Logan was the first to speak. "I've missed being with you like that."

"Me too my love. It's been a long time coming."

Logan closed her eyes feeling relaxed in Amaris embrace. She didn't know if she would ever feel comfortable in their home again but being like this with Amaris was like old times.

"I want to take you away; can I do that?"

"Where baby?"

"It's a surprise. We've been so focused on your rehab; we can finally breathe now. We haven't had the chance to celebrate my transplant and you doing so well in rehab."

"Ok baby, you can take me anywhere you'd like. When do we leave?"

"In a couple of weeks, after the release of my movie. I have press week and then I'm all yours." Logans movie was already receiving great reviews from critics. She felt so blessed to be living her dream, a dream she didn't know if she'd be there to see. They missed the premiere because Amaris was still in the hospital and Logan refused to leave her side. Her family went and represented her instead. Logan didn't care about missing the premiere, she was just happy she was there to see it come into fruition.

"A few weeks, I can live with that. Will it be more of this?" Amaris motioned between the both of them while wiggling her eyebrows.

Logan laughed. "Oh yeah, definitely more of this." Logan planned to get reacquainted with her wife in every inch of their room on vacation.

"I'll pack our bags."

EPILOGUE

"**D**o you hate me for what I did?" Logan rested her head against Amaris's thigh as they sat on the beach in the back of their private villa in Bora Bora. They'd enjoyed it so much on their honeymoon Logan thought it would be a good idea to have a permanent space there. Amaris was in love when she walked into the villa and couldn't believe it was theirs. She planned to visit whenever their schedules allowed it.

Logan had promised Amaris they would finally talk about what happened on their trip so here they were.

"When I realized what you did, I didn't know what to think. How do you hate someone for wanting to give their life for yours? But I thought about going through life without you and it didn't feel worth it. To know you died so that I could live, I don't know how I would have lived with that."

Amaris ran her hands through Logan's locs. "I'm sorry, baby, I didn't think about the guilt you might feel from me doing what I did. After you had your last seizure that night, I knew in my heart you didn't have long. Writing that letter to you was the hardest thing I had to do but I found comfort in knowing I would still be close to you."

Logan looked up at Amaris lovingly. "Amaris, you are my life, my everything. Going through life without you would have been a tragedy for me." A tragedy Logan might not have recovered from. Thinking now about Amaris no longer being on this earth sent a wave of sadness over Logan. So quickly she'd d become everything Logan wanted in life and so quickly that all could have been over.

Amaris leaned down to kiss Logan. There was that spark, the spark she felt the first time they kissed, the moment they reconnected, the times they'd made love. Logan was her everything. She was her person, her twin flame. She thanked the universe for giving her a second chance to do life with Logan. "Do I know you?"

Logan chuckled while kissing Amaris's hand. "Maybe we met in another life, maybe we've met in each life we had. Maybe our souls are aligned to find each other in each life we have because I will find you again, Amaris, and have another beautiful life with you."

Amaris felt her heart flutter at Logan's declaration. "You know, Mrs. Maddox, I'm okay with that."

www.ingramcontent.com/pod-product-compliance
Lightning Source LLC
Chambersburg PA
CBHW030149310726
48970CB00005B/1659